SPHINX

SPHINX

T.S. LEARNER

SPHERE

First published in Great Britain as a paperback original
in 2010 by Sphere
Reprinted 2010 (three times)

Copyright © Tobsha Learner 2010

Hieroglyphs © Stephen Raw 2010

The moral right of the author has been asserted.

A CIP catalogue record for this book
is available from the British Library.

ISBN 978-0-7515-4347-6

Typeset in Caslon by M Rules
Printed and bound in Great Britain by
Clays Ltd, St Ives plc

Papers used by Sphere are natural renewable and
recyclable products sourced from well-managed forests and certified
in accordance with the rules of the Forest Stewardship Council.

Mixed Sources
Product group from well-managed
forests and other controlled sources
www.fsc.org Cert no. SGS-COC-004081
© 1996 Forest Stewardship Council

Sphere
An imprint of
Little, Brown Book Group
100 Victoria Embankment
London EC4Y 0DY

An Hachette UK Company
www.hachette.co.uk

www.littlebrown.co.uk

In memory of Troy Davies
1959–2007
Maverick, muse and emotional anarchist

Author's Note

This is a work of fiction written to entertain, inspire and intrigue and should be read as such. Any similarity to a living person or actual institution is entirely coincidental.

Many of the historical characters and their back stories are factual. For example, Nectanebo II did disappear mysteriously at the end of his reign. The character of Banafrit, however, is a literary device. The Antikythera mechanism – the oldest piece of machinery in existence, dating back two thousand years – is authentic, therefore the hypothesis that it might have had predecessors is logical.

Finally, the author would like to make it clear to her readers that she strongly condemns the illegal removal of antiquities from Egypt and any unauthorised exploration, commercial or otherwise.

SPHINX

Prelude

Now, when I look at the desert, I am reminded of the year I spent in Egypt – the most definitive of my life. I never fail to be amazed by how sand resembles granules of glass, orbs made by grains colliding with each other as they shift, trickle and blow in invisible clouds across the horizon.

And I am reminded of how, if I'd had the eye of God that year, if I'd had some omnipresent aerial vision that could have wrapped itself around all the deserts of the world, I would have seen that when sandstorms settle they settle in patterns and those patterns make a cipher – a hidden prophecy.

1

Abu Rudeis oilfield, Western Sinai, Egypt, 1977

In the distance a dust devil skimmed along the horizon, its trajectory zigzagging with uncanny intelligence. The Bedouin believed such dust storms to be the restless spirits of those who lay unburied, bone-naked, lost in the harsh desert. Was this a bad omen? Worried that the roughnecks might think so, I glanced over. The fieldworkers, big fearless men, their overalls blackened with grime and oil, were paused in awe, tools in hand, staring at the phenomenon.

The rumble of the generators rolled out over the sand like the growling of some colossal animal, across the patch of ground where the pump jacks and rigs of the Abu Rudeis oilfield stood, the derricks sentries against the bleached sky. Captured by Israel in the 1967 war, the oilfield had been returned to Egyptian control only two years before – in November 1975 – and army tanks still patrolled its perimeters. I could see one now, slowly cruising in the distance. With the Israeli border not far away this was a combustive landscape. Despite recent attempts by Egypt's President Sadat to normalise relations between the two countries, the atmosphere was tense, the whole area a tinderbox. It felt as if any sudden movement – a jeep careering off course, a bout of careless yelling – might trigger another jaw-rattling exchange of fire.

Over at the control tower, the rest of the crew were hovering, waiting for me to give the final command to start drilling. A jeep was parked nearby with its door open, the driver tuning his car radio, the bulge of his pistol rippling under his jacket as he moved. Country and western music collided with the melancholic voice of singer Mohamed Abdel Wahab, the plaintive Arabic ballad blasting out with the heat across the blindingly white plains.

'Mr Warnock!' the driver shouted, pointing to the fake Rolex watch that had appeared from under the sleeve of his jellaba. I nodded and swung around to face the newly constructed rig. The derrick hung suspended over the rocky ground; the crew gathered by the control panel stared at me, tense with anticipation, watching for the thumbs-down: the signal to begin drilling. My assistant, Moustafa Saheer, catching my eye, grinned and nodded.

In the same instant I lifted my hand to signal 'go' there was a huge explosion. I threw myself to the ground, a burst of gunfire followed.

An image of Isabella, my wife, shot through my mind – she was stepping out of the shower, her wet hair hanging down to her waist, her smile enticing, wry. It was eight weeks earlier – the last time I'd seen her.

Lifting my head carefully I glanced over my shoulder. Just a few metres away, spewing oil had ignited into a single blazing pillar. 'Blowout!' I shouted, frightened that the fire would spread to our own well. Already the crew were clambering down, frantic, limbs tumbling over limbs. Nearby, a panicked soldier sprinted towards the inferno, firing his automatic rifle uselessly into the air.

'Get in! Get in!' the driver screamed to me. Running for my life, I bolted for the jeep.

We drove back to the camp in silence as black smoke billowed alongside the road. Moustafa stared out of the back window at the blazing oil well, now a flaming tower receding into the distance.

He had trained in Budapest and spoke perfect English with a private-school accent, but it had been his methodical analysis of data as well as his easygoing camaraderie with the roughnecks – an asset in politically anxious times – that had impressed me. This was the third project I'd hired him for, and we had developed a concise communication based on an understanding of each other's personalities and boundaries; essential out in the field where it was often too noisy to hear anyone speak.

'All those months of calculation gone.' Moustafa's expression was lugubrious.

'C'mon, at least it's not the new well burning. The company will cap the fire and we'll start our drilling a few weeks late.'

'A few weeks is still a great deal of money. This is bad for my country.'

After President Nasser nationalised the Egyptian oil industry in 1956, he insisted that local men replace the mainly Italian, French and Greek fieldworkers. But when Nasser died of a sudden heart attack in 1970, his heir, Anwar El Sadat, had introduced an open-door policy again. The consultancy company I worked for – GeoConsultancy – was part of that policy. I'd been brought in by the Alexandrian Oil Company to assess whether they should drill south of the existing oilfield and develop a deeper, as yet untested, reservoir. This landscape was second nature to me, a place where my soul sprang into thirsty agitation. I read terrain like the blind read Braille. Known as The Diviner, I had a reputation as the best geophysicist in the industry, famous for my ability to discover oil. But the moniker made me uncomfortable: it seemed to suggest that I had some mystical talent. In reality, I was meticulous in my scientific research but also prepared to take the extra gamble many others were frightened to.

After six months, with the help of Moustafa, we'd finally convinced them that the new field was worth the risk.

The sound of the explosion still rang in my ears but my heartbeat steadied slowly. I turned back towards the skyline; dusk had reduced the sea to an inky charcoal and the rippling waves glittered randomly. The sky was a burnt orange; the off-shore oil rigs were silhouetted on the horizon like marooned ships with bizarrely oversized masks, islands of industry. It was a sight that never failed to inspire me. I sniffed my fingers; they smelled of smoke and burning oil. The blowout had thrown some things into perspective. Isabella, for one. The last time I'd seen her we'd fought and we hadn't spoken since. When I threw myself on the sand to save myself from the billowing flames, I was suddenly convinced that we would never get the chance to be reconciled. The thought that I might never see her again was devastating.

Oil geologists spend a lot of time by themselves, analysing seismic data or studying core samples on site. You develop a certain self-sufficiency, the roar of your own blood filling your head until you find yourself deaf to other people. But after five years of marriage I had become welded to Isabella. We were the same animal, both of us fascinated by the way history folded itself into the ground, the trail of clues left by previous civilisations.

As a marine archaeologist, Isabella's hunting fields were the valleys and cliffs of the sea floor. Now, driving along the coast road that hugged the eastern edge of the Suez Canal, I wondered whether she had continued with her underwater exploration, even after our heated argument about it. She was searching for an ancient object, an astrarium, which she believed was a prototype of the Antikythera Mechanism, an artefact dating back to the times of Cleopatra and possibly even earlier, found off the coast of Rhodes in 1901. The Antikythera Mechanism itself was an anomaly: nothing as mechanically sophisticated had existed for over a thousand years after its construction. Nevertheless Isabella was convinced that it must have had predecessors. My wife was a maverick in her field, famous for making discoveries based on a few facts and an intuitive sense of where a site might lie. Her hunches were often uncannily correct – something that unnerved many of her contemporaries. She had been researching the astrarium for years and now believed she was in the last months of her quest, having narrowed her search to Aboukir Bay near Alexandria, where the drowned suburb of Herakleion lay, close to the submerged island of Antirhodos, home to Cleopatra's palace, all destroyed by a tsunami twelve hundred years earlier. Against my advice (and the cause of a series of bitter arguments) she'd recently embarked on a series of illegal dives. There was a new desperation to Isabella's obsession and it had begun to frighten me.

By the time we arrived at the field camp and pulled up beside the cluster of corrugated-iron worker cabins, I'd decided that regardless of what the company demanded I would fly back to Alexandria early the next morning.

Eight hours later the well was still burning, despite the efforts of a ground crew working around the clock. The sand berms that the tractors had pushed up around the well had contained the blaze, but thousands of dollars' worth of precious oil continued to go up in smoke.

'It is impossible to put out the fire, my friend.' Mohamed, the manager of the oilfield and an usually cheerful man in his forties, appeared defeated. His large moon-shaped face seemed to have deflated around the collar of his stained boiler suit and his eyes glared out from below a soot-smeared brow. 'Forty men, their equipment and who knows how many gallons of expensive foam and the bastard is still burning. Any minute now the rest will go up and I will have an even greater catastrophe on my hands. A curse on the Israelis.'

'This wasn't sabotage,' I said. 'This was bad luck and maybe some negligence.'

'Negligence! We do what we can with the equipment available, but we are still catching up after the Israelis ruined the wells. Is that my fault?'

'I think it's time to look for some outside help,' I suggested carefully.

'Never! Our roustabouts will get it under control eventually.'

'"Eventually" will be too late.'

I tried to contain the anger in my voice. Mohamed was quite capable of compromising the machinery to avoid losing face.

As the manager scowled at me, Moustafa, who had been listening to our exchange, stepped forward smoothly. I didn't stop him. Both of us knew he had the temperament and diplomacy to deal with the site manager's bursts of grievance, usually aimed indiscriminately at both government and private enterprise. Such tantrums had got three of my best field hands fired already.

Moustafa's tone was conciliatory. 'Mr Warnock did not mean to insult your professionalism, Mohamed. It is a major fire and it's going to take the best team around to extinguish the blaze. He merely meant to suggest that perhaps you might consider bringing in outside expertise.'

I glanced out the office window. A poisonous-looking fog billowed above the blaze, snaking out across the landscape and staining everything in its path.

'I know a firefighting company run by a Texan called Bill Anderson,' I said. 'He's not cheap but he's the guy. He could be here within forty-eight hours.'

I'd first met Bill Anderson in Angola. After an abortive negotiation with a rebel leader and self-appointed oil tycoon had failed to materialise, my company had hired a small plane to fly me quickly out of the country. Bill had been in nearby Nigeria, putting out a government oil well that had been sabotaged by the same rebel leader, and had about as much affection for the region as I did. Between us we'd managed to persuade the manager of the local airfield to let us hide in his cellar until the next available Cessna arrived. We'd had nothing except a bucket, a crate of whisky and a pack of playing cards. By the end of the second night, we were violently disagreeing over philosophy, religion and politics. By the morning, we were lifelong friends.

'Forty-eight hours! I haven't got forty-eight hours!' Mohamed slammed his desk in frustration.

'You still have thirty intact wells, plus a brand-new drilling rig just waiting to go. You have forty-eight hours.' I scribbled down Anderson's telephone number. 'I'm going back to Alex until this is fixed. I can't open a potential new reservoir with this going on above ground – it's too dangerous.'

'The company won't like it.'

'That, my friend, is your problem.'

Mohamed sighed. 'One week, Oliver, then I promise the fire will be out, all the wells will be pumping again and you can start your drilling, *inshallah.*'

'God willing indeed.' I tucked the phone number into his breast pocket. 'You know where to find me.'

It was about five in the morning by the time I got back to Alexandria and the weather was deteriorating rapidly. There was no phone at the company villa we were living in, which was not unusual – telephones were rare in Egypt and most people had to go to the post office to book a call. So I had been unable to warn Isabella of my return and I was apprehensive about having to surprise her. Despite her own dangerous exploration dives, Isabella did not approve of the hazards I faced in my own profession. But she knew nothing about the explosion and I didn't intend to tell her about it. All I craved now was a truce and to have her back in my arms.

I hauled my luggage as quietly as possible across the cobbled back lane towards the old colonial villa. The security guard was just finishing his night shift and he let me in through the wrought-iron back gate; the enclosed garden was a sanctuary from the storm now buffeting the palm trees. Tinnin, the Alsatian guard dog, began to bark at the sound of my footfall. I murmured his name and he dropped to the ground whimpering, ears flattened.

As I pulled out my key I watched the window of the housekeeper's flat carefully. Ibrihim was a cautious, taciturn man; he was also a heavy sleeper. I shut the oak door behind me and slipped into the large entrance hall. The canaries in their old-fashioned wire cage twittered wildly as the wind rattled the shutters of the French windows. I closed the windows quickly and hurried to calm the birds.

The house had been built in the 1920s and was an idio-syncratic blend of cubism with Islamic architectural overtones. The villa itself had once housed the representa-tive of the original British-owned Bell Oil Company, as it was known before Nasser nationalised it. It had been one of the most desirable postings in colonial Egypt, enabling the well-spoken aspirational English employee to socialise with the wealthy European families who used to run both the cotton and oil industries. Families like Isabella's – Italians who had migrated in the mid-nineteenth century and had built up powerful dynasties over the preceding century. A photograph of Nasser now hung where the portrait of the original owner had once been – a wonderful metaphor for the toppled ruling class. One evening, smiling furtively, Ibrihim had shown me the usurped and now hidden portrait – with a fez perched above his jowly Edwardian face the old patriarch looked like the ultimate colonial pasha, a dethroned prince exiled by revolution.

In the political chaos much of the original furniture had also been abandoned. Like many Alexandrian Europeans during the Suez Crisis in 1956, the plant manager had fled overnight but the Art Deco furniture, sofas and wall hang-ings remained; mementos of obscene wealth, all lovingly maintained by Ibrihim.

The bedroom door was ajar. The curtains were drawn and it was dark inside; I almost stumbled over an oxygen cylinder abandoned on the floor next to a wetsuit and a diving mask. In the dim light I could just make out Isabella's sleeping form sprawled on top of the bedcovers.

Quietly, I switched on a side lamp. There were maps spread out over the rugs – the spidery cartography of the sea floor, a parallel subterranean landscape, seductive in its mys-tery. In the middle of this pile lay a sheet of paper showing a drawing of a metal contraption: a fantastical device of dials and cogs held together in a wooden casing. The dials were engraved with a series of marks or symbols, like clock faces. I knew this was a fictional depiction of the astrarium drawn by my art-student brother Gareth. Isabella was close to Gareth, closer than I was in fact, and had commissioned the illustration after briefing him from snippets of visual research that she had amassed over the years. And now here it was – my nemesis, the one thing we always argued about – placed like a shrine in the centre of the floor.

Oblivious to the outside world, Isabella had fallen asleep with her clothes on. As I picked my way across the scattered papers it was easy to imagine her exhausted, falling across the bed after a day of diving. I didn't have the heart to wake her.

Instead, I sat in a battered leather armchair and watched her. The moonlight filtered in to illuminate her strong face.

Isabella wasn't a beautiful woman in any conventional sense of the word. Her profile was just a little too angular to be considered feminine, her lips a little too thin. She had no breasts to speak of, I could almost span the width of her hips with one hand, and there was a constant hunger in the way she held her body, a tipping forward as if she was always ready to run. But her eyes were exquisite. Her irises were black; a kind of ebony that changed to violet if you stared long enough. They were the most startling aspect of her face; disproportionately large, the rest of her features seemed to fall away from them. Then there were her hands – beautiful working hands with long fingers – tanned and worn, showing the hours immersed in water or spent painstakingly piecing together ancient objects.

Outside the villa, a nightjar churred. Isabella stirred, groaned and rolled onto her side. I smiled and sighed, regretting our argument and the subsequent long weeks of angry silence. Isabella was how I anchored myself: to culture, to emotion, to place. And I was a man who craved place. I had grown up in a mining village in Cumbria and sometimes even now, in my dreams, I saw the sweeping plains of Ordovician limestone, the landscape of my childhood. I was drawn to solidity, to the slower-evolving manifestations of nature. If I were to describe myself it would be as a listener, a man of few words. Isabella was different. She used language to define herself, to ambush the moment and talk it into history. Nevertheless, she was able to read stillness, especially my stillness. That was the second reason why I'd fallen in love with her.

Isabella did not move. Finally I couldn't help myself. I leaned over and she woke, consciousness travelling slowly across her face to finally form a smile. Without saying anything she reached up and wrapped her arms around me. I sank down and joined her on the bed.

Isabella's sexuality was an organic part of her nature; a spontaneous wildness that kept us both excited. We made love in exotic places: a telephone booth, beneath the tarpaulin of a boat in full view of the busy Indian port of Kochi, on the Scottish moors. But whatever the context, Isabella liked to stay in control. With her eyelashes brushing my cheeks, we kissed and I caressed her. Soon it felt as if there was nothing but the flame of her irises, her hardening nipples, her wetness.

I lay there afterwards, curled around her as she slipped back into sleep. Staring across the room, I listened to the sound of the rain lashing the windows. My last thought was one of thanks – for my marriage, for my life, for surviving. One of those moments of clarity one has in the dead of night: a quiet realisation that this might be happiness.

2

Two hours later I woke to find Isabella standing by the open balcony door; hair flying wildly, naked against the early morning, the silk curtains swirling dervishes propelled by the wind.

'Isabella, it's freezing!'

Ignoring me, she stared out at the thunderous clouds low over the trees. I got out of bed, grabbed a dressing gown and wrapped her in it, then shut the doors.

'Please, can we get some sleep?'

'I can't. Oliver, how many years have I worked towards finding this astrarium? Ten? Fifteen? And it will be today, I know it!'

I glanced back at the window – the sky was as dark as it had been yesterday. 'That's not diving weather.'

'I'm diving anyway.'

'Can't it wait a couple of days until the storm blows over?'

'No. Oliver, you don't understand—' She broke off, staring into the distance. I decided to change my argument.

'I'm assuming you have back-up with you – some of the French archaeologists, the Italians?'

Apart from an English archaeologist called Amelia Lynhurst, and a new young French academic who had just set up offices near the Stadium, marine archaeology was virtually unheard of in Alexandria, despite rumours of Cleopatra's sunken palace in the bay. Up until recently the political situation, dealing with poverty and the needs of Alexandria's citizens, had taken precedence.

Isabella smiled wryly. 'I'm afraid it's only me and Faakhir.'

Faakhir Alsayla was a young diver with whom Isabella had been working over the past few months. Although he was trustworthy and enthusiastic as well as a great diver, the young Arab was not an archaeologist.

'Christ, Isabella.' I would have preferred her to be part of an authorised team. It was dangerous to dive illegally in Egypt, a country understandably nervous of both clandestine military surveillance from its enemies and of further plundering of its ancient underwater treasures. The only way to do it legally was to be accompanied by an Egyptian official and a recognised team of foreign archaeologists, rules by which Isabella never really abided. She was a rebel in her own field and was not liked for it. But whatever her professional standing she was often lucky in her chosen sites. A mixed blessing, it was this mysterious accuracy that was the cause of both suspicion and fear from her peers.

We seemed to share this gift of divination, something I refused to discuss. I'd always felt that to have acknowledged this shared intuition meant I would be undermining not just my scientific training but also the fierce atheism I had adopted in reaction against my strict Catholic upbringing.

'Let's talk about it later.' I tried to pull Isabella back towards the bed, with no success.

'Oliver, I have to dive today! It's all planned. We've found the site of a Ra shipwreck that I'm sure belongs to Cleopatra.

It dates from the Battle of Actium. The astrarium could have been on board – the Greek historian Siculus mentions such an object being given to Cleopatra at her coronation.'

'What's the rush? You've waited years. Surely it can wait a few days?'

'I don't *have* a few days.' Her desperation seemed to have reached new heights and I didn't fully understand the nature of her distress: all I knew was that Isabella could easily become intractable. I looked at her, searching for another tactic.

'Sweetheart, the whole area's a military zone.' I slipped an arm around her waist.

'I've made provisions. There'll be an official on the boat.'

'Really? Or is this some dubious character you've bribed?'

She shrugged off my arm. 'I'm making that dive, no matter what!'

But under her anger I thought she looked apprehensive. Perhaps about us, the marriage, our careers. But, if I hadn't known her better, I might have assumed it was fear.

'So you really believe the astrarium was aboard this ship?' I asked, more conciliatory. 'Why would Cleopatra take it into the middle of a raging sea battle?'

'She was desperate. The political alliances of the time had shifted, putting her and Mark Antony into a dangerous position while Octavian tried to establish his power. She knew that Mark Antony was delusional about his military supremacy. She also knew that if Octavian won, he would murder her lover and sacrifice their children. This was a woman who had staked all on winning. Siculus described the astrarium as a powerful weapon that could predict when to sail and when to attack. She must have taken it to help her lover.'

I struggled to keep my expression neutral. I believed in a

world of cause and effect: crushed carbon made diamonds; crushed limestone, marble; compressed organic material, oil. This was my world: palpable, exploitable. Isabella's world was far more spiritual: there was a karmic logic to the outcome of events; the personal had an immediate impact on the political, the micro on the macro. I thought this a misinformed perception; an anthropocentric outlook that bred complacency; the determinist's investment in the notion of meaningful destiny.

'If Cleopatra had the astrarium and it was able to influence the outcome of the battle, why did she flee and abandon Mark Antony to Octavian?' I asked.

'I don't know. But if it had been me, I would have fought to change my fate right up to the last minute. The astrarium would have saved her, I know it.' Her obsessive tone worried me. Again, the desire to protect her shot through me but I knew that to stand between Isabella and her quest would mean the end of our marriage and certainly any respect she held for me. A fiercely independent woman who had consciously fought both her family and her culture for the right to pursue her profession, I had no choice but to trust her judgement. Nevertheless there was something unsettling about this particular dive that I couldn't quite place my finger on – all of her obsession seemed to be leading to this one event.

There was a huge clap of thunder outside. A violent gust of wind threw open the French windows and pushed over a cane chair.

'That's cyclone weather,' I told her as I secured the doors. 'You are *not* diving today!'

'It's too dangerous for me not to dive!' she yelled.

Isabella was almost hysterical by now and I knew it was pointless to continue to argue.

'You can dive tomorrow, first light,' I said, pulling her into an embrace. 'I'll go with you, okay? But this day is for us. We'll do something nice. Isn't it the anniversary of your grandfather's birthday? We could visit your grandmother. By tomorrow morning the storm will have cleared and visibility is going to be much better.'

'You don't understand,' she murmured into my chest. But she let me guide her back to bed.

Back then I thought we had all the time in the world.

Already the salty tang of the sea air was discernible above the exhaust fumes and the wafting scent of incense billowing from jars placed outside night stalls, an odour tainted by the ubiquitous but faint smell of sewage. Isabella wound up the taxi window; we were driving down the Corniche – the long seafront path that swung around the glittering curve of the Eastern Harbour. We stopped at a red light and I glanced across at the cafés on the sidewalk. Huddled around small tables were groups of men, some dressed in pale brown jellabas and blue turbans, the traditional dress of the fellahin, others in Western clothes, sharing the large hookah pipes with their colourful corded stems snaking out into the mouth of the smoker. Inside one of the cafés a black-and-white television blared out to a small argumentative knot of men and youths. A football game was playing. A penalty was being taken and a sudden cheer catapulted through the men, reminding me of England and the long afternoons spent watching football with my father and brother.

I turned back to face the Mediterranean. The emptiness of the panorama was in stark contrast to the frenetic metropolis nestled up beside it. Liberating the eye, this elemental minimalism was always a comfort to me. It took me away from humanity, from the mistakes we make, the noisiness of life. In Alexandria, as in the rest of Egypt, this polarity was exaggerated. The desert touched the sea, just as the green fecundity of the delta surrounding the Nile and its canals butted right up against the sand. It was said that Alexandria had a front door and a back door and little else.

North-west of the bay, out there under the waves, lay Isabella's archaeological site. A place where once the great sea battle between Mark Antony and Octavian had taken place, it was easy to imagine the long ancient wooden battleships, oars creaking as they raced against each other, galley slaves lighting the flaming balls to catapult them high across the waves, the battering rams ready. Isabella had grown up among myths of Cleopatra's subterranean city Herakleion, and family friends would tell stories of swimming amongst strange sunken statues, ruins of palaces. Tales that buried themselves deep in her psyche, drawing her irredeemably to their mystery. I couldn't help being proud of the explorer within her, regardless of how it impacted on our relationship. Reaching across, I took her hand as the taxi continued down towards her grandmother's villa.

The wealthy suburb of Bulkely still retained some of its original mansions, wrought-iron gates enclosing gardens of tumbling bougainvillea, Lotus trees and blossoming cacti as well as palm trees. Isabella's family, the Brambillas, had once been one of the key dynasties within the large and influential Italian–Alexandrian community. Isabella's father, Paolo, had died shortly after the Suez Crisis in 1956 when, in reaction to the military attack on Egypt by the French, British and Israelis – an attack triggered by President Nasser's decision to nationalise the Suez canal after the US and Britain withdrew an offer to fund the building of the Aswan Dam – Nasser took control of all of the foreign-owned companies and exiled many of the old colonial class. President of the Italian Rowing Club, the Rotary Club and owner of a large and highly successful cotton-ginning mill, Paolo had been transformed from owner to manager overnight and the factory that processed the cottonseed had been handed over to the fellahin who had worked the cotton fields for centuries. The humiliation had been too much for the Don and he had died of a heart attack several weeks later. Cecilia, his young wife, remarried within the year and moved back to Italy, leaving her eight-year-old daughter with her in-laws to be brought up.

Isabella had barely talked to her mother over the years. Her grandfather Giovanni Brambilla, a man broken by the death of his son and the decline of the family, had retreated into the two passions that had always preoccupied him – hunting and Egyptology – until his death ten years ago. Now his widow, Francesca Brambrilla, was forced to rent out the top floor of her villa and had been pawning her jewellery for decades. Nevertheless, she retained her loyal Sudanese housekeeper, Aadeel, who had come with her as part of her trousseau. Although Aadeel was an official tenant of the villa these days and not an indentured employee, he still wore the uniform of the pre-Revolution servant: a red turban and traditional Egyptian male attire. It was the last act in a drama that both were determined to play out: obsolete roles from a bygone era.

The Brambilla villa, although dilapidated, was still impressive. A familiar sense of intimidation rose in me as the taxi pulled up in front of its marble-pillared entrance. Isabella's background was one of assumed wealth, even when most of the money had been lost. But I'd come from nothing. I'd grown up with a miner for a father and an Irish Catholic mother who was deeply religious, yet had outraged her own parents by marrying a Protestant. It had always seemed to me that she'd never quite forgiven my father for seducing her away from her own family. She was a piano teacher who had greater aspirations for her children than did my pragmatic, deeply stoic father who thought it good enough for his sons to follow him down into the mine. Despite this ongoing feud, my parents' marriage had been one of great love and after my mother died a couple of years ago my father had become as lost as a rudderless boat.

My childhood had taught me that if there was a God he'd certainly abandoned my parents to their hardships. It seemed to me that the poorer you were the more religious you were likely to be – an abdication of taking responsibility of one's fate – and it had led to my abandonment of Catholicism, to socialist tendencies at university and finally to my material aspirations.

As we both climbed out of the taxi we noticed a yellow Fiat sports car. 'That's Hermes's car,' Isabella said with a wary tone to her voice. 'That'll make it an interesting encounter.'

I glanced over, surprised. Normally Isabella would have been enthusiastic about seeing Hermes, one of her few mentors.

'I thought Francesca hated him?'

'Exactly, but today would've been my grandfather's birthday and Hermes always visits, as he did when my grandfather was still alive. Nonna is just too well-bred to refuse him.'

Hermes Hemiedes, an Egyptologist, had been an old friend of Isabella's grandfather. When Giovanni Brambilla died, Hermes had formed a relationship with the granddaughter, sharing a fascination – obsession, I thought – with mysticism, astrology and spiritual philosophies. A very reputable interpreter, he and Isabella spent hours together poring over hieroglyphs that she needed translated. Isabella trusted him completely and although I didn't approve of Hermes's influence over Isabella in mystical matters he had a dry wit that I found appealing.

We had finished our lunch and were now drinking coffee in the conservatory, waiting for the traditional dish of marmalade that completed the meal. Francesca and Hermes sat opposite, Francesca in a chair that was reminiscent of some eighteenth-century wooden baroque throne – one of the antiques she hadn't been forced to sell. At eighty years old the matriarch still had the upright stance of a dancer and was the embodiment of classical European grace. She made me think of 1930s Rome – her dyed black hair sculpted into a short crisp wave, the creased olive skin suckered against the bones of a lineage bred for power and beauty.

In contrast, Hermes lounged in a leather armchair. His hair was long, its silver roots merging into dyed purple-red locks that descended to his shoulders. He could almost have passed for an elderly woman, an illusion helped by a remarkable lack of facial hair. His eyes were golden brown with a tinge of yellow in the irises, indicating a curious ethnic mix somewhere in his ancestry. The shape of his face suggested the Sudan while the thinness of his lips gave him a European look. His hands, gnarled by arthritis, bore witness to his true age, which Isabella had told me was around seventy.

A silver dish filled with marmalade was placed on the table, ten matching silver spoons curving out of the thick golden paste like swan's necks. They represented the members of the family, most of whom were long dead. Aadeel placed four glasses of water on the pearl-and-wood inlaid

table. Quickly, I washed the bitter-sweet taste of the marmalade down with the water, then reached for the small cup
of viscous coffee.

Isabella could not relax. She stood up, walked to the
window and pulled open the shutters. Her agitation seemed
a conductor for the lightning that flashed across the sky. The
distant boom of thunder sounded out a moment later.

Francesca sighed in exasperation. 'You think you can wish
away the weather, Isabella? Sit down. You are making me
nervous with all this pent-up energy.'

'Your granddaughter needs to be out there fighting the
elements to find her holy grail,' Hermes said with theatrical
relish. 'Archaeology is a noble calling. It defines the pioneer
within us.'

'Please, Hermes, don't encourage her,' I said. 'At least not
in this God-awful weather.'

'Barry Douglas has dived in worse weather,' Isabella said,
still staring out at the darkened sky.

'Barry Douglas is a self-confessed risk taker,' I retorted.
'He's not interested in anything unless it's highly illegal and
involves sexual conquest.'

Isabella stifled a laugh while Francesca glared at me disapprovingly.

Barry Douglas was a mutual friend of ours, a flamboyant
Australian who had lived in Alexandria for years. He
restored archaeological artefacts – his speciality was anything made of bronze. When he wasn't working he could be
found in the bars, where I often joined him, his irreverent
humour and earthiness a respite from the frenetic pace of
the city.

Francesca turned to me. 'You must tell my granddaughter
to abandon this ridiculous quest of hers. It's exactly those
kinds of obsession that destroyed my husband.'

'Nationalisation destroyed Giovanni, Francesca,' Hermes murmured.

Francesca glanced nervously towards Aadeel. Even I knew Hermes had transgressed; it was dangerous to voice such opinions in a country still caught in the difficult transition from a past of colonial feudalism to a more democratic socialism. And lately President Sadat's efforts to place Egypt into the free world market had caused food riots. Overnight, ration cards were worth nothing, and as it became near impossible to get rice, bread, even gas to cook with, the people revolted.

'Shhh! I will not tolerate such radical beliefs in my house! I have the safety of my family to think about,' she hissed.

The open hostility between the two old associates was now palpable. Isabella intervened.

'*Basta!* Nonna, this discovery is going to establish my reputation, you wait and see.'

'It will finish you,' Francesca replied ominously. 'We should never have let you go to university.'

I sensed an argument looming. Isabella had delighted her grandfather but appalled her grandmother by getting into Oxford to study Archaeology at Lady Margaret Hall; Francesca was traditional and had envisaged a prestigious marriage for Isabella. Instead, she'd got me.

'So you would have been proud of me if I'd hooked a billionaire like my mother?' Isabella snapped back.

Francesca made a small spitting motion into her palm. She hated her daughter-in-law. 'I suppose I should be thankful that at least you are married,' she said. 'The fact that he is English does not make me so happy.'

She turned to me and said sharply, 'You know the English interned my husband in a concentration camp out here in the desert during the war.'

'Along with all the other nationalists who opposed the Allied forces, they had no choice. Grandfather would have volunteered to fight for Rommel; the English were protecting themselves. Besides, to call it a concentration camp is exaggerating, Nonna. After all, Grandfather was a card-carrying member of the Fascist party,' Isabella interjected before I had a chance to respond.

'He was a nationalist, he loved Italy, and, yes, he wore Mussolini's shirt until Il Duce introduced those ridiculous race laws. They were the finish for the party here in Alex. We all knew each other then – Jews, Copts, Catholics, Greeks. It wasn't a problem in those days.' Francesca sighed deeply and visibly restrained herself from making the sign of the cross. 'British and a non-believer as well. What did I do to deserve this?'

'He is a scientist – of course he is an atheist, Francesca,' Hermes cut in.

'It was a conscious choice,' I told her. ' You'd be pleased to hear that I was a bitter disappointment to my Irish-Catholic mother.' Despite myself, I couldn't keep the defensiveness out of my voice. There was a pause. Then Francesca spoke with an intensity I had never heard before.

'Science cannot explain everything, Oliver. There are many mysteries in life.'

'For once, Francesca is right.' Hermes smiled at me, a charmingly open smile, almost like that of a child. It was hard not to trust the natural warmth of the man.

'So this is where you inherited your mysticism from,' I said to Isabella, nodding towards Francesca.

The old woman leaned forward and gripped my arm with a surprising strength. 'You are wrong. She inherited it from my husband. Giovanni was the mystic. I keep what little faith I have left for my postcard collection of saints.'

She released me; her sharp nails leaving an echo in my flesh.

'He was the magus, a visionary,' Hermes added with a sigh, and for a moment a curious truce was drawn between the two old people, almost as if Giovanni himself had stepped into the room.

Isabella turned back quickly from the window. 'Careful, Nonna, I have sheltered Oliver from our darker family secrets. I don't want him to think we are all crazy.'

'But you all are,' Hermes said, and they both broke into laughter.

Ignoring them, Francesca turned back to me. 'Oliver, this is Egypt. I've got my own god, but there are countless others. And sometimes the most rational people find themselves caught up in the inexplicable. Like my granddaughter and this quest for the impossible.'

'She will find the astrarium, I know it,' Hermes concluded.

The statement was delivered with a prophetic smugness that irritated me. It seemed to have a similar effect on Francesca.

'On the other hand, maybe Isabella's search itself is a metaphor,' I replied, before she could speak.

'A metaphor for what?' Francesca smiled wryly.

'For her to find where she truly belongs.'

There was an awkward silence during which I realised I'd stumbled upon a truth that resonated for everyone in the room. Suddenly Isabella sprang up again.

'None of you understand how important this is!' Furious at being talked about like a child, she began pacing. 'Say they prove that the Antikythera Mechanism was able to track the orbits of the planets and the position of the Sun. Do you realise this will prove that the ancient Greeks knew that the Earth wasn't the centre of the universe? Now imagine if I discovered an earlier prototype – say Babylonian or even Egyptian – that had the same function. My discovery would entirely change our view of antiquity! Not only would it force a complete revision of our understanding of ancient engineering, the existence of such a device would also change our notions of ancient navigation, and radically push back the date of our understanding of the first astrolabe. I could prove that the Dark Ages were in fact far darker than we imagine. But not only that, the astrarium could give us so many answers. It would be the discovery of a lifetime.'

'Discovery or no, Isabella, you are a fool to keep diving in the bay,' Francesca said emphatically. 'Not only because of the weather, but sooner or later you will run into trouble. We are all watched everywhere we go – by the military, the secret police, the friend you thought you could confide in.'

'Your granddaughter is experienced. She will be safe.' Hermes put out a hand to reassure the elderly woman.

Pointedly she ignored it. 'No one is safe. Everyone suspects everyone else of being a spy. We publicly welcome Sadat's open-door policy but inflation has made us all desperate. Remember that when people look at us, they still see the old order. Be on your guard, granddaughter. Don't delude yourself – they are all watching, waiting for you to make one mistake.'

'I know how to look after myself,' Isabella replied dismissively. 'Besides, my big strong husband is coming with me on the dive.'

Isabella reached out and curled her fingers, a small fist of heat, into my hand. An amnesty.

I turned to smile at Francesca, but she stared back in hostile indifference. 'Oliver, it is foolish to think your oil money will protect you.'

3

Back at the villa, I lay on the bed watching Isabella undress brusquely with that characteristic efficiency of hers, as if clothes were an irritant she needed to rid herself of: it was both amusing and erotic at the same time, and I loved the way she seemed to battle her own femininity.

I reached over, picked up a thrown stocking and handed it back to her. 'Where did you meet this official you're taking on the dive?'

She sat down at the dresser. 'At a lecture at the French Archaeology Society.'

'He could be working for anyone. Why can't you let yourself be supported by a proper team of archaeologists?'

'Right, and let them steal ten years of research from under my nose? Amelia Lynhurst already suspects I'm diving for the astrarium. I've heard a rumour that she knows I'm close to finding it. She'd do anything to get her hands on it,' she replied grimly. By now she was dressed only in bra and pants.

Amelia Lynhurst, Isabella's mentor when she began at Oxford, had lost a great deal of credibility after the publication of a controversial paper about a mysterious priestess of

Isis who she claimed had lived in the time of the Thirtieth Dynasty, during the reign of the Pharaoh Nectanebo II. The paper was controversial because there had been little evidence that the priestess had ever existed. Despite this, Isabella had remained close to the Englishwoman until they'd had an irreparable falling-out during Isabella's second year of university. She had never told me why they had argued.

'Will you stop worrying?' Isabella went on impatiently. 'Faakhir's cousin, who owns the boat, has got friends who work for the coastguard.'

'Sweetheart, if you're caught, it'll be prison for Faakhir and his cousin and the end of your career here.' I was trying to tread carefully to avoid yet another row.

'We're not going to be caught. I'm not hauling up a huge statue, just a very small bronze artefact. Besides, your work is far more dangerous than mine.'

'My work is authorised exploration.'

'Bravo, but you're still blasé about the risks you take.'

She was right – I was being hypocritical. The places my company sent me to were invariably dangerous terrain or in a state of political upheaval. But at least my presence was authorised rather than clandestine – I didn't like the idea of Isabella falling foul of the dangerously fickle labyrinth of Egyptian bureaucracy. It could endanger both our careers.

'Why not cancel for a few days?' I suggested. 'I could try to get some extra sonar equipment through GeoConsultancy—'

'Oliver,' Isabella interrupted. 'This is non-negotiable. The boat's been arranged. It has to be tomorrow! There's no more time.'

The fatalistic tone of her voice jolted me out of my exhaustion. Tensing up, I stared at her for a moment, uncomprehending. Then a kernel of remembrance uncoiled in the back of my mind.

'This isn't about that prediction, is it? Isabella, you know it's complete bullshit.'

We'd had this debate many times before, dating right back to our very first meeting in Goa. Isabella had just come from seeing a mystic who, amongst other things, had given her her astrological chart, which included not only the time of her birth but also the date of her death. Through the years she remained convinced of its accuracy, despite all my arguments to the contrary. She'd never given me the exact date but it must be looming closer for her to feel this panicked.

She broke angrily away from me. 'You just don't get it, do you? That Newtonian you carry around inside you refuses to believe that there might be other principles – less conventional, perhaps, but just as valid. At least I'm honest about my methodology.'

I tried to stop myself becoming defensive; I hated it when Isabella slipped into what I perceived as irrational mysticism. Sensing my shift in attitude, she turned towards me.

'Come on – I've seen you out there on the oilfield, in your bare feet, sniffing the air. It's not just science you rely on, but you simply won't admit it!'

Now naked, Isabella threw herself down onto the bed beside me. I suddenly realised she was shaking. Horrified, I pulled her into my arms. 'What is it?'

There was a pause. 'Tomorrow is the day Ahmos Khafre predicted I would die.'

'You're not going to die,' I finally said warily. 'It's all superstitious nonsense. This dive is too dangerous, Isabella.'

She stared up at me, thinking.

'No,' she finally replied. 'This is my last chance to find the astrarium. We will dive tomorrow.'

'I'm still coming with you,' I snapped. 'I'm not going to allow anything to happen.'

Isabella rolled on top of me, her slim body pressed against mine as she stared solemnly into my eyes. I tried smiling but her face stayed serious, her gaze boring through any pretence, as if she were trying to look beyond the banter that had become the veneer of our relationship. I knew that I had no option but to support her. Isabella did not believe in compromise, emotional or otherwise. For her, this would have been surrendering to mediocrity. She threw herself recklessly from one experience into another. This impulsiveness was one of the reasons I had first been attracted to her. A characteristic so opposite to my own controlling nature, it had always provided a healthy counterbalance, but recently it had become something I couldn't protect her from, as much as I longed to.

'What is it, sweetheart?' I asked, unnerved by her unblinking stare.

She appeared to be on the brink of speaking, but then hesitated before kissing me instead, her long hair falling either side of my face in a wave of musk.

I always wanted Isabella. I never understood why that was – maybe the differences between us created a space, a place I could eroticise. I couldn't tell you how; it just worked. The touch of her lips, her fingers, the scent of her neck, made me stiffen. She was the first woman with whom I had truly understood the notion of desire, a thirst that was intensely emotional, not just physical. She was home to me; we made our own nation.

I pulled her down to me and, finally, she smiled.

I was woken an hour later by Isabella thrashing about in the bed. I shook her and she woke up – her heart racing against my chest; her face veiled with sweat.

'The same nightmare?' I asked.

'Yes, except I don't know if it's a nightmare or a memory. This time it was clearer, more specific . . .'

She faltered, staring into the distance as she forced herself to remember. I waited, knowing that, for her, part of the exorcism was in the telling.

'There's a platform,' she said slowly, 'with a group of people standing on it. They're dressed bizarrely, like animals.'

'Maybe they *are* animals?' I said.

She waved the suggestion away. 'No, they are humans, real people. There's a man with the head of a dog – a jackal, I think – crouching by a large set of scales. Then a tall figure with the head of a bird, a big bird holding a quill, and a man dressed in white – he looks terrified. There's blood on his robe. Another figure's holding him – this one has the head of a falcon – and they're in front of a throne. There's a figure sitting on the throne – maybe the god Osiris . . .'

'A ritual, perhaps?'

She was silent for a moment, then suddenly clutched at my hand. 'Incredible! I've just worked out what it is, after all these years. It's the ceremony of the weighing of the heart, Oliver! I've shown you the pictures, remember?'

The Ancient Egyptians believed that after a person died their heart was weighed by Osiris. Depending on the purity of the heart, the deceased was either allowed to pass into the afterlife or was denied entry – a terrifying concept for them. The idea of the ritual disturbed me, partly because of its sheer grotesqueness but also because it reminded me of my mother's attempts to indoctrinate me with a notion of sin.

'But why would I dream such a thing?' Isabella said, now almost more distressed. 'Over and over?'

'It's probably a motif you return to when you're stressed – maybe a fear of being judged by your peers?'

'But it's so clear – the detail of Osiris's headdress, his eyes, the terror of the man waiting to be judged, the heat of the flaming torches on the walls . . . I'm telling you, it's like I have lived this. I just can't remember . . .'

'Buried memory?'

The thought that she'd already lived through this seemed to frighten her even more. Finally she said, 'If it is, maybe it should stay buried.' Restless, she got out of bed and went over to her desk.

'Isabella, you need sleep.'

'I couldn't possibly sleep now. Besides, going over the plans for tomorrow will help relax me.'

Naked, she put on her reading glasses and switched on a desk lamp, illuminating several maps of the bay and the seabed. I knew she referred to two sources of expertise on the geography of the harbour. One was Kamel Abdou el Sadat who had campaigned tirelessly to try and get the Egyptian authorities to fund exploration. The other was an earlier enthusiast – Prince Thosson, who had created early twentieth-century aerial maps of the bay. And it was these two men's own hand-drawn maps that now lay before her. She picked up a ruler and pencil and began to retrace her route for the dive, the defencelessness of her bare shoulders an innocent contrast to the intense expression on her face. My gaze moved down her body, along her legs curled together under the table and to the tattoo on her ankle – a sparrowhawk with a human face turned in profile. It was her Ba, the Egyptian representation of the soul after death. Traditionally these birds were sparrowhawks unless the deceased was a pharaoh in which case they were falcons – although, depending on the period of history and the school of thought, the Ba could also be a butterfly or even a heron. Isabella had had the tattoo for as long as I'd known her.

She'd told me she'd got it on a drunken trip to London with a couple of her wilder girlfriends when she'd been a student. Isabella loved the hieroglyph for the Ba. It was like her personal totem. The Ba was always considered attached to the body and was only freed in death after which it could fly anywhere, even into open sunlight.

Isabella talked about Bas often, describing how, for Egyptians, they also represented individuality, the emotional characteristics that made up a personality – even a person's own morality and inspiration. The other elements were Ka, the life force, defined as the spirit that entered the body at birth, Ren – name, Sheut – shadow, and Ib – the heart. A third significant hieroglyph was Akh, which depicted the successful union of the Ka and Ba that enabled the deceased to progress to the afterlife. A successful passing-over into the afterworld could only take place if the Ba was united with the Ka at the moment of death. If this union did not happen, the soul was thrown into oblivion, an annihilation that was the equivalent of Hell for the Ancient Egyptians whose afterlife was an imagined parallel world full of earthly pursuits and pleasures. Isabella herself was terrified of such a fate.

As I stood and walked over to the desk I noticed Isabella slip a small envelope under the ink blotter: a movement so tiny and mostly blocked by her turning her back to me that a second later I wasn't quite sure whether I'd imagined it. She swung back around and smiled. 'Recognise this?' she said, and held up the drawing of the astrarium I'd seen on the floor the night before. 'It's a great rendering, I really think it's going to look like this. Gareth's a genius.'

'Oh, I don't know about that,' I replied gruffly; I couldn't help thinking about my brother's complete inability – genius or otherwise – to look after himself both physically and financially. I took the drawing from her and peered at it. The elegant ink drawing showed the jagged teeth of cogs set against more cogs, while another perspective demonstrated how the interior workings fitted within a wooden frame. Beneath the diagram was a series of six symbols or letters of an ancient script. I hadn't noticed them before. 'What's this? It doesn't look like Greek – is it meant to be Ptolemaic?' I asked.

'It is, but this is a cipher made of hieroglyphs. The Ptolemaic rulers took every opportunity to link themselves to Ancient Egyptian beliefs in order to legitimise themselves. I've found evidence that this cipher may be written on the mechanism itself. It's a phrase from a temple wall, an Isis temple, only recently discovered. I had Gareth write it down, because he's so good at riddles.'

'Have you solved it?' I was intrigued despite myself.

'I have an idea, but I'll wait until I have the astrarium before I reveal my theory to a cynic like yourself.'

'Be careful of anything Gareth suggests,' I said warningly, handing her back the drawing. 'He's such a conspiracist.'

Isabella threw her hands up in mock exasperation. 'You see? No wonder I don't confide in you. I'm too frightened of being ridiculed.'

'Come back to bed, please?' I begged, smiling.

Dawn was creeping under the blinds but by my calculations there was at least an hour before we had to get up for the dive. Sighing, Isabella switched off the desk lamp and skipped across the room. As she slipped in beside me, the familiar fragrance of her body was an immediate comfort.

'You'll always look after Gareth, won't you? He needs you, even if he'll never admit it.'

'Of course I will,' I answered, trying to ignore the fatalistic undercurrent in her voice.

My brother Gareth, born sixteen years after me, was an unexpected menopausal baby, adored by my mother but regarded as a late financial burden by my father. I had hardly known Gareth when he was a child, but when I did visit I would take him out for long walks across the moors, describing the rock formations in the hope that it would instil some greater ambition than my parents' aspirations. It must have worked, for at the age of twelve he'd announced that he intended to become a landscape painter. We were close in those days and I would often make the effort to travel to Cumbria to see him. But suddenly, at sixteen, he began to reject openly both my parents and myself. He would argue furiously with my mother, and would not talk to my father for days. The first time he slammed the phone down on me I was devastated by the sense of alienation. I had loved the wild imagination and trust in the young Gareth: it was as if another, more sullen and closed individual had hijacked him. By the time he arrived in London to start art college he was already addicted to drugs. Despite this and determined to be supportive of his career as an artist, I'd tried openly to win him back. Regardless of my efforts it was always Isabella to whom Gareth turned in times of distress – our relationship from then on was never quite as it once had been.

Sighing, Isabella curled up against me. 'If anything should happen to me, Faakhir will know what to do with the astrarium.'

I pulled her closer, her leg over my torso, my arm slipped under her waist. 'Nothing's going to happen.'

'No, Oliver, you must listen to me: you must guard the astrarium with your life. If the astrarium really is all that I believe it to be, then a lot of people will want it, but it is crucial to keep it safe. Don't trust anyone, except Faakhir. Follow your instinct – your natural gift will lead you. It believes in you even if you don't believe in it. There is a journey and a destination for the astrarium.'

'What do you mean?' I yawned, tired from a long day and the prospect of getting up again soon.

'I don't know yet. There is so much we don't know until I find the mechanism itself.' She sighed. 'All I know is I have a feeling that when we find the astrarium it could throw us into much danger. You'll just have to trust me. Promise?'

I nodded and, reaching down, kissed her deeply, and there it was – a simple pledge given simply. With hindsight I wonder whether if I had argued with her, had made the case that perhaps sometimes it's good to leave some treasures undiscovered, old hurts and dramas dormant, unanalysed, never to be returned to – would I have persuaded her not to have taken that dive? Maybe, maybe not, but I wasn't that kind of man in those days. Then, with all the arrogance of a young gun who'd achieved a certain status and who believed Nature favoured the hard-working, I assumed our lives would go on for ever.

The boat – a small fishing vessel aptly named Ra Five, with an old rusting cabin and a pile of mended fishing nets on board – chugged determinedly against the incoming tide, ploughing through the great webs of seaweed the storm had thrown up in the days before. Faakhir's cousin Jamal, a short muscular man in his late fifties with the calloused and scarred hands of a working fisherman, guided us out towards the bobbing red buoy that marked the dive site. He was the owner of the boat and, as Isabella had again reassured me, part of the coastguard, and had therefore secured the official permission necessary for her to take the boat out and make the dive. I wasn't sure whether to believe her or not. Jamal's constant smile was betrayed by a nervousness in his eyes and I suspected bribery had played its part. But I knew better than to ask.

Hanging over the cabin controls was a miniature Michelin man, and a plastic hula-hoop girl with a painted green grass skirt hung alongside the eye of Horus as I steadied myself against the chipped wooden panelling.

'Careful, you might fall overboard,' Omar, the official Isabella had told me about the night before, joked. He was a plump man with a badly fixed broken nose and a thin white scar running vertically across one heavy eyelid down to his cheek. He wore a fluorescent pink life jacket strapped over his clothes and appeared to be taking little interest in the proceedings. After suffering two centuries of the illegal excavation and export of its ancient statues and artefacts, Egypt had finally established a policing system that required all archaeological sites to have at least one of their officers present. But even if Omar was really such an officer and not just moonlighting, I strongly suspected that Isabella had deliberately underplayed the significance of the astrarium.

Faakhir stood in the doorway of the cabin. He had a clumsiness on land that completely belied his grace when in the water. When I'd first dived with him I had been astounded not only by the fluidity of his movements but also by his uncanny ability to locate objects on the seabed, even in the murky waters of Alexandria's harbour. The fishing hut in Al Gomrok he'd grown up in had a number of small Ptolemaic objects placed casually next to a radio or an old family photograph. Objects his father and grandfather had either caught in their nets or hauled up from the seabed over the decades. Faakhir himself had seen submerged statues and pillars, many of which had become reefs over the aeons, attracting schools of fish: the reason why the fishermen fished there in the first place. But there were levels of Faakhir's diving expertise that were unfathomable to Isabella and he was always strangely vague about where he'd trained.

'The Mediterranean makes brothers of us all,' he'd once said to me. 'She is like a language – you either speak her or you don't.'

'Are you going to venture in, my friend?' Faakhir asked me.

I wasn't too keen on diving, feeling slightly claustrophobic underwater. Also, I wanted to keep an eye on Omar. 'Maybe later. I'm happy to watch for the time being.'

'Oliver, wait until you see the shipwreck for yourself,' he said dreamily. 'The royal boat is a skeleton but you can still see its shape. To imagine, Cleopatra herself would have sailed in it!'

Isabella appeared, an oxygen tank slung over her shoulder. 'Ready, Faakhir?'

Faakhir smiled. 'I have studied the map so many times I could swim to the site blind.'

'With the amount of sand that's shifted in the last few nights you probably will be. You know the drill. Let's cover the area evenly, side by side, until something registers on the metal detectors.'

Isabella's voice had the clipped authoritative tone she adopted when she was nervous, and I felt another stab of apprehension.

'How long will you be?' I asked.

'We've narrowed down the location to a few feet with the help of side-scan sonar. We have a window of opportunity of about three hours.'

'A mystery thousands of years old! We are going to make history – I know it.'

Faakhir's excitement was infectious and I couldn't help smiling. 'Just stay safe,' I told them both.

'Don't worry.' Isabella was impatient as she handed an oxygen tank to Faakhir.

Two metal detectors – clumsy Soviet-designed devices the navy used for detecting underwater bombs – lay on the wooden deck. Isabella and Faakhir placed the attached headphones over their ears and tested for sound. Both of them sat concentrating, eyes shut as they strained to hear the dull bleeping, already lost in concentration on the task at hand. There was a strange intimacy to the act and, for a moment, I found myself irrationally jealous.

The plan was that they would swim along the seabed at a distance of about half a metre from the bottom. As soon as they heard anything, they would signal me and I'd lower a steel tube, which they'd then sink around the bronze artefact. The tube would be lifted off the seabed with the artefact preserved in the mud packed around it. Later, they would clean and desalinate the artefact, first in a bath of salt water and then in fresh water.

Opening her eyes, Isabella checked her watch, then stood decisively. Faakhir followed and solemnly they pulled on their diving masks. Isabella sat on the side of the boat before she threw herself backwards into the sea. A moment later, Faakhir – flippers kicking like black fins – disappeared into the blue. Jamal and I carefully lowered the metal detectors after them. Within minutes the only evidence we could see of their presence underwater was the movement of the rope leading down to them and the dull torchlight that rapidly vanished in the rippling depths.

Omar was sitting on an upturned lobster cage, his head tilted towards the sun as if he were sunbathing. I was convinced his indifference was disingenuous.

He leaned towards me. 'Mr Warnock, we are very pleased

with your wife's work. We think she has much talent. But maybe a little crazy too, *non*?'

Hiding my distrust, I smiled and nodded.

I took my own seat on the deck and stared back at Alexandria, its skyline of hotels and apartment buildings broken by the occasional distinctive minaret of a mosque. It was hard to believe that Isabella might finally locate her holy grail.

I sat back remembering the first time Isabella had told me about the astrarium, sitting there at that bar in Goa. The establishment was a small bamboo-and-brick structure run by a German hippie and her Hindu husband. Incense burnt in the corner and the Rolling Stones played incessantly through a small tinny speaker. Appropriately named 'Marlene Chakrabuty's Sanctuary from Hell', they were famous for their Bloody Marys – my favourite cocktail. The air was constantly filled with the treacly aroma of hashish and an autographed cover of the Abbey Road album hung proudly above the bar.

I had just finished a job with Shell and was consumed by the ennui I always experienced after a successful exploration. Then I lived solely for the elation of the chase, the feeling of using all my senses, the intellectual rigour of the geological calculations involved as well as the emotional groping – the blind intuitive flash that always came to me standing out there in the field, sniffing the air, feeling the vibration of the rock beneath my bare feet; the roustabouts joking nervously amongst themselves as they watched me take off my shoes and socks to stand there in silence, eyes shut, reading the land under my naked soles.

In those days I was always running to the next job as quickly as I could. It was the exhilarating rush of finding the next potential new oil reservoir and not the money that kept me running. From what, I never really knew, not back then – I just knew there was some part of myself I had been denying for as long as I could remember. I was thirty-three, a dangerous age for a man, a craggy lump of graceless Anglo-Saxon masculinity drooped over his bar stool.

I'd grown up in Cumbria, between the Lake District and the Irish Sea. Out there your body forms an island, a wind-battered automaton of pounding legs and flaying arms. Hot breath warming icy cheeks in the folds of a scarf as you tear jagged through the antediluvian landscape. This self-sufficiency, the dogged struggle against the elements, starts to define you and before you know it, you have become a curmudgeon – bristling, impenetrable and ready to deal with a hostile world. Not the most attractive proposition and I knew it. But none of these characteristics had deterred Isabella.

She'd introduced herself by dropping a necklace of amber beads into my Bloody Mary. I looked up and was startled by the vivid energy that seemed to dance around her face – the ferocious intelligence that sharpened her features. I pulled out the amber beads, sucked the vodka off them and, after holding them up to the light, guessed that the amber came from Yantarny, Russia. To my surprise she seemed to find the fact that I was a geophysicist intriguing and, determined to engage me in conversation, she'd sat down next to me and demanded that I buy her a drink. I remember noticing how she seemed a little wild and reckless, almost as if she were determined to shake off some recent trauma. But back then India was full of lost souls.

Three whiskies later Isabella was telling me about her visit to Ahmos Khafre. My seduction plans were momentarily derailed. I had a strong aversion to mysticism and disliked the dispossessed Westerners I often came across floating aimlessly, with their long hair and loose mock-native clothes, through the same geography as myself. However, I found myself suspending disbelief when Isabella went on to tell me about the topic of her doctorate.

'It's a kind of portable astrarium – a mechanised model of the universe that doesn't just tell mean time and sidereal time but also incorporates a calendar for movable feasts, and has dials illustrating the movements of the sun, moon and the five planets known to the ancients. Leonardo da Vinci saw one that was built during the Renaissance – he described it as "a work of divine speculation, a work unattainable by human genius . . . axles within axles." Another was found in 1901 – the Antikythera Mechanism. My hypothesis is that an earlier prototype existed.'

'And your mystic?'

'Ahmos Khafre – you should meet him. He's a really serious archaeologist as well as a world-famous astrologer.'

'Before you go on, I'd better warn you I'm a complete sceptic.'

'I don't believe you.' Isabella hiccupped and I guessed she might be drunker than she realised. 'A sceptic does not use sorcery to tell me the exact place my amber came from.'

'That wasn't sorcery, that was just training, extremely good detective work and a tiny bit of guesswork. Plus . . .' I held the beads up again. 'I recognise the fossilised insect in this piece as the rare Slavic wasp.' It was a ruse I often applied to cover guesswork – the trickster covering his tracks with a pseudo-fact.

She stared at me, her huge black eyes widening.

'I think, Oliver, that you are a man who is not entirely integrated with both his intellect and intuition. But that's okay: we will be good for each other – I can make you whole and you can protect me.'

Isabella's quaint use of English and her Italian accent had

me hooked, but her uncanny observation made me uncomfortable. I decided that if I was to bed her it would be sensible to steer her away from any further analysis of my personality.

'So let me guess: your mystic told you about a wonderful but deeply cynical Englishman with an interesting Northern accent . . .'

'Not if you intend to ridicule me.'

'I promise to keep an open mind.'

'Really?' Her lack of guile was utterly disarming.

'Cross my Newtonian heart and hope to die.'

Isabella smiled. Then, after finishing her drink, she moved closer.

'Years ago, Ahmos Khafre was given a letter rumoured to have been written by Sonnini de Manoncour, a naturalist who had travelled with Napoleon's troops. He wrote that he had come across information that a ship carrying Cleopatra, retreating from the Battle of Actium and sunk in the Alexandrian Bay, had been carrying a famous astrarium. One day I'll find that astrarium, I know I will. I have to.' She hesitated as if she were about to tell me something else, something of greater importance. Then in the next instant she looked pensive. I remember, even to this day, that intensity. Her narrow triangular face collapsing into vulnerability and, to my great surprise, I instantly wanted to rescue her, a sensation that only fuelled my desire.

'Can I be with you tonight?'

I could barely hear her over the noise of the revellers behind us and, sitting there wanting her in all my low self-esteem, I thought I had misheard. It was only after our lovemaking later the same night that Isabella told me about how Ahmos Khafre had also insisted upon giving her a birth chart that predicted the date of her death. Furious at the irresponsibility of such an action I'd sat up in bed and had tried, unsuccessfully, to persuade her that it was all superstitious nonsense. I'd failed. We were married three months later.

I stared down at the murky water, incredulous at how we'd come from there to here and that Isabella had actually carried out her quest.

My reverie was broken by Jamal's shout – the rope was twitching. Was it possible she'd actually found it? Against my reservations, I felt some of the same elation that Faakhir had shown earlier. If this was it, this was truly a momentous event in history. I tugged the rope, the signal to Isabella that I was ready, and she replied with four twitches. I fastened the steel clip attached to the thick tube to the cable and lowered it into the water; in seconds it had disappeared, sliding down to the divers below.

Jamal reached into the back pocket of his jeans and pulled out a battered packet of Lucky Strike cigarettes, which he offered to both Omar and me. I'd given up smoking a year before because I'd noticed it was affecting my sense of smell – an essential asset for my oil hunting – but that morning I lit up.

'Now we wait,' Jamal announced ponderously, then began to hum 'Stayin' Alive' by the Bee Gees under his breath while Omar stared fixedly out at the horizon. I exchanged glances with Jamal. It was as if our thoughts drifted up with the cigarette smoke – independent patterns curling around each other, then merging in a secret shared anxiety: what if we get caught?

A speedboat roared past, seemingly coming out of nowhere. Startled, my stomach tightened as I steeled myself for a raid by the coastguard. But Omar leapt to his feet and waved. A man on board waved back and the boat continued on its course.

Omar smiled, reading my expression. 'Don't worry, he is a friend. Besides, we have nothing to hide.'

I had the distinct impression that he was enjoying my discomfort.

Just then a flock of pigeons flew overhead. Both men looked up at the sight of the wheeling birds.

Jamal cursed under his breath and glanced nervously at the shoreline. 'That is not good,' he muttered.

'A bad omen,' Omar confirmed grimly, his gaze following the swooping mass.

'It's just pigeons,' I said, wondering why they were so agitated.

'Look again, my friend,' Jamal said, and pointed. 'These are land birds flying away from the land.'

'Perhaps they're flying towards an island.'

'What island? There is no island – just Cyprus, too far for pigeons. No, something is not right. Maybe the storm is returning, or perhaps something more dangerous.'

I was relieved when Isabella and Faakhir surfaced in a great rush of silver bubbles. Pushing her mask up to her forehead, Isabella's ecstatic face appeared.

'We found it, Oliver! Isn't that amazing? We have it! The tube's sunk and fitted – all we have to do now is lift it out! I've found the astrarium!'

4

Isabella handed the metal detector up to me and hauled herself back onto the boat. Faakhir, smiling, climbed up after her while the others hung back, inexplicably tentative.

'We should go back now, make the final dive tomorrow,' Jamal announced, glancing at the horizon.

'Absolutely not! The site will be covered again by tomorrow. We have to retrieve it in the next hour, before the tide comes through!'

Isabella's tone was demanding and urgent. I glanced at the men and saw an expression cross Jamal's face, so fast I think I was probably the only one who noticed. I'd seen it before with some of the Arab oil workers: resentment. It was difficult for them to take orders from a woman, no matter how much they respected her.

Faakhir, sensing potential conflict, put his hand on his cousin's shoulder. 'Please, we are so close, and if we dive tomorrow we'll have to start all over again.'

Jamal glanced up at the flock of pigeons – now barely a speck on the horizon. A particularly high wave lifted the

boat and a couple of dull thuds sounded as the floats lashed
to the sides bumped against the hull.

'Okay. But be as quick as you can.'

I picked up a spare mask and oxygen tank, 'I'm coming
with—'

'Oliver, I don't need . . .' Isabella began.

But Faakhir put a hand on her shoulder. 'Isabella, we
could do with the extra help.'

Isabella glanced back at me. 'Okay, but you'll have to
follow orders, understand?'

Stifling my claustrophia I nodded; there was no way I was
going to allow Isabella to take any extra risk by being under-
staffed.

The site was illuminated by an underwater floodlight fixed
by a rope. It was eerie swimming down towards the light – I
had the strange sensation of an inverted world in which the
sun lay beneath us. The water was cloudy, but as we neared
the seabed the site came into view – a suspended oasis surrounded by darkness. Clouds of fish hovered like a swarm of
moths, attracted by the floodlight.

At first the ship looked like some kind of unusual reef, a
sudden manifestation of coral and molluscs jutting out from
the seabed, but the hazy outline of what appeared to be a
sphinx's head and shoulders stood out from the base. Closer,
the features of the statue took shape. Algae had covered
everything but her face, which, unlike many of the images
I'd seen in the past, had a human asymmetry about it. The
arched nose and large eyes were surprisingly naturalistic and
seemed to hold a wry humour. The creature stared back at
me through the cloudy water with a beauty that was palpably
and jarringly real. Was it a relic from the nearby submerged
island of Antirhodos, which had once housed Cleopatra's

palace, swept in by the massive wave that had destroyed the whole area thousands of years before?

Isabella swam into view, gesturing towards the rest of the site. Pivoting slowly, I saw how the seabed had taken on the impression of the hull of a ship, with only the basic ribs of its construction still imprinted on the mud. Isabella hovered over the site, indicating the rim and handles of the steel tube, which now held the bronze artefact, its circular edges having been sunk down around it, deep enough for the object to be lifted along with the sea mud packed tightly around it.

She unhooked the floodlight and shone it onto the tube. Faakhir clipped a hook to one of the handles so the tube could be winched to the surface once we'd freed it from the seabed. He gave me the thumbs-up sign and we each took one of the handles and began to pull the tube slowly out of the mud. It wasn't easy. I felt the muscles in my arms tighten and my mask began to steam up from perspiration. Through the clouds of dislodged sand I could just make out Faakhir's straining face.

Unexpectedly, the mud released its grip and the tube began to lift away. Finally a foot and a half of steel gleamed dimly through the greenish water. After waving her hands in excitement, Isabella tugged on the cable to alert the crew on the surface. The steel tube began its ascent.

As it moved, I thought I heard a distant thud, a dull echo underwater. Then the water itself seemed to shift in transparent planes. The fish shot away in panic, breaking the natural patterns of their shoals. Just as I turned towards Isabella, the whole area was plunged into darkness. Suddenly my sense of claustrophobia was intense. Panicking, I struck out wildly, hoping to touch the others. My fingers became entangled in seaweed and my chest heaved with blind dread. The darkness stretched ahead into a bewildering void.

After what seemed an eternity, the floodlight spluttered back on. But now the beam was pointing away from the site at an extreme angle, illuminating the descending clouds of stirred-up sand.

An earthquake. Somewhere in the jumble of my panicked mind, a thought crystallised. I looked up for the supply line. It arched above me, intact – but where were the others?

Isabella. I peered frantically through the thick fog of disturbed mud, but nothing was visible. I had the disorientating sensation of suddenly being entirely alone. Terrified, I spun around, looking for her. Nothing, not even the glimmer of a diving mask. Then I caught sight of a small white hand curling upwards through the clouds of sand. Isabella! I lunged towards her, my heart banging wildly against my ribs.

The sphinx had slipped sideways and pinned her leg against the sea floor. A silver cascade of bubbles gushed out from the oxygen-tank pipe where it had torn away from her mask.

The gravity of the situation didn't hit me immediately; I suppose it was a combination of shock and disbelief. As I hovered there in the drifting cloud of mud I felt thrown out of the moment, almost as though I was an observer. I hesitated – a fatal mistake.

Then, almost magically, Faakhir was beside me and both of us were swimming frantically towards Isabella. A cloud of pink blood now threaded its way through the water; her loosened hair floated like delicate seaweed.

I tore away my mouthpiece and tried to place it in her mouth while Faakhir prised the statue off her leg. But her mouth lolled open and she was already unconscious. Faakhir and I placed our shoulders against the sphinx and pushed. As it lifted from the seabed, I pulled Isabella's crushed leg free. Holding her limp body to mine, I swam full pelt towards the light filtering down from above.

We burst through the water's surface to the sound of shouting. Frantic, I pushed Isabella up towards the outstretched arms, then clambered into the boat myself and crouched over her body where it lay on the deck. My hands seemed like huge clumsy paws as I tried to pump the water out of her chest; I felt the shock of her cold lips as I gave her mouth-to-mouth. Pump, breathe, pump, breathe. It seemed like hours.

The others stood by dumbly, silenced by the horror of the scene. The terrible, almost unbelievable images seared into my memory: the water trickling from the edge of Isabella's mouth, Faakhir's blanched face as finally he pulled me away from the lifeless body, her limp hands. All the while, the steel tube containing the astrarium stood on the deck, glinting in the sun.

'Isabella? Isabella!' In disbelief I shook her, my whole body trembling uncontrollably. Then I collapsed on the deck alongside her, cradling her to me.

Above me, as if at a great distance, I heard Faakhir shout suddenly. I glanced up to see Omar standing over us, a small revolver in his hand. He looked almost embarrassed.

'*Ana asif, ana asif.* I'm sorry this is necessary.'

The sight of him pointing the gun while apologising profusely was so incongruous that the three of us could only watch in frozen surprise as he tucked the mud-packed cylinder containing the astrarium under his arm.

'What are you doing? Are you crazy?' Jamal shouted.

'Excuse me for resorting to such extreme measures, but this object is infinitely more valuable than you imagine.'

Omar's voice was clipped and bizarrely polite. Then he aimed the gun upwards, as if about to shoot a warning signal into the air.

A blind anger roared through me. Not caring whether I lived or died, I sprang towards Omar and punched him on the jaw, so hard that he fell to the deck, dropping the cylinder. It rolled to the side of the boat and lodged against the railing. His eyes rolled into the back of his head. He was unconscious.

Suddenly terrified, I stared down at Omar's body. 'Who is he?' I blurted out.

Faakhir lifted one of Omar's arms and shook it, as if testing that he really was out cold.

'A nobody. A middleman,' he said. 'He doesn't worry me. It's who he might be working for that is the real concern.'

Faakhir's calmness and professional control was staggering. Somehow, in the midst of extreme distress, I registered that he too wasn't quite what he appeared.

I dropped to the deck and cradled Isabella in my arms again, beginning to realise the impossibility of bringing her back to life, the sky and the deck receding from me. I was in shock.

Jamal picked up the fallen gun and aimed it at Omar. Faakhir grabbed his cousin's wrist. 'Stop! Kill him and we're all finished!' He took the gun, then squatted beside me, gripping my hand. 'Oliver, you must listen! You must let me go now so that I can keep the astrarium safe. But I promise I will return it to you.'

Water seeped from Isabella's wetsuit, forming a pool around my knees. Her hand lay outstretched on the deck, the fingernails already bluish.

Faakhir shook me. 'Oliver, concentrate. For Isabella!'

I nodded now, unable to speak.

He turned to Jamal and said something in his own dialect. Immediately they hoisted Omar's unconscious body into the small life raft hanging from the side of the boat, then lowered it into the sea. Finally the reality of the moment came rushing painfully back,

'What are you doing?' I asked. My voice sounded oddly emotionless.

'Don't worry,' Faakhir said. 'The current will carry him ashore. He will be found alive within hours. But this way I have more time.'

He picked up the cylinder with the astrarium inside and then sat on the edge of the boat. 'Oliver, when you get back to shore with Isabella's body the harbour master will have to contact the police immediately. If they interrogate you, it is important that you don't mention I was on this boat. You have never heard of the astrarium. You and Isabella were on an innocent tourist dive. Understand?' Faakhir's face was grim. 'Oliver, do you understand?'

'I understand.'

Faakhir took my hand.

'I will see you in a few days, my friend,' he said. 'I will come to you. If this really is the actual astrarium, then Isabella would want you to take it back where it belongs.'

Before I had a chance to ask any questions, he'd slipped backwards into the water and, with a ripple of his black flippers, disappeared from sight.

Jamal slowly steered our boat back to shore. I stepped onto the jetty carrying Isabella's body wrapped in a blanket. I remember talking to her, telling her everything was all right, I was there to protect her and everything was going to work out, my voice sounding curiously distant. Behind me, I was vaguely aware of Jamal arguing with the harbour master.

Minutes later a police car and an ambulance screeched up to the kerb. Before I'd even reached the Corniche an ambulance officer was guiding me towards the waiting stretcher. I laid Isabella's body gently onto it, arranging a limp hand that had fallen loose, tucking her hair carefully around her face, still murmuring to her, part of me refusing to comprehend the reality of her death.

Two police officers stepped up and, apologising, politely asked me to go with them. Ignoring them, I continued to stroke Isabella's cold face, her fingers that were stiff beneath my own.

'Mr Warnock, we are sorry to inform you that you must accompany us to the police station. Please.' Slipping an arm through each of mine, they pulled me away and marched me towards the police car.

Over my shoulder I watched my wife's body being loaded into the white van. It was the last time I ever saw her.

5

☥

The police held me for over a day, convinced that Isabella had drowned planting sea mines and that I was a spy. They also interrogated me about Faakhir and his involvement with Isabella, even claiming he was my wife's lover in an attempt to break me down.

In a monosyllabic voice, I repeated the same story like a mantra: we had wanted to see the ancient underwater sights for ourselves, we assumed we had official permission to dive in a military zone and the earth tremor had taken us completely by surprise, causing Isabella's drowning. Over and over they asked why Isabella, as an archaeologist, hadn't had a whole team assisting her and whether I had heard of anyone called Faakhir. I denied his existence again and again. I felt as if I was still underwater, mouthing words that floated on the other side of a glass wall separating me from an outside world.

At dawn I was freed, apparently due to a phone call from Henries, the British consul. I couldn't face going back to the villa; instead, I found myself stumbling through the streets towards the Brambilla family home. Time had stopped for

me, refusing to spill over into the tragedy that had now
become my life. I can't remember how, but what seemed
only a minute later I was standing under the stone arch of
the entrance, too petrified to ring the bell. When I did, and
Aadeel opened the door, my unshaved face, sullied clothes
and violent trembling told him everything.

'Mr Warnock, we thought they would never let you go,' he
murmured, ashen with grief.

'What have they done with the body?' I asked.

'She is already in her coffin. We bury her tomorrow afternoon.' Aadeel's face crumpled. 'I have known her all her
life. She was the only reason my mistress still lives,' he whispered, his large frame now folding in on itself, squeezing
grief tight.

I reached out to him. His shoulders were heaving. But I,
the Englishman, could not weep. Grief had locked my emotions in, like a frozen river with its water trapped inside the
ice.

'Oh Lord, take this soul, torn from us before her time, and
transport her into heaven,' the priest intoned in Italian.

I stared at the coffin standing beside the freshly dug
grave, the darkened recess as intriguing as a secret chamber.
I wanted to smash open the wood and rescue my wife.
Sudden bereavement is illogical, irrational. It refuses to
believe the obvious. The scent, the physical warmth of skin,
the weight of her head on your shoulder: the memory of
these sensations stays suspended, waiting for the departed to
return and confirm the internal illogical truth that beats on
relentlessly – one that tells you that they haven't really died
at all but are only hiding.

The priest began a Latin chant; his incomprehensible
words emerging in a solemn murmur, and I found myself

furious – at a God that had allowed such a futile death, at the world, even at Francesca for hijacking the funeral arrangements.

It was a family tradition for the Brambillas to bury their dead within two days and because Francesca hadn't been able to reach me during my interrogation at the police station she had taken it upon herself to organise everything, from the funeral parlour through to the Catholic service at St Catherine's Cathedral. The whole event appeared brutally fast to me, as if Isabella had been drawing breath only moments before we were putting her into the ground.

The only thing left to me was the grim task of breaking the news to my own family. I had called my father first. His reaction had been one of initial disbelief followed by an irrational insistence that I should return to England immediately as if my own life might be in danger. Dialling my brother's number had been more difficult. I was frightened that the news might set off one of Gareth's lapses into addiction, but it had to be done. I'd been blunt and to the point; anything else felt evasive. Afterwards he had fallen into a long silence, then, to my annoyance, launched into a Buddhism-inspired soliloquy about reincarnation. I knew his emotional clumsiness was unintentional but it still distressed me. His rant turned into weeping. That was Gareth, always oscillating between bravado and fragility.

The Valium the company doctor had prescribed made my head swim. The sun danced in streamers, catching the shimmering feathers on the more ornate hats of the women – a second of visual distraction, a brief respite from the crushing emotion that overlay everything. I couldn't bear to think. I hadn't slept since the accident, unable even to shut my eyes without seeing Isabella's body lying limp on the wooden deck. That last conversation we'd had about Ahmos Khafre and his terrible prediction kept floating back into my head. And part of me was furious at the idea that Isabella had allowed herself to be influenced by it, as if, maybe, her believing in it had made it real, and in doing so had ensured her own demise.

I glanced at Francesca who was standing on the other side of the grave, propped up by Aadeel. She was dressed in an elegant mourning dress that must have dated from the 1950s, but her granddaughter's death had withered her overnight. Standing beside her was Hermes Hemiedes, his hand absently stroking the old woman's frail arm. He returned my gaze, his blank stare devoid of emotion. I looked away.

The sound of wood scraping against gravel jolted me out of my reverie. The casket touched the bottom of the grave and the ropes were pulled out. A bird swooped over the cypress trees and down towards the open grave, the move-ment of its wings catching my eye. It was a sparrowhawk. It reminded me of Isabella's tattoo, her Ba. Abstractly, part of my mind wondered whether this was her spirit freed from her body. The thought helped distract me for a moment. I was interrupted by a gentle nudge to my elbow and turned to see Aadeel there, holding out a spade. The male relatives were expected to cast the first shovels of soil into the grave. I took the spade and stared down at the polished surface of the coffin; the strata in the banks of reddish sandy soil around it changed as the grave deepened. A geophysicist committing his wife to the earth; I didn't want to do it. I didn't want to give her up.

The crying of the mourners mingled with the ambience of the world beyond the high walls of the cemetery: the squeal of tram wheels, the clip-clop of horses' hooves, the midday call to prayer from a nearby mosque, the imam's voice threading through the air like a thin purple ribbon. Could

Isabella hear any of this from inside her coffin? I couldn't help wondering, trying to distract myself from the excruciatingly tight band of grief now squeezing my heart and lungs. The moment swelled and burst into the next while I stood there, paralysed, dreading the rain of soil against wood, the rattle that signified finality.

The Brambilla family headstone was a large altar dominated by a statue of the Madonna. Set into the marble, in circular frames like lockets, were sepia photographs of the dead: her father, Paolo; Isabella's great-grandfather and his wife; her great-uncle who had been killed in the Second World War; a spinster aunt. I looked for Giovanni Brambilla's photograph, but he appeared to be missing. Below the miniature portraits were empty frames, yawning sinisterly. The idea that a photograph of Isabella would appear there, in a solemn pose that betrayed her exuberance, horrified me.

The warmth of hands wrapping themselves over mine brought me back. Aadeel had stepped up behind me, and together we shovelled the first spadeful of earth into the grave.

Several ancient black Mercedes cars stood outside the cemetery gates, waiting to drive the mourners to the wake. Wanting a moment of solitude, I broke away from Francesca and her entourage and walked towards a row of cypress trees. A man emerged from behind a statue and approached me so swiftly I was barely aware of him until he was in front of me.

'Monsieur Oliver Warnock?'

Startled, I looked up. The man was short and looked to be in his fifties, with heavy-lidded eyes that blinked like a tortoise's. He looked vaguely bureaucratic in his ill-fitting suit and embroidered fez and, disorientated, for one absurd moment I wondered if I knew him from the Egyptian Oil Ministry in Cairo. He glanced around nervously, then pulled me behind a high gravestone.

'You don't know me but I know you,' he said. 'And I have met your wife. Unfortunately, after her demise.'

I assumed he was one of the cheap psychics that operated like parasites amongst the elderly European community. He noticed the repulsion in my expression.

'Many apologies – let me explain. My name is Demetriou al-Masri. I am a coroner at the city morgue. My condolences, Monsieur Warnock. Forgive this interruption but there is something I must tell you.'

'Were you working that night?' I asked him.

'Yes, of course, but this is a strange thing, Monsieur Warnock. Is it okay if I speak frankly?'

'I suspect I wouldn't be able to stop you.'

'Alas, in my profession there are many things that cannot be said delicately.'

A mourner passed us and tipped his hat. Al-Masri lowered his voice.

'Monsieur Warnock, it is my great misfortune and, I believe, my duty to have to tell you that by the time your wife's body arrived at the morgue it was missing several of its internal organs.'

His expression was grim yet nervous, as if he were committing some terrible crime by giving me the information. My mind reeled as I tried to grasp the simple facts.

'You mean there was an autopsy?'

'I mean that several of the organs had been removed before the body came under my jurisdiction.'

Nauseated, I leaned against the gravestone. The idea that Isabella had been violated in such a manner was abhorrent.

'Impossible,' I murmured. 'What is it you really want?' I

was still clutching at the idea that the man may be trying to extort money from me somehow.

'It is terrible to be the bearer of such bad news,' he said. 'But I must tell you, the liver, the stomach, the intestines and the heart were gone. I have seen this only once before, twenty years ago. Interestingly, the victim was an Egyptologist, female and about the same age as your wife.'

'Isabella's heart was gone?'

Again, he looked around nervously. 'Please, it must appear as if I am simply offering my condolences. Even the statues have ears in Egypt.'

'Why didn't you report it?'

'Because, my friend, my relationship with the authorities is tenuous enough without further aggravation, you understand?'

I nodded; I understood exactly.

He moved closer. 'Do you know anything about the art of mummification?' he whispered.

'A little.'

'Then you will know that these organs had great significance to the Ancient Egyptian priests. They would place them in a series of Canopic jars, each with a stopper that symbolised the god that would protect the deceased's journey into the underworld. What I don't understand is why the heart was taken as well. Traditionally it is left in the body as it is essential for the ancient ritual of the weighing of the heart. Without a heart, your wife would stand no chance of entering the afterworld. She would be, as you Christians say, condemned to purgatory.'

'But why would someone commit such a disgusting crime? My wife was a Catholic.' Not entirely relevant, perhaps, but I was still grappling with the enormity of the revelation and the man was clearly distressed by the spiritual implications of the theft.

'And I am a Sunni Muslim with a Greek Orthodox grandfather. In this city, religion is not a simple issue. I hope your
wife's spirit will find peace.' He bowed, said, 'Good evening,
sir,' and slipped away through the gravestones.

I lingered in the shade of the murmuring branches, an
overwhelming sense of powerlessness pinning me to the
gravelled path. How could any intelligent person believe in
the spiritual dimensions of mummification? And why had
they chosen Isabella's body for such desecration?

6

Our car weaved slowly through the narrow streets towards the Brambilla family villa. I glanced at Francesca, her profile rigid in grief.

I had to ask. 'What happened to Isabella's body after the ambulance collected her at the jetty?'

'She was taken to the city morgue, and then to the funeral directors in the morning. The Brambillas bury their dead swiftly – it is a tradition in our family.'

'You're positive there was no autopsy?'

'Please, we have just laid my poor granddaughter in the ground. Do we have to talk about such matters now?'

'Francesca, you were in control of the arrangements while I was being held by the police. I just need to know if there was an autopsy,' I persisted, determined to get a straight answer.

'Of course not,' she snapped back. 'Is this something to do with that idiot official who approached you at the cemetery?'

I thought she hadn't noticed, but she peered at me sharply, her frail frame dwarfed by the huge crimson leather seat, and again I was struck by how she had aged since the drowning.

'You know him?' I asked.

'Alexandria is a village. A village of chattering monkeys making mischief. There are many truths here and some of them dangerous. Be careful, Oliver, otherwise you will find yourself fighting for your own truth along with the rest of us.'

A marquee had been erected over the villa's courtyard and beneath it stood a long table covered in a variety of both Arabic and Italian pastries. Subdued waiters in tails served coffee and everyone spoke in muted whispers. I knew Francesca couldn't really afford the wake, but when I'd offered her money she had been insulted. Façade was all that many of the European diaspora had left, but it was essential to them to maintain that illusion of wealth.

For the first time, I took note of who had attended my wife's funeral. There was Cecilia, Isabella's errant mother, whose beauty isolated her from the others, the usual elegantly dressed Italian pensioners who formed Francesca's social circle; also the British consul, Henries, who had recently liberated me from the Alexandrian police, and his wife. On our first encounter, Henries's reaction to my northern English accent had been supercilious, and when he realised the high status of the Alexandrian family I had married into he had done nothing to conceal his amazement – neither of which responses had endeared him to me.

I spotted a representative from my company's client, The Alexandrian Oil Company – Mr Fartime, the man who'd employed me as a consultant. Catching my eye, he nodded in sympathy. Despite the arguments he used to have with Isabella at the occasional cocktail party, usually over benign issues like the environment, I liked the man. Standing near him was a middle-aged European woman in an ill-fitting grey tweed suit, her flushed face betraying the unsuitability of such an outfit in Alexandria's heat. Amelia Lynhurst. I saw her glance towards me, and then become distracted by the sight of Hermes Hemiedes, still at Francesca's elbow. To my surprise, her expression changed to one of apprehension and she turned away quickly.

A tall, handsome man in his early thirties approached me, his veiled wife beside him. Ashraf Awad, son of Aadeel, Francesca's housekeeper. He had grown up with Isabella and their friendship had lasted into adulthood. I didn't like to think I found Ashraf threatening, but I suspected his relationship with Isabella had more than once slipped into something approaching intimacy. An ardent socialist and supporter of Nasser, Ashraf had completed his engineering degree at Moscow University, which had appealed to Isabella's left-wing leanings. 'Meet the new Egypt' had been the way she'd always introduced him; she'd seen his education and political fervour as a manifestation of the better side of Egyptian nationalism. Ashraf had visited us once in London en route from Moscow to Cairo. He had slept on our couch and dominated our dinner parties for a couple of weeks, captivating the women and outraging the men with his fervent discourses on socialism and the Middle East. I sensed that he'd never fully approved of me, but Isabella had loved him. In many ways he'd been the brother she'd never had. More importantly, through him she had seen a way she could fit into this new post-colonial society. Noting the full abeyya his wife was wearing and Ashraf's traditional clothes and newly sprouted beard, I wondered about 'the new Egypt'. Why and when had he become a fully practising Muslim?

To my surprise, Ashraf began to weep as he reached to grasp my hand.

'Oliver, my friend, it is a tragedy, a real tragedy. I have lost a sister, you a wife. But Isabella, she had courage. More than perhaps we will ever know.' He embraced me; embarrassed, I patted him awkwardly on the back.

I had always secretly envied the openness with which Middle Eastern men expressed their emotions. I couldn't remember my father ever embracing me or Gareth. A hand on the shoulder was the best we could expect, and as a child I had craved the ponderous intimacy of that deceptively casual gesture. In Egypt, men kissed, held hands; fathers openly caressed their sons. I watched Ashraf's tears with secret envy. My grief hadn't broken yet and I wished I could weep like that now.

Francesca, determined to follow protocol, interrupted Ashraf's condolences and guided me to a podium at one end of the marquee. It held three ornate chairs.

'You, as the husband, sit in the centre. I am on your right, while the mother,' Francesca spat the word with ill-hidden disgust, 'sits on your left. People will pay their respects and we shall conduct ourselves with proper decorum. Then my duties as a grandmother will be over.'

Cecilia collapsed into her chair. She moaned quietly, her painted mouth opening and shutting like a beached fish. There was a self-conscious theatricality to her grieving that appalled me, and I noticed Francesca glaring disapprovingly at her.

Despite Isabella and I having been married for five years, I had never met Cecilia before now. Isabella had described her mother as having a pathological fear of intimacy. 'It makes her claustrophobic to spend time with her own daughter,' she'd told me one night after an argument on the phone with Cecilia. 'She doesn't like to be reminded that she gave birth. This is a woman who is running from her past and she is terrified that one day it may trip her up in the shape of a resentful daughter.'

I could still hear Isabella's scornful tone ringing in my ears. She had reason to be resentful. As far as she was concerned, her mother had abandoned her. Seeing Francesca's reaction towards Cecilia now, I suspected the situation might have been a little more complex than that.

The Valium was beginning to wear off. I desperately needed something to defend myself from encroaching grief and the tedium of greeting a parade of strangers, but there wasn't a drop of alcohol to be seen.

A man gestured to me from the other side of the marquee. Francesca had pointed him out to me disdainfully earlier on. It was Cecilia's husband, Carlos. He was at least ten years her senior and wore the uniform of the wealthy European: panama hat, linen suit, loafers and gold cufflinks that caught the sunlight. Excusing myself, I got up from my chair and walked over to him. He shook my hand, introducing himself. Then, taking my arm in a familiar manner, he guided me behind a marquee, out of sight.

'Here, my friend, some grappa from the village I grew up in.' He pushed a silver hip flask into my hand.

I unscrewed the top and took a long, grateful swig. The alcohol burned my throat and seared through to the top of my head, but it obliterated the moment, which was what I wanted.

'I am sincerely sorry we meet in such circumstances. These Brambilla women – before you know it they have swallowed your balls. Cecilia loved her daughter, you have to understand that.'

'She had an odd way of showing it,' I replied. I tried to remember what line of manufacturing Carlos was in, but failed to do so in the fog of tranquillisers and grappa.

'It is far more complicated than you or I know, my friend. When Paolo died the grandparents insisted on keeping the child. That Giovanni, he was a crazy man, obsessed with the mystical. He could hypnotise people, like snakes can. If you ask me, all the Brambillas are crazy. As for Francesca, she is still angry with Isabella's father for dying so young.'

I nodded, slightly doubtful, but thanked him for the grappa and returned to my seat. Francesca gave me a disapproving glare, but she was preoccupied with the Italian guests and couldn't reprimand me further.

I was dismayed to see that my first English-speaking visitor was Amelia Lynhurst. I had first met her at a cocktail party at the British Consulate. The English middle-aged Egyptologist was famous for dressing in a tweed twinset even in the full summer heat, much to the amusement of the Arabic members of the prestigious Smouha Polo Club who had created a betting ring around these legendary appearances. And I always had the impression that she was frozen in another era, as if the post-war Kensington of the late 1940s she'd left had stayed preserved in aspic – gas meters, rationing, dingy flat and fog all waiting, suspended in time, for her return. At that first encounter she'd launched into a passionate monologue about oil exploration destroying the natural world – or Gaia, as she insisted on calling it, to my great irritation. She had also attempted to cross-examine me about Isabella's research, and I'd found myself taking an uncharacteristically intense dislike to her. She seemed hungry for new information, perhaps for a thesis that would re-establish her ruined reputation. Whatever her intention, I didn't trust her.

'I'm surprised to see you here, Miss Lynhurst.' I failed to keep ambivalence out of my voice.

'Perhaps you didn't expect me,' she replied. 'But please understand, I had a great fondness for your wife, particularly during our time together at Oxford.' She leaned forward and lowered her voice. 'In relation to other, more pressing matters, I hope you understand the implications of harbouring an undeclared antiquity, particularly one of such spiritual value. This country is in the throes of a delicate resurrection and these are perilous times. Such an antiquity has powers that you, a man of prosaic interests, could never understand. Others, however, do. If the wrong people were to get hold of such a device, it could prove very dangerous indeed.'

Startled by her directness I felt myself become defensive. Had Isabella been correct in her suspicion that Amelia Lynhurst had known how close she was to finding the astrarium? I decided it would be wise to feign naivety.

'Oh, we always kept our work very separate,' I replied casually.

Amelia looked sceptical. 'Oliver, if you need my help in any way, you must visit at any time. I'm not sure whether Isabella had a true idea of the value of the object she was researching . . .'

Her voice faltered and she glanced over my shoulder. I was surprised to see what I thought was a glimmer of fear in her eyes. I turned to see Hermes Hemiedes coming towards me, followed by the priest who had conducted the funeral.

'I really must leave now.' Amelia pressed her hand into mine, then walked away.

Hermes stepped onto the podium, an ironic smile playing over his thin lips. 'Such women are dangerous because they never appear so,' he remarked as we both watched Amelia leave the tent.

'Oliver, Isabella's death is a profound loss.'

He embraced me and I was enveloped by a wave of musk and the scent of the cologne he was wearing – a sharp green tone undercut with a darker shade. In my heightened emotional state, it smelled like the aroma of physical decay. I pulled back, stiffly self-conscious.

'Thank you. I know Isabella respected you greatly, which was rare for her.'

He laughed – a hyena's bark. My eyes fastened on a curious pendant around his neck: a silver depiction of Thoth, the baboon moon god whom the Ancient Egyptians believed gave hieroglyphs to mankind on behalf of Ra.

'The very bright can be very arrogant,' Hermes said. 'I helped make her who she was: uncompromising.'

'So I understand.'

He moved closer, enveloping me in that nauseating aroma again. 'If Isabella did indeed find the astrarium, you should know that the device is very valuable to a lot of people, all of them far less scrupulous than myself.'

He pulled a card from his breast pocket and slipped it into my hand. 'If you respect the ambitions of your dear wife you will visit me sooner rather than later. Dusk is the best time.'

I glanced at the address, recognising it as the old Arab quarter to the west of the city. When I looked up again, the Egyptologist was making his way through the mourners, his slightly uncoordinated stride parting the crowd. I wondered briefly what he would make of the coroner's revelation.

Now tired of the event, I decided to leave too. I stood, but was prevented from stepping down from the podium by Francesca's hand on my wrist.

'Oliver, you cannot leave now.'

'I can and I will,' I told her. 'It's time I began my own mourning.'

I had never been so defiant with the old woman and she didn't try to dissuade me.

I was amazed to find that it was near nightfall. A hantour, a small horse-drawn cart, was waiting outside the Brambilla villa. The driver, a rake-thin middle-aged man in traditional clothes, was leaning up against the villa wall and smoking. He threw away his cigarette and stood upright when he saw me.

'Please, get in,' he said quietly but with authority.

Wanting to walk, I waved him off.

'No, for you it is free. Please, Monsieur Warnock, I insist.'

I hesitated, wondering whether he was a member of the secret police, but there was a dignity to his stance and something in his open pleading face that made me trust him. Foolish, maybe, but exhaustion and grief had made me weary. I got in and asked him to take me back to the villa at Roushdy.

We drove through the narrow lanes of the city. The air was fragrant after the recent rain and the soft clip-clopping of hooves lulled me into a gentle trance. The sense of motion postponing the terrible loneliness I knew awaited me back in the villa, confronted with remnants of my life with Isabella.

The cart slowed alongside a low archway that seemed to lead into a darkened courtyard. A man wearing a headscarf that covered most of his face suddenly hauled himself into the cart. He was carrying a bag over his shoulder. I reared back, jolted out of my reverie. To my immense relief, Faakhir's face emerged from under the dark blue cloth.

'Say nothing,' he whispered. 'The astrarium is in the bag by your feet. I promised Isabella that I would deliver it safely to you. She said you'd know what to do with it. Oliver, guard the astrarium with your life. I don't know exactly what its powers are, but there are people out there who believe they can use it to destroy everything we have worked for in this country – political stability, peace, an economic future . . . and worse.'

With a clatter of wheels we pulled up outside the villa.

Framed in an upstairs window was the lonely silhouette of Ibrihim, switching the lights on ready for my return.

'You must take the astrarium to your friend Barry Douglas. You can trust him. He will be able to open the container and carbon-date the astrarium to tell you what exactly it is. This you must do – for Isabella. You know I loved her too.'

I grabbed his arm. 'Why are you risking your life, Faakhir? Who do you work for?'

Smiling enigmatically he shook off my hand. 'Stay safe, my friend.'

He leaped out of the cart to disappear into the shadows.

7

I had arranged to meet Barry Douglas at the Spitfire, a small bar just off the Sharia Saad Zaghloul – one of the main avenues in Rue de l'Ancienne Bourse. Established in the 1930s, it had been popular with the Allied troops posted in Alexandria during the Second World War. The proprietor – an Anglophile – had proudly installed a small plaster bust of Winston Churchill draped by a Union Jack in the window. Inside, it was perpetual twilight. This was one of Barry's favourite haunts.

Barry Douglas had quickly become one of my friends as well as Isabella's; I was attracted to his maverick sensibility and classic Australian intolerance for bullshit. We shared a strong disdain for pretence and class-related snobbery. What I didn't share was his love of all things mystical and spiritual, a characteristic he had in common with Isabella.

I hesitated at the bar's doorway. When I'd arranged this meeting with Barry I hadn't had the courage to tell him about Isabella's death. Each time I had to tell someone the news it was like living through the drowning all over again and I dreaded that sensation of being swept back into the moment. Besides, I told myself, he was bound to have heard – news tended to sweep through Alexandria like wild-fire. Steeling myself, I stepped inside. On the walls hung a gallery of old photographs, dusty black-and-white shots of smiling young men in khaki, arms around each other, ham-ming it up for the camera – Brits, Canadians, Australians, New Zealanders, the occasional Scotsman in a tam-o'-shanter. Some of them looked like children in ill-fitting uniforms: narrow adolescent shoulders lost in jackets; huge rabbit eyes staring out across time, tiny beads of fear buried in the centre of their pupils and defying the wide smile beneath. It couldn't have been easy defending a territory that many locals regarded as stolen anyhow; dealing with an ambivalent Arabic community not to mention the Italian–Alexandrians – people like Isabella's father – some of whom had already left to fight with Mussolini or the Germans.

Glancing around, I couldn't see Barry, so I sat at the bar and ordered myself a Bloody Mary. I looked at the photos and couldn't help wondering how many of those young sol-diers were now lying in the El Alamein war cemetery. There were seven thousand tombstones there, stretching out in frightening monotony – the most poignant of them marked seven unknown soldiers, five unknown soldiers and so on. Comrades blown apart, then thrown together in unimagin-ably macabre embraces.

'Christ, you're a bloody sorry sight.' Barry Douglas's unmistakably Australian voice boomed across the bar. He pulled up a bar stool beside me and attempted to perch his massive body on the seat. 'Fucking stools are made for midgets. Aziz!' He yelled at the proprietor who was busy wiping glasses. 'When are you going to get some decent fucking chairs?'

Aziz shrugged, humouring the Australian, who, I knew, was a dedicated regular.

Barry turned back to me. 'At least the beer's cold. How are yer, mate?' He wrapped a huge arm around me and pulled me into a bear hug.

I turned my face away, terrified my reserve might break down. And it might have if I hadn't been momentarily over-whelmed by the combined smell of Brut aftershave, stale sweat and hashish emanating from Barry's ancient leather jacket. He released me to wipe a tear away.

'That was some tragic funeral. Hate them myself. When I go to join the great Buddha in the sky I want my physical remains cooked up in some delicious cordon-bleu stew so my molecules are recycled in a meaningful way.'

That was the trouble with Barry: you never knew if he was being serious or not.

'You were there?' I asked. I must have been sleepwalking through the whole ceremony. I hadn't seen him.

'Wouldn't have missed it for the world. I was right at the back, getting stoned. Didn't want to upset the natives.' He blew his nose into a large embroidered handkerchief. 'At least the Catholics put on a good show, unlike the Proddies. You can't have a decent burial without some decent bloody ritual. But Isabella? It wasn't her time.' He thumped the bar to emphasise his point. 'It wasn't her fucking time!'

A furtive couple in the corner looked up from their tête-à-tête, a lone Cypriot sailor turned to stare, and a stray cat bolted from under one of the tables. The bar-music tape clicked over and a Kinks track filled the sudden silence – the incongruous youthful yearnings of another world.

Without prompting, Aziz slammed down a glass of beer in front of the Australian.

Barry Douglas was one of those rare individuals whose

flamboyance and maverick attitudes worked like an electric shock – his childlike sense of the absurd was both liberating and infectious. Forty-five, he stood at six foot three, weighed twenty stone, and had a tangled mane of steel-blonde hair and a matching beard that made him look like some Viking god. His skin, permanently sunburnt, had the wrinkled deeply tanned look of the Caucasian in Africa. When drunk he looked and behaved like an outraged bull, but when sober he was capable of charming even the most unapproachable women. The local Arabs loved him, and he had lived in Alexandria for so long that they regarded him as a lucky talisman. His clashes with the municipal police were legendary, but even they tolerated his regular escapades with affection. An avid diver and surfer, Barry claimed to have grown up more in the ocean than out. He described his occupation as 'marine expert', though expert on what exactly was never clear. I'd always thought treasure hunter a more appropriate description, but the longer I knew Barry the more he revealed himself to have extraordinary talents in the most surprising areas.

He'd left Australia in the late 1950s and ended up on the coast of California by the early 1960s, where he'd become involved in some of the early LSD experiments conducted at Berkeley. This had led to a complete revision of all Barry's ambitions. He abandoned academia for adventure and managed to land a job as a diver with Jacques Cousteau, which began his infatuation with shipwrecks. Dissolute as he was when he wasn't on a quest, once he started the hunt he became dangerously focused – a real shark. According to Isabella, the Australian was one of the best restorers of gold, silver or bronze ancient artefacts around and his phenomenal ability to carbon-date wood accurately was legendary within the archaeological community.

After his stint with Cousteau, Barry had continued to work his way around the world and had finally settled in Alexandria. A self-declared sexual compulsive, he was as capable of monogamy as a buck hare and regarded marriage as an abhorrent and outdated institution. Although this hadn't prevented him marrying three times: once to a Hindu, once to a Thai Buddhist and once to a Muslim, all disastrously.

'I loved Isabella, you know.' He took a few deep draughts of beer and stared at me. 'I know you're English, but for Christ's sake, Oliver, show some emotion. You're freaking me out.'

I glanced down at my wedding band. 'Can't, not yet. But I suppose in a few days I'll break down into a blubbering mess.'

Barry's stare drilled into me, his grey-blue irises swimming in a sea of broken capillaries. 'You do realise,' he said, drawing in the air a circle that encompassed the bar, the customers, Aziz in the corner reaching for a cigarette, 'that all this is an illusion, this quantum foam of particles, matter, bodies, neurons. She's still with you, in your—'

A wave of anger swept through me. I didn't want his sympathy. 'Cut the bullshit, Barry. I'm an atheist, remember? I haven't got some nice little spiritual fairy tale to fall back on.'

'I'm not talking bullshit. You can't really think that all we are is mortal flesh and blood? The Ancient Egyptians had it right. There's a whole world beyond this perceived reality we're experiencing right now. I know – I've been a witness to the cosmos.'

'Too many illegal substances, if you ask me.'

Defiant, Barry held up his lager. 'Hey, maybe you're right! Maybe old Barry's grey matter is just a little too fried. But I've met guys with thrice my IQ, physicists, who'd agree with me. Still doesn't change the fact that it wasn't Isabella's time.'

He drained the glass. Following his cue, I finished my own drink and ordered another round.

'You know I was with her when she drowned. I tried to save her . . .'

'Mate, there was no way anyone knew that tremor was going to hit. No way – underwater earthquakes happen all the time. Anyhow, what the hell was she doing diving in the bay? That's strictly no-go. Let me guess: you guys are both MI5 and you were combing the seabed for military secrets.'

Aziz leaned over. 'Don't joke, my friend. In Alexandria, even the snakes have ears.'

'Yeah? And the mice have cocks.' Barry, miming paranoid, looked under the table, then over the counter.

Ignoring the Australian's bravado, I lowered my voice. 'They've already interrogated me about the dive – for twenty-four hours straight. In the end, the oil company phoned the British consul who bailed me out.'

'Bloody bastards, no respect for the grieving.' Barry's tone changed, serious now. 'But Isabella was onto something, wasn't she?'

I looked over to Aziz, who was busying himself out of earshot with some glasses – a deliberate retreat, I suspected. I turned back to Barry.

'She did find something. An object she was convinced was historically important.'

'And?'

'I need you to carbon-date whatever wood you can find. I think the artefact inside is bronze. At least, that's what Isabella thought.' Faakhir's last words flashed through my mind. I'd taken the bag home but hadn't got much further than pulling out the steel tube containing the astrarium. 'I can hardly bear looking at it, Barry, it's just history to me. None of it means a thing – not set against her life.'

Barry must have driven the company car back to the villa – I was certainly too drunk to do so. The lights were all off except for a small lantern burning on the first floor. Ibrihim had stayed up, I noted appreciatively as I staggered to the front door. In those first few days I'd overheard him weeping behind the door of his small room. He had retreated into a formal reticence since Isabella's drowning, as if death, after entering the house, was an important guest who had to be treated with special reverence. The housekeeper had covered all the mirrors, and had given away a small kitten Isabella had adopted, claiming it would be bad luck to keep the animal.

As I fumbled drunkenly with the keys, Ibrihim opened the front door. A practising Muslim, he strongly disapproved of drinking. He frowned as I stumbled into the hallway, Barry catching me before I fell.

'Monsieur Warnock is stricken with grief,' the Australian explained solemnly, before belching.

Ibrihim winced in disgust at the stench of alcohol coming from my clothes. 'Indeed,' he replied, regaining his composure. 'I have heard that strong coffee is beneficial for such grief. Shall I make some?'

'Excellent idea,' I answered, hoping I wasn't slurring my words. 'My friend and I will take it in the drawing room.'

Barry followed me into the large room and whistled as I switched on the lights.

'Geez, I can never get over how luxurious this place is. Get used to this shit and it'll be the beginning of your moral demise, not to mention your socialist credentials.'

'What socialist credentials?' I slurred.

'Mate, Isabella dobbed you in.'

'I was a student – I only joined the illustrious Socialist
Party of the once-Great Britain so I could get laid. All I
wanted was to get out of my parents' two-up, two-down and
avoid going down the mine. And I succeeded – so shoot me,'
I concluded, a little more defensively than I'd intended.

'Oh, c'mon, you're a runner – like me.'

Barry grabbed a First World War British helmet that sat
ceremoniously on a sideboard, placed it on his head at a
rakish angle and started goose-stepping across the parquet
floor.

'You think that if you stop, all your past – your shitty
childhood, fucked-up love affairs, compromised ethics and
your working-class background – will catch up with you in
some catastrophic collision. Bang, bang, you're dead.'

'Something like that.' I sat on the floor, suddenly overwhelmed by the events of the day; the funeral, the wake as
well as the bizarre encounter at the cemetery. 'Barry, I'm too
bloody drunk and miserable to philosophise.'

Mercurial as ever, the Australian's mood changed
instantly. He replaced the helmet and helped me to my feet.

'Right, then, mate – lead me to the golden calf.'

I unlocked the door to the bedroom. We didn't usually lock
doors in the villa but Faakhir's urgent warnings had somehow
penetrated the fog in my mind. It was the least I could do.
The steel tube sat in the middle of the bedroom floor where
I'd left it earlier, still oozing mud and sea water onto the
carpet. Crouching down, Barry tapped against the tube's side.

'Still in there, is it?'

'According to the metal detector. It's some kind of nautical instrument – at least, that's what Isabella believed. She
also mentioned some kind of wooden casing.'

'Nautical instrument? What era are we talking?'

I hesitated. I guess if I hadn't been drunk I mightn't have been so candid, but Barry's face seemed so open, his ruffled blond hair standing up like the quills of an outraged porcupine.

'Ptolemaic, I think – Cleopatra's time.' I knew Isabella had traced it back to Cleopatra, but I wasn't sure if the device was supposed to be even older. I wished now that I'd listened more closely to Isabella's sometimes tangled explanations.

Barry's eyes narrowed. 'Impossible. Nautical instruments don't date back that far.'

'I thought you were the one always going on about how we limit ourselves through our conventional perceptions and expectations.'

'The quote is "the expectations of our perceptions", you pissed bastard. Mate, you're holding out on me – what exactly did Isabella think she'd found?'

'Some kind of astrarium with supposedly supernatural properties.'

Barry's eyebrows shot up.

'According to Isabella,' I added quickly.

'Excellent – that clears up a lot of bloody things. Oliver, I know you're a cynic but let's look at the Ancient Egyptians' comprehension of magic. It was inseparably entwined with religious worship and intellectual pursuit. For example, Isis was known as "Great in Magic", having been told the secret name of the Sun-God. The god Thoth – god of the written word – was also a god of magic. Thoth's task was to classify the creations of the superior deities – Osiris, Horus, Ptah, Amon and Ra. This gave him tremendous power.' Barry relished any opportunity to talk about the Ancient Egyptians and he was clearly in his element. 'Any self-respecting magician – like myself, for example – would have a well-stocked library; magicians were expected to read every holy word, comma and tome of Thoth's, the idea being that the knowledge would make them as powerful as the god himself. I'm telling you, the concepts were far more bloody sophisticated than the history books make out, and maybe, just maybe, the buggers were right.'

'What's this baloney got to do with the astrarium or astrolabe or whatever the hell it is?' I asked.

Barry dipped a finger into the mud inside the steel tube and tasted it, oblivious to my disgust. 'Mate, if this is an instrument once used by a magician, you have to adopt their mentality and treat it accordingly – with respect and fear. This artefact, as you insist on calling it, could still be formidable in the right hands. In the hands of someone who knows how to use it. If Isabella was right, then it was constructed hundreds of centuries before the Enlightenment, before the separation of church and state, religion and science, before the compartmentalising of the psyche. Not that I expect a repressed bastard like yourself to understand,' he concluded affectionately.

I pointed at the steel tube. It stood there, upright, like some obelisk of ill portent.

'Magical or not, or whether it still has power, just remember Isabella drowned for that bloody piece of irrelevant history,' I said, a little more bitterly than I'd intended.

Barry reached into the top of the tube and, with the edge of his fingernail, carefully scraped away some of the mud to reveal the edge of what appeared to be a wooden casing.

'This looks way too well preserved for Ptolemaic. You sure Isabella didn't have her dates mixed up?'

'You know Isabella – she was obsessive and thorough in her research. But – you'll love this – it was a mystic called Ahmos Khafre in Goa who finally convinced her it existed.'

'*The* Ahmos Khafre?'

'I imagine so.'

'That bloke's legendary. He was one of the greatest mystics of this century.'

'Yeah, along with Houdini, Crowley and Mickey Mouse. Legitimate or not, Khafre had a total hold over Isabella. So there it is – myth made real,' I finished dramatically, sitting on the floor myself.

Barry peered back into the tube. 'I'll have to take it to my apartment to desalinate it, then carbon-date the wooden casing. Jesus, Oliver, if Isabella was right, do you know how significant this could be?'

To my dismay, Barry's face had lit up with the same kind of maniacal excitement I'd seen so many times in my wife. I'd debated whether to ask his opinion about Isabella's missing organs but now decided against further encouraging his obsession with mysticism.

'Take it, but please get some results quickly,' I said. 'I have to figure out what to do with the bloody thing before I get back to Abu Rudeis next week.'

I watched from my balcony as Barry walked off down the alleyway, the shaggy outline of his mane visible between the branches of the magnolia tree. Night was Barry's natural domain, along with the subterranean underwater world. He was fearless. Actually, I suspected it wasn't so much fearlessness as active risk-taking – an irresistible compulsion to seek out any situation that would challenge his faculties. It was because of this that I had known he would take the job.

He turned the corner and vanished. Exhausted, I leant against the wall, the night air playing across my face. My shirt, damp with sweat, stuck to my back and I realised how much I had begun to fear sleeping, how I'd started to be afraid that with each passing day my memory of Isabella would fade and eventually she would leave me completely – a terrible, infinite abandonment.

I dragged myself back into the bedroom. The bed was large and low; an embroidered quilt with mirrors sewn into it lay over the top – one of Isabella's Indian acquisitions. I dreaded sleeping in that bed alone and the thought of finding it empty of her in the morning was overwhelming. The reality of Isabella's absence had started to grow like an invisible force that threatened to eclipse my own desire to keep living. And I knew that if I didn't sleep now I probably risked having a breakdown.

Stripping off my shirt and trousers, I walked into the bathroom. As I reached into the bathroom cabinet I knocked over a tin of talcum power, spilling it over the window ledge. I looked at it forlornly for a moment but realised I was too drunk to deal with it. I decided to clean it up in the morning.

I brushed my teeth and, in an attempt to sober up, plunged my face into a basin of cold water. As I stood there, the water pressing into my nostrils and against my lips, I couldn't help thinking of Isabella's drowned face and how she must have felt. Had she panicked, had she fought to stay with me? I needed to know. I needed to get inside her consciousness – I needed her back. For a moment, I was tempted to breathe in and join her.

I waited until my lungs were bursting, then, spluttering, lifted my face, now streaming with water.

I pulled away the scarf Ibrihim had used to cover the bathroom mirror and barely recognised the face, covered with stubble, that stared back. Exhaustion and grief had hollowed my cheeks. Surprisingly, I welcomed my altered appearance: it delineated transition from the person I had been before Isabella's death to the person I was now. I decided I would stop shaving from now on to emphasise the delineation. I was determined; this new alien Oliver would face sleeping in the empty bed; would block out the hours of lovemaking that had taken place there, the faint scent of Isabella that still lingered on the linen, the taste of her skin imprinted on my senses.

I re-entered the bedroom and threw myself onto the quilt. In seconds I was asleep.

The sound of a door clicking woke me. I forced my eyes open and craned my neck to check the digital alarm clock. It read 3.45 a.m. but as I watched the digits didn't appear to flip over. The bloody thing's broken again, I thought, and was reaching over to switch it off when a noise from the bathroom made me swing around. The door was closed but light shone out from beneath it. I froze. I couldn't remember leaving the lamp on.

Then I heard it again – a rustling sound, like someone moving about. A puddle of water began to seep out from under the bathroom door. Slowly I got up.

Inside the bathroom, the art deco lamp had been switched on, illuminating the pink marble tiles. The bathroom sink was empty, gleamingly clean; a normalcy that was comforting. The sound of water swishing against the bathtub broke the silence. I stopped in my tracks. Suddenly I was aware of another presence in the room; fear crept up the back of my scalp, stretching back the skin. My immediate thought was that it had to be Isabella, yet I knew that wasn't possible.

I turned around slowly. A hand hung over the edge of the bathtub – a woman's hand, long fingers blanched by water and death. My heart pounded against my throat as I forced myself to walk over to the bath. Each step brought me closer to a terror I knew I had to face.

Twisted, the curve of one buttock pressed up against the porcelain, her skin as white as a beached cuttlefish, Isabella's corpse floated in the bathtub. Her eyes were closed; her lips a faint violet. I was close to screaming. The room felt like a vacuum, as if all sound and air had been sucked out of it. I couldn't tear my eyes away. A great bloodless gash ran down the centre of her body and her wet hair floated, suspended like tendrils. Her other hand lay palm up in the water, the fingers plaintive in their curled pleading. As I watched trans-fixed, her eyelids flickered, then opened.

I screamed and woke again in my bed. Terrified, I looked across at the bathroom door. The room was dark and silent.

8

The scent of kosherie – a local rice, lentil and pasta dish – floating up from the kitchen woke me. Ravenous, I sat up, only to sink back, flattened by a pounding hangover, onto the pillows. I waited a couple of moments, then bellowed for Ibrihim, who confirmed that it was indeed past midday.

Gingerly, I made my way to the bathroom. A series of bird-claw prints were clearly marked in the talcum powder that I'd spilt on the window ledge the night before. The window was ajar, yet I felt sure I'd shut it. Could a bird have flown in through the open shutters of the bedroom while I was sleeping?

The Ba tattoo on Isabella's ankle flashed through my mind. Then I remembered the events of the night before. Isabella's presence had been so vivid. Had it been real? My terror had been real enough. My mother's warnings of souls caught in purgatory for sins left unconfessed came flooding back to me. As a child I'd hated the fear these tales engendered in me; they had seeded my determination to live unfettered by superstition. But Isabella had lived a 'good' life. I suddenly thought again of the bizarre encounter with

Demetriou al-Masri after Isabella's burial, the horror of her missing organs. Had being buried incomplete condemned her somehow?

Crazy lapsed-Catholic nightmares, I told myself as I stood naked in the middle of the bathroom. This isn't rational, it's just coincidence – the dream, the fact that a bird flew in during the night. This is grief stringing together a narrative.

Turning the shower on, I stepped into the cold water, letting it pummel my face and shoulders in an effort to exorcise the images of the night before. But Isabella's gaze of entreaty and bewilderment had seared itself into my memory.

I stepped out, wrapped a towel around my waist and went to the library.

The small square room was panelled in dark oak and had brass trimmings. The walls were lined with bookcases, many of them filled with Isabella's books. The volume I was looking for was on a top shelf, between works by Robert Graves and Giovanni Belzoni: *The Meaning of Ba*.

I opened the book at a photo of a wooden effigy of King Tutankhamen on his funerary bed. He was flanked by two wooden birds: one with a human face, his Ba; the other showing the face of the sun god, Horus, signifying that Tutankhamen's Ba was that of a pharaoh, a living god. I turned to the next page and began reading:

The hieroglyph used to write 'Ba' was a jabiru stork, while in funerary art it was represented as any bird with a human head and sometimes with human arms. Whatever its image, the Ba was always considered to be attached to the body and was freed only in death, after which it could fly anywhere, even into sunlight.

Trees were often planted near graves to provide shade for the soul-birds before they soared up towards the stars, taking with them all that had made the deceased human. The Ancient Egyptians facilitated such departures by building a false door or window into a wall of the tomb.

I remembered that Isabella's Ba tattoo had her own profile. She'd told me she'd had it tattooed on her ankle to ensure her path to the afterlife. She had been deadly serious about it and there was something unnerving about the tattoo – its vulnerable profile with the distinctive nose and large eye; its bird legs and large claws seemingly poised for flight.

Was it possible that I'd experienced some kind of visitation of Isabella's Ba, that Demetriou was right? I entertained the notion for an instant, then immediately dismissed it as ridiculous. But a sliver of doubt remained. Haunted by the travesty of Isabella's desecrated body, I knew I had to find out why it had happened and how.

Banging, loud and persistent, on the front door below startled me, followed by the sound of Ibrihim's footfall as he ran to answer it. I leaped up, Faakhir's warning flashing in my mind. Or maybe it was the police, come to search the villa on some flimsy excuse. Instead, I heard Barry's voice roar up the stairs.

'Mate! Get yer clobber on! I'm taking you out!'

The Union restaurant was one of the last bastions of colonial Egypt. A favourite of Alexandrian society before nationalisation, it still retained some of its earlier glamour. The head waiters were dressed in black suits (now frayed at the cuffs and collars) and bow ties, while the lower waiters wore white skull caps and brown jellabas. The ornate pink and brown wallpaper had started to peel and the velvet curtains were blotched, but the piano was still polished and the pianist wore real diamond earrings. At the height of the Union's glory white caviar had been flown in from Iran with French foie gras and Scottish salmon readily available. Now the kitchen was dependent on the black market. On a good day it was possible to order Australian lamb chops, mint sauce and couscous and be swept up by a nostalgia you knew wasn't your own while a head waiter pointed out where Montgomery used to sit and which table was Churchill's favourite.

Barry was a close friend of the maître d'hôtel, Photios Photaros, who was the nucleus of all society gossip and knew not only all the old power players of the European diaspora but their children and grandchildren. He was the story-keeper. Photios, having heard of Isabella's drowning, had placed us at his prize table, in an alcove near the pianist who was playing a mournful rendition of 'La Mer'. The maître d'hôtel had also supplied Barry with his customary bottle of Johnny Walker Black Label whisky.

I'd thought initially that Barry had come back with some exciting news about the astrarium but it turned out he was scheduled to meet an American journalist, keen to get Barry's view on the local reaction to Sadat's peace initiatives with US President Carter. Convinced that no grieving man should be left alone for long, Barry had insisted I accompany him while the astrarium was desalinating back in his apartment, a process that could take a few days.

'Do you believe in ghosts?' I asked him. It wasn't even late afternoon and I was on my third whisky.

'Mate, I believe in everything except mountain trolls in red caps and bells. Although having said that, I have actually seen a few trolls in red caps and bells – I just didn't believe in them. I've never seen a ghost, though, not drunk, stoned or on the stairway to heaven. Why?'

I finished my drink. The whisky's trickling warmth hit the back of my skull and then coursed down to my stomach. I needed anaesthetising, even if it only made me forget momentarily.

'Nothing. But do you think there may be a psychological reason why someone would think they're being haunted?'

Barry looked at me. 'I dunno . . . guilt, grievance, a sense of unfinished business? But if this is to do with Isabella, forget it. It's more likely her sudden absence has left a shadow; a presence you still expect. I used to get a lot of that back in San Francisco when I was tripping. Also, you have to take into account that time is not linear.'

My heart sank; it had been foolish to expect any empirically based explanation from the Australian. 'So tell me about this journalist,' I asked wearily. Barry accepted the change in the subject of the conversation without comment.

'She's the Middle Eastern correspondent for *Time* magazine. She's here covering the Carter–Sadat–Begin dialogue, got some absurd idea that Sadat might actually take the initiative on the peace process. Some bright spark told her I was the bloke for the local gossip.'

'Probably terribly earnest and naive as all hell,' I suggested cynically.

'Who cares as long as she's buying?'

Just then a visible ripple ran through the male diners in the restaurant, the kind of reaction that indicates the arrival of an attractive woman. Barry and I looked up. A glamorous small blonde woman in a black cocktail dress stood at the door, scanning the tables. In an instant Photios was at her side. He pointed out our table to her and she began weaving her way towards us. We both watched, a little amazed.

'Stone the crows, she's a looker. Tuck the bib in, Oliver, we have company.' Sweeping his great mane away from his face, Barry sat up straight in his chair.

As the journalist drew nearer, her face came into focus. To my utter astonishment I realised I knew her. It was like seeing a phantom from the past, and I couldn't suppress a shudder of emotion at the sight of a face I had once been obsessed by. She arrived at our table and reached out to shake hands with Barry. She obviously hadn't recognised me yet – but then, it was nearly twenty years ago that we had been lovers.

'Barry Douglas?' Her familiar deep rich voice sent a ripple of memory through me that was almost painful. I couldn't tear my eyes away. She still hadn't looked in my direction.

'It might be,' Barry joked.

'Rachel Stern, *Time* magazine.' They shook hands.

Barry turned to me. 'And this is Oliver Warnock, the best geophysicist in the oil biz. He's a bloody great mess at the moment so I hope it's all right if he joins us?'

Rachel Stern met my gaze and I watched the flood of recognition sweep across her features. To my satisfaction she blushed briefly.

'But we know each other. Oliver, how are you?' Rachel's expression now indicated nothing but a smooth diplomacy. She was older – a wrinkling at the corner of those dark blue eyes whose slant betrayed a faint Mongolian gene somewhere in her Russian heritage – but the rest was as I remembered: the strong nose and chin, the disproportionately full mouth, the play of humour around her lips, the same shock of fuzzy blonde hair that stood out triangularly from her head. However, a sharp intelligence and tangible confidence had replaced the air of curiosity that had defined the young woman whom I'd known as a student.

'Rachel Stern?' I asked.

'Stern's my married name – *was* my married name.' She sat at the table and called the waiter over. 'Can I get you boys another bottle?'

After a quick glance at my dazed expression, Barry said to the waiter, 'Johnny Walker Black Label and a plate of olives, please.' He turned back to Rachel. 'I trust it's courtesy of *Time* magazine?'

Rachel smiled. 'You bet.'

I tried not to stare; I still couldn't quite believe it was her. Perhaps it was the fact that I was already quite drunk, perhaps it was the surreal nature of coincidence, but it felt as though another strange twist of fate had just punctuated my life.

I'd first met Rachel Rosen, as she'd been then, at a cocktail party in London in the early 1960s. The host, a mutual friend, was a caustic but erudite Marxist I knew through the Imperial College branch of the Socialist Party of Great Britain. I was in the second year of my degree and Rachel, several years older, was completing her Master's degree in International Relations at the London School of Economics. We began our relationship after an argument about Stalin and we had lived together for over a year. My first older woman and first real love, Rachel had steered me towards all kinds of cultural sophistication and some of the friends she'd introduced me to then were still friends now. But I was very young and very intense and, finally, I suspect it had been this intensity that drove her away. The affair finished when she left abruptly for New York because of family issues – at least, that had been her excuse. But I was eternally grateful for one thing: Rachel had been the only person at that time who really believed in me, both as a professional and as someone able to transcend his background. And that, to a twenty-three-year-old with a huge working-class chip on his shoulder, had proven invaluable.

As the waiter placed the fresh whisky bottle in front of me Rachel turned to me, her expression composed but open. 'How nice to see you, Oliver. I heard on the grapevine that you'd ended up working in the Middle East, but I didn't expect to find you in Alex.'

'I'm working at the Abu Rudeis oilfield. I'd be there now, except . . .'

My voice faltered; I couldn't actually say the words.

'Oliver lost his wife recently – a bloody tragedy,' Barry said bluntly.

'Oh, I'm so sorry.'

The concern in Rachel's voice was genuine. I turned away, frightened that I might actually cry. The room swayed slightly. Despite knowing I was drunk, I couldn't repress the urge to tell Rachel about the drowning, as if telling someone from my past might somehow put Isabella's death into perspective. Before I could help myself I'd launched into an explanation.

'Isabella is – was – a marine archaeologist, top of her field. She was conducting a series of dives in the harbour. She was obsessed with this astrarium, a ridiculous piece of tin. I couldn't stop her from making this dive . . .' I downed my fourth whisky. 'I was with her when she . . . when she drowned.'

Barry coughed and the spell was broken. Rachel reached out and squeezed my hand, then let it go.

'I can't even begin to imagine how terrible it must have been for you,' she said. 'And so far from home.'

'Home? I travel so much I don't even know where that is any more.'

I couldn't keep the bitterness out of my voice. I poured myself another whisky.

Barry put a hand on my shoulder. 'Mate, don't you think you should take it easy?'

'Not tonight – tonight I intend to forget who I am.'

'Fair enough, but I reckon you should sit on that drink for a while.' He turned back to Rachel. 'So Henries, that silly English bugger, told me you're reporting on the Egyptian reaction to Carter's peace-brokering? I tell you what, President Sadat's a brave bastard even to be talking to the Israelis. Do you know how unpopular that is with the locals? Half of them lost sons and brothers in the last two wars. And let's not mention the Saudis and the Syrians – they'd have Sadat's head on a stick if he made peace. There's a lot of mad bastards out there who would give up their mothers to sabotage such a thing, and they're going to go to all sorts of extreme measures to make sure it doesn't happen. And what about young Colonel Gaddafi over in Libya? We've got the Eygptians demonstrating outside the Libyan embassy and the Libyans storming the Egyptian embassy in Libya. Trust me, I'd be very careful if I were you before I started poking around. The whole region's a time bomb just waiting to explode.'

'Sounds like I've got the right guy. You willing to help me?'

'Tell you what, come over on Thursday night when the old fellas play their backgammon and I'll introduce you to the local elders. Big respect for guru Barry.'

'I'll do just that.'

They clinked their glasses together in a toast. I watched, vaguely aware that the alcohol had started to make me feel belligerent.

'You can't be naive enough to believe that Carter will actually achieve anything?' I leaned toward Rachel, swaying a little.

'I really think the players are committed this time,' she replied cautiously. 'That's half the battle.'

'You and I both know that Sadat and Begin need their people behind them. The Israelis don't like Carter.'

'And they didn't like Kissinger. Listen, Carter's talked to Sadat, Hussein and Rabin. Next week he'll be with the Syrian president in Geneva. Camp David will produce results. Sadat wants peace. He's an Egyptian nationalist; he's not into pan-Arabism. He's a practical individual, not a sentimentalist. There are economic reasons why Egypt would seek peace with Israel.'

'Sure, we all know how practical. The Yom Kippur War – remember that little peace initiative? Sadat went to King Faisal to convince him to flex the only muscle he knew the region had over Israel and the West.'

'Right. Well, maybe now he wants to recoup the benefits. Maybe he's an oilman now, like you,' Rachel teased.

'Hey, I just find the stuff. I see it as my vocation.'

'And what a huge waste of talent. You might know the region but you're wrong about Sadat. Besides, he lost the Yom Kippur War – even more reason to seek peace.'

I lurched on with the argument, feeling as if I was watching myself from the outside. 'Egypt only just lost; that war was far closer than you know. People remember. It was only four years ago; a lot of young men were slaughtered – on both sides.'

'And they're tired of the killing.' Rachel finished her whisky. 'Why oil, Oliver? I'd have thought with your background you'd have pursued something a little more egalitarian, maybe even ecological?'

'Market forces intervened. Happens to the best of us. Right, Barry?'

'No, mate. Yours truly has held on to his socialist credentials, not to mention the credo of Buddha.'

'Bullshit. But here's to American optimism, anyway.' I lifted my glass. 'Long may it reign.'

The others ignored the toast, and I could see from Rachel's eyes that she'd already passed judgement and found me wanting. But I was beyond caring.

'You are angry,' she said.

'I'm a realist. I've been working in the region for over ten years. It's not enough to get a few politicians to agree – you have to change a whole nation's prejudices and fears. It's a complicated mess that's not going to be solved by a fast-talking peanut farmer.' I failed to keep the sarcasm out of my voice.

'Old stories can have new endings. I'm sticking with my optimism. It's been great catching up – and again, I'm really sorry about your wife. No doubt we'll bump into each other somewhere soon.'

Rachel turned to Barry and handed him a card. 'This is my hotel, I'll see you Thursday.'

Then, to my surprise, she leaned over and kissed my cheek. 'Bye, Oliver.' Her perfume transformed me back into the combustible youth I'd once been, desperate to impress.

I watched her leave, her confident bearing so different from that of the over-eager young woman I'd once known.

'You've had enough, mate. I'm taking you home.' Barry plucked the half-full glass from my hand.

'We have a past,' I said.

'I can see that. For a stitched-up Pommie you've got taste.'

'I'll assume that's a compliment. Don't worry about walk-ing me – I'll get a taxi.'

'Listen, before you go . . .' He pulled me closer and dropped his voice. 'Last night I came across an old friend, a local. Now it just so happens this bloke used to be the son of the gardener who worked for the Brambillas back in the 1950s, when Isabella's grandfather ran the joint.'

'So?'

'So we got talking about the drowning and he tells me he's heard that it was Giovanni who killed Isabella.'

'That's ridiculous. Giovanni's been dead for years.'

'You don't understand – he told me that the grandfather put a curse on the granddaughter. Marked her for an early death. Apparently he was considered a great sorcerer by the locals.'

'Giovanni Brambilla?'

'Mate, I'm only telling you what the bloke said. But put it this way: he was shaking with fear when he told me.'

'It's just superstitious nonsense – Isabella's grandfather adored her. It was an accident, Barry, I was there. A stupid, avoidable accident.'

'Nevertheless, I'd be asking the grandmother a few questions if I were you. There was something odd about Isabella's childhood, even for around here.'

I speculated about how well he'd actually known Isabella. Better than I'd realised, I guessed.

'How long is the carbon-dating going to take?' I asked.

'A few days, if you're lucky.' My heart sank. I felt I owed it to Isabella to keep a close eye on the astrarium.

'I'm due back at Abu Rudeis tomorrow.'

'And if I need to contact you?'

'We have a satellite phone out on the field, for emergencies. Ibrihim has the number. But, Barry, maybe best to keep a low profile about the astrarium, yeah? Just make sure it's safe.'

Barry pulled me into another of his bear hugs. 'Don't look so worried, mate. You can rely on me.'

9

Bill Anderson was waiting for me at the tiny airstrip in Port Said, with a car and driver.

'I thought I'd stay an extra night and catch up with you,' he said. 'My crew left for Texas this morning.' Bill was a big muscular man just beginning to run to fat, his broad Texan physique incongruous next to the slender Arab driver waiting to drive us back to the camp. He extended his hand, a massive paw, the calloused palm abrasive against my own. 'My sympathies, Oliver. I couldn't believe the news when I heard. It's a rough life, that's for sure, rough and unjust.'

The intensity of his concern embarrassed me and again I found myself wrestling with my emotions. I nodded and we both climbed into the back of the car in silence.

On the way to the camp we drove past the capped oil well. Floodlit, the well was surrounded by a circle of burnt and charcoal ground; debris from the explosives that had been used to cause the fire to implode and extinguish itself.

'Took a week to figure out the configuration,' Bill said. 'It was probably sheer bad luck but I wouldn't rule out sabotage. Capping it was a bitch, took way too long – fortunately we didn't lose anyone. This one was a mother, that's for sure.'

'Where are you off to next?'

'Libya – there's a problem at Sarir. That should be exciting,' he added ironically.

I turned back to the open window. Being back in Abu Rudeis was disorientating; my mind kept playing tricks on me, as if I'd slipped back in time to before the drowning. I kept expecting Isabella to ring on the satellite phone; for her to be still in Alexandria, at the villa, waiting. It was a seductive illusion.

The moon had painted the desert in black and white, with just a faint hint of azure streaked across the horizon. The vast scale of the landscape placed human life into perspective. But my grieving had flattened my emotions and the usual sense of cleansing I associated with the desert was absent. And the uncomfortable suspicion that I might have unwittingly endangered Barry by leaving the astrarium with him tugged at the back of my mind.

Anderson interrupted my reverie. 'I looked at some of your core samples and the seismic. I hope you don't mind?'

Actually, I did mind. I was fiercely private about my data and, as always between the research and the actual drilling, I was plagued by the vague sensation that I'd missed something in my analysis. This one was a particularly unpredictable risk, however. The seismic had indicated the possibility that the field extended out a good way, and the sonar readings had been promising. But the subsurface was a jigsaw of geological features and although I had taken my usual intuitive leap in my assessment – something only Moustafa had been party to – the idea that we might not hit black gold now played on my conscience.

'Not at all, as long as you don't change career and suddenly become the competition,' I joked, trying to cover my annoyance.

'No chance. I like gambling but I'm not that much of a risk-taker.'

I noticed the driver glance at his rear-view mirror as he reacted to Anderson's sharp tone. I lowered my voice. 'Is that what you think I am – a gambler?'

'We're all gamblers in one way or another, Oliver. But you have to admit this one's a fairly long shot.'

'Did Johannes Du Voor ring you?'

The chief executive officer of GeoConsultancy was a difficult man. He had no conventional training as a geologist or geophysicist but had fallen into the oil business via shipping after his time as a supplies officer in the South African navy during the Second World War. A perfectionist, Johannes Du Voor had an ambivalent relationship with the notion of risk. As a small consultancy that depended on fewer than a dozen large corporations as clients, GeoConsultancy couldn't afford mistakes. Initially, he'd accepted that some of my methods were a little unorthodox, but lately he'd been pushing me to back up that final ten per cent of sheer instinct with data. I had tried fudging it, but sometimes my hunches were so inexplicable that even I couldn't account for them. Understandably, the bigger the commission, the more nervous Johannes became.

'We bumped into each other in the executive lounge at Austin,' Anderson said. 'Boy, that man can talk. I don't think he realised that you and I know each other as well as we do. The guy didn't look well, I have to say, and he was kinda morbid.'

'He has an eating disorder. In that he eats too much, I mean. What else did the old bastard say?'

'He asked me if you're angling to set up your own consultancy, walk off with his clients.'

I laughed. The idea that I could be that underhand seemed absurd. 'The guy's paranoid,' I answered. 'He just doesn't understand the way I work.'

The trouble with Johannes Du Voor was that he imagined the rest of humanity to be as ambitious as he was, particularly the few he recognised reluctantly as more talented than himself. He'd recruited me directly out of Imperial College and for two years had insisted I work as his assistant in the field. On our first job together I realised he'd made a mistake; that he was out by nearly a kilometre. It was an important job – the first well in a new structure in Angola – and millions were at stake. I had pored over the seismic data, tested the core samples myself and walked the field while sniffing the air. At the risk of being fired, I'd offered him my alternative interpretation. Johannes had listened and had trusted the leap my instinct was pointing to despite his own calculations. To his credit, he corrected the proposed drilling angle. Then told me that if I was wrong he would not only fire me but he would also go out of his way to ruin my ongoing career. We struck oil that day but our relationship altered profoundly after that. He respected this inherent talent of mine, but even so every new exploration was like free-falling all over again for him.

The car pulled up beside the new drilling rig – untouched since I'd left two weeks earlier. The drill bit hung above the deck, its steel gleaming in the floodlights, poised like some vast mole ready to begin burrowing. Nearby, a deep-water well had been drilled to tap bore water to cool the rig in operation. Generators and various other pieces of equipment stood in the long shadow cast by the drill, like a silent audience awaiting a performance. It was bizarre to think that this massive contraption had remained unchanged, as if frozen in time, while my own life had gone through such devastating upheaval.

I made a quick appraisal of the equipment and the operators waiting at their controls. Then I raised my thumb, just like I had only a few weeks ago, moments before the explosion, and jerked it downwards. The giant diesel motors burst into life and the drill started to rotate as the stem was lowered through the deck. Nearby, engines turning the turntable pumped away the rubble and mud.

Anderson, standing next to me, slapped me on the shoulder. 'Rotary drilling – don't you love it!' he shouted over the noise. 'Ultimate penetration!'

Ignoring him, I watched the process for a few minutes. This initial stage was always nerve-racking: one had to pray that the drill bit was the correct selection for the rock. So far it was holding.

'I hear rumour there's an oasis about fifty miles from here,' Anderson interrupted my concentration. 'The guys told me there's a 1920s Arab-style hotel and it's great swimming.'

'I should stay here.'

'C'mon, there's nothing going on that your assistant can't handle. Man, you're suffering a loss. You need some time to gather yourself. I know how that feels.'

I glanced back at the rig. Anderson was right. It would take two days before the drill had gone deep enough so that it could change direction and enter the pay zone. Maybe a desert drive would burn away some of my sadness.

The road was little more than a track. I drove the company jeep like a madman. Somehow the prospect of dying out here attracted me; an instant way of escaping the grief that now shadowed me.

Inland, the Sinai was endless scrub broken by the occasional sand dune. My eyes played tricks, turning the clock back to repopulate the dunes with primordial trees, an inland sea, swooping gulls against a kinder sky. Once, areas of Egypt had been moister, the weather more tropical. There had been swampland, hippopotami in the Nile, lions and crocodiles, but the desert had always been the kingdom of the snake, jackal and scorpion, the domain of harsh death. Many of the Ancient Egyptian icons reflected this. Anubis, the jackal-headed god of embalming and cemeteries, was an embodiment of the stalking jackal at the edge of the desert, inching his greedy way towards the ravaged corpse; Ammut, the terrifying crocodile-headed goddess to whom the hearts of sinners were thrown during the weighing-of-the-heart ritual, was a manifestation of the real predators in the murky waters of the Nile. As my imagination sketched the fecund past against the arid horizon, I was reminded of Isabella's recurring nightmare and then of the horror of her missing organs. When I got back to Alexandria I would need to find out more. What kind of individual or organisation might have authorised the desecration of a body? And what of the other Egyptologist whom the coroner had told me about, the young female corpse he'd seen years before with the same organs missing? Was there a link?

'Anderson, have you ever heard of an illegal organ trade here in Egypt?'

He looked perplexed by the question. 'Not here. Asia, maybe, but not in Egypt – why? You missing something?' he joked. Then he realised I was serious.

'No,' I lied. 'Just thought I might have stumbled onto something.'

'Wow, that's kinda heavy.'

'Forget I even mentioned it.'

We fell back into an uneasy silence.

Two hours later we arrived at a fork in the road. There was nothing on the horizon in either direction.

Anderson studied the map in frustration. 'Jesus, I thought you said you'd been there before.'

'I have, but I had a local driver,' I answered, smiling.

He swore and tried to trace on the map the way we'd come.

I jumped out of the jeep. Immediately the heat hit me like a furnace; punching me in the lungs and almost sending me reeling. I stood still, shallowing my breath, then wrapped the scarf I was wearing over my head and across my burning cheeks. I loved this elemental pain, this pushing-up against the tediousness of physicality, the proximity of death and the sharpness of life it brought with it.

Just then I heard the distinct plod of camels' feet, followed by a shout in Arabic. A group of five Bedouin men emerged from behind a small dune, leisurely making their way down to the desert track, their headdresses and robes catching the breeze. They stopped their camels and stared at the jeep.

Uncertain of my reception, I waved. One of them waved back. Then the chief whipped his mount on its flanks and galloped towards me, the animal moving with surprisingly elegant strides.

From inside the jeep Anderson whistled. 'Hope your Arabic's good,' he muttered as he climbed out.

'It depends on how thick his dialect is.'

Close up, the hennaed beard of the Bedouin was startling. Now I could see the end of an AK-47 assault rifle poking out from under his saddle. He stared at Anderson. I followed his gaze; the Bedouin had noticed the old army ID tag from his service days in Vietnam that the oilman still wore.

'May peace be with you,' I said hurriedly in Arabic, hoping to distract the Bedouin.

Ignoring me, he pointed aggressively at Anderson. 'Soldier?'

'Say nothing,' I murmured to Anderson, praying that the normally loquacious American would stay silent.

By now the others had ridden up. They formed a sullen bunch, staring over the chequered scarves covering the lower halves of their faces, wary, waiting for a cue from their leader as to how to react.

'Not any more,' I answered in Arabic, pointing to Anderson's grey hair. 'Old.'

Unconvinced, the Bedouin chief's suspicious gaze travelled across Anderson's T-shirt, flared jeans and ancient sneakers.

'Old body, young mind,' the Bedouin said, deadpan.

Behind him, the other four tribesmen burst into laughter. Anderson, sensing an affront, swung around to me.

'What's he say?'

'He says you look very strong for a man of your age.'

Anderson narrowed his eyes in disbelief. 'Jesus, Oliver, just ask him where the oasis is.'

'The oasis is half an hour's drive from here. You take the left track,' the Bedouin replied in perfect English. 'Be careful – the desert can be dangerous.'

He swung his camel around and they were gone.

The gravelly tones of JJ Cale floated out from Anderson's radio, mingling with the rustling of the date palms above us. We were lounging beside a small lake surrounded by a green fringe of reeds and palms. Its surface mirrored the turquoise sky yawning above it. Set back a short distance was the low-lying hotel, its white-yellow desert-mud bricks making it barely discernible. Its Moorish architecture, with narrow slits for windows and with arches leading to an enclosed walled garden that was cool and shady even at midday, made it a refuge from the incessant heat.

I lay on a beach towel, left behind by some long-departed tourist and taken by me from the hotel, the grey flannel embroidered with 'P&O, Suez Cruises'. Next to my head sat the satellite phone borrowed from the oil company. My contract stated that I was to be contactable at all times in case of possible crisis in the field – so where I went the phone went too. Above me, a thick serrated palm trunk leaned over the lake, its reflected counterpart swaying slightly with the movement of the water. It was a perfect isochronism, a parallel world in reverse where anything was possible. I sat up, intrigued by the notion.

Anderson, in voluminous crimson bathing trunks, a copious amount of suntan lotion smeared over his reddening face and chest, lay in full sun, resembling a beached starfish. A thick, crudely rolled joint hung between his fingers. He sat up, took a long drag of the marijuana and, holding his breath, handed it to me. After exhaling he fell back onto his towel.

'Boy, how good it is to stop the brain.'

I inhaled gingerly; I had never liked to lose control and marijuana wasn't a favourite of mine, although Isabella had smoked it regularly, claiming that it stimulated her imagination. Personally I thought it stimulated nothing but paranoia, but, for fear of sounding unfashionable and old, I'd never asked her to stop indulging. My preference was alcohol, and I'd never tried any of the stronger hallucinogens and stimulants around at the time – LSD, mescaline, cocaine. But now I was willing to try anything to stop my mind from slipping into introspection. The smoke hit the back of my throat and seared my eyes. Seconds later a sense of psychological dislocation seeped through my body.

'This is strong. Where did you get it?'

'Afghanistan – it's opiated. They always prioritise my equipment so I'm never searched at airports.'

'Sounds useful.'

'Sure thing, buddy, but I draw the line at firearms and radioactive waste. A man has to have some morals.'

I stared across the lake, the colours blurring into smudges of brilliant blue, emerald green, white-yellow. An ibis flew low over the water's surface, its wings a languid progression of semi-circles rising and falling in a spiral of feathers.

'Do you know why I do what I do?' Anderson's voice was distant and slightly slurred, and my own increasingly inarticulate mind struggled to register the fact that he sounded very stoned.

'For the money, I suppose, maybe the danger.'

'Wrong on both counts. You know I was in Nam?'

'Sure.'

'Well, back around '68 – 17th September 1968, to be precise – my platoon was ambushed by the Vietcong and I found myself crouched among three friends with their guts spilling out. I was the only one left standing. I can't tell you why – wasn't reflexes, wasn't clever thinking, it just happened that way. I missed my death day. That's what I truly believe: I missed my death day and now here I fucking am – amen.' He took another drag of the joint, then stubbed it out on a rock. 'But I know, in my heart of hearts, I was truly meant to die that day.'

I lay there thinking about Isabella, her fear of Ahmos Khafre's prediction of her death day. Was that really the day she had drowned? Then there was the vision I'd had of her in the bathtub, the fact of her stolen organs and her own terror of her Ba and Ka not being united and ending up in an Egyptian purgatory. I waited for Anderson to continue. I'd never considered him a religious man or even particularly philosophical; in fact, I'd always assumed him to be the opposite: a realist willing to work for anyone for the right price, regardless of his politics.

'Couldn't it have been simply luck – the angle of fire?' I asked finally.

Anderson rolled over and stared at me, the whites of his eyes reddened. 'Christ, another cynic.'

'Organised religion is the scourge of the world. Look what it's done in this region.'

'That's economics, colonial history and territory and you know it. Anyhow, I'm not talking about religion. I'm talking about the natural span of a man's life and what kind of meaning we bring to our time here on this damn planet!'

Anderson's voice was loud – he was too stoned to realise how loud. I glanced around: the place was deserted except for a peasant woman on the opposite bank doing the laundry. She squatted at the water's edge, her long slim wrists emerging from her robes, her reddened hands a fury of soap suds as she scrubbed the clothes with a pebble on a rock. She looked across at me, then went back to her washing.

I turned back to Anderson, wondering whether to humour the huge bear of an ex-soldier or to be honest.

'You know, one of the things Isabella and I disagreed on most was her belief in all this voodoo. It used to amaze me that an educated, intelligent woman could believe in astrology and Ancient Egyptian magic, that some kind of invisible force directed her in her archaeology. I just don't buy that. Everything is what you see: gravity is gravity, the laws of physics are immutable and all mysteries are explicable. We're complex animals run by our hormones and ultimately not very important in the grand scheme of things. No more, no less.'

There was a short pause during which I realised we were

engaged in the meandering philosophising that smoking marijuana always led to. But I was on a roll, I couldn't stop myself; it was as if I was talking out the events of the past two weeks, trying to incorporate them in a framework that made some logical sense. But why was I so angry? Was I angry with Isabella for dying in her search for something that she believed was a spiritual object – a magical one, even, if some of the old accounts were to be believed?

'We live and then we die,' I continued. 'People live on in memory; that's the only kind of immortality available, unless you believe in wrapping desiccated corpses in linen and building huge triangular tombs over them. I don't. I'm worse than an atheist; I believe in expendable biology. Maybe that's why I'm terrified of forgetting Isabella because that would mean she'd really left me. You know, that moment when she stops appearing in my dreams and I find I can't remember her face.'

There was another long silence. Intoxicated, I gazed up into the vast blue. Suddenly I realised that the circling dot above me was a hawk patiently stalking over its hunting ground.

Bill lifted his sunglasses and peered at me, genuine emotion crinkling his eyes. 'She'll never leave you – you know that, don't you, Oliver?'

'I guess not.'

Another silence fell upon us, as dense as wood.

Bill collapsed back onto his towel. 'Tom, one of the guys who died with me in Vietnam, a real close friend, had this private joke with me. When we were under fire he'd call me Jerry. Tom and Jerry, see? Humour was his way of dealing with terror; no one else in that platoon, hell, on the whole planet, knew this little joke we had going between us. Anyhow, a couple of weeks after his funeral in Austin, the army put on a commemoration dinner for the platoon – most of whom had perished with Tom. So there I am, dressed up like a Thanksgiving turkey, thinking how much Tom would have hated all this hypocrisy and pomp, and I'm looking for my place name on the table. And there it was: Jerry Anderson – not Bill, Jerry – in black ink with a small cartoon of a cat and mouse. It was a sign, you know – Tom joking with me, reminding me that he was still out there, watching.'

'I'd love to believe that random events may have a special significance,' I said, 'but I can't. Maybe it's my scientific training – who knows? – but if I had an experience like that I'd just see it as someone's ill-conceived joke.'

'That's bullshit, Oliver. I've seen how you work – not all of it's based on cold logic, not in this game.'

Uncomfortable with the knowledge that he was right, I changed the subject. 'You still haven't told me why you became a firefighter on oil wells.'

Anderson trailed a hand into the water. The drips falling from his fingers appeared huge: deliciously welling miniature worlds of cool, cool water.

'Maybe I just like tempting the gods. You see, every time we set those explosives I'm waiting to die. Just can't shake off the sensation that I'm living on borrowed time.'

'Survivor's guilt?'

'Like I said, I missed my death day, brother. It's as simple as that.'

We lay there flattened by the sun, both very conscious of the unspoken statement hanging awkwardly between us. Finally Anderson spoke.

'Listen, I didn't mean to suggest that Isabella's accident was—'

'Yeah, I know,' I cut in. Then I stood up and waded into the shallow lake.

At the edge the water was warm. I slipped off the bank and moved into the deeper part where it became colder. After taking a deep breath I dived down, four strokes through the greenish water, sand below, the dark stripes of reeds shooting up towards the light, caressing paintbrushes against my body. The cold jet of the current travelling over my burning skin was soothing; my fingers making splayed frog-hands in the aquamarine light filtering from above.

I swam further down and along the bottom. A small group of large fish hovered above me, metal-blue in the subterranean sun, then darted away, glinting like thrown silver coins. In that moment I felt something pass by me, something large. Nothing was visible. Ripples ran along my skin, making my body hair stand on end. Treading water, I rotated as fast as I could, just in time to catch the sight of feet and naked legs disappearing into a forest of weeds.

A second later, Isabella loomed out of the lattice of long floating leaves, her loose hair weaving around her face, her breasts luminous. Terrified, I froze, drifting slowly down, as she smiled sadly at me, her face a translucent moon filtering through the green. Then, indicating that I should follow, she turned and swam away with that characteristic kick of hers. This is no ghost, I told myself, fighting blind panic.

I followed, only to lose her in the shadowy labyrinth. I searched, fighting the dangerous tangle, stirring up clouds of mud, but found nothing. Lungs bursting, I made for the surface.

Gasping, I broke through, limbs flailing. Disorientated, I struggled for breath for what felt like minutes, then managed to clamber onto the bank where I lay curled on the ground.

I became aware of a strange dull whirring sound – my satellite phone was ringing. I sat up. Anderson was on his feet, waving frantically.

'Are you okay?' he shouted.

Shaking, I got to my knees, trying to compose myself, but Isabella's face still hovered in front of my eyes. I leaned against the sandy bank.

'Fine. I just shouldn't smoke and swim!' I yelled back.

The satellite phone continued to ring.

'Answer it!' I shouted, and then I was back in the water, swimming towards him.

10

Barry's excited voice sounded distant, as if he were yelling from the bottom of a ravine. 'Oliver, this thing, it's amazing, mate. It's definitely an astrarium, but I've never seen anything even remotely this mechanically sophisticated.'

'What do you mean? It's an ancient artefact.'

'That's what's blowing my mind. It isn't bronze but some other alloy, which might explain why it's so well preserved. It seems to have some unusual magnetic properties – there's a cog-like device at the centre with what appear to be two magnets – looks as if it's meant to spin. Totally freaky. But get this, mate, the first time I carbon-dated the wooden box I thought I was hallucinating, but I've checked it five times now and I'm getting the same result over and over!'

'What result?'

'Mate, this astrarium isn't Ptolemaic, it's way older – Pharaonic. I found two cartouches on it – the cartouche of Nakhthoreb, otherwise known as Nectanebo II. That makes it Thirtieth Dynasty, which in itself is bloody unbelievable! But what is even more freaky is the cartouche I found next to it – of Ramses III. You know when that was, Oliver?'

'I have an idea.' My voice broke in terror. An uncomfortable blend of fear and excitement was making it difficult to talk.

'The Twentieth Dynasty, Oliver!' Barry yelled down the phone. 'I reckon around 1160 BCE, time of frigging Moses!'

My throat was dry and my heart felt as if it was thumping against the wall of my stomach. If the astrarium was Twentieth Dynasty it was well over two thousand years old. The Pharaohs weren't meant to have this kind of technology. If confirmed the discovery would force a complete reassessment of history, the beginning of civilisation, and our understanding of the Ancient Egyptians. It also meant the astrarium was immeasurably valuable, priceless beyond any reckoning.

'That's not possible. You've made a mistake.' I fought to keep my voice calm.

'Mate, I don't make mistakes.'

'Okay, I'm going to get back as quickly as I can. Meanwhile, I want you to keep this quiet. Barry, listen to me. Not a single word to anyone.' Overwhelmed, I sat back on the ground, fighting a sudden dizziness. In my mind I saw Faakhir, then Amelia. Hermes. Isabella's face. Her unbelievable excitement had she been around to witness this.

'Oliver, this is the discovery of the century.'

'Just promise me you'll lie low. I don't want either of us ending up in jail for stealing an antiquity. I'll be back in a couple of days. And, Barry, for Christ's sake watch your back.'

The line cut out before he had a chance to answer. I glanced over my shoulder. I was relieved to see that Anderson was fast asleep on his towel and the peasant woman washing her clothes had disappeared.

I flew to Alexandria four days later. I took a cab from the airport straight to Barry's apartment on the Corniche. The apartment block was one of those neoclassical buildings constructed at the turn of the twentieth century and had a crumbling magnificence. Barry had lived there for years, and had an arrangement with his Syrian Christian landlady, Madame Tibishrani. Now a voluptuous widow in her early sixties, she lived on the first floor with her handicapped daughter. She maintained Barry's place during his long and often inexplicable absences and operated as an unofficial postbox, dutifully collecting his mail. She adored the Australian and was fiercely protective of him, as well as tolerant of the numerous young travellers (almost always female) who'd turned up to stay over the years.

The apartment was on the third floor, with a large balcony that wrapped around the corner of the building. The cab dropped me off.

The sun had begun to set – a blood-red eye staring over the sea already streaked with the darkening clouds of night – and the call to prayer echoed: a lone melodic wailing that never failed to stir something elemental in my soul. The stately white Abu El Abbas mosque with its two domes and slender tower reaching to God like an outstretched arm dominated the square.

Small distinct groups of worshippers had begun to walk to the mosque. The smell of the sea blew in – a crisp breeze tainted with the scent of distant shores – and the familiarity of it saddened me. I glanced back up at Barry's apartment block. My heart missed a beat. I immediately noticed that something was wrong. The birdcages that usually hung there were missing and the shutters on the doors were closed. I'd never seen it like that before.

The doorman let me into the building without a word, then resumed his position in a plastic black chair by the stairwell. I raced up the stairs. Barry's apartment door was shut; the magic eye carved into it to ward off evil stared back at me as if to mock my growing sense of dread. I lifted the brass knocker and banged. There was no reply.

There was a creak on the stairs behind me; Madame Tibishrani's platinum beehive appeared on the landing below. The rest of her followed, incongruously dressed in an elegant black evening dress. She gasped, startled to see me.

'Monsieur Oliver, you have given me a scare. It has been so terrible, you cannot imagine.'

She hurried up the stairs and joined me outside Barry's door. Even in this dim light I could see that her eyes were swollen from weeping.

'I'm trying to find Barry. Isn't he in?'

Sighing, Madame Tibishrani stroked my hand. 'My poor Monsieur Oliver, have you not heard? Barry is no longer with us.'

'What do you mean?'

'He had an accident. The police say it was suicide, but I don't believe it, Monsieur Oliver. Barry would never have killed himself. Never.'

The news ran me through like an electric shock. Reeling, I leant against the wall. I couldn't believe that Barry was actually dead – it didn't seem possible that such a spirited bull of a man could suddenly no longer exist.

'Do you have the keys?' Fighting grief I made an effort to stand, pushing against the barrage of memories of Barry in this apartment – the evenings we'd got drunk together listening to the Rolling Stones, the political arguments that always ended in Barry resorting to standing on his head while making some grand statement that was totally irrelevant to the debate, reducing both Isabella and me to hysterical laughter, the night he got arrested for prophesying naked from his balcony, the day I walked in and found him feeding twenty of the local street kids.

'Of course I have the keys.'

'Let me in, please . . .'

'But the police . . .'

'Madame Tibishrani, please. I need to see for myself.'

She glanced down and up the stairs – that furtive look of fear so common in Egypt – then turned back to me.

'*D'accord*,' she whispered. 'But you cannot tell a soul it was I who let you in. The police have been here so many times that I think Barry must have been in trouble with the authorities.'

She pulled a bunch of keys from her pocket and, after wrapping the latch with a handkerchief to muffle the sound, opened the door.

The smell was awful – musty, with an overlay of old incense, stale cigarette smoke and cat piss. But there was something else that assaulted my senses – the sense of past violence. Death hung in the air, making the back of my scalp prickle. It was dark, almost pitch black: the heavy velvet curtains were drawn across the windows. Broken glass splintered under my shoes as I made my way across the lounge room, my feet bumping against books scattered across the floor.

'When they searched the place they made such a mess, but I have orders not to disturb it,' Madame Tibishrani murmured from the safety of the doorway. 'No respect for property, no respect for the dead.'

I drew the curtains, then opened the balcony doors to let in the sea breeze. Illuminated, the apartment showed itself to be in a state of total chaos. Books had been pulled from the bookcases lining the walls and flung to the floor, as if the intruders had been looking for secret compartments behind the shelves. Several of Barry's prized beanbags had been ripped open with a knife and the stuffing scattered – it looked like a tidal wave of foam had swept through the apartment. Despite a growing sense of horror I found myself looking for blood smears – on the walls, on the furniture. There weren't any. A leather armchair, its cushions neatly slit, stood in the centre of the room. I collapsed into it, the cotton stuffing pushing up around me.

'What happened?' I asked.

Madame Tibishrani stepped gingerly into the apartment. Barry's cat, a thin black and white creature called Thomas O'Leary, appeared and wrapped itself around her ankles, miaowing. She picked the animal up and stroked it absent-mindedly.

'It happened two days ago. I was wondering why I hadn't heard from him – normally he visits every Thursday night and I make him pigeon . . .' She blushed; it was an Egyptian belief that roast pigeon was a powerful aphrodisiac. 'But last Thursday there was not his usual knock on the door, so I went up . . .' Her face crumpled as she tried not to weep. 'His front door was unlocked, but this wasn't so unusual – you know how Barry believed in keeping his door open for every no-hoper to drop by. Anyhow, I went in and that was when I found my poor friend.'

She pointed at the chair I was sitting in. 'He was in that chair, with a needle in his arm and a leather string . . . what do you call it?' I leapt up out of the chair, disturbed by the thought that I was sitting where his corpse had been found. Covering my squeamishness, I turned back to Madame Tibishrani.

'A tourniquet?'

'*Oui*, like a tourniquet, wrapped further up. He was dead; I think maybe for a day already. But I don't understand . . .

Barry was not a heroin addict, of this I am sure.'

She was right. Despite his indulgence in many recreational drugs, Barry had always been vehemently anti-heroin. Besides, Alexandria wasn't the easiest place to purchase such a drug. And Madame Tibishrani was right. There was no way that Barry, a man who'd sucked every sensation he could out of life and relished it, could have killed himself. Why? It didn't make sense. The astrarium. It had to be. Was it murder, or possibly some kind of assassination, perhaps ordered by some higher authority? Did they find the astrarium? Or had Barry hidden it? My mind reeled as I absorbed this terrible reality. Then another thought occurred to me. If they were prepared to kill Barry, they were quite possibly prepared to kill me. I had to find the astrarium.

This has got to be a set-up, I thought as I looked around the ravaged room. Someone had killed Barry and then searched the place. And I had the impression they'd left frustrated; frustrated enough to be wantonly destructive.

'I pray for him,' Madame Tibishrani said. 'You know, if it is suicide his soul will not be able to enter heaven. I spoke to the priest about it but he is adamant . . .'

As Madame Tibishrani continued worrying about the possibility of Barry's condemned soul, I found myself wrestling with my own conscience. Had Barry died because I'd given him the astrarium to carbon-date? Was I directly or indirectly responsible for his death? And who would be so determined to lay their hands on it that they'd kill to get it? Who even knew that it was here? Who was Faakhir frightened of? I shivered and glanced involuntarily over my shoulder. Madame Tibishrani's raised voice broke into my thoughts

'They tried to tell me Barry was cooking up drugs in his home laboratory. Such ignorance! The police, the secret police and the municipality officials have been harassing me constantly since the accident. An Englishwoman even came and questioned me – what gave her the right! I look at her and I think she cannot ever have been Barry's lover; in fact, I doubt whether she has ever had a lover—'

'Can you remember her name?' I cut in urgently. I had a sneaking suspicion I knew who she meant.

'Adelia Limeherst, she called herself. When I tried to stop her from entering the apartment, she pushed me aside and looked anyway. Crazy, *non*?'

So Amelia had been here. How on earth would she have known that Barry had the astrarium? Although, the more I thought about it, the more obvious it became. Our friendship was well known, as was his ability to carbon-date and Isabella's obsession. It wouldn't have been difficult to make the connections. I walked carefully around the room, trying to ascertain what could be missing. A huge glass tank stood against one wall – an aquarium filled with tropical fish of which Barry had been immensely proud. It appeared to be the only undamaged object in the room. Uneasily, I found myself wondering what the fish would tell me if only they could speak. I wasn't sure I wanted to know. I turned back to the landlady.

'Did the woman leave with anything?'

'Not a thing! So many questions, though, Monsieur Oliver. She even asked about you and your poor wife.'

'Outrageous. Madame Tibishrani, do you think you could give me a few moments alone? I would like to say goodbye to Barry in private.'

Again, tears filled the landlady's eyes, making me feel guilty for deceiving her. But I couldn't search the room with her there.

'Normally I would say no, but out of respect for you and your poor dear wife who were so close to him . . . Besides, I need to feed poor Thomas. Just call me when you have finished.' And she left, the miaowing cat in her arms.

Now I was even more convinced that Barry had been murdered. What I needed to know now was whether he'd had time to hide the astrarium; and if so, where? And then, the more pressing question: who was behind this?

I sat back down in the leather chair and tried to place myself in Barry's mind, follow his line of vision. Where could he have hidden it? Battling the desire to leap up and rummage wildly through the debris I focused my mind, closed my eyes, then opened them. My gaze immediately fell on the fish tank. Nothing obvious had changed and, when I looked inside, the sand and silt seemed to have been there for ages, undisturbed. I stared at it for another minute, then got up restlessly, a sense both of panic and fear rising in me like bile. The police – or even Barry's murderer – could return at any moment and I needed to move quickly.

I decided to check the other rooms. In the bedroom, the futon Barry slept on had been slashed, and the three wooden crates he'd kept his clothes in had been overturned – trousers, sarongs, underwear and wetsuits spilled out in a tangled mess. The sight of his adored surfboard, with a line from Jack Kerouac's *On the Road* lovingly written on it, made me falter. Suddenly furious at the vandalism, I kicked the wall. A poster slid to the floor, drawing my gaze down to a small shrine to Buddha. The figure of the deity had been smashed – nearby, his beatific face gazed up from his severed head. Beside it lay a statuette of Thoth, the Ancient Egyptian god of magic and words – Barry's favourite god. But where was the astrarium? Somewhere outside the apartment a floorboard creaked. Glancing over my shoulder I froze, battling the sense that I was not alone. I waited. Nothing. Carefully and quietly I then walked into the bathroom where Barry had constructed his home laboratory.

Metres of blown glass tubing – vacuum lines – were clamped to metal frames suspended from the ceiling, the tubes threading around and over each other like some bizarre sculpture. The basin had been turned into a workbench, on which stood a small bar fridge, a hammer, a file – still spotted with flakes of dark wood – and a mortar and pestle.

I opened the fridge cautiously, nervous about what I might find. Sitting on the grimy plastic shelves were several corked glass flasks filled with liquid nitrogen – one of the necessary components of carbon dating. A couple of them trailed curling wisps of vapour from leaky stoppers. Alongside them was an unopened can of Foster's beer. For a moment I was tempted to open it and drink to Barry's health – a ghoulish sentiment I knew he would have appreciated. I was interrupted by the sound of something smashing in the room next door. I jumped, then, pressing myself against the wall, lifted a heavy pair of pliers from the bench as silently as I could. Holding it high like a club I inched towards the half-open door, expecting some thug to appear at any minute. Just then a starved-looking kitten wound its way around the doorway. Staring up át me with huge pus-infected eyes, it began miaowing pitifully. Relieved, I dropped the pliers: just another one of Barry's waifs.

I breathed a sigh of relief, then returned to my search, more desperate now. I knew he must have carbon-dated the device in the laboratory, but where could he have hidden it?

Further along the bench a Pyrex beaker was suspended over a Bunsen burner. I lifted the beaker and sniffed – inside were tiny charred fragments of charcoal. Apart from the flakes of wood on the file and a tiny amount of dark dust – ground wood, I assumed – in the mortar, there was no sign of the astrarium or its wooden case. Ten minutes later, I had to give up, my heart heavy in my chest. Whoever had killed Barry now had the astrarium, the artefact that Isabella and Barry had died for and had given into my trust.

After making sure the front-door lock clicked behind me, I walked down to Madame Tibishrani's apartment. She answered my knock with rosary beads clutched between her fingers.

'Well, did you make your peace?' she asked me.

'Not entirely. Has there been a funeral yet?'

'*Mon Dieu*, I wish. But no, the poor man is still in the city morgue. They are waiting for the Australian consul, apparently – there is a small problem locating Barry's nearest living relative. Although there has been no problem with living ex-wives. Apparently, all three have been informed of his death, and all are claiming that they are still married to him. Barry was such a romantic.' I left hastily before the landlady began weeping again.

The nearest working phone line I knew of was at the Alexandrian Oil Company office. I went straight there. After practising my Australian accent, I rang the central police station and told them that I was a relative of Barry's ringing from Australia and that I was after further details of the circumstances of his death. The officer investigating the case told me politely but firmly that as drugs had been found in Barry's body, they had dismissed the case as accidental suicide, a drug overdose, but his body was still in the morgue awaiting collection. Apparently, one of his long-lost wives had claimed the body but hadn't yet shown up. When I asked about the ransacking of the apartment, the officer laughed and told me that drug addicts were known for their wild parties. As I put the telephone down I had the distinct impression someone had provided the financial incentive for the investigation to be closed down prematurely. Were Barry's killers part of a bigger and more powerful network than I imagined? The idea set a chill running down my spine. Egypt was not a place where you'd want to be up against the authorities. Nonetheless, I decided to visit the morgue to see if I could find out more about Isabella's missing organs, but also to try and catch a glimpse of Barry's corpse. Maybe there'd be a clue or a hint. And at least it would give me a chance to say goodbye.

11

The morgue was located to the west of the city, in the old Turkish quarter. On the way there I'd almost been sure that the taxi I was travelling in was being followed, but just when I was about to tell my driver to take a deliberately confusing detour, the small red Fiat trailing us had peeled off into another laneway, disappearing from sight. I arrived at the grand nineteenth-century building trying to convince myself that my fear wasn't real, that I'd begun to slip into paranoia. It wasn't working.

At the sweeping marble reception desk I asked to speak to Demetriou al-Masri, the coroner who had approached me at Isabella's funeral. The sour-faced man behind the desk told me with ill-concealed relish that Wednesday was Mr al-Masri's day off and that I should come back tomorrow. Quietly I explained that I was here to see the body of a dear friend. The thirty Egyptian dollars offered under the table seemed to soften his attitude. He called over a youth lounging against a wall and instructed him to take me to 'the European'.

The room was freezing. The sound of a generator battling

to maintain the sub-zero temperature filled the room, adding to the sensation that I was now standing in a strange ante-chamber that had some unspeakable ritualistic function. A chemical smell of embalming fluid pricked at my nostrils and sent vague fingers of fear fluttering across the back of my scalp. This was where the new guests were kept, the youth informed me, grinning: the drowned, victims of road accidents, or beggars found curled up in doorways. Each corpse had its own plinth of marble, and one could make a guess at the age and shape of them from the silhouettes of the bodies that were all covered by grimy white sheets; I couldn't help wondering if Isabella's corpse had lain on one of them. Irrationally, I found myself imagining how cold the marble must have been against her skin, and how if I'd been there I could have swept her up in my arms and wrapped a blanket around her to warm her.

The mortuary attendant pulled the sheet off Barry's corpse. The mane of tangled hair made him look like some majestic statue of Neptune in repose, the white-grey pallor turning his flesh to alabaster. The eyes were open and filmed with a whitish-blue sheen, his chin was unshaven, his cheeks sucked back to the skull in death. In his chest was a huge T-shaped wound – a crude incision that ran from his belly button up to the centre of the collarbone, as if they'd peeled back the chest cavity – roughly stitched with black thread. I assumed they had carried out an autopsy to confirm the cause of death. To see him so still was shocking. Leaning across, I closed his eyes.

The attendant, noticing my emotional reaction, nodded respectfully and left to have a cigarette in the corridor.

The refrigerated air sank into my bones. I shivered, then glanced down at Barry's feet; they were bony, the veins a topography of congealed life stopped mid-pulse. I looked back at his huge barrel chest and the skin below it that hung grey and slack. I kneeled, retching.

Mastering my revulsion, I stood and examined his body for signs that might illuminate the real cause of death. I lifted his beard: under the tangled mass of grey and blond hair was a thin purple bruise. My breath caught in my throat. I'd seen this once before in Nigeria, on the body of a field worker left propped up on a fence around a well – murdered as a warning to the oil company I was contracted to at the time. Barry had been garrotted. I glanced at his arm and the puncture mark left by a needle – the stigmata of the addict. Whoever had killed him had injected him with heroin after his death to make it look like an overdose. My guess was that they had tortured him to find out where he'd hidden the astrarium. Maybe they hadn't meant to kill him, but he'd died anyway.

I was furious. 'You were never a junkie and you did not commit suicide.' My angry voice bounced off the shiny white tiles.

Tenderly, I tucked Barry's arm up against his body. As I did so I noticed a greenish-blue colour staining his finger-nails and fingertips. I knew that colour – I'd seen it underwater, during dives. Algae.

It took an hour to get back to Barry's apartment through the traffic along the Sharia Saad Zaghloul. As the cab sat there, sandwiched between an open truck full of exhausted-looking soldiers and an hantour, I felt someone's stare burning through the window. I turned and met the gaze of a man sitting at a table outside a café. I reeled back in shock when I recognised the scarred face of Omar, the supposed official who had accompanied us on the dive for the astrarium. The sight of him transported me instantly back to the boat and, momentarily, I was paralysed by a surge of grief. I stared at him, unable to look away.

The truck in front of us accelerated and my driver was quick to follow suit. We swung into a side lane and away from Omar. Relieved, I promised the driver triple the fare if he went as fast as he could. We reached the Corniche fifteen minutes later.

I raced back up to Madame Tibishrani's floor and persuaded her to lend me the keys for one last time. Moments later I was inside Barry's apartment.

I pressed my face up against the fish tank, the cool glass humming under my skin. On the bottom stood a kitsch statue of Jesus, his feet buried in gravel and his painted eyes turned beatifically towards heaven. He was framed by a stream of silvery bubbles that bounced up behind him through a pump concealed in a plastic treasure chest. Next to this little ensemble was a Richard Nixon doll entwined with a plastic mermaid who appeared to be fellating him – a classic example of Barry's deeply irreverent humour. Then I noticed what I hadn't seen before: the metal edge of something half-buried at the back of the slope of gravel. An angel fish, fins rippling like the wings of a hummingbird, swam down and began nibbling at some algae growing on the edge of the object. I immediately recognised the colour of the algae from Barry's fingertips. I peered closer. Between the waving waterweed and the bubbles of the air pumps, part of a smallish box was visible, about the size of an eighteenth-century mantelpiece clock. Despite a thin layer of algae, I could see the serrated edges of two discs. So that was why Barry's killer, or indeed myself, hadn't found it. It looked as if it had been in the aquarium for months, indiscernible from the other marine ornaments.

Transfixed, I switched on a reading lamp and hauled it

over to the tank, pointing the light directly at the object. Instantly, thin lines of glittering bronze were illuminated – a tiny inscription written across one of the discs.

'Barry, you clever bastard,' I announced. I turned to make sure that all the blinds were pulled down, then plunged my hands into the tank.

Back at the villa, I asked Ibrihim to bolt the front gate, then stood quietly in the shadow of the gates for a moment, waiting to see if I'd been followed. I was both nervous and excited, weak from the adrenalin surge I'd experienced in Barry's apartment. The weight of the astrarium in the rucksack across my back felt ridiculously light for an object of such extraordinary impact and although the drive back had been uneventful I'd been edgy, feeling myself watched from every corner. The quiet residential road we lived on appeared empty except for a thin Arab youth who was lounging against the wall of the villa opposite, staring blankly across at us. I was just about to confront him when Ibrihim pulled me back. Apparently, he was the mentally handicapped son of a local gardener.

I took the astrarium up to my bedroom again – it seemed the safest and most private place in the villa. Even then I found myself bolting the bedroom door. I pulled the blinds down. I lifted the device out of the backpack and sat down, drinking in the sudden silence. I'd been determined to be neither fearful nor too reverent. I failed miserably. Out of its container the astrarium was far smaller and more innocuous-looking than I'd imagined – dirty and sodden, it certainly didn't look like the powerful weapon that Isabella and Faakhir had described. But there was an undeniable mystery about it and, because Isabella had talked about this the day we'd met, I almost felt that it brought some of her presence back to me. This was hers, in life and in death.

As Barry had said, the metal resembled an alloy – bronzy in colour but slightly grainy and sparkling, almost as if it had been mixed with diamonds or something flinty. It reminded me of one of the rare-earth metals. Intrigued by the way it glinted in the lamplight I couldn't help myself. Holding my breath, I ran my finger across the surface, focusing on the silvery, slightly coarse texture. I had seen a metal like this before – samarium, which had strong magnetic properties, particularly when combined with cobalt. As such metals were hard to mine for – even today – I couldn't imagine how the Ancient Egyptians would have had the technology, never mind the expertise, to refine such ores. Still, I knew they had been fascinated by metallurgy. Isabella once told me that the Ancient Egyptians believed the natural chemical changes in such metals to be so magical that through them a lowborn fellah's destiny could be transformed into that of the most powerful pharaoh – a kind of ancient alchemy. I'd found this idea intriguing, particularly when I discovered that they had developed a use for magnetic iron ore derived from meteorites and tektite glass in their ritual instruments and had considered such iron ores to be sacred. Could the astrarium be made from a similar metal? My study was interrupted by a flurry of shouting outside. Throwing a scarf over the device I rushed to the window and peered down through the shutters. Outside, Ibrihim appeared to be arguing with the man who delivered our heating oil. I listened intently; they were fighting over a bill. I dropped the shutter and returned to the desk, my heart still thumping from fear.

When I examined the astrarium more closely, it appeared to be a series of cogs built around three main discs, their faces visible through a peephole in the top of the box. There was a main pivotal rod that provided the central axis for the cogs and discs, finishing in what looked like a keyhole at the front. Presumably, one inserted a key or some similar device to start up the mechanism. There were inscriptions in various languages engraved on both the discs and on the body of the astrarium itself; some in hieroglyphs, the others I did not recognise. But the whole appearance of the instrument seemed familiar to me. Fear, and the trepidation of the explorer – the same feeling I got when solving a particularly complicated piece of geological substructure – had began to creep up from the base of my spine.

I suddenly remembered Gareth's drawing of the astrarium and ran to Isabella's desk to search for it. I found it and placed it next to the device. It was uncanny how closely they resembled one another, except that the actual device was larger and more complex than they had envisaged. I looked at the cipher written at the bottom of the drawing, then peered again at the inscriptions on the astrarium. With a shock, I realised that the first two symbols of the hiero-glyphic inscription matched Gareth's lettering. Excitement rushed through me and I caught my breath; I had never really believed it but Isabella had been right. This was it. This was the actual astrarium she had been searching for all those years.

Two small balls – one gold, the other darkened silver – jutted out from behind one of the discs: the Sun and the Moon, I guessed. There were five other smaller copper balls – probably the five planets visible to the naked eye: Mercury, Venus, Mars, Jupiter and Saturn. It reminded me of a miniature orrery. It was almost inconceivable to think it might be more than two thousand years old. I peered into the central chamber, where, with the aid of a torch, I could just about make out the two magnets that Barry had men-tioned. Each sat on its own axis. What would it take to set them into motion?

I returned to Isabella's desk. The ghost of her presence hung in the air. I remembered her sitting there in the lamplight that last night, pensive as she studied the illustration of the astrarium, her long fingers trailing along the edge of the paper. For a moment I allowed myself to remember the scene, seeing her again, naked, her hair spilling down her back. It felt inconceivable that I would never be with her again, and yet here in my hand was the one thing she'd been searching for, the ultimate achievement that she had died for. I stared down at her desk, lost in thought. Then, my thoughts suspended in the stilled air, I remembered something else. That small gesture, almost invisible, the slipping of something under the ink blotter. I broke open the desk lock. Atop a pile of papers sat an envelope, my name written on it in Isabella's distinctively neat hand. Staring down, grief clutched at my chest. I fell back into the chair, waiting for it to pass.

I propped the envelope up against the lamp stand, stalling the moment of opening it and glancing at the papers it had been lying on. On top of the pile was a yellowed document with the title *Nectanebo's Priestess and the Pharaoh's Ba*. The author was Amelia Lynhurst. This had to be the thesis that Isabella had told me about, the one that had finally discredited the Egyptologist.

I forced myself to look back at the sealed envelope that had my name on the front. Why hadn't Isabella trusted me more? Why had she held back about the significance of the astrarium, the danger involved in finding it? She'd trusted Faakhir with the truth but not me. Had I been so unapproachable, so cynical, so disbelieving?

Resolved to face whatever she had to say to me from beyond the grave, I opened the envelope quickly. Under my fingertips the expensive notepaper felt like silk, like her skin. A trace of her distinctive scent – a mixture of musk and jasmine – was faintly discernible. Closing my eyes, it was easy to imagine her heavy hair brushing across the paper, leaving its own olfactory signature.

13th May 1977
Alexandria

Oliver, forgive me, I've never been completely honest with you. All those years ago, Ahmos Khafre did not only tell me my death date; he also told me I might have been able to save my own life if I discovered the astrarium in time.

My love, there are people I know who will guide you. But the astrarium has a mind of its own. It will lead you to them, if you let it. As I write I hear your voice chastising me for such superstitious beliefs, but the world I grew up in had no borders between magic and myth, the living gods and the dead. Through them I have been a witness, and through you I thought I would escape them. I will always love you.

Isabella

'Don't you dare try to give meaning to a pointless death, Isabella!' I shouted, swept up by sudden rage. 'No one could have predicted that earth tremor. No one! Not even me!'

I punched the cushion on the chair, anger and frustration pounding through me, and the fabric ripped, sending feathers flying up into the air. They floated back down to the floor like lazy snow, covering the envelope at my feet.

The call to afternoon prayer sounded: haunting and melodious. Time was passing. I walked over to the balcony window. Below I could see a gardener pruning a magnolia tree. The simple intent of his gestures seemed so real against the extraordinary events that had begun to shape my choices. Yes, I was intrigued, but rational instincts told me to stay away. And yet, there was Isabella, her hands outstretched, asking me to carry on. I worried that she had never confided fully in me because she feared I wouldn't have believed her. If I had been less scornful of her 'voodoo', taken her seriously, could I have saved her? This would be my way of pursuing Isabella's quest and, in some ways, absolving myself of the guilt that I now felt about not supporting her in the past. Out of nowhere the image of Barry's clouded eyes appeared like a warning. Determined to jolt myself out of a sense of growing dread I opened the doors and shutters and shouted down to Ibrihim, instructing him to bring me some lunch. Then I picked up Amelia Lynhurst's thesis.

On the inside page was a portrait of a beautiful woman. The caption read *High Priestess Banafrit*. The patrician nose, long almond eyes and full mouth were profoundly human in their flawed asymmetry. I would have recognised this face on the street. In fact, it almost seemed familiar to me. The more I looked at it, the more I was convinced that I'd seen it before, but where? I read the text below the illustration.

This depiction, discovered on the wall of a Hathor temple, is thought to be the only remaining representation of Banafrit (meaning 'of the beautiful soul') who lived during the reign of Nectanebo II in the Thirtieth Dynasty (360–343 BC) and dedicated herself solely to the Goddess Isis, the queen of all goddesses, endowed with magical powers unrivalled in the Pharaoh's reign. Banafrit's other titles included Divine Adoratrix and God's Wife. Her power exceeded that of the High Priest and was only slightly less than that of the Pharaoh. As the supreme High Priestess, Banafrit would have worn the royal uraeus cobra on her brow; and would have appointed her own successor to ensure that her magic remained within the Isis sect.

I looked at the illustration below the title. The central figure, a high priestess, sat on a throne and was dressed in a long-sleeved ceremonial robe with red and blue ribbons and a tall pillbox-shaped headdress with flowers sprouting out of it. In one hand she held a sistrum – a rattle-like musical instrument associated with the goddess Hathor – and a garland of morning glory, the hallucinogenic bindweed, lay across her lap. A sparrow was perched at her feet next to a small pot. She was surrounded by handmaidens playing tambourines and wearing dark rose mantles over white gowns, similar pillbox headdresses adorned with a single blue lotus flower, and gold bands high around their necks. The caption told me that the image had been found in a tomb in Hierakonpolis on the Nile and was one of the very few depictions of an Isis festival rite. This particular scene had been dated to the reign of Ramses XI in 1000 BC, but the ritual had been carried out through the ages and it was known that Banafrit had performed similar rituals.

> *Little is written about this powerful but enigmatic figure, although it is reported that several sphinx statues commissioned by Nectanebo were reported to have carried her facial features.*

I paused, realising where I'd seen the face in the illustration. It was the face of the sphinx that had pinned Isabella to the sea floor. How was that possible? Banafrit and Cleopatra had been three hundred years apart. A shiver ran through me; it was as though the priestess herself was trying to reach out to me through all those aeons. I thought back to my conversation with Barry, straining to remember every detail about the astrarium he'd mentioned. He'd talked about Ramses III, who lived in biblical times – he'd mentioned Moses, hadn't he? – and then of Nectanebo II, whom Isabella had often spoken about. Ramses. Moses. Nectanebo. And here was Amelia's Banafrit, High Priestess of the Isis sect, a cult who worshipped her, a legendary magician. And then there was the sphinx found at the underwater site of Cleopatra's shipwrecked Ra boat. Was it a bizarre coincidence or did it mean something? I couldn't dismiss an underlying fear that someone or something was directing my research. Isabella's words about the astrarium guiding me forward rang into my ear and although I had dismissed it, and still did, as impossible, I couldn't shake the feeling that there were too many crossing lines and too many links in the chain for it not to have a significance. I began reading again.

One of the greatest honours that could be bestowed upon a mortal, such privileges were usually reserved for royalty, further strengthening the hypothesis that Banafrit had been Nectanebo's youngest sister. There is also strong evidence that she was his lover. Some might say the love of his life.

The hieroglyphs found below this mural describe Banafrit's vision of Nectanebo II's Ba trapped in his tomb. Unable to fly in and out, it had perished, condemning the Pharaoh to eternal exclusion from the afterlife. It is possible that Banafrit, clearly a consummate strategist to have achieved such a powerful position, had heard rumours of an assassination plot and was using the vision as a metaphor to warn her Pharaoh. The hieroglyphs also mention a skybox, already legendary in the time of Nectanebo II for being able to inflict magic on the sea, sky and earth. It was this that Banafrit sought out to ensure the fortune and destiny of her beloved Pharaoh. Here the inscriptions become too heavily vandalised to make complete sense but a passage later talks of a following or cult that sprung up around the charismatic priestess. I believe I have

*uncovered evidence that proves this cult continued to exist
well into the era of Cleopatra who herself might have identified with Banafrit.*

So there was the connection, I thought, although I had no
idea what it meant. I leafed through the rest of the pages,
most of them about the Isis cult and speculating about
Banafrit's relationship with Nectanebo, the various ways she
supported his reign and kept him from harm.

*Interestingly enough, Nectanebo himself was immortalised
through an account from a translation of an ancient manu-
script entitled 'The Dream of Nectanebo' in which Nectanebo
dreams he overhears the sky war-god Onuris complaining
about his uncompleted temple. When Nectanebo woke he
immediately summoned the priests who told him everything in
the temple was finished except the hieroglyphs. Nectanebo
employed the best hieroglyph-cutter around, one Petesis.
Unfortunately, Petesis was distracted from his task by a beautiful woman whose name meant 'noble Hathor'. Hathor was
the goddess of love and drunkenness, but she also personified
destruction. At this point the account ends abruptly, so we'll
never know exactly how angry Onuris was with the Pharaoh.
I like to believe his fury might have had something to do with
Nectanebo's demise and eventual disappearance. And, to me,
the strange way the scribe suddenly stopped writing seems to
tell a story in itself – as if he himself might have been killed, a
murder that would have prevented him from completing his
task and revealing the whole story . . .*

A photograph of a sarcophagus followed, described as
Nectanebo II's empty coffin, now housed in the British
Museum.

Idly examining the photograph, I wondered why this paper had been so contentious within the archaeological community. It seemed fairly innocuous to me – the language conversational, the legends and myths telling a believable story. Not perhaps a clearly proven hypothesis but certainly insufficient grounds to ruin Amelia Lynhurst's entire academic career. The reference to the skybox intrigued me. Isabella must have made a connection between that and her astrarium. I sighed: what was my role in all this? Whatever it was, I needed to listen to my own instincts and work out where the astrarium rightfully belonged. But that had to be soon, and not only for the sake of my own safety. I had to keep it out of the wrong hands.

I noticed the change in the light outside; evening had fallen without me realising. I glanced towards the astrarium, still illuminated by the desk lamp. It threw a shadow now – the unmistakable silhouette of a robed woman, tall and statuesque. Then, terrifyingly slowly, the shadow turned to profile: the full lips and arched nose clearly defined.

Outside, Tinnin the guard dog started barking. Then came the sound of running footsteps. My heart leapt, my whole body tensing as I got ready to defend myself. The footsteps died away and by the time I swung back to the astrarium the shadow had vanished. Had I imagined it?

12

The next morning I was due at the Brambilla family's lawyer's office for the reading of Isabella's will. Having lost the astrarium once, I'd decided not to let it out of my sight. So I packed it into a rucksack and slung it over my back. And just before I'd left the house I'd taken Gareth's illustration and hidden it at the back of my bookshelf in a dusty and boring-looking tome on accountancy.

The office of Popnilogolos and Sons was located in the banking district, two buildings down from the Alexandrian Oil Company headquarters. Dreading another encounter with Francesca Brambilla, I pushed open the heavy brass door. Mr Popnilogolos's secretary showed me into his office.

'Am I early?'

I glanced around; the heavy oak desk was surrounded by piles of documents stacked against the walls. In the centre sat two ominously empty chairs, like props waiting for actors to breathe life into them. I stepped over a stack of files towards one of the seats.

'Don't worry, Madame Brambilla is late as usual. She regards it as her perennial right.' Mr Popnilogolos, an elegant man in his mid-fifties, his hair oiled back, immaculate in a black suit and blue tie despite the sweat prickling at his forehead, offered me a cigarette which I declined. He pulled out a box file from the top of a heavily stacked cabinet.

'The Brambillas . . . well, I'm afraid, your wife's estate was not worth very much. I hear Cecilia was at the funeral?'

I nodded. Encouraged, he continued.

'An exquisite woman. We all wanted her, you know, but Paolo was the only one who was not too intimidated to propose. He was frightened of nothing – except his father Giovanni, I suppose. An eccentric man but dangerous too.' He swung around, clutching the box file to his chest. 'Here we have it . . . Signora Isabella's will.' Popnilogolos sat down behind the desk and sighed ponderously. 'Such a tragedy – appalling. The strange thing is, your wife came to see me only a week before her death. At the time I thought it bizarre: usually clients think about making their wills when they are somewhat older, not in their twenties and bursting with health.' He looked up at me and must have caught the look that passed over my face. I knew that Isabella had taken the prediction seriously but I was shocked at the extent to which she'd gone to prepare. He continued without further hesitation. 'Of course, I was happy to oblige, and her foresight was fortunate. You do realise Giovanni Brambilla left his house to his granddaughter upon his death? Which – technically, at least – made Isabella her grandmother's landlady. And now possibly yourself. Fascinating.' He smiled; leaving me with the distinct impression that the lawyer was indulging in a little *schadenfreude*. Before I had a chance to question this surprising information we heard his secretary welcoming another visitor.

'Speak of the devil,' the lawyer said, with a wink, and stood to open the door.

*

Francesca Brambilla settled into a chair where she sat stiffly upright, clutching her crocodile-skin handbag as if it were a barricade in a storm.

'Are you comfortable, Madame?' the lawyer enquired.

'As comfortable as possible, given the unnatural circumstances. It really should be my will you are reading, not my granddaughter's,' she snapped back.

I tried to catch her eye but she barely acknowledged my presence.

'Indeed, life is tragically unpredictable – as we Alexandrians know too well,' Popnilogolos responded smoothly. He turned to me. 'Monsieur Warnock?'

'You may proceed.'

He cleared his throat and began reading: 'I, Isabella Francesca Maria Brambilla, bequeath all of my estate, including the Brambilla Villa, my books, research and collection of artefacts, to my husband, Oliver Patrick Warnock. To my grandmother I leave the jewellery I inherited at the time of my father's death. Dated 7 May 1977.'

The two of us waited; I sensed we were both expecting something more conclusive – some kind of absolution, even.

'Is that it?' I asked finally.

The lawyer nodded, then turned to Francesca. 'You do realise what this means, Madame Brambilla?'

Francesca's hand shook as she grasped the ivory head of her cane. 'This will was written seven days before her death?'

Mr Popnilogolos smiled weakly. 'Perhaps Madame Warnock had a premonition?'

The old woman swung around to me. 'Has this got anything to do with you?'

'I promise you, Francesca, I had no idea that she'd made this will. Nor that Giovanni had left the house to her.'

A difficult silence settled over the room like dust. Francesca's deep voice stirred it up as she finally spoke.

'My husband and I had a disagreement towards the end of his life. There were aspects of his behaviour that I did not approve of. Rewriting his will was Giovanni's way of punishing me. I don't think he ever imagined that Isabella would die before me.' She turned back to me. 'Does this mean you wish me to move out of the villa? You are the new owner, apparently.'

'So it appears.'

Watching her discomfort, it occurred to me that there was a way of taking advantage of the situation.

'Mr Popnilogolos, would you give us a few minutes of privacy?' I asked.

'Certainly.' After a short bow, the lawyer stepped outside.

'I'm happy to allow you to stay on in the villa on one condition,' I told Francesca.

She narrowed her eyes angrily. 'Which is?'

'You tell me the truth about what happened to Isabella's body. Why was she buried without her heart?'

The elderly woman's cane fell with a clatter to the parquet floor. 'She had no heart?'

'No heart, no internal organs.'

Francesca seemed shocked but, at the same time, not completely surprised. As I watched, another expression – one of realisation – swept across her fine wrinkled features.

I picked up the dropped cane. 'You know something, don't you, Francesca? What is it? You must tell me.'

'I know nothing,' she replied tersely. 'I am as horrified as you.'

Clutching the arms of the chair, she rose to her feet. 'If you wish to evict me, I would appreciate at least twenty-four hours' notice.'

And without another word, she opened the door, pushed past the lawyer waiting outside and left.

I walked down towards Mohammed Ali Square, where the Bourse, Alexandria's cotton and stock exchange, had once stood. It had existed for centuries in one form or another. E. M. Forster had written about it, even ancient Arabic writers such as Ibn Jubayr. A symbol of old colonial Egypt, the Bourse had been burnt down in the hunger riots earlier in the year. You used to be able to hear the cries of the bartering merchants every morning. Now the site had been reduced to a vacant lot that functioned as a temporary car park. Somehow it seemed emblematic of modern Egypt.

As I made my way through the narrow streets I kept thinking about Isabella's missing organs: had it really been an ambulance waiting for her body on the jetty or something more sinister? Thinking of Isabella's empty body made my heart clench with new grief, but it also seemed like a message, like another piece in the puzzle, seemingly unlinked and yet integral to my understanding of where to go from here. She'd said I would know what to do, had said it trustingly, unquestioningly, and I couldn't disappoint her. Conscious of the weight of the astrarium on my shoulder, I reflected on the experts I knew and who I could trust to help me work out what to do with the device. Faakhir's grim expression as he warned me of those who would use it to destroy the region's political stability came back into my mind. What did he mean by this – an undermining of President Sadat's peace initiative? There was little stability in the Middle East anyhow: Egypt had been at war with Israel only two years before and that war had been triggered by OPEC nations holding the world to ransom over oil prices in the early 1970s. It wouldn't take much to destabilise what little progress both President Sadat and the US president Carter had achieved so far. And who knew how Israel might receive Sadat's overtures – there was little or no trust on both sides of the border. But how could the possession of an ancient astrarium have an impact either way? Maybe there was some kind of strong historical symbolism that had suggestive power over Arabic/Israeli relations. Or was it some kind of devastasting weapon? I could have speculated for hours but in the end it almost didn't matter whatever my conclusion might be – obviously there was someone out there who believed absolutely in the power of the device. And they were prepared to kill to get hold of it. I walked without thinking, taking little notice of what was around me. But that was a luxury I'd soon not be able to afford.

Sensing a presence, I glanced behind me. A veiled older woman scurried behind a food stall. Frowning, I ducked behind a pillar; a minute later she re-emerged to run after a small child whom she caught and scolded. I rested against the wall. Was I losing my abilities to think analytically? My rationalism? I'd lost a wife and a friend. I was carrying a priceless artefact on my back and I seemed to be walking into some kind of geopolitical battlefield in a country torn by modern ambition and ancient beliefs, all of which would unhinge the sanest of men. No, I thought firmly, the astrarium was real, Barry's carbon-dating was indisputable and Isabella's own belief, one in which she had invested her life, deserved respect. But it was no doubt a massive task to undertake. Had Isabella realised the implications when she'd made me promise I would embark on the venture if necessary? The pragmatist in me struggled against such an esoteric responsibility. I had work, I had the oilfield to look after, I needed to rebuild my world, and yet I'd made a promise that was now turning into the most significant of my life. I was compelled to carry through her task even at the risk of losing everything – even my life. I had no choice. I walked on, quickening my pace to get out of the back alley. Whatever my reservations, I needed to glean as much information as I could from as many people as possible. Both Hermes Hemiedes and Amelia Lynhurst had offered their help, but could I trust them? Isabella had been close to Hermes, but I didn't have quite that relationship with him. He unnerved me somehow and I was never sure about his own agenda. Amelia seemed knowledgeable but her conflict with Isabella made me hesitate. And her reaction to Hermes at the funeral had been bizarre. Had she felt frightened or threatened by him? There were political divisions and conflicts within the archaeological world that were beyond my understanding. I'd witnessed first-hand Isabella's frustrations over such struggles, as she herself had fallen victim to them again and again. Purely in terms of the archaeological community the astrarium was an enigma whose ramifications I couldn't even begin to comprehend.

My mind turned to Amelia Lynhurst's thesis and the reference to the sphinx statues that had Banafrit's features. It almost felt as if Isabella herself was some kind of sphinx, challenging me to solve a riddle the answer to which, I suspected, lay beyond the conventions of my thinking.

A loud whistle cut through my thoughts. Startled, I spun around. A policeman stood at the busy intersection of Salaymar Yussri Street and El Nabi Daniel directing the traffic.

Opposite stood the broken pillars of the Roman amphitheatre. Kom el-Dik was the only official archaeological dig in Alexandria. One day Hermes had taken Isabella and me there for lunch with the Polish archaeologists – an amicable group of survivors who tolerated the Soviet rule of their own country with ironic irreverence. I remembered the easy camaraderie between Hermes and Isabella. They spoke often and if she ever needed to sound out her archaeological theories it was Hermes to whom she usually turned. The decision was made. This was not only mine but also Isabella's journey and it would have been her starting point. Crossing the road, I made my way to the tram stop that I knew would take me west into the old Arabic quarter.

The tram was nearly empty. An old man, his jellaba stained with marks of the day's work, slept with his head lolling back; a lone schoolgirl sat next to him, painfully self-aware in the way of all adolescents; a group of intense young men huddled in a corner talking rapidly, their hands a flurry of illustration – university students, I concluded. Opposite me was a middle-aged woman, well dressed in Western clothes. She smiled, one eyebrow cocked suggestively. Ignoring her, I stared out at the passing streets, holding the astrarium safe in my rucksack on my lap.

Suddenly, with a screech of brakes, a car pulled up beside the tram. Lost in thought, I gazed down at it and froze in shock. For the second time in twenty-four hours I saw Omar, in the car's back seat. He had already seen me. Coolly he smiled up at me, then leaned forward and, pointing up to my window, tapped the shoulder of the man in the front passenger seat. The man swung around.

He had a distinctive angular face with a heavy jaw, dark eyes set deep. His expression was one of cold menace, cruelty and a kind of terrifyingly intense hatred. For a few moments the world seemed to recede around us and I was suspended there, my gaze locked with a stranger's. Fear and inexplicable terror gripped me. Then the lights suddenly changed and the tram lurched forward. An elderly woman who had just climbed aboard fell to the floor, pomegranates scattering from her shopping bag. Several of the students rushed to help her up, blocking my view of the car. Taking advantage of the distraction, I leaped down from the other side of the tram and ran down a side alley.

13

I took the circuitous route, so by the time I reached Hermes Hemiedes's apartment block it was early afternoon. The smell of frying fish filled the dim foyer and from somewhere in the building came the sound of a wailing baby. As I entered, a mangy dog curled in the corner lifted its solemn head and gazed at me blankly. Then, as if it had completed its duties as guard dog, it flopped back to the ground.

I glanced at the list of residents – the name Hemiedes was written in gold lettering next to the words PENTHOUSE APARTMENT. A handwritten sign in Arabic announced that the lift was out of order. I began hauling myself up the stairs.

The view from the roof was spectacular. In front of me, Pompey's Pillar arched up into the sky, flanked by two sphinxes. Made of red granite, it had been erected in AD 300 to commemorate the Roman emperor Diocletian, who had saved the city from famine. It was a magnificent sight, with the city behind the Pillar stretching back to the Mediterranean. I turned back to the roof garden. The top floor of the penthouse was a small roof-terrace apartment that housed a cane sofa and chairs with plenty of cushions, all shaded by a canopy of vines growing out of huge clay vases. Brass wind chimes hung like strange fruit between the branches, their atonal chimes accompanied by the strains of David Bowie's 'Ziggy Stardust'. It was a bizarre combination. I sat down tiredly, wondering again about the man I'd seen with Omar. It couldn't be a coincidence, could it? But who was he and who was he working for? The Egyptian government eager to protect the country's artefacts? No, it felt infinitely more sinister than that, and even now, sitting in a secure apartment, I found it difficult to shake off an insidious sense of foreboding. It was becoming impossible to feel safe in Alexandria.

The boy who had let me in – whom I presumed to be Hermes's companion rather than his servant – placed a pot of mint tea and a glass on the low table in front of me and began to pour. Dressed in a sari, with gold hooped earrings, kohl smeared over each eyelid and wearing purplish lipstick, he looked about thirteen years old and was incredibly effeminate in his movements. The classic catamite, I thought: a local tradition that stretched back for centuries. He'd told me in halting English – with a strong American accent – no doubt picked up from watching black-market movies – that Hermes was taking his customary midday walk and would be due back around three. The speech had been accompanied by a series of fluttering flirtatious gestures.

His gaze wandered to the rucksack I'd placed beside me on the couch and, protectively, I put a hand on it. He grinned, an absurdly innocent smile. Then, to my amazement, he took off the sequined scarf draped around his thin narrow shoulders and began to dance to the music – an outlandish pirouetting that seemed to be an exaggerated version of contemporary Western dancing that he must have seen once or twice. He sang along in a high falsetto that dipped occasionally when his voice broke; it was strangely beautiful and poignant to hear this child-man's voice interweaving with Bowie's lyrics.

He moved towards me, gyrating his hips in a clumsy seduction attempt. I wasn't sure whether I should laugh, cry or run.

'Usta!' Hermes's voice bellowed out from the open French doors, followed by a sharp clapping of hands. The boy immediately stopped his dance and went sulkily to the record player to take the LP off.

Hermes stepped onto the terrace. I stood up to greet him. He was dressed in an embroidered caftan and a pair of pearl earrings shone between the strands of his lank dyed hair; a matching necklace hung around his wrinkled neck. He resembled some kind of latter-day alchemist who'd bought his accessories at an upmarket duty-free shop. Clicking his fingers he ordered the boy to leave us.

'I apologise,' he said. 'The silly child wants to be a rock star and live in New York. Still, perhaps he is not entirely without talent. It's so nice to see you, Oliver. Please, sit, finish your tea.'

I placed the rucksack on the table in front of him and took a deep breath. Then, before I had a chance to regret it, I opened the rucksack. 'I've brought you something,' I said. 'Something on which I need your expert advice.'

Hermes opened the rucksack and pulled out the astrarium very gently. Almost as if he were making love to the object, he peeled off the tissue I'd wrapped it in. Finally it stood revealed on the glass-topped table. Hermes muttered what sounded like a prayer and sat back.

'My poor Isabella, so close to her discovery . . .' He looked at me. 'Has anyone else seen it?'

'Only one other person and he's dead. I suspect he was murdered.' If I'd expected Hermes to be shocked I was disappointed.

'People have accidents so easily these days. I like to regard such unfortunate events as historical phenomena. After all, it is a very accidental era we're living in,' Hermes replied cryptically.

I frowned. That was one interpretation, I supposed. But it showed his slightly irritating tendency towards mysticism, albeit a slightly darker, more elemental form than Isabella's.

'I am honoured that you have brought the instrument here.'

'I was hoping you might be able to translate the inscriptions on the discs,' I suggested tentatively.

'I will certainly try.' The Egyptologist pulled a pair of glasses from his waistcoat pocket and peered through them. 'There are two languages I recognise immediately – Greek, Babylonian and of course there are hieroglyphs, but there is a fourth I don't know. It will take time – I have to make a rubber impression of the etched letters. Leave the instrument here and I will have the translation finished by tomorrow evening.'

I hesitated, not wanting to leave the instrument overnight but also acutely aware that its very presence here might endanger Hermes's life. I couldn't bear the idea that I might be unwittingly responsible for another murder. The vision of Barry's dead body – the fingers curled over in rigor mortis, the purple thread running around his garrotted throat – flashed through my mind. I looked up to find Hermes watching me closely.

'I can give you four hours. I'll wait here while you work.'

'Please, you must trust me.'

'Four hours, Hermes. I have my reasons.'

He stared at me, then laughed and reached out to shake my hand. 'A cautious man is a wise man.'

'A cautious man is a living man and I made a promise.'

'I fear the astrarium will demand further sacrifices. Do you think you were followed?'

'I lost them.'

'Good. There are spies everywhere in Alexandria; everyone wants to ingratiate himself with someone. Such shocking promiscuity. Come, you will wait in my reception room.'

I followed him back into the apartment. One wall of the small reception room was covered in photographs, most of which looked as if they dated from the 1930s and 1940s. I peered closer – they all appeared to be of lavish social occasions: polo matches, beauty contests on Stanley Beach, yachting races, opera nights. There were even images of a masked ball: characters in ornate evening dress but tribal from the neck up, frozen in time as if caught in some clandestine illegal rite. With a shock I recognised some of the famous faces of people standing next to a younger, slimmer Hermes Hemiedes who smiled arrogantly out of the photographs as if he were already conscious of the awed gaze of the viewer. Lawrence Durrell, Daphne Du Maurier, King Farouk, Lord Montgomery, Maria Callas. The Egyptologist had even been photographed with Winston Churchill.

He sighed wistfully. 'The glory days, when Alexandria was a real metropolis. Nowadays there is such a grinding earnestness – sometimes I wonder whether I am witnessing the death of imagination itself.'

'Don't worry: imagination hasn't died, it's just been replaced by paranoia.'

Hermes laughed and I found myself warming to him more than usual.

'You know, I attended many of these events with

Isabella's grandfather Giovanni,' he continued, unable to conceal the sadness in his voice.

'What was he like? I've heard so many stories . . .' I asked gently.

'Oh, Giovanni was a wonderful fellow, a visionary in his own right. We shared some proclivities – a weakness for ancient beliefs, you could say. However, he had strong opinions and he wasn't frightened of alienating people. He adored Isabella, she was his little princess. She was such a serious little girl. We visited a lot of sites together. Did she ever tell you about Behbeit el-Hagar? A minor site, but an important one in relation to the last days of the empire.'

'The empire?'

'The great reign of the Pharaohs.' The nostalgic tone of Hermes's voice made it sound as if he'd lived through it himself. 'When there was real magic in spirituality, the kind of power we don't even have the imagination to envisage today. That's why people are so fascinated by those times now. They sense that a great mystery has been lost.' Again, he seemed to drift off into a waffling romanticism and I decided to steer him back to reality.

I turned away from the photographs. 'I apologise for the urgency, but I have to return to Abu Rudeis as soon as possible . . .'

Ripped out of his wistfulness, Hermes's dreamy expression suddenly changed to one of wariness. He looked over his shoulder to where the boy had disappeared. When he spoke, his voice was quieter, hoarse almost.

'Oliver, the astrarium is a precious antiquity, priceless to us archaeologists, but many would also see it as a working tool – you do understand that?' His hands gripped my jacket lapels and he shook me slightly as if to underpin the urgency of his warning. 'It may even be regarded as a weapon in the wrong hands.'

Disturbed by his warning I drew back. He let go of my jacket.

'Whose hands, exactly?' My fear forced me into bluntness. 'Government, political groups, private individuals?'

'I have an idea,' Hermes sighed, then his expression seemed to close over. 'But I'd like to keep my theories to myself for the time being. Just remember, whatever your other priorities may be, that to treat the astrarium as anything less than extremely powerful would be very foolish.' He gave me a last little shake and nodded several times. 'Be careful, Oliver, that's all I'm saying.'

I didn't know whether he was warning me about the people who were after the astrarium or the artefact itself. 'I am only investigating the astrarium for Isabella's sake,' I finally replied cautiously. 'I don't believe in astrology or ancient mysticism.'

'Even so, you must appreciate that there is much about the material world that we do not understand. And there are certain individuals who have gifts . . . gifts of interpretation—'

'And naturally you'd describe yourself as one of them?' It was impossible to keep the irony out of my voice.

'Rest assured that I am not alone in that assumption.' His quiet confidence was almost convincing. 'Please, take a seat. Usta will bring you more mint tea, but now I really should get started.'

He left the room and, emotionally exhausted, I sank back into the embroidered silk cushions. Four hours later, I was woken by Usta.

Hermes was working in a study at the back of the apartment. The astrarium stood on a table: sheets of tracing paper covered with pencilled inscriptions lay beside latex casts of the machine's discs – the faint imprints of the hieroglyphs were visible in the raised rubber.

Hermes placed the first page of the transcribed hieroglyphs before me. 'First, let me say that this instrument is indeed the predecessor of the Antikythera Mechanism, as Isabella had anticipated.'

I nodded, curious to know whether he would also confirm Barry's findings.

After a glance at me, he continued. 'It is not of Cleopatra's era, but originally from that of the Egyptian Pharaohs – the Twentieth Dynasty to be precise, the reign of Ramses III, one of the great kings of Thebes. Interestingly, there are two cartouches, two signatures, if you like, of two great Pharaohs. The first is Ramses III, who I imagine was the king who commissioned the construction of the device, the second cartouche is of Nectanebo II, who ruled over the fading years of that whole era – the Thirtieth Dynasty.'

'Jesus, Barry was right.' I spoke aloud without realising it.

Out of the corner of my eye I saw Hermes look up at the mention of Barry's name. He started to speak but I was distracted as I scanned the lines of hieroglyphs. The inscriptions on the bronze wheels were tiny, barely millimetres tall. In the larger format, I recognised a couple of them – the sign for the Sun that doubled for Ra, the god of embalming, and that for Anubis, symbolised by the jackal's head. I reached out and touched the serrated edge of one of the cogs. A device from the times of the Pharaohs. Historically priceless. But was that reason enough to kill for it? Or to die finding it?

Hermes interrupted my reverie. 'What do you know about the Thirtieth Dynasty, Oliver?'

'I know it was roughly 400 BC.'

'Indeed. By the time Nectanebo II came to power, Egypt was little more than a banana republic, only kept safe from being annexed by Persia through the employment of Spartan mercenaries. Nectanebo II faced two major challenges at the beginning of his reign. The first was to hold on to power; the second, to balance the ever-threatening Persians and their sophisticated weaponry with the dangerous greed of the Spartan mercenaries who were employed as Egypt's protectors. More than anything, the young king had to unite Egypt, to restore the nation's self-esteem. In some respects there are parallels with Egypt today . . .' Hermes's voice drifted off before he recovered his train of thought. 'Nectanebo rebuilt Egypt's confidence in three ways. One was by reminding his people of Egypt's former glory days, when it ruled the known world and the Persians and Greeks were primitive upstarts by comparison. The second way was through reinforcing his influence with priests, peasants and the intelligentsia by emphasising his alliance with the gods. This led to the third way: building as many temples as he could during his reign. An astrarium, one that was already legendary in its own time, a spectacularly magical object that one of the great Ramses pharaohs themselves had once owned, would have been a powerful political symbol for Nectanebo. By owning this he could claim direct lineage to Ramses and also to the gods themselves, Isis particularly, the most powerful of the goddesses, to whom this device was dedicated.'

'And what about the first owner, Ramses III?'

'Ramses III is known for living through the time of plagues and for fighting off what were described as the Sea People, possibly war refugees from the devastation of Troy. There is some conjecture that he was also the pharaoh at the time of Moses and the Exodus. There are many who believed Moses himself was a great magician.' Hermes looked at me pointedly. 'There is even a mention in the New Testament: "Moses was learned in all the wisdom of the Egyptians, and was mighty in words and in deeds." Remember, Moses was brought up in the Egyptian court and in ancient Egyptian parlance "wisdom" meant knowledge of the occult. There are even two papyri from the fourth century called *The Hidden Book of Moses*, describing magical rituals for meeting the gods and how to glean predictive information.' I started nodding impatiently, and Hermes hurriedly brought the conversation back to the astrarium. 'Some of the hieroglyphs on the device describe the function of the "skybox" as having power over sea, sky and earth. There is a legend that Moses used a magical astrarium stolen from Ramses III to part the Red Sea . . .'

Hermes's last words lingered in a moment of silence and I felt a great trembling sweep through me – the idea that the astrarium might have biblical significance terrified me more than anything, a residue emotion from my childhood as I remembered my mother reading some of the more frightening passages from the Bible to me. Sitting up straight I tried to shake off my irrational fear.

'You can't mean—'

'Let me finish,' Hermes snapped back. 'It would only take the rumour of owning such a potentially terrifying weapon to serve Ramses's battle strategy and strike terror into the hearts of his enemies.'

I digested this for a second.

'And the inscriptions on the device confirm this?'

'Well, the astrarium itself consists of three primary discs behind which a far more complex mechanism sits. The largest outer disc is made of an alloy I don't recognise; it appears to be etched with a scaled-down version of the

Dendera Zodiac – based on Egyptian astrology. The next disc describes the movements of Venus and Mars – Hathor and Horus to the Egyptian astronomers. The final disc follows the trajectories of Jupiter, whom the Egyptians identified with Amun-Zeus, and Saturn, the dreaded deity Seth.' Hermes paused to sip some tea. 'As to the inscriptions themselves, the majority are written in Egyptian hieroglyphs. Some are simply instructions on how to operate the mechanism. Some describe the history of the machine and chronicle its feats. There is a small amount of Ancient Greek, but I suspect this might have been added later – during the time of Ptolemy. There are a few lines of Aramaic, suggesting that Hebrew scholars were also involved in its construction and there is also acknowledgement of Babylonian astronomy, which the Egyptians respected too.' He looked at me thoughtfully.

'There is also mention of a key, called a Was, which is a reference to the staff of dominion carried by all sky deities.' Hermes pointed to the small keyhole-like cavity I'd noticed before at the centre of the discs. 'It appears to have been hand-operated.'

'But the key is missing.'

'Indeed. I suspect that in ancient times there would have been an official keeper of the Was. Possibly he drowned in the shipwreck and the Was key was lost; or perhaps he survived and the key is who knows where? But one thing is clear: reunite the key with the astrarium and you have a very powerful, very dangerous device at your service. Just look at this . . .' He held a sheet of the traced Greek inscription under the light and began reading. '*This illumination of the skies and of Fate* – I use the word "Fate" here loosely as it is the nearest translation I can think of but the actual word suggests greater free will than the contemporary notion of

Fate. Really, it is a combination of passion and destiny.' He paused, whether from awe or for effect I couldn't tell. '*This illumination of the skies and of Fate is the inherited property of Her Majesty and earthly manifestation of Hathor, Aphrodite and Isis, Cleopatra VII . . .*'

As Hermes looked at me, I noticed his hands were trembling with excitement.

'It does appear that Cleopatra was quite possibly the last owner of the astrarium,' he said. 'But there is something that disturbs me . . .'

'What's that?'

'It's this.' He pushed an almost blank sheet of paper towards me. I recognised the cipher that I'd seen in Gareth's drawing. 'Do you know what it is?' he asked. I saw no reason to lie.

'I've seen it before. Isabella already knew of it when she was searching for the astrarium. She told me it was a cipher.'

'But did she tell you what it meant?' Hermes stared at me searchingly and for a moment I thought I detected in his eyes a paranoia bordering on desperation. He looked away quickly.

'She never got the chance,' I replied slowly. Instinct told me not to tell him that my brother might have the answer to the riddle.

'I found it standing alone below the main body of text,' Hermes said, watching me carefully. 'For the life of me, I cannot decipher it. But its isolated position indicates its importance.'

Despite the long hair combed back over the domed forehead, the rouge smeared roughly on each hollowed cheekbone, there was something entrancing about Hermes. I could see why Isabella had been so captivated by him: it was impossible not to find his passion and his depth of expertise compelling. He was one of those individuals who swept others up in his enthusiasm. His animated explanations, his obvious and infectious excitement made me struggle with my usual detachment.

He picked up another paper.

'The translation of the hieroglyphs is as follows: *Whoever sets his birth date upon these dials will change/transform the path of his Ka. I will give to the slave the life of the Pharaoh; I will make Anubis bark the date of his demise.* So the astrarium is also a predictive tool. In fact, I believe one of its predictions might have been the reason why Nectanebo fled Egypt. Some say he went to Ethiopia or the Macedonian mainland. Others believe that Aristotle was really Nectanebo II, and that he tutored his nemesis, the young Alexander, in the sciences of mathematics and astronomy.'

From somewhere in the apartment came the sound of cutlery being rattled, a tap turned on, then off. Both Hermes and I looked around, startled. It was hard to stay in the present, to avoid being thrown back into the history that seemed to emanate from the artefact itself.

'Isabella said the astrarium would prove that the ancient world knew long before Copernicus that the Earth rotated around the Sun,' I commented thoughtfully, trying to anchor my thinking to a familiar reality, to ground myself.

'My friend, you and I both know that isn't the only thing at stake here. I fear you are letting your own prejudices dictate your perceptions.'

'And I fear that, as in quantum physics where the observed particle is influenced by the observer, this astrarium's purpose changes according to the expectations of whoever is examining it. It seems to become a metaphor.' We looked at each other, locking stares as if in battle. Hermes was the first one to lower his gaze.

'In any case, what we think is irrelevant,' the Egyptologist countered. 'The Ancient Egyptians believed that the most important principle of life was to maintain a balance between Maat, universal order, and Isfet, universal chaos. The astrarium was constructed as a means of restoring balance, a way of controlling chaos and evil, personified by Seth, and harmony and light, personified by Isis and Ra. Ramses and Nectanebo were both worshippers of Ammon, also known as Amun-Re. Amun symbolised concealment and mystery, while Re represented visibility and transparency. The name Amun-Re united this duality in the one god – a duality of light and dark. The astrarium could be used in the same dual capacity: to predict positive events such as the correct positions of the planets for successful navigation, it could lead you to treasure and predict auspicious dates for magical rituals and the like, and it could foretell negative events, such as the loss of a battle, the parting of water to save a people or drown an army, or even one's own death date. The deciding factor was the true – or, in modern parlance, unconscious – motivation of the user.'

I shook my head. 'You're trying to tell me that the astrarium itself makes a judgement about the true motivation of the user?'

'Oliver, this machine has a soul, a kind of independent will. That is what the Ancient Egyptians believed. And I'm inclined to agree.'

'That's ridiculous.' I hadn't heard anything more preposterous in my life. Hermes held up his hand as if to silence me.

'It would be dangerous to ignore me, Oliver. You don't have the slightest idea of the astrarium's importance or the danger it brings. Most of us live the unexamined life – we live in Isfet, in chaos. Seth rules this century, my friend. But

what's more important is that there are those who seek influence at such times. Amelia Lynhurst, for example, is a
woman with dangerous aspirations.'

'Really? Why do you think that?'

'She was very possessive of Isabella when she was at
Oxford – the relationship was more than that of mentor and
student. Isabella was impressionable, putty in the older
woman's hands. For Amelia to seduce her was unethical. To
abandon her was worse.'

I wasn't entirely surprised to hear Isabella had had an
affair with a woman – her understanding of sexuality had
been far more fluid and open-minded than mine. Isabella
had been ten years younger than me and her experiences
were very different from my own. My generation had been
shaped by the drabness of the economic deprivation that
followed the Second World War. Isabella had been luckier,
benefiting from the economic boom and cultural openness of
the 1960s. But Amelia Lynhurst? I just couldn't quite believe
it.

'That was the real reason for them falling out?' I asked
incredulously.

'Believe me, Amelia does not have either your or
Isabella's interests at heart when it comes to the astrarium,'
Hermes told me. 'If you go to her, not only will she betray
you to the authorities; she will claim discovery of the instrument and use it to promote her own ambitions.'

Hermes's warning echoed the concerns that Isabella had
expressed. I looked at him, speculating as to his agenda, but
I had invested too much already. I had to trust him.

'What do you know about Banafrit, Nectanebo's priestess?' I asked tentatively.

'How do you know about Banafrit?'

'I found Amelia's treatise on her in my wife's possessions.

Amelia claimed that Banafrit sought out the astrarium to help her pharaoh Nectanebo.'

Hermes looked at me with interest. 'So you know a little more than you have suggested, Oliver.'

'That doesn't make me a believer,' I replied disparagingly.

'Amelia Lynhurst always had an obsession with Isis, and I believe, apart from any professional glory she might gain, she's spent so much of her life proving that Banafrit, high priestess of Isis, both found and rededicated the astrarium to Isis that she has obvious vested interest.'

The detail was slightly lost on me, so I simply shrugged. Hermes looked at me firmly. 'As I said before, this is still a working mechanism. It can manipulate the destiny of the individual who dares operate it but it can also wield a greater power. This is a fledging nation, Oliver, and there are those who seek to overthrow the current regime. There is a history of dictators, people corrupted by power, seeking out religious relics imbued with occult power. Think about Hitler and his obsession with the "Spear of Destiny", an artefact that was meant to have speared Jesus Christ in his side and that was rumoured to confer invincibility upon its owner. Hitler sent officers across the globe to find it. Your astrarium has just as much legend attached and that legend speaks of power, power that still exists today. No wonder there are people who would do anything to gain possession of it.'

Fear swept through me as belief and disbelief battled in my mind. 'It is still a working mechanism missing its key,' I finally pointed out, looking back at the astrarium.

'Again, I urge you to leave the mechanism here. I will try to find the key for you.'

In another place, at another time, I might have rejected outright such an obvious manipulation. But sitting in that richly decorated room, the lamplight catching the bronze dials of the astrarium, Hermes's face rapt in anticipation, I was almost convinced by his explanations. Egypt had that effect – it was impossible to escape the history and mystical lineage of the land, no matter how sceptical one might be. But there was something else at stake here: Isabella's commitment to the astrarium that she had died pursuing. At first I'd thought the authorities were simply trying to reclaim a prized possession. Now, I realised there was far more to the device than I had possibly imagined. A valuable artefact, a cult object, a powerful tool capable of destruction and resurrection – at least that was what others seemed to believe. Follow your instincts, Isabella had told me, and my instinct now was to learn more before surrendering it. 'No, I'll hold on to it for the time being,' I said firmly. 'I want to continue my own research. But thank you, Hermes, your help has been invaluable.'

His face closed over and, to my surprise, for a second I thought I detected a glimmer of fury. 'As you wish,' he finally muttered.

Intensely aware now of the fragility and antiquity of the device, I wrapped it up carefully again and placed it into my rucksack. 'I just have one last question, Hermes. What's the significance of a manifestation of a person's Ba?'

He replied almost grudgingly. 'If the deceased's Ba is seen after burial, it usually means that person's task on earth is unfinished and their soul cannot complete its journey to the underworld.'

As I left the building, I had the distinct impression of invisible wings brushing past my cheek.

14

I wound my way back to the city centre, my mind a whirling mass as familiar axioms battled a multitude of new hypotheses. With each step, the astrarium in the rucksack on my back bounced against me. I kept thinking of Hermes's warning about the power of the device; then I remembered Barry's explanation of the Ancient Egyptians' belief in magic, their intertwining of religious worship, intellectual pursuit, sorcery and science.

Walking helped me organise my thoughts; it was a habit borne of my childhood wanderings across the Cumbrian Fells. As the rhythm of the streets pounded up through my legs a destination began to take shape in my mind. A couple of old men were playing Shesh Besh outside a shoe stall. I glanced down at the backgammon pieces, calculating the moves necessary to win, and then made my own decision. I would go to the cemetery to talk to Isabella, to take her the astrarium.

It was illogical, but this time, unlike in the oilfield where I'd legitimised my decisions with science, I was relying solely on my intuition. Now I truly had become the Diviner – the realisation felt painfully ironic.

I walked on up Bab el-Mulouk back towards Rue Sherif and past the Antiques Market towards Cairo Station Square. My path was broken by two long queues of people; women in one, men in the other, all clutching their ration cards, snaking out of a gamaya – the ubiquitous co-op grocery store where the locals collected their rationed food: meat, rice, oil and flour. Such queues formed with each new shipment of rare imports, simple things like New Zealand lamb, butter and tea. Once commonplace, such items had now become scarce in the economic tumult created by Sadat opening up Egypt to the free market earlier that year.

Here, towards the centre of the city, the buildings became more Westernised, and the old cosmopolitan Alexandria, elegant and ostentatious, began to appear: the old Lloyds Bank building, the Banco di Roma and the Bank of Athens – all originally landmarks of colonialism that were now under the banner of the National Bank of Egypt. I passed Bank Misr with its balconies and arches, more Ottoman than classical, then walked past the Anglican church of St Mark, and the old offices located in ornate neoclassical city blocks. Along Fouad Street the grand villas started appearing: Villa Salvago, Villa Sursock, Villa Rolo – phantoms from a past world.

As I weaved between the pedestrians I became aware suddenly of the sound of a motorcycle behind me. I'd been so lost in thought that I didn't know how long it had been trailing me. Realising I might have been followed from the moment I left Hermes's apartment I glanced around wildly. A cab hooted next to me, the gesturing driver touting for business. I leaped in and instructed him to take me to

Chatby Cemetery, just as the sound of the motorbike engine grew louder behind me.

As the cab pulled away I glanced out the rear window, trying to catch a glimpse of the motorcycle. There it was, weaving its way towards me, dodging in and out of the chaos of pedestrians and horse-drawn carts. For a terrifying moment I thought I saw the menacing face of the man who had been in the car with Omar earlier that day. Then a minibus crammed full of commuters got in the way, and by the time it had passed, the motorcycle was gone.

ISABELLA FRANCESCA MARIA BRAMBILLA
B: 31/1/1949
D: 14/5/1977.

I stared at the engraved letters and numbers, their crisp edges confirming their newness. Isabella's face, wryly smiling, gazed up from the black-and-white photograph set into the large marble headstone next to the oval portraits of her father and uncles. Once again, I noticed the absence of Giovanni's photograph. It seemed inconceivable that he would not be buried with his family and I wondered about the etiquette of asking Francesca directly about it. I glanced back at Isabella's photo: it looked as if it had been taken at her first communion; I barely recognised her. It represented a period of her life I'd never had access to and I found myself momentarily flooded by a strange jealousy.

It horrified me to think of Isabella lying in that grave incomplete. Had I failed her in death? Despite my own lack of spirituality, I couldn't shake off the disturbing thought that Isabella would not be able to rest until her heart was returned to her, that her Ba might be trapped in this life for ever. I knew rationally that this couldn't be the case but beneath it all I felt my pragmatism slowly beginning to erode. Despite my protestations to Hermes, I could feel myself being swept up in the great epic history of the astrarium. Stress, sheer physical exhaustion as well as my constant battle against grief had left me vulnerable, ungrounded. Had I begun to see meaning in arbitrary patterns? Imagined pursuers, ghosts in shadows, even symbols in dreams? Had I begun to imbue coincidence with meaning? Was I practising some kind of bizarre heuristics? Either way, it was undeniable – my parameters of reality were beginning to slip.

Carefully I laid the astrarium, still inside my rucksack, onto the marble slab covering Isabella's grave. I waited – for what I wasn't sure: perhaps a sign that she was finally united with the object she had spent years searching for. The seconds ticked by into minutes. There was nothing, just the creaking of a tree branch and a faint breeze; time breathing out.

I concentrated on an old wreath of lilies propped up against the headstone, the petals now brown and curling. One bloom had broken loose and fallen onto the grass. I crouched to pick it up and suddenly noticed a small hole at the far end of the marble slab. I kneeled down and looked closer: it was a chiselled hole about four inches deep and three inches across. Someone had even bothered to give it the appearance of a miniature door with an etched outline. I hadn't seen it when we'd buried Isabella, yet somehow the image seemed hauntingly familiar.

'Oliver?'

The voice was feminine, lilting and Italian in its accent. I looked up: Cecilia, Isabella's mother, stood at the head of the grave, her expensive Chanel suit looking ridiculously out of place. In one hand she held a small bunch of chrysanthemums; the other was trying to stop the breeze ruining her coiffured hair.

'I'm so sorry,' she said. 'I have disturbed you in a private moment.'

Realising she'd assumed I was in the middle of a prayer, I stood swiftly, dusted my knees and, worried that she might notice the chiselled hole in the tomb, stepped quickly back onto the pathway.

Cecilia reached out and took my hand between her gloved fingers, her gaze travelling over my tired face, new beard and crumpled clothing. 'You poor man. We never think of the young and the talented dying. Such deaths are an obscenity, a joke against God, don't you think?'

Unlike her daughter, Cecilia was tall and had a Tuscan blonde beauty honed by the polish of Rome. Slender and green-eyed, she seemed entirely aware of the power of her own attractiveness. She was only eight years older than me, which made her a very youthful forty-six. To my great chagrin, a spasm of involuntary desire shot through me like electricity. To make matters worse, I had the impression that Cecilia sensed my dilemma. I pulled my hand away.

Smiling faintly, she crouched down to place her bouquet next to the lilies. My words spilled out nervously as I tried to distract myself from the sight of her skirt riding up her thighs.

'I couldn't stop her making that dive. God knows I tried, but she was insistent. Still, I can't help thinking that if I had . . .'

'Oliver, it was an accident, the consequence of a chain of events that led to a moment you had no control over. Who is to say whether that moment might or might not otherwise have happened?'

She glanced apprehensively around the cemetery, then stepped closer. 'I know Isabella would have told you terrible things about me.' Cecilia's voice was little more than a whisper. She paused, as if waiting for me to protest. I did not.

'You have to understand,' she continued, 'I was bullied into letting Isabella go. I knew very quickly that I had made a grave mistake. But I was only twenty-five when I was widowed, and Giovanni Brambilla was a very frightening man. He was immoral, desperate to influence events beyond his control and he channelled a lot of that through Isabella. He even began to involve her in his activities – activities that were not appropriate for a child. He is powerful even now, even beyond the grave.'

'What kind of activities?' I asked, intrigued. I wasn't convinced by her casting herself in the role of victim but there was something about Giovanni that I found immensely fascinating.

'Once, when Isabella was about nine, Francesca wrote to tell me that she was worried about the way Giovanni had started to involve Isabella in some strange "performances", rituals, with a group of followers. I immediately bought a plane ticket, but when I tried to get back into the country they refused me a visa. There was no reason for it and I couldn't help but think that Giovanni had somehow used his influence to bar me. After that, whenever I confronted Francesca about it she denied she'd written to me at all.'

'Isabella had nightmares,' I told her. 'The same one again and again. A gathering of people performing a ritual – one of the Ancient Egyptian rituals she'd studied . . .'

Cecilia's face fell in horror. '*Mia povera figlia!*' she murmured, near to tears. Her anguish was so real that I felt more sympathetic towards her. I was just about to speak when behind us a twig snapped and we both turned. I glimpsed a movement between the trees, the flash of a figure now hidden.

Cecilia's expression changed instantly to one of fear. 'We should go. People here will go to any lengths to reinvent their history, even their recent history,' she whispered.

We started walking back to the entrance. The cemetery appeared empty but the strong sense of being observed remained. I shivered. Above us, the cawing of ravens filled the blank sky. I grasped Cecilia's hand briefly. For the second time that afternoon she smiled.

'You know, Isabella did finally contact me, about a month before her death. No letter, just a box of photographs from our early days, from when her father was alive. I cried when I opened it. But don't you think it is strange? Not to hear from your daughter for so long, then out of the blue she sends you old photographs a month before she dies?'

As I waved Cecilia's Mercedes off, my heart heavy with memories of Isabella and fear about her past, I suddenly remembered where I'd seen the miniature door before: it was like the portal engraved into the wall of an Ancient Egyptian tomb; the symbolic door that allowed the deceased's Ba to fly in and out.

Who would have carved such a thing into Isabella's gravestone? And who would have watched me make that discovery? I looked around one last time. But the cemetery lay deserted in the fading light of the afternoon.

When I arrived back at the villa I discovered that Mr Fartime, on behalf of the Alexandrian Oil Company, had engaged an extra guard at the gate for additional security. He'd told Ibrihim he'd been concerned by my interrogation after Isabella's drowning. But also, with the growing food shortages and rationing, there had already been a few attacks on Westerners and I knew that Fartime felt responsible for my safety.

Although it was reassuring to see the burly but friendly guard, smiling in his makeshift uniform and waving from the gate, I still didn't trust the security of the villa. Later that night, knowing that Ibrihim was away making his annual visit to his mother in Ar-Rashid, I waited until I noticed the guard dozing on his stool by the iron gate. Then, as quietly as possible, I made my way into the garden. I wrapped the astrarium in canvas and buried it in a wooden box beneath one of the magnolia trees – a temporary hiding place should anyone break into the villa. As I paused, spade in hand, I glanced up at the waxing moon. The Egyptians thought the moon was a resting place of ascending souls and, staring up at the luminous pock-marked surface of the orb, it seemed a strangely reasonable concept. Just then there was a rustling of wings and something flew across my gaze, too fast for a bird. Startled, I dropped the spade, then cursed myself for taking fright. Half an hour later I finished planting a small pomegranate bush with shallow roots over the top of the astrarium, smoothing down the soil so the earth didn't look disturbed. It was only after I went back inside that I remembered how Persephone had been tricked by Hades into eating seven pomegranate seeds, condemning her to stay with him in the underworld for seven months of each year. It was a disturbing association.

It was past midnight. I sat on the edge of the bed clutching the Valium that the company doctor had prescribed for me, wondering if I could, again, face that wave of treacly darkness, the loss of sensory control that now allowed me to sleep.

I decided against taking the pill and climbed into bed. Staring at the ceiling and the shifting shadows of the tree branches thrown by the street lamp outside, my eyes closed finally, and I drifted off.

I dreamed I was in sunshine. Bright light, a beach perhaps, the sense of a soft grainy surface beneath my

sun-warmed skin, then the soft weight of another body curling around me. I recognised the shape and scent instantly. I
didn't dare open my eyes in case I frightened her away, but
the urge to see her overwhelmed me.

I opened my eyes and found, to my relief, that I'd stayed
dreaming. Isabella stared back at me, her eyes filled with
that dark violet I had lost myself in so many times. Smiling,
she lowered herself down onto me. The touch of her skin
almost threw me into consciousness. It felt indisputably
real – the warmth, the velvet moisture, the intimacy of her
scent.

In wonder, I reached up, threading my fingers through
that thick veil of hair, the familiarity of touch quickening.
Her lips caught my lower lip, the promise of other caresses
silently mirrored in the lovemaking of our mouths; a kiss
that sprung open all the memories of our earlier embraces.
The first weeks of our courtship, when we would make love
all night, then stumble around the markets of Calcutta drunk
with exhaustion; when just the smell of her hair would make
me hard, her voice whispering out all our future plans, spinning patterns against those tropical nights. This and every
other moment ran through my mind like the patterns of a
kaleidoscope, but by now her mouth had started to travel
down my chest, her long cool fingers as real as the taste of
her, her lips a tight band of heat throwing tremors down my
thighs.

Suddenly the memory of her death reverberated through
me like one of the subterranean explosions I'd choreographed.

15

☥

It was well after midday when I woke. The sun was a crimson prickling against my eyeballs, forcing the lids open. I lay there in that delicious non-state like an amoeba, happy for a time, until a burning sensation across my shoulders threw me into full consciousness. I sat up and reached behind me to touch my smarting skin. My fingers were sticky with blood.

I got up and walked over to the mirror: four deep scratches ran across my shoulders. I touched them – it felt as if I'd caught my back on a row of pins or nails. Then I remembered the dream, the lovemaking with Isabella. I studied the marks again, but they seemed too closely spaced for fingernails.

I flung back the covers on the bed; the bottom sheet was spotted with blood. Several long black hairs lay on the pillow. I picked one up and wound it around my finger. Isabella's? It was a crazy thought. But part of me wanted it to have belonged to her, for the dream to have been real. Just then I noticed a tiny brown feather halfway down the mattress. I lifted it and blew it across the bed. Could it have come from one of the pillows?

The miniature doorway chiselled into Isabella's gravestone came to my mind. I went to the library and looked up Nectanebo II in one of Isabella's reference books. Some of the information I'd gleaned from Hermes and from Amelia Lynhurst's thesis was there, along with a photograph of the Pharaoh's empty sarcophagus and a sidebar with information about it. It was now housed in the British Museum. I studied the photograph again, looking vainly for new clues. I noticed the sidebar was credited to Hugh Wollington of the British Museum. Hugh Wollington. Presumably the man was an Egyptologist but I couldn't remember Isabella ever mentioning him. Perhaps he'd be able to give me more information about the astrarium. Moses, Ramses III, Nectanebo, Banafrit and Cleopatra were all linked to the astrarium. Maybe Hugh Wollington had more information about how they were connected and maybe he knew whether there was any correlation between the hieroglyphs inscribed on the astrarium and those on Nectanebo's sarcophagus. I didn't yet know quite how to ask without showing him the astrarium itself but maybe I could work out a way en route. I was gripped with a growing excitement. I hadn't been home in a long time. This might be what I needed to gain some perspective alongside new information, and a trip to England might get me away from the clutches of those looking for the astrarium. An image of a helmeted face on a motorcycle suddenly sprang up in my mind, followed quickly by those of Omar and his sinister sidekick. It would be good to be free of this constant paranoia of being followed. But, almost as importantly, going to England would allow me to see my father and Gareth for the first time since Isabella's drowning. At the thought, a wave of desire to be with family and in familiar surroundings engulfed me.

I was interrupted by a knocking at the front door. Carefully, I looked through the peephole: a youth of about sixteen waited on the other side. I recognised him from the offices of the Alexandrian Oil Company.

'From Mr Fartime,' he told me, handing me a note as I opened the door.

The garish modern decor of the Alexandrian Oil Company's headquarters on Sherif Street reflected Mr Fartime's personal dilemma. He regarded himself as a twentieth-century entrepreneur trapped in a nineteenth-century paradigm that barely creaked along. He'd done his utmost to defuse the classical proportions of the office with oddly inappropriate modern furniture, but he hadn't been able to apply the same modernisation to the organisation of the company and was constantly bombarding me with long anecdotes about the antiquated bureaucracy he was forced to work within.

As I entered his office, Mr Fartime struggled out of the white leather chair he'd been sitting in, a copy of *Time* magazine still in his hand. I noticed the cover featured a smiling Noam Chomsky. Before I had a chance to wonder what Mr Fartime made of the American activist, he'd tossed the magazine onto his desk and was reaching out to shake my hand.

'Thank you for coming so quickly, Oliver. Again, my condolences on your terrible loss . . .'

'Thank you,' I replied, reflecting that the last time Mr Fartime had seen Isabella had been at a dinner party during which they'd argued over the ecological merits of the Aswan dam. Fortunately the dispute had been interrupted when the hostess – a well-to-do Syrian-Egyptian socialite with many connections to the European community – had lost a microphone concealed in her low-cut evening dress. She was leaning across the table to make a point when the device fell out and landed in the soup tureen. The American ambassador had fished the microphone out and remarked, 'If you must spy, Madame Abdallah, allow us the honour of supplying you with the latest technology. Our Soviet friends tend to be a little clunky in the design department.' At which the whole table had burst into laughter. But although the evening had ended up on a light note, I remember being acutely aware of the fact that every guest must have left wondering whether their safety in Egypt had been compromised by some unfavourable remark they'd let slip about the regime.

I sat down opposite Mr Fartime, wondering if he too was recalling the occasion.

He indicated my beard. 'My friend, have you joined my more religious brothers?' he joked – a reference to the bearded Muslims who had started to appear more often in the Westernised city recently.

I smiled. 'No, no new-found faith. I've just been too busy to shave.'

'I understand. I trust the additional security at the villa is to your liking?' he went on. 'I was concerned by the unduly rough treatment you received at the hands of our esteemed police force after your wife's demise. The Alexandrian Oil Company may be a government institution but we like to look after our consultants, especially our "Diviner". I promise that from now on we will be better hosts.'

Mr Fartime's English was a quaint mixture of Victorian phrasing and Arabic proverbs. Despite Isabella's reservations about his politics, I had always liked the man. Nevertheless, I watched his face carefully now. Were his comments a way of assessing my response to the police interrogation? Perhaps even an attempt to find out whether Isabella had discovered anything during that final dive?

'The extra guard does make the place feel more secure,' I replied carefully, 'so thank you. But I'm sure this isn't the reason you called me in so urgently. Is everything all right at the field?'

'More than all right. The drilling rates are holding up nicely. Diviner indeed. No, this is a personal matter.'

I shifted in my seat, a little nervous now, racking my mind for memories of any transgression I might have committed.

'I have received some news of your younger sibling Gareth,' he said quickly.

I sat up. The last phone conversation I'd had with my brother came back to me: the broken words, his sudden weeping at the end. Ever since my mother's death, my brother had become more isolated, despite the entourage that hung around him. Then there was his addiction – the self-aggrandising that came with amphetamine use, the manic phone calls. And, in the throes of these depressions, Gareth had always turned to Isabella for emotional guidance, a lifeline now cut off.

'He hasn't—'

'He is alive, fear not,' Mr Fartime cut in. 'His female friend rang the office this morning looking for you. Your brother has taken a turn for the worse, as they would say in England. His friend seems to think you should return to England as soon as possible to provide some guidance. She was most insistent – a rather strong-willed young woman.'

Mr Fartime's smile was entirely without irony and I sensed that his concern was genuine. Gareth had mentioned a girlfriend on the phone, Zoë, but I'd never met her. At least she sounded responsible, I thought. I'd been concerned that Isabella's death would cause Gareth to relapse and the promise I'd made to her to look after him reverberated now in my mind.

As if reading my thoughts, Mr Fartime leaned across the desk. 'I had a brother too, once. He was ten years younger. I lost him in the 1973 war. There are many things I would have done differently if I had been given the chance, and knowing my brother better would have been one.' He paused, a little embarrassed at venturing into such intimate terrain. 'Go to him, Oliver. The company is happy to give you four weeks. The field can spare you and, given your own personal circumstances, it is the least we can do.'

There was another awkward pause as he stared down at his shoes. 'I knew your wife's father, you know. My father worked as his manager at the cotton mill – before 1956, naturally.'

'Naturally,' I repeated, surprised once again by how entangled Alexandrian society was.

'We trust that you will return at the end of those four weeks, Oliver. There is more work to be done at Abu Rudeis, and after that minor earthquake . . .'

He coughed politely, embarrassed that he'd had to refer to the tremor that had killed Isabella. The memory of the sphinx tumbling down to the sea floor flooded my mind. I quickly shut it out, not wanting to think about it here.

'The fault line reached as far as the oilfield?' I asked instead, genuinely surprised. 'I thought it was an underwater tremor. Why wasn't I told?'

'The well was undamaged, and you had enough trouble to deal with at that time.' Mr Fartime coughed again.

'I'll be back by early June, I promise. The reservoir is my project too, don't forget.'

'I will keep the villa vacant for you,' he said, with a nod. Pushing back his chair, he hauled his large frame upright and shook my hand again. 'Tell me, what was your wife really looking for during that dive?'

The question came so out of left field that I struggled to retain my composure. I thought quickly. 'A rare fish,' I said. 'You must remember what an ecologist she was?'

Mr Fartime chuckled. 'Alas, I'm afraid I do.'

When I returned to the villa I found Ibrihim waving an ancient pistol around wildly as he berated the new guard in loud and abusive Arabic. Behind them a broken kitchen window was visible. As soon as Ibrihim saw me his face fell.

'Monsieur Oliver, you must tell this lazy dog of a guard that he cannot fall asleep on the job! Otherwise we will all be murdered in our sleep! Praise Allah, nothing has been stolen from the villa this time. Next time we might not be so lucky. Please, you have authority.' He dragged me over to the sheepish guard. Questioning the man, I found out that the villa had been broken into while Ibrihim was visiting the mosque. The guard, who had indeed fallen asleep, had been woken up by the sound of breaking glass and had managed to chase off a youth. I tried to get a further description of the youth, but it was already evening and the guard hadn't got a clear view of the intruder's face. But he was sure he'd been wearing a gun. No ordinary thief, then. As I stared up at the high iron gates I wondered how the intruder had managed to scale them and climb over the spikes at the top. Certainly the surrounding brick walls were too high to climb. The irrational idea that he might have flown over flickered through my mind. I dismissed it instantly, horrified at my own mental fragility. Undeniably, though, any sense of safety within those four walls was gone and I was determined to get out of Egypt before my pursuers caught up with me – or before I lost my mind completely.

As soon as the others had gone back into the house, I walked around to the back and checked on the astrarium. Its burial site appeared undisturbed, the soil untouched, but now there was no way I could leave it buried there.

I spent the next day organising my trip back to London. Throwing myself into packing was a way of distracting myself from my growing anxiety about leaving Isabella's grave behind. I couldn't help feeling that I was abandoning her, but I needed to see Gareth. I was worried about the call that had been made to Mr Fartime and the uneasy feeling that Gareth's addiction had begun to consume him played on my conscience. Suddenly, an idea occurred to me. Perhaps Isabella had told Gareth a little more about the astrarium when she'd asked him to produce the drawing? I crossed the room to the shelf and pulled out the paper hidden at the back. If anything, he might be able to solve the cipher. He'd always been brilliant at puzzles. I pushed the paper deep into the inside pocket of my backpack.

That evening I sat on the bed, Isabella's letter in my hand. Her distinctive handwriting pulled images of her like threads from my memory – Isabella cheering with my brother during a Carlisle United match; Isabella giving a paper at the Royal Archaeological Society in London; Isabella dancing wildly in the flat to the Rolling Stones.

I looked back at the short note.

Oliver, forgive me, I've never been completely honest with you. All those years ago, Ahmos Khafre did not only tell me my death date; he also told me I might have been able to save my own life if I discovered the astrarium in time.

The fact that Isabella had really believed the mystic, to the point of changing wills and building bridges with Cecilia, made me realise how profoundly our cultural and philo-sophical outlooks differed. If I'd had the courage to confront those differences when she'd been alive, instead of hoping that she'd grow out of them, could I have saved her? A sickening sense of guilt swept through me: I should have stopped her from diving that day. We should never have come back to Egypt.

I walked over to the balcony and glanced down at the garden. The buds on the pomegranate bush that I'd planted above the astrarium were beginning to unfurl. It was as if I could feel the presence of the astrarium through the thick canvas in which I'd wrapped it, through the wooden box, through the foot of soil above it. And as I kept staring, I had the distinct impression it was staring back. I shook my head as if to rid myself from its influence. It wasn't real, simply the power of suggestion. But Hermes's words kept coming back to me. *Do not underestimate the astrarium.*

But how was I going to get it to England? If I took it in my luggage there was the chance I'd be arrested at the airport for attempting to smuggle an antiquity out of the country. I couldn't afford another interrogation. Perhaps I could just take the pages with the transcribed hieroglyphics that Hermes had given me – would they be enough information for Hugh Wollington? But the more I thought about it, the less I wanted to leave the astrarium behind. I was bound to it now, committed. It was part of Isabella and so part of me too. And if whoever wanted it was prepared to kill Barry, I knew it was only a matter of time before they got past the security here. I had to take it with me.

Then I remembered Bill Anderson's boast days earlier.

I met the Texan at the Alexandria Sporting Club. Once a prestigious country club where only the privileged few could be members, it had its own racetrack, croquet and lawn-bowls lawns and an eighteen-hole golf course. The large reception room with its Tudor-style wooden beams and hunting trophies reminded me of an English country house. After the incident at the villa I'd been alternately favouring as somewhere to meet public places or the maze of the back alleys where it was impossible to be followed. The two of us sat sipping mint juleps on a terrace looking over the immaculately mown lawns and ornamental topiary, the gentle thud of tennis balls echoing in the distance. In one corner of the room sat a dignified older gentleman wearing a red pasha hat and a red carnation in his blazer. He was holding court with a group of women who must have been well into their seventies, dressed in faded but elegant day dresses and hats. We watched as he kissed the hand of one of the women, who laughed coquettishly.

'Who's that? Methuselah?' Anderson asked, grinning.

'That, my friend, is Fargally Pasha, once known as the King of Cotton and past friend to kings, film stars and dictators,' I answered. 'Now condemned to his memories.'

'We all end up like that sooner or later,' Anderson quipped and raised his glass to the old man.

Smiling, Fargally Pasha toasted us back.

Anderson turned to me. 'So what's this mysterious favour I can do for you?'

I leaned forward. 'In the Sinai you said you could get anything through Customs under the guise of emergency equipment.'

'Wasn't I under the influence of an illegal substance at the time?'

'Come on, Bill, I'm serious. There's something I need to get back to London; something Isabella cared about very deeply.'

He stared at me, then thoughtfully stirred his cocktail with the sprig of mint that decorated it. 'How big is it?'

'It's stored in a box about eighteen inches by twelve. If it were opened, no one except a very experienced archaeologist would recognise it.'

'Jesus, Oliver, you're not getting into that game?'

'If you think I intend to flog the damn thing to the highest bidder, you're wrong. It'll end up back in Egypt sooner or later. I'm just carrying out Isabella's last wishes – and trust me, it's not what I want to be doing.'

Anderson's eyebrows shot up in disbelief. 'The best I can do is fly it direct to Aberdeen on the company's private plane, then have it couriered down to London. If it's marked with the company's insignia, no one's going to open it.'

'That's good enough. How quickly?'

'I can organise for you to put it on the plane yourself, and it should get to London a couple of days after you. My equipment flies on ahead of me.'

I lifted my cocktail glass in a toast. 'Anderson, I owe you.'

'And I intend to collect.' He clinked his glass against mine.

16

On the afternoon of my departure I visited the Brambillas' villa. When I arrived, Francesca was sitting in a reclining chair, her eyes shut, in the walled courtyard in a small circle of sunlight beside the pond. Several carp, hopeful for food, weaved over each other in a blur of pale gold, gathering under her shadow where it fell across the water.

The garden was still beautiful despite its neglect. Frangipani branches cut a pattern across the sky and vines trailed across some of the paths. Someone – probably the teenage son of the lodgers – had spray-painted a rough facsimile of football goalposts on the stone back wall and scrawled *Viva Al Olympi!* It was peaceful, safe.

I sat down in an empty chair beside Francesca, wondering whether to wake her or not.

'So you have come to evict me?' she said abruptly, her eyes still closed, her voice resounding through the courtyard like the cry of a tragedienne.

I stayed silent, and after a moment she opened her eyes and gazed at the weaving mess of fish.

'I just want some answers, Francesca.'

'What kind of answers?'

'Why was Isabella's body violated?'

'If my granddaughter's body was violated I know nothing about it.'

I tried to read her face but it was as tightly closed as her knotted hands.

'I would love to believe you, but I don't,' I replied carefully.

She sighed, still staring down at the fish. 'Do you have any idea how terrible it is to be born on the wrong side of history?' Only now did she look at me, her gaze bitter. 'Of course you don't; you're English.'

'I was born on the wrong side of class.'

'That's different. You can buy yourself out of that situation, as you yourself, Oliver, have done,' she replied harshly. Then she reached into a pocket and pulled out a cigarillo.

Reaching into my own pocket, I offered her the gold Gucci lighter that a Saudi client had once given me. Francesca lowered her face towards the flame and the tip of the cigarillo burst into a glowing ember. She exhaled; a great curl of white smoke hung on the still air.

'No,' she continued. 'To be born on the wrong side of history is to be trapped in great sweeping circumstances over which one has absolutely no control. This was our country. Mohammed Ali personally invited my grandfather, a civil engineer, to Egypt, placed him into his cabinet. And my grandfather built roads, waterways, great architectural feats. But even if my family's hearts were Egyptian, their souls were Italian. This was what I was taught, and it was not a contradiction.'

She was becoming hysterical. Aadeel emerged from the villa – I guessed he had been listening – and hurried over to the elderly woman.

'Madame, the lodgers,' he murmured, pressing a blue pill into her hand.

'A curse on them,' she muttered, but took the pill with a sip of water from a glass that Aadeel held out. Then she waited, ostentatiously disregarding the servant until he slipped back into the house.

'My son was also an idealist,' she said, more calmly. 'We all thought that Mussolini, like Julius Caesar, would unite Alexandria with the Mediterranean world. We were not alone in this delusion: the Greeks thought the same, only their great dream was the old Ptolemaic order – Athens and Alexandria. Dreams like that have their own fuel – economic polarity, the ambition of a new order where everyone knows their natural place.'

Francesca's philosophising riled the humanist in me. 'There is no such thing as people having a natural place,' I interjected.

But the old matriarch was determined to finish her tirade. 'Those soldiers marched into that desert knowing they were going to die, and many did. The rest were herded together and interned, like animals. That was the first time this family was on the wrong side of history. The second time was Nasser and the revolution. Even then my son stood firm. "Times will change, Mama, you'll see. Our time will come, we just have to wait," he told me – the fool. The third time was the Suez Crisis; again, it was the English who let us down. Do you know what they call that incident here in Egypt? The triad of cowardice – the French, the British and the Israelis. We Italians, along with every other European, lost everything overnight. The Jews were the first to leave, or disappear mysteriously in the night. Others followed. But not this family. Paolo was determined. "So now I am the manager of my own company, but I will own it again, you will see, Mama." The wrong side of history, Oliver – it killed him, thirty-seven years old. And we, his parents, had to watch him die of humiliation!'

Again, I could see Aadeel hovering in the gathering twilight. Indifferent to his anxiety, Francesca continued. 'Paolo's death turned Giovanni into a desperate fool. And desperate men reach out for all kinds of false hopes. He thought he could use the old ways, the ancient ways, to change things back. I had no choice – I had to pretend I didn't know what was happening. In the end, it was all Giovanni had left.' I waited for her to say more, but she didn't.

'Is this to do with the "performances" you wrote to Cecilia about?' I prompted finally.

'You have been talking to Cecilia?'

'She mentioned a few things . . .'

'She is a liar! Giovanni worshipped Isabella. We were parents to her, not grandparents!' Francesca fell back into her chair, exhausted by her fury. 'I have said enough. Throw me out of my own house, but I refuse to divulge my husband's secrets.'

'What about your granddaughter? Doesn't she deserve respect?' I grabbed her hand; the wrinkled liver-spotted skin was as thin as rice paper. 'Francesca, they stole her heart.'

She snatched her hand away, her face closing over like stone. 'You should have protected Isabella. Isn't that what husbands are for?' she said with quiet spite.

In the branches above us, a dove began to coo, an ironically peaceful sound considering the tension between us. Enraged, I battled the impulse to hit out at the old woman.

'I told you, I know nothing.' She tried to stand, her elbows shaking wildly as she grasped the sides of the chair. 'Aadeel, begin packing our things! We are to be evicted!'

Her shouting startled the dove, which flew noisily out of the tree, dislodging leaves that showered down over the old woman's shoulders. She did not brush them off.

Aadeel glanced at me.

I stood. 'It's all right. No one is going to be evicted. I just came to say goodbye. I'm going away for a few weeks.'

Francesca sank back into her chair. I waited, unable to pull myself away without a final goodbye from her.

'Of course you're going. The English always do,' she muttered into the descending dusk.

I sat back against the leather upholstery of the oil company's ancient Bentley, the rich smell of the interior mixed with the driver's cigarette smoke. After taking a deliberately meandering route to the little airstrip I'd placed the astrarium into the cargo hold of Anderson's jet earlier that day and the thought of it flying on ahead of me was consoling; as if something of Isabella would be waiting for me upon my arrival in London. Cocooned in the car, the painful events of the last month seemed to stream behind us like the wake of a ship.

I wound down the window and the music of the city – honking vehicles, the cries of the street vendors, the bells on the horses' harnesses – rushed in. Old Ramadan decorations stretched gaudily between two buildings, tired tinsel and paper ribbons waving palely. Twilight. Already the streets were bustling with night shoppers; street pedlars selling figs, dates, peanuts, fresh fish caught that day – their wares carefully spread out on sheets of canvas; young women with extravagant hairstyles and Western clothes hurrying home from offices and shops; the old men holding court at the café tables.

The memory of Isabella's childlike pride at showing me her city, her hand holding mine in this very seat, sputtered on and off like a faulty fluorescent light.

'The airport?' the driver shouted over the traffic noise. 'We go to airport, right?'

'*Shukran* – thank you.'

I turned back to the window, trying to suppress an unexpected wave of sadness. Leaving is not losing her, and memory is a kind of afterlife, I told myself, but I found no consolation in the observation.

The car headed out towards the airport, past the sewage works and the satellite towns beginning to spring up around the outskirts of Alexandria, and into the cool desert. The oil refinery's flaming towers roared up against the darkening horizon like great primordial torches and finally my panic began to flatten out. With the blind sky yawning above the speeding car, I thought how Isabella would have loved this night.

17

London, June 1977

The hazy English sunlight was a shock after the glare of Egypt. The drive from Heathrow took me through the factorylands, into the outer London suburbs, then on to Chiswick with its large Victorian houses and gardens, into denser Shepherds Bush, past the terraced boarding houses of Notting Hill and finally into West Hampstead. The suburban landscape dragged me back into the smells, sights and sounds of England.

I stepped out of the taxi. There was the faint sound of reggae music, birdsong, and the feel of that particular humidity that always laced the early summer air – a languid sensuality that invariably surprised even the Londoners. I glanced at the Victorian terrace; our flat was located on the top floor. The curtains were pulled across. Staring up it was as if I saw Isabella parting them and peering down, her anxious face searching the street for me in that way she always did when she was expecting me back from a trip. But the curtains stayed closed and my legs almost buckled underneath me from grief.

'You all right, mate?' The taxi driver leaned out of his open window.

I nodded, and turned to lift out my suitcase. The cab drove off, and as I carried my luggage up the pavement I noticed the twins from next door watching from their front garden, one nonchalantly picking his nose while the other scratched a scabby knee. Children of a recent divorce, their working mother was rarely home and Isabella had often brought them up to our apartment for tea and the Turkish delight that Francesca sent from Egypt.

'Mister Warnock!' called Stanley, the older brother, now hanging from the garden gate, his prematurely aged face peaky and worried. I turned reluctantly: this was the moment I'd been dreading.

'Where's Issy?' he demanded, his voice trembling with anxiety. 'You've not gone and got divorced, 'ave yer?'

'Stanley, I've just got in from a long flight and—'

'She's left yer, 'asn't she?' Alfred joined his brother on the gate, the two of them glaring at me in defiant accusation, blond hair shaved tight against their narrow skulls, precocious in their distrust of all things adult.

I hesitated. They had both adored Isabella. She'd even taught them a few words of Italian, which they'd repeated solemnly in atrocious North London accents, captivated by her expressive gestures – *buongiorno, buonasera, arrivederci*. Momentarily overwhelmed, I sat down on my suitcase, unable to reply. There was the creak of the gate as it was swung open. A minute later I felt small cool fingers slip between my own.

'Mister Warnock, it's bad, innit?' Stanley stood in front of me, his eyes wide with a sense of tragedy that belied his age.

I stared up at him. 'I lost her,' I whispered.

'Lost her? How can you lose a whole person?' Alfred, incredulous, still hovered behind the gate. But one glance at Stanley's trembling lip and I knew that the older twin had understood.

'C'mon, Alfred.' With his eyes screwed tight, Stanley led his brother back to their front garden.

Our flat was in West Hampstead, a suburb filled with the dispossessed middle class: the divorced, the bachelors, the perpetual spinsters alone in their studio apartments huddled around the electric kettle. But it was my favourite part of London; I liked the semi-urban location. The apartment was tiny – I'd purchased it at the beginning of my first job, using the position as leverage to secure a mortgage. It had been a momentous occasion: I was the first member of my family ever to own property, and at twenty-four I felt I was already soaring above a cycle of poverty that went back generations.

It was a one-bedroom apartment, really a glorified attic conversion. The kitchen was the size of a large cupboard with a view of next door's concreted courtyard. The lounge, which doubled as the dining room, was split-level; a small set of wooden steps led up to a sleeping area with just enough space for a double bed. The ceiling was so low that I could hardly stand. The best thing about the place was the small roof terrace that lay beyond the double windows of the sleeping area. It was located between two tall Victorian red-brick chimneys: a sanctuary hidden from the windows of the surrounding buildings that offered an unencumbered view of north-west London. When the weather was good, I'd carry out the large telescope I kept folded against the bedroom wall and set it up on its spindly tripod. Beyond the orange city sky, the stars were my metaphysical ladder, a way to escape the claustrophobia of both London and the apartment.

I pulled my suitcase along the entrance hall and onto the
staircase. The paintwork was battered and splintered, the
carpet stained and worn by a thousand tenants before us, and
the strong smell of curry wafted down from the apartment of
the young Indian Sikh couple who lived on the first floor. I
paused on the landing.

'Oliver?' My neighbour peered through his partially
opened front door, the door chain still on.

'Hello, Raj,' I said.

Sighing with relief, Raj unlatched the chain and stepped
out. He was wearing a sweaty vest, a white turban and the
trousers of his bus driver's uniform. His eyes were tired and
anxious.

'Just come off the night shift?' I asked, surprised by the
pleasure I felt at the familiar sight of him.

'That is right.' He reached out, his voice cracking with
emotion. 'Oliver, your brother told us about your terrible
loss. My wife and I are most grieved – you know we both
loved Isabella very much.'

'Thank you.'

I could see Raj's sari-clad wife hovering shyly behind him.
Shaking his hand, I tried to hold down the balloon of emotion now banging against my ribcage. Embarrassed, Raj
tactfully turned back to the apartment.

'Aisha, he is back.'

His wife, her slim figure radiating a glasslike fragility,
offered me a biscuit tin. 'Please, you must be tired and
hungry, and your fridge will be empty. I made some samosas
for you. Please?'

Thanking them both profusely, I slipped the tin under my
arm.

After the door closed behind them, I stood staring up at
the next landing, my own front door, achingly evocative with

its blue paint and brass doorknob, beckoning through the banisters. Clutching the biscuit tin as a drowning man might hold on to a buoy, I made my way up the stairs.

The flat was a darkened cavern that stank of stale cigarette smoke and frying bacon. With all the curtains drawn, it held the gloom of somebody else's life, a past I now barely recognised. Even in this dim light I could see several dirty plates on the floor, a dressing gown thrown across the television. A lava lamp glowed in the corner, its nebulous wax mass congealing in slow motion like an alien fungus.

Isabella had insisted that Gareth should have a set of keys so he could use the flat as an occasional retreat from the frenetic world he existed in. It was obvious he'd stayed over and failed to clean up after himself. I picked up the plates and carried them into the kitchen. Well, at least he's eating, I reassured myself. The task of dealing with my brother's latest bout of addiction loomed; a depressing prospect.

I turned off the dripping tap and went back into the lounge. It was a time capsule, the objects within which might themselves have been submerged – the dust and microscopic human debris from a lifetime before, a lifetime suspended in the still air.

I climbed the wooden steps to the sleeping area. Isabella's dressing gown hung on a hook on the wall. Burying my face in the silk, I breathed in deeply. The smell of our sex still lingered in the folds, the love twistings of leg and skin.

Kneeling on the floor, I buried my head in this tent of memory, wondering if I could go on. I was free-falling in her absence. If I was entirely honest with myself, I think I might have been waiting for some kind of external sign to give me a reason to continue, for Isabella to talk to me from beyond that invisible wall that divided the dead from the living.

There was nothing but silence. Then, slowly, the sound of

a distant ice-cream van playing a tinkling 'Greensleeves' and the roar of a plane passing overhead came into focus. And suddenly I wanted to wipe all of it away – the clinging labyrinth of Egypt, the astrarium, the incessant misery of loss.

I grabbed the steel waste-paper bin, pulled open the chest of drawers and began to pull out Isabella's clothes: sweaters, blouses, skirts, lingerie – all ghost clothes now, a ghost I was determined to exorcise. I stuffed as much as I could into the bin, then carried it onto the roof terrace. I emptied a bottle of lighter fluid over the clothes and held a match to the pile.

Sliding down, I sat with my back to the wall. As each item crinkled and then burst into flames, I remembered the occasions when she'd worn it: an Indian cotton dress flying around her tanned legs as she danced at a rock concert; a business suit she wore for her lectures; a nightdress she would put on, without consciously realising the signal she was sending, when she wanted to make love.

Emotionally exhausted, I curled up and closed my eyes.

The sound of footsteps woke me. Silhouetted against the afternoon sky was a young woman, her wild hair framing her face like a mane.

'Oliver?' she said.

Disorientated, I stumbled to my feet. I must have slept for hours.

'I'm Zoë. Gareth's girlfriend. Sorry.' She indicated the open window that she must have climbed through to reach the roof. 'I was audacious. I let myself in. Gareth had the keys. He doesn't know you're back or anything . . .'

'You're forgiven. So you're the person who rang my office in Alex?'

Zoë stepped into the shade and finally I could see her

clearly. She wore Dr Martens boots, purple fishnets and a blue lurex ball gown that flared from the waist, her hennaed hair fell to her shoulders, and her face had a Pre-Raphaelite beauty that formed a jarring contrast with her dress. Despite the heavy purple eyeshadow, she looked ridiculously young.

She looked me up and down candidly; to my annoyance I found it a disarming sensation.

'You look like him, only older,' she said.

I moved the subject onto safer ground. 'Is Gareth all right?'

'Depends on what you classify as all right. He's playing tonight so I thought you could come and see for yourself. Personally, I've never seen him so self-destructive.'

'In what way?'

She looked me fully in the eye, then decided to be honest. 'Speed. I mean, we all indulge. It's just that with Gareth it's got so bad that he's frightened to sleep. Like really frightened, as if it might kill him to close his eyes. Most of the time he's rational, but then he'll start talking about people coming to steal his soul.'

'That isn't rational.'

'Isn't it?' Zoë replied with a nonchalant irony.

Reaching into the still-smouldering bin, she pulled out one of Isabella's half-burnt bras, all underwiring and lace, and held it up. 'I don't think everything is rational.'

She waited for an explanation of the burning clothes; I didn't give her one. She dropped the smouldering bra back into the embers. 'I think we have a few things in common.' She flung out the remark as if it were a paradox.

'Apart from my brother?'

'An interest in stone, rock . . .'

I glanced at her quizzically.

'Didn't Gareth tell you?' she continued.

'Afraid not – we've never talked much, my fault as much as his,' I replied, wondering now how much he'd told her about me.

'I'm a sculptor – I work in marble.' Zoë's earnestness was endearing. 'You're a geologist, aren't you?'

'A geophysicist, that's far less romantic.' I smiled. 'How old are you?'

'Does my age preclude the possibility of being taken seriously?'

'As an artist or a woman?'

'I'm asking you.'

'I think' – I leaned forward to emphasise the point – 'I'm old enough to be your father.'

'But you're not my father. And, if you have to know, he died last year in a road accident and I suspect he was several years older than you.'

Suddenly her façade of hardened indifference slipped away. I fought the impulse to hug her.

'I'm sorry.'

Zoë flinched. 'So, you see, we have something else in common.' She glanced out at the rooftops before turning back towards me. 'I met your wife once, at the squat. She told Gareth to break it off with me – she thought I was too intense, and probably too young.'

I laughed. 'That sounds like Isabella – she was always giving him advice about his love life.'

'It's okay, she was right. I *am* too intense ...' Her voice trailed off and she indicated the smouldering bin. 'It's hard to find the words ...'

'That's because there aren't any.'

She nodded and, squatting down against the wall, lit a cigarette.

'Marble's made from seashells crushed together over

millions of years, isn't it? That's why it has that translucency – the light of all those ancient oceans.'

'Exactly,' I answered, smiling. 'And oil is made from organic matter crushed together over millions of years, and that black-gold tint is the treacly light of money shining through.'

'But isn't working just for money ultimately corrupting?' Zoë persisted.

'I'll let you into a secret. It's not the money but the hunt that gets me excited. Finding something I can sense is there.'

She nodded. 'I feel that when I look at a piece of marble. I see the shape hidden in the rock, then release it by carving.'

'Bingo, that makes three things we have in common,' I joked.

Zoë's expression wavered, then settled into seriousness. 'So what do you think happens to us when we die, when we're crushed together over millions of years?'

I stared out over the languid summer evening; the laughter of children playing below floated up with the faint scent of mown grass. 'We become one with the universe, nature recycling itself. It's that simple,' I answered finally.

'Nothing's simple.' Zoë threw her cigarette away. 'I'm eighteen, in case you're wondering.' She stood up. 'She's still here, you know.'

For a moment I thought I'd misheard. 'Sorry?'

'Your wife, she hasn't left yet. She's still here, all twisted up in your shadow.'

'Look, I hardly know you—'

'Oops, I'm being audacious again, sorry. Sometimes I speak out of turn. You'll have to put up with it. Come to the gig tonight – please. Gareth really respects you. He'll be thrilled if you are there. I wouldn't have rung if I didn't think the situation was serious.'

Zoë smiled; a poignant half-smile that softened the ferocity of her make-up. There was an unnerving maturity about her despite her youth, and her beauty was hard to ignore.

'He doesn't know you're back or that I rang you,' she continued. 'Proud family, your lot – Gareth would rather die than ask for help. I'm sorry about your wife. She must have been amazing. Gareth took the news really badly.'

'They were close.'

'The band's playing at The Vue. They're on in an hour so we should get moving.'

I hesitated. I hadn't reckoned on the possibility of actually seeing my brother sing. In fact, I'd never seen Gareth's band play – that had been Isabella's domain, and I'd semiconsciously avoided the gigs, a part of me terrified that he might not be as talented as I hoped. I needed to believe in his future in the way my parents had never believed in mine, which meant I needed him to be good, really good.

I glanced out over the rooftops, the urban regularity jarring after the skyline of Alexandria. The sun had begun to slip behind the horizon.

'Come on, come with me,' Zoë said. 'It's got to be better than hanging around here. But there's no way you're wearing that daft suit.'

18

The Vue was an old ballroom that someone had decided to recreate as a rock-music venue. Apart from some fluorescent ceiling hangings and a stage backdrop with a massive black 'A' on a red background ringed by a circle, the original decor looked relatively intact. Ornate plaster reliefs decorated the balconies and a huge crystal chandelier hung from the ceiling, imaginatively strung with pink electric lights, while a strobe painted the walls in blindingly blue-white staccato flashes.

The bar, located on an upper balcony, was encircled by large booths and had a neon sign depicting Betty Boop having sex with Mickey Mouse pulsing over the counter. I pushed my way through the crowd, cradling a vodka and four pints of Guinness. By the time we'd arrived, the band were backstage preparing to go on and the bouncers wouldn't let us see them. Zoë had guided me to the bar, pointed to where Gareth's housemates were waiting, and told me to buy the drinks. I reached the table, self-conscious in the battered leather jacket that Gareth had left at the flat and which Zoë had forced me to wear.

I felt I'd entered some kind of Hieronymus Bosch netherworld populated by young women and men dressed in the most fantastical outfits and hairstyles. They lounged against the walls and on the chairs; a couple even appeared to be having sex on the table of one of the booths, oblivious to the incurious bystanders. Another couple sported bright pink mohawks over a foot high; the man, a good deal shorter than his girlfriend, reminded me of a bizarre peacock. His eyes were carefully outlined with black kohl and eyeshadow, while the shaved halves of his scalp either side of the stiff pink spikes glistened like a pale pancake. A torn T-shirt held together by oversized safety pins sat under a black leather jacket covered in zips and studs, and his skintight trousers were made of rubber. His girlfriend wore a leather bra – the kind of thing one might purchase from a sex shop – and a tartan miniskirt, under which the suspenders holding up her fishnet stockings were clearly visible. The two of them had a tribal grace, and the male youth particularly, with his long naked skull and aquiline features, reminded me of a pale version of some of the Nubian tribes I'd seen in central Africa. I'd never thought the English could be capable of such decorative and imaginative dressing, and for one bizarre moment I speculated whether such fashion wasn't a brilliant fusion of colonial-era Britain and the urban dispossessed.

Gareth's housemates were seated in one of the booths, Zoë beside them. I placed the drinks down on the table, then sat opposite. They looked as out of place as I did, I couldn't help noting with some relish. They were a curiously eclectic group who looked like they had nothing in common except the squat they lived in – in Harlesden, a semi-industrial, unprepossessing suburb on the outskirts of north-west London. The narrow Victorian terrace was one side of a whole cul-de-sac that had been marked for demolition until Gareth and his friends had taken illegal occupancy eighteen months before. Despite my disapproval, I couldn't help admiring the energy they had poured into repairing the place – clearing the ancient sewage drain that led under the street, emptying the back garden of litter, replacing the shattered windows.

'Excellent, my friend – the beverages have arrived intact despite the unruly herd,' Dennis announced.

At forty, he was an active member of the International Marxist Group and a borderline schizophrenic: a passionately literary character who, when he wasn't reading Nietzsche, worked as a bookie. Next to him was Philippe, a short corpulent Frenchman with long hair who had come to London to escape military service, or so Gareth had told Isabella. My brother had apparently recruited the draft dodger at an anarchist meeting.

The third housemate was a diminutive thirty-year-old Irishman called Francis, with straight red hair that ran down in flat streaks to his waist. He sported a matching goatee. Never seen without his embroidered beanie, he resembled a studious garden gnome.

'Thanks, Oliver, you're a gentleman and it won't be forgotten,' he murmured in his soft southern Irish brogue as he reached for his drink.

A tall stunning pneumatic blonde in bondage trousers and a net vest sauntered past; her pendulous breasts were clearly visible, as were her large pierced nipples. All three men paused, glasses in mid-air.

'Would you look at that? An angel in hell and I know exactly the man to deliver her from such terrible damnation,' Francis said admiringly.

'Be my guest – these punky girls look like their pussies

have teeth. Me, I would have concern for my manhood,' Philippe responded before sipping cautiously at his Guinness.

Dennis turned to Francis. 'You don't get it, do you? The desecration of the body is an anti-beauty statement, and yet the desecration itself becomes a fetish, then a subculture with its own individual ways of delineating beauty – so all this protest becomes self-defeating. It's a loop. All of history is just loop after loop.'

'Jesus, Dennis, I bet you're fun in bed in a modernist kind of way.' Francis swung around to me. 'What about you, Oliver? Does that bird lift your wick or what?'

'Francis! The man's just become a widower – he's not interested in getting laid,' Dennis retorted. 'Sorry, Oliver, my associates are emotionally insensitive at the best of times. Francis didn't mean to be offensive.'

'No offence taken,' I replied, concluding that the only way I was going to survive the night was to get drunk.

'Leave the poor bastard alone,' Zoë ordered. 'Can't you see he's in culture shock as well as acoustic.' She turned back to me. 'But don't worry, the girls here won't bite – unless you ask very, very nicely.' She grinned wickedly.

Luckily, any further humiliation was staved off by the lights dimming. The MC came on stage and immediately the audience broke into a chorus of wolf whistles. 'The Alienated Pilots!' he screamed through the microphone.

Dennis rose to his feet, his face cadaverous under the fluorescent lights. 'Well, comrades, it's time the troops turned up for the parade,' he announced solemnly and began making his way to the front of the stage.

We all followed – except Francis, who took the opportunity to finish off our beers.

From the back of the darkened stage came a low drum roll

and then a cymbal clash. A follow spot flicked on, illuminating my brother in a pool of blue-white light. Gareth looked like a beautiful sixteenth-century Spanish carving. His bared torso was a washboard of cascading pale ribs with a bleeding heart crayoned onto his chest; his leather trousers were slung low on his hips that were ringed by a studded belt. His head was tilted back, his eyes shut. A crown of plastic barbed wire was pushed low over his forehead, pearls of fake blood rolled down over his cheekbones, and he held the microphone clasped in one hand like a sceptre. He lifted his muscular arms up as if in crucifixion. The religious references appalled me – clearly he hadn't escaped our mother's influence. He looked thin but not emaciated; I hoped, against all the evidence, that Zoë's concern for him had been unwarranted.

The audience fell into awed silence. I couldn't help thinking how proud Isabella would have been of Gareth at that moment. I almost felt her standing beside me in the dark, radiating excitement. Instinct made me turn, half expecting to see her face, but instead I found myself glancing at Zoë, who was staring at a space just above me. I looked over my shoulder, wondering what she'd seen, but there was nothing. As if in answer, she suddenly reached out and fluttered her fingers above me, almost as though she was shooing something away.

Then, her face avid with anticipation, she leaned across and whispered into my ear. 'The trouble with your brother is that he has no continuity – he reinvents himself from moment to moment. But that's exactly what will make him famous.'

Zoë looked like some magical sage, her kohl-rimmed eyes shimmering silver under the lights. Suddenly Gareth's voice rang out over the crowd.

'This is for Isabella – may you shine on for ever,' he

announced, and a great sweep of emotion rushed through me.

The next minute, he burst into low gravelly song, his body throwing itself into pose after pose: a svelte Pierrot with the stance of a bullfighter. The effect was undeniably sensual and I couldn't help wondering what had happened to the small child I used to take walking on the Downs. 'The Fens have shadows,' he'd once told me. 'But when night comes the shadows fly away and leave the Fens alone, all cold and shivery.' I'd never forgotten the passion of his six-year-old conviction, and now there it was, up on the stage.

My love wears green
Like the dragonfly she shines
Slices my heart into shimmering pieces
My love wears green . . .

The chorus was a pounding cacophony of guitar chords that ignited the audience. At the front, a row of skinheads leaped up and down, their shaved skulls glistening with sweat. In a violent frenzy they pushed aside the surrounding spectators as the lights changed to a deep blood-red strobe fragmenting Gareth's movements like time-lapse photography.

She takes the mighty
And strikes them blind
She sleeps with all my friends
Yet swears she's mine
My love wears green . . .

It was as if my brother had been transformed into someone whom I'd had no idea existed under that indolent façade. There was an old-world Celtic quality to his lyrics despite the punching brutality of the chorus. The next three songs had the same lurching romanticism as the first – seductive ballads splintered by violent refrains. At the edge of the stage near Gareth's feet, a small group of girls had gathered, their faces illuminated as the spotlight swung into the crowd like a beam from a lurching lighthouse. Each girl appeared to be undergoing a private dialogue with the sinewy figure, as if he were singing for her alone. They reminded me of worshippers at an altar, transfixed, transported. It was hypnotic to witness and, suddenly envious, I found myself imagining what it must be like to hold such power.

Just then a boy who looked about fifteen, a Union Jack safety-pinned to his vest, pushed past, spilling his beer down the front of my trousers. I reeled around but he carried on regardless, stumbling into the swaying audience. The three vodkas I'd consumed collided with my exhaustion in a sudden dizziness. I made my way through the crowd and leaned against the wall, looking on as my brother sang his way through a kaleidoscope of emotion.

Gareth's dressing room was far less glamorous than I had imagined it would be. Painted white, it had a chipped mirror glued to one wall, a battered Formica table covered in sticks of stage make-up, empty beer cans and ashtrays spilling over with cigarette butts. In one corner stood a steel clothes rack on wheels with various performing outfits hanging off it.

Wearing sunglasses, Gareth leaned against the edge of the table. He was surrounded by a small crowd of groupies, fans and band members, with a beer can in one hand and Zoë nestled adoringly under his other arm. Under the fluorescent light I could see that sweat had run rivulets through his make-up. He appeared jittery, still high from his performance, but I also recognised the influence of amphetamines in his manic gestures.

He caught sight of me. 'Oliver! Oliver! I can't believe you're here! I almost didn't recognise you with that beard.' He addressed his entourage. 'Everyone, meet my brother – fresh from the land of the Pharaohs!'

The small crowd stared at me, then, seemingly disappointed at my ordinariness, turned back to their drinking and chattering. Pushing his way through them, Gareth took off his sunglasses and pulled me into a hug. The shock of the embrace made me freeze.

'Did you like the dedication?' he asked. He smelled of cigarettes and Old Spice aftershave.

'It was really moving.'

'I'm so sorry about Isabella.'

Hating myself for the inherent awkwardness of the men in my family, I pulled away. 'It's been terrible.' My voice broke despite my reserve.

'You're home now. It's good to see you.'

I changed the subject. I couldn't bear to talk about Isabella, not now, not with Gareth. 'You were brilliant out there. I couldn't believe you were my brother.'

'Did you all hear that? Oliver here thought we were bloody brilliant!' he shouted to the room. 'And he's a bloody Tory!'

His entourage grinned inanely and nodded in dumb approval.

'I'm not a bloody Tory,' I muttered, embarrassed.

'Yeah, but you're a capitalist – same bloody thing.' He suddenly swung back to the others. 'Fuck off! The lot of you!'

They paused, murmuring amongst themselves, wondering if he meant it.

'Now!' he yelled, spittle flying.

The room emptied in minutes.

Gareth turned back to me, grinning. 'Oh, the sheer power of celebrity. They're sheep, the whole bloody lot of them.' He extracted a crushed cigarette packet from the back pocket of his tight leather trousers and lit up a crooked cigarette, inhaling deeply. 'Fuck, it feels so wrong – without Isabella you're nowt. She was your inspirational self, your evolved feminine side, she made those exploitative mud scramblings of yours poetic.'

Gareth's speech tended to oscillate wildly between an ornate Oscar Wilde-style patter and contemporary slang, as if his personality was some grand work in progress whose foundation hadn't quite settled yet.

'The word is "geophysicist" and it's not mud, it's oil.' I looked into his eyes, trying to gauge the size of his pupils. 'You're speeding, aren't you? Do you know we're all worried sick about you?' My voice reverted to the northern accent of my childhood as I spoke – the tongue of my family.

Gareth pushed me away and put his sunglasses back on. 'Give me a break. You've been gone for months, and Da's been on my back every bloody week.'

'When did you start using again? I thought we talked about that—'

'Isabella talked about that. You were never bloody interested until now. Did you bring her back?' he demanded abruptly.

'What?'

'I thought maybe you'd bring the ashes back or something.'

I stared at him – the amphetamines were making him manic. 'Isabella had a Catholic funeral, it was what her family wanted.'

'I just thought we could have our own service – you know, scatter her ashes on the Heath or something. I could have sung. Isabella liked my singing.'

'Christ, you're unbelievable.'

I turned to walk away, but Gareth reached out and put his hand on my shoulder.

'Listen, I'm sorry, all right? It must be hell for you. I know I wouldn't have survived it. You two were symbiotic: silence and song.'

For a second a window opened onto the man he might become; rarely had I heard Gareth sound so sincere. I decided to take a risk.

'Gareth, you made a drawing for Isabella, a drawing of the astrarium . . .'

His whole demeanour changed; it was as if he sobered up instantly. He went to the door and, after checking that no one was loitering in the passage outside, closed it. 'Come back with me tonight, Oliver, back to the squat. We need to talk.'

Gareth's bedroom, on the top floor of the terrace, had black walls and a dark blue ceiling onto which he'd stuck fluorescent decals of planets and stars – a fictional galaxy that in no way resembled the Milky Way or any other known astral body. He lay on a mattress on the floor, while Zoë and several others of his entourage – Philippe, the drummer, a couple of drunk bouncers – lounged around the room. I sat awkwardly beside my brother, my back hard against the cold wall, the discovery that he was virtually never alone a growing source of irritation.

Gareth had just turned off the light to display his celestial artwork and the others were staring reverently at its greenish glow.

'I'm telling you, on this hash it's better than the Sistine Chapel,' Philippe murmured, curled up on a beanbag.

'You should see what it's like on acid.' The drummer rolled over onto his back, high as a kite.

'Yeah,' Zoë affirmed in a reed-thin voice.

'Gareth,' I hissed, 'I thought you wanted to talk to me alone.'

'We are alone.'

'No, we're fucking not.'

'I meant existentially.'

'That's it – I'm out of here.'

I struggled to my feet but Gareth grabbed my arm.

'I'm sorry. Listen, don't go, we'll talk in a minute, I promise.' He pulled me towards him. His breath stank of Guinness. 'How did she die really? Did she find the astrarium? Is that how it happened?'

I paused, my mind reeling in the dark. I hadn't realised he'd known Isabella had been diving for the astrarium in Alexandria.

'She drowned searching for it,' I whispered.

I wasn't going to tell him we'd found it. It wasn't that I didn't trust him; simply that I wanted to protect him. I couldn't bear the idea of putting him in the same danger I'd unwittingly put Barry. Perhaps I'd already endangered Gareth's life simply by coming to his house. I couldn't shake the overwhelming sense of being shadowed, and if, God forbid, someone did corner him and question him at some point it was safer that he knew nothing.

'Come with me.' Gareth pulled me to my feet.

We stumbled our way to the door, tripping across outstretched legs and splayed arms, and provoking a chorus of expletives. The tiny room he took me to was lined with cardboard egg cartons and illuminated with a single naked electric bulb. A battered desk with a sound-mixing board on it ran along one wall, while opposite stood a small book-case holding titles such as Rimbaud's *A Season in Hell*, John Fowles's *The Magus*, *Ways of Seeing* by John Berger – all the usual reading for a twenty-two-year-old art student.

'This is my workshop,' he said. 'It doubles as a recording studio and drawing space. Only a privileged few are allowed in. There are fans out there who would give their virginity just to get through that door.'

'You're safe then. I lost my virginity years ago,' I joked.

'Thank fucking Christ for that.' Gareth reached for the copy of *A Season in Hell*. 'This is what I think you're after.' Between the pages was what looked like a slightly rougher draft of his drawing. 'She showed you this?'

'Yes, the night before she . . .' I faltered, unable to say the words. Hands shaking, I pulled out the drawing he'd done for Isabella.

Gareth put his hand on my shoulder, a brief reassurance.

'Did she explain the symbols at the bottom?' he asked, keeping his hand on my shoulder for another brief moment. I sighed and shook my head, scrutinising the drawing.

'She said she was going to tell me when she had the actual astrarium in her hands. But I know you'd worked on the cipher together.'

Gareth's demeanour changed instantly. He pulled him-self upright, sweeping his hair back over his forehead, then grinned. 'I was always good at puzzles, remember?'

He paused, seemingly to collect all his energy. Then, like some kind of alchemist, he held his hands above the page before running his finger over the letters as if they were Braille. I'd never seen him so concentrated before: eyes shut, his features twitching slightly as if the paper itself was talk-ing directly to him alone. He opened his eyes suddenly, then folded the paper carefully so that the symbols lined up against each other. 'I'd been staring at it for hours. There was something about the symmetry or lack of it that kept annoying me.'

He held up the paper. The way he'd folded it made it apparent that the symbols were actually halves of whole symbols or hieroglyphs; and once each symbol sat against its opposite, eight letters became four. He pointed to the four new hieroglyphs.

'They're basic Egyptian hieroglyphs you can look up in any library: Singing/Song, Stick/Reed, Put in/Placed, Hathor/Lion, Mouth. The translation is: "When the singing reed is placed in the lion's mouth the sands will echo." We spent hours before you guys left for Alexandria trying to understand the context – what such a phrase might be doing on an astrolabe, a time calculator. Then, weeks later, it came to me. I was on a bender – I'd been up for days. Anyway, in the middle of the night I had this epiphany – it was just a couple of weeks before Isabella drowned. I booked a call through to her immediately and asked her, "What if the reed was a key and the lion's mouth a keyhole? What if the astrarium required a key?" There was a long silence and then she said quietly, "My God, Gareth, you've solved it. Ten years of searching and you've solved it." I'll never forget her voice.'

'Isabella was always a little dramatic,' I said, my own voice hoarse. Grief mingled with guilt, and a strange jealousy that she'd taken Gareth into her confidence and not me.

'Look, it's an ancient riddle,' he said impatiently, 'some kind of metaphoric instruction. But now we'll never know, will we?' He looked at me questioningly.

I avoided his gaze, anxious that he'd guess the astrarium had been found, even that I had it in my possession. He wasn't fooled.

'Oliver, you haven't . . .'

'Listen, the less you know the safer you are, understand?' I snapped back, more aggressively than I'd intended.

'You're in danger, aren't you?'

Dropping my gaze, I didn't reply. I don't think Gareth had ever seen me more vulnerable and I could see him struggling as he tried to square this new persona with the fearless entrepreneur he knew me to be. After a moment he turned back to the photocopy.

'Okay, I know nothing. But there's something else you should know about this inscription. I think the way the cipher's constructed is symbolic in itself. Two halves that mean nothing until they're put together. It re-emphasises the key idea. I reckon that the astrarium, if Isabella had ever found it, would have been incomplete. It needs something else – its other half, most likely the key – to be activated. Two halves making a whole – it's almost like a love story. There you are, that's Gareth the drug-fucked Romantic's version.'

I looked back at the hieroglyphs, trying to keep my face blank to cover my amazement. Intuitively Gareth had understood the need for the Was, the key to the device.

A noise outside the door startled me and I shuffled the papers together quickly. I could see that Gareth was unnerved by my fear. Reaching out, I put my hand on his shoulder. 'You're to tell no one about the hieroglyphs or their meaning, understand? This is important – important for me, important for Isabella. You're to destroy the drawing and forget about the whole thing. Promise?'

He nodded solemnly.

'And I want you to come and stay with me,' I continued, determined to persuade him while he was vulnerable. 'I'm only here for a couple of weeks, but it'll give you a chance to get clean. And, frankly, I could do with the company.'

Gareth's body stiffened at the mention of his addiction. Immediately he began to slip back into the nonchalance of the junkie. 'I can't do that – I have art school, gigs, it's impossible . . .'

'Please?'

'No, Oliver.' His voice had dipped into a tone of sullen aggression and I knew there was no point in arguing.

'Then at least ring me every day to let me know you're okay?'

'That I can do.'

He pulled his lighter out of his trouser pocket and lit the corner of his piece of paper, watching the page curl and turn to ash.

'Goodbye, oh sister mine,' he whispered.

19

That night, too drunk and jet-lagged to make my way home, I slept in Gareth's bed. He'd gone to stay at Zoë's place. I collapsed onto the sheets beneath an old quilt that I recognised from my childhood. With my head buried in a pillow that smelled of patchouli oil and stale sweat, I fell asleep instantly.

Isabella appeared to be sitting on the pebbled lane that I recognised from my childhood, the road that ran outside my father's house. Her black hair spilt over her olive skin and she was clothed in the embroidered dress that she'd married me in. Looking up at me, she smiled, then threw two small grey stones onto the concrete as if she were playing jacks. As they hit the concrete, the stones began to spin; balanced on their ends, they turned faster and faster, like two magnets spinning around each other.

I awoke not knowing where I was, the angled walls of the darkened bedroom completely alien to me. I stared up at the ceiling covered with glowing fluorescent stars and planets. As I watched they dissolved into a greenish fiery loop, travelling faster and faster until they lifted away from the ceiling and swooped towards me in the shape of a body in flight.

I woke again, this time for real, drenched in sweat, dehydrated, the beginnings of a hangover pounding my temples.

When I got back to my building it was early morning and as I made my way wearily up the steps I passed Raj in his bus conductor's uniform. He stopped me.

'Oliver, a parcel was delivered early this morning. When you were not there they rang my bell instead, so I brought it up. I hope it brings good news.' Before I could thank him he'd hurried off to work.

A box marked 'Private Air Delivery' was sitting outside my front door. I instantly recognised the insignia of Bill Anderson's company, Runaway Wells, and my own scrawled handwriting. As if propelled by my nightmare the astrarium had arrived.

Set on the Formica kitchen table, the mechanism looked as if it were from another world entirely. I sat down at the table, part of me hoping the cogs might have assembled themselves into working order during the journey to reveal their secret. But the device continued to sit there motionless.

The outer bronze dial etched with symbols for the five major planets glinted dully under the light. The middle dial, made of a silver-like metal, was etched with Greek zodiac symbols – the twins, the archer, Taurus the bull – along with the crocodile and the ibis. The smallest dial, made of a gold alloy, was etched with Egyptian hieroglyphs and seemed to contain the centre of the mystery.

I peered through the small opening at the base of the main shaft around which the cogs turned. Hidden in the middle of the mechanism were two magnets facing each other – small grey discs that looked like stones; a little like

the pebbles in my nightmare. They appeared to be waiting – to be set spinning?

If I found the key to activate the mechanism, would that
put Isabella's spirit to rest? Was it possible, in some abstract,
esoteric way, that she herself had ended up living out one of
her worst fears, hovering in a halfway world – a trapped soul?
If I found the Was, would the astrarium give up its destiny?
Isabella had a plan for it, one with me in mind. What could
it be?

Through the thin wall, the abrupt ringing of my neighbour's alarm clock made me jump. I was being ridiculous, I
told myself; the nightmare meant nothing. Still, the vividness
of it haunted me. I needed to work out what the astrarium
could do and then find a safe place for it, for Isabella's sake, for
mine and, if Hermes was to be believed, for the safety of the
fledging and fragile structure that was the new Egypt.
Suddenly, the enormity of the task overwhelmed me.

I reached for the telephone and called the operator to get
the number of the British Museum.

The sarcophagus stood in an alcove in the large hall.
Hieroglyphs encircled it, describing the life of Nectanebo
II – his military conquests, his wives, his palaces and wealth.
They also narrated the journey he would take in the afterlife,
even though the sarcophagus had never actually fulfilled its
function.

I was acutely aware of the astrarium in the rucksack as I
walked slowly around the granite coffin studying the hieroglyphs. I stopped at a small doorway etched into the side –
the gateway for the Pharaoh's Ba. What had happened to
Nectanebo II? Had he died in some obscure corner of Africa?
Or had he ended up as an official in some foreign court,
living under a secret identity?

Suddenly the desire to reach out and run my fingers across the hieroglyphs was overpowering, as if by touching the gateway I would be able to tell where the Pharaoh's restless Ba still hovered – Greece? Iran? Egypt? If I lifted out the astrarium now and held it up against the tomb, would there be some kind of synchronicity between the two?

I scanned the display hall – the security guard had turned his back. Quickly, I reached out and stroked the carved surface, the narrative whispering out from under my fingertips.

'Wonderful, isn't it?'

Snatching my hand back, I swung around. A stocky man in his late forties with bright red hair, a large band of eczema covering his forehead, stood before me. Despite his naked pate, he sported sideburns that ran thickly down each cheek. He was dressed in maroon corduroy trousers and an orange shirt, the vivid colours giving the impression that he was compensating for his unprepossessing physical appearance.

'Don't look so worried,' he said. 'People touch it all the time, they can't help themselves. It's compulsive – subconsciously we're all searching for a gateway into the afterworld.'

He gave a bark of a laugh riddled with irony, then held out his hand. I shook it tentatively.

'Hugh Wollington. You must be Oliver Warnock.'

'I am. Thanks for making the time to meet me.'

'My pleasure. Besides, it's flattering to be sought out. I don't get that many enquiries – my area of Egyptology is rather specialised.' He looked at me appraisingly and I suddenly had the fleeting impression that his surprise at my phone call hadn't been entirely genuine. I quelled my feeling of unease – I needed to get a step further, and Wollington was my one chance.

I turned back to the tomb. 'So tell me, is it true no one knows where Nectanebo II is buried?'

'He fled Egypt, abandoning his post, so to speak—'

'After retreating to Memphis . . .'

'You do know your stuff.' Wollington began pointing out the various inscriptions. 'Here the scribes have written how the Pharaoh was known as the Great Magician. Nectanebo II was famous for building a record number of temples and thereby reminding the populace of his own divinity – basically using mysticism and religion as tools for political propaganda. Irrational to our way of thinking, especially in the context of modern politics—'

'Oh, I don't know. Apparently the King of Saudi Arabia frequently consults astrologers about political decisions.'

'He does indeed. Do you know the king?'

'Not personally, but I worked on some of his oilfields.'

'I know the whole family. I worked for one of his distant relatives – Prince Majeed. An interesting chappie, a little heavy-handed with his subjects, but then that is the way to get things done out there.' Wollington smiled, clearly warming to his subject. I was happy to let him talk – the less I had to say the better. 'I was Majeed's personal curator for a number of years. He had amassed an extraordinary collection of antiquities, many of them of great religious and mystical significance. Ah, yes, I loved the Middle East. I was posted out there in the 1950s when I was still in the army – it's a landscape that burns away all affectation, don't you think? But you'd know all about that in your industry.'

'I don't know – plenty of affectation in oil.'

We both laughed again, and despite myself I warmed to his enthusiasm, our shared love for a country so difficult, so intense and fraught as Egypt. His passion seemed to be anchored in a pragmatism that was appealing after Hermes Hemiedes's fantastical interpretation of Egyptian theology; and the fact that he was ex-army was reassuring – it grounded him somehow.

'The challenge is to put yourself into the cultural mentality of the Ancient Egyptians,' Wollington went on, 'virtually
impossible for a Judaeo-Christian Anglo-Saxon living in a
modern democracy. But if you can imagine a total belief in
the power of sorcery, and a regular dialogue with a whole
swarm of deities whom one had to appease and second-guess
in order to survive, then you begin to get the picture.' He
pointed to a particular hieroglyph. 'This tells us that at one
point Nectanebo decreed that he was the living embodiment of Horus – an astute political decision, as this was a way
of using the myth of Horus's defeat of Seth as an allegory for
his own power over the Persians. As a marketing strategy it
worked brilliantly until—'

'Until they invaded for the second time.'

'Exactly. Nothing like a second invasion to destroy one's
reputation for invincibility.' We both laughed again.

'I've been fascinated by Nectanebo II since I was a student,' Wollington said. 'It's the combination of military
strategist, wizard, spiritual visionary and the puzzle of his
disappearance. I was an impressionable youth, always looking for heroes, probably because I was so patently unheroic
myself – anything to get out of Hendon, you see. Suburbia is
a great motivator. I suppose that's why I joined the army, but
you can blame Luxor, the ancient city of the Pharaohs, for
making me into an Egyptologist – seems like centuries ago
now.'

His evident intelligence endeared him to me even further. I wondered if I could trust him.

As if he read my hesitation, he lowered his voice. 'I heard
about your wife, Mr Warnock. Archaeology is a small community. My deepest condolences – Isabella's death is a great
loss. I met her at a conference once. She was a lovely woman,
passionate about her subject. So many of us are fossilised old

sticks – I mean, reassembling shards of ancient pottery can make one rather introspective . . .'

Smiling, I glanced at the sarcophagus. The desire to take out the astrarium and place it next to the hieroglyphs was almost unbearable. I turned back to Hugh Wollington, teetering on the edge of confession. I needed his expertise desperately, and he seemed to have respected Isabella. In that second, I made a leap of faith.

'If I told you I have with me an artefact that might be Pharaonic, would you examine it for me?' My words spilled out recklessly.

He drew back, startled. 'You do realise possession of such an object could be illegal?' He looked at me searchingly. Momentarily, I wavered; worried that I'd just made a disastrous mistake.

'I realise I'm taking a huge risk trusting you,' I said. Then I lowered my voice. 'My wife found the artefact just before she drowned.'

Hugh Wollington glanced at the rucksack. 'Please, come this way.'

He led me into a vast hall and towards the colossal granite head of Amenhotep III. The beatific expression of the young Pharaoh was somewhat ruined by the fact that he was missing most of his chin and the royal false beard that was an indication of his deity-like status. Had the false beard been hacked off by early Christians in an attack on the old pagan icons? Or had the rough handling of irreverent English sailors destroyed it during transportation on some nineteenth-century sailing ship? Either way the young Pharaoh now suffered the indignity of gazing into infinity while missing half his face. Taking me by the elbow, Hugh Wollington guided me around the statue.

There was a discreet door set into the wall behind it.

As we stepped through, the lofty ambience of the museum gave way to the civil service's atmosphere of musty neglect. Here was the private face of the institution, a labyrinth in which historians made fetishes of their particular domain – Greek, Roman, Celtic – absorbed in their individual worlds, like fishermen throwing out their nets and painstakingly hauling in each forgotten clue. Several small offices led off the passage and some cell-like rooms were visible through glass windows, their occupants bent over lamplit desks, busily categorising and assembling new exhibits, restoring the old, casting moulds from the broken – an ants' colony of activity.

We arrived at a door painted hospital green and embellished with a small brass plaque bearing the legend H. W. Wollington.

'The W stands for Winston, in case you're wondering. My mother was a huge Churchill fan,' Wollington remarked cheerfully as he pulled out from a waistcoat pocket a key attached to a chain. 'Welcome to the inner sanctum – beyond the yellow brick road.' He ushered me in.

The strong odour of preserving fluids assaulted my nose immediately. I recognised the smell from the laboratories that Isabella had taken me to: acids to eat away layers of calcification, along with desalination chemicals. I moved towards the desk by the window and glanced outside. Then, carefully reaching into the backpack, I drew out the elaborately wrapped package. Slowly I unpacked the astrarium, then placed it on the desk where it sat glinting under the lamplight. Wollington inhaled sharply – almost in wonder – then sighed.

'Fascinating.' Holding up a magnifying glass, he bent over the device. 'The first thing I notice are the cartouches – the royal insignia.' He pointed at two lines of hieroglyphs one above the other, both enclosed by rounded borders – a little like long imprints of seals. One, I noticed, contained the hieroglyph of the royal falcon. Wollington continued eagerly. 'The distinctive ostrich-feather motif suggests the astrarium belonged to Nectanebo II. The second cartouche, which theoretically would have been that of the original owner, is that of Ramses III. See here, the heiroglyphs reading "Use-maat-re mery Amu". *Re is powerful in truth, beloved of Amun, Ramses, ruler of Heliopolis.* Of course, adding a cartouche is common practice in the attempt to make fake antiquities look authentic. Two cartouches is over-egging the cake, so to speak. But back to the device itself: a mechanical ephemeris to navigate destiny might be a good way of defining this artefact. Although, in truth, the existence in Pharaonic time of a sophisticated object such as an astrarium is highly unlikely. Egyptian astrology was considered a sacred science to be kept out of the hands of the uninitiated, which means that most of what we know of it today is only surmised – educated guesses based on the belief systems of contemporary cultures. Unfortunately, we have no other points of reference.'

'So I'm discovering when it comes to my own ability to suspend disbelief,' I joked.

'Easier for some than for others; it really depends on your own spirituality. But you must remember that Nectanebo II believed absolutely in his own mystical powers, as did his followers. In fact, in his own time and in the generations to come, he was considered one of the greatest sorcerers and astrologers ever to have existed. Of course, his mysterious disappearance only added fuel to the myth. Some say he still lives to this day.'

I was a little shocked to see not a trace of irony on Wollington's face now.

He smiled as if to reassure me, and continued: 'If the myth of immortality is to be believed, that is. It is extraordinary what lengths humanity will go to in the search for eternal life. There was a huge export industry in mummies between the twelfth and seventeenth centuries – Europeans believed that drinking a concoction containing powdered mummy would make them live longer. It proved such a profitable export that the Egyptians resorted to sending over far more recent desiccated corpses.' Wollington smiled ghoulishly. 'Even now, American tourists spend large amounts of money bribing tomb guards to allow them to sleep overnight in the pyramids in the belief that this might extend their lives. An astrarium like this, a machine that could control one's destiny, might also have been assumed to confer immortality – such an idea would certainly have seemed reasonable in Ancient Egypt.'

I sensed a change in his attitude towards me – a definite coolness underpinned by something else: a concealed arrogance. Now I was almost starting to suspect that he might be concealing his real personality under an assumed eccentricity.

'I have heard of the existence of the astrarium before,' Wollington went on. 'It has become something of a holy grail amongst certain archaeologists, not only for your wife.'

He walked over to a filing cabinet and after rummaging around finally pulled out a facsimile document. 'This letter, dated 1799, was sent from Alexandria by Sonnini de Manoncour to Napoleon. It details how although he failed to find the Ramses/Nectanebo skybox, he had the good fortune to find a section of an inscribed stone tablet which he was convinced was of great religious and magical value. As you can see, the letter was bequeathed to the British Museum by the Coptic Egyptologist and mystic Ahmos Khafre.'

I realised this had to be a copy of the very letter that

Isabella had seen all those years ago in Goa. Fascinated, I tried to make out the ornate archaic French script, but Hugh Wollington all too quickly put it back into the cabinet.

'So Ahmos Khafre was reputable?' I asked, trying to sound casually interested.

'As an Egyptologist, his reputation was impeccable. As for his other beliefs, I'm not one to pass judgement. But the letter has been proved authentic.'

'How did the museum get hold of it?'

'Khafre bequeathed all his possessions and writings to us – some were more useful than others. Interestingly, he told the museum exactly when to expect them.' He paused, perhaps for effect. 'He predicted the date of his own death, you see – to the hour. Amazing.'

I frowned, as much because of the smug glee in Wollington's voice as the actual morbidity of the matter.

Wollington pulled on white cotton gloves and lifted the astrarium to examine the underside. 'It's always amusing to see how these fakes work.'

I was startled back to reality. 'Fake?'

'Yes. I'm sorry to tell you this is probably a forgery – possibly seventeenth century. Most likely constructed for an alchemist as part of his collection of tricks to convince prospective clients. Any object that could be associated with Nectanebo II, the great Egyptian magician Pharaoh, would be marvellous for setting the scene.'

I stared at him. I knew he was lying. The question was why.

'I tell you, I was there when my wife excavated it from the sea floor.' It was hard to disguise my anger at Wollington's superciliousness. Through the glass partition I could see other museum officials looking up from their desks at the sharpness in my tone.

'I'm sorry to disappoint you. I didn't say it wasn't an *expensive* forgery. Besides, as I said before, it is ridiculous to think that something of the Pharaonic period, and as complex as this, would be in such pristine condition.'

His tone of voice had become distinctly patronising, and only served to convince me further that the artefact was genuine. So he wanted the astrarium as well. But why the clumsy attempt at deception? Even if he managed to persuade me of its worthlessness, surely he couldn't believe I'd leave it with him?

'As a geophysicist, I can tell you such preservation is rare but not unheard of,' I said. 'Sometimes the mud on the ocean floor is so dense that oxygen can't permeate it. It also appears that the mechanism might have originally been preserved in oil, which would have created a watertight seal.'

'Mr Warnock, you are clutching at straws,' Wollington said, his smile a grimace. 'Naturally I understand you are upset, given the circumstances of its discovery.'

His earlier wry humour appeared extremely disingenuous now, a fake benevolence designed to both make me trust him and lower my guard. Instead, a steely and thinly disguised aggression now ran under his voice and I noticed that his whole body had tensed up as if he were preparing to fight. I moved back behind the chair, my mind switching to an animal instinct, the prey preparing to run from the hunter.

'Well, if it's a worthless fake, I'll just take it home,' I said in a deliberately casual manner, stretching out my hand to take the artefact. Unexpectedly, his own hand shot out and closed around my wrist. I yanked it back but Wollington was surprisingly agile for a man of his bulk.

'Actually, as I warned you earlier, there are protocols to be observed, even for fakes.'

Wollington's whole tone had changed and I caught a

glimpse of the soldier beneath the academic – a quiet but palpable violence. I felt momentarily intimidated and my anxiety mounted. For a moment we struggled. Then, just as quickly, he reverted to a neutral friendliness, releasing my arm.

'Look, it won't take long. If you don't mind waiting here?'

He smiled, an open, reassuring smile now. Reluctantly, I sat down. Perhaps I was being paranoid. I watched through the glass partition as he entered the adjoining office and approached an officious-looking colleague. They exchanged a few words, then looked at the partition. Their gazes didn't connect with mine and I guessed it must be one-way glass. They appeared to be arguing. The older man reached for the phone but Wollington grabbed his arm, preventing him from picking up the receiver.

Wollington's shirt sleeve rode up, revealing a tattoo. Then, just as quickly, he gestured and the tattoo disappeared. Although it was hard to be sure from that distance I thought I recognised the distinctive shape of a Ba, a tattoo similar to Isabella's. The unexpected congruence of images hit me with a jolt.

The sound of a door slamming nearby galvanised me into action. I put the astrarium back into my rucksack and left the office as fast as I could without attracting attention.

The museum's entrance hall was milling with tourists. I stood at the foot of the broad marble stairs. On the far side of the hall I noticed a museum official scanning the crowd. I ducked behind a pillar. Just then a lift door opened and five security guards, serious in their intent, stepped out. At the orders of their superior they separated and began pushing their way through the tourists and museum visitors. I could see they were looking for someone. I glanced around wildly;

nearby a heavily pregnant young mother with a small child was struggling with a stroller. The child had just begun bawling. Lowering my head I made my way across and offered to help. Without waiting for a reply I soothed the child, strapped her into the stroller and escorted both mother and child towards the exit. Pushing the stroller, I walked right past the guards as I smiled and chatted to the thankful woman – we must have looked like the epitome of a young family. No one gave me even a second glance. But as we walked past the reception desk a phone rang. A young girl answered, then looked over in my direction. Mustering all my acting abilities I ignored her. I must have been a foot from the revolving glass doors when she called the guards over. Without a word, I handed the stroller back to the mother and exited as fast as I could without panicking. Outside I broke into a run, flagged down a taxi and jumped inside.

As the cab swung around the corner I caught sight of the security guards racing out of the building. I ducked down in my seat.

20

That night I lay in bed torn between exhaustion and the fear of having another nightmare about Isabella. My body was rigid with tension. Eyes wide open, I watched the shadows on the ceiling. It was impossible to relax. I'd bolted the front door and actually pushed a cupboard against it but it had felt like a ridiculous attempt to keep out the inevitable raid I was expecting. Surely Hugh Wollington could trace me to the apartment if he really wanted to. Suddenly an unearthly howl sounded outside. I jumped, terrified, steeling myself for some supernatural visitation. The howl was followed by a low growling and a miaow – cats fornicating. Relieved, I laughed at myself, then glanced at the alarm clock. I was amazed to see it was already five in the morning. Abandoning the bed, I decided to distract myself. I needed to find out if Isabella had left any clues amongst her London papers. Knowing how extensive her research had been, I was hoping she might have jotted down some notes indicating to whom and where the astrarium belonged, if found. I couldn't carry the device around for ever. I needed to get rid of it as soon as possible. While I was reaching up to a top shelf for a box file, a book became dislodged from a lower shelf and fell onto the carpet. It was a collection of English poetry. As I picked it up, an inscription on the inside cover caught my eye: *For Isabella – all my love, Enrico Silvio, Oxford 1970.*

Slipped between the pages was an old black-and-white photograph. A group of people stood poised in front of an archaeological dig, a strange formality to the composition as if they were members of a travelling group or club. In the front row, crouching down and smiling into the camera, was a very young Isabella. Her hand rested on the knee of the woman seated behind her – Amelia Lynhurst. To my surprise Amelia had once been quite attractive. Seated next to her was Giovanni Brambilla, Isabella's grandfather – I recognised him from the family photographs. He wore a safari suit and an embroidered fez, and looked authoritarian even in his eighties, his deep-set eyes and heavy eyebrows scowling at the camera. Standing behind him was an effeminate-looking man with long hair who stood in profile – a younger Hermes Hemiedes. On his other side stood a strangely familiar figure, a man in his late thirties with a mop of unruly hair and a piercing gaze. He wore a British army uniform and the facial features stood out immediately despite the unfamiliar framing of hair – Hugh Wollington. So he had known Isabella, but not from some conference. I paused. I felt somehow like a voyeur, reaching back into Isabella's past, more so here, surrounded by the objects she'd lived with. I glanced up. The room was beginning to fill with the bluish light of dawn. Again, the unsettling feeling that I was being directed, that I was only part of a puzzle, the shape of which remained obscure. I shivered, filled with a sense of foreboding. I'd escaped the threat in Egypt, or at least I thought I had, but now, after the incident at the museum and while I stared down at the photograph of Hugh Wollington's face, the net felt as if it was once more closing in.

On the back of the photograph were inscribed the words:

Behbeit el-Hagar, 1965.
The ceremony of innocence is drowned;
The best lack all conviction, while the worst
Are full of passionate intensity.

The lines of poetry resonated. I glanced at the book in which the photograph had been hidden – was there any connection? I searched through it and found the three lines in Yeats's poem 'The Second Coming':

Turning and turning in the widening gyre
The falcon cannot hear the falconer;
Things fall apart; the centre cannot hold;
Mere anarchy is loosed upon the world,
The blood-dimmed tide is loosed, and everywhere
The ceremony of innocence is drowned;
The best lack all conviction, while the worst
Are full of passionate intensity.
Surely some revelation is at hand;
Surely the Second Coming is at hand.
The Second Coming! Hardly are those words out
When a vast image out of Spiritus Mundi
Troubles my sight: somewhere in the sands of the desert
A shape with lion body and the head of a man,
A gaze blank and pitiless as the sun,
Is moving its slow thighs, while all about it
Reel shadows of the indignant desert birds.
The darkness drops again; but now I know
That twenty centuries of stony sleep

Were vexed to nightmare by a rocking cradle,
And what rough beast, its hour come round at last,
Slouches towards Bethlehem to be born?

What had the group been excavating? I remembered
Hermes telling me about Behbeit el-Hagar, an important
site in relation to the last days of the Pharaohs. Was it linked
to the astrarium in some way? And why had Hugh
Wollington lied to me?

I touched the inscription on the inside cover, the slight
indentation unfurling a whole scenario in my imagination.
An affair, lovemaking, that lay embedded in my wife's past,
secret, unshared; the shadowy figure of a man she'd never
told me about. Each new disclosure about Isabella's past
separated us further. How well had I really known her? Was
the woman I'd loved an artifice? A composite of all that I'd
wanted her to be rather than what she actually was? The
idea was too distressing to dwell on. I needed to believe in
us, in the authenticity of the marriage – there was little else
left.

I glanced back at the name, racking my memory. Enrico
Silvio. I'd never heard it before. I knew the Yeats poem was
about the end of Christianity – my mother had made me
memorise it as a child – but the imagery reverberated in different ways: the circling falcon that had lost its master, the
sphinx galvanised into a slow awakening by the possibility of
the end of the known world, the crowing of the desert birds
flying wildly around the blinking eyes of the colossus; it was
an allegory that felt uncomfortably relevant to my own dis-
integrating world.

I looked around the room, thinking. Isabella had a collection of old address books that she had never thrown
away. They had to be somewhere. I searched the room

several times. Eventually my gaze fell on a collection of old bags hanging from the back of the door. I went through each of them carefully. Finally I got lucky. It was the beaded shoulder bag I remembered her wearing when we were courting – I knew she'd had it since her student days. The inside smelled musty and the torn silk lining was stained with perfume, lipstick and crumbs of what I suspected might have been hashish. I turned the bag inside out. Slipped between the lining and the bag itself was an address book. I opened it; the handwriting – a simpler, more looped version of the script I'd known – made my heart lurch. I sat down and turned tentatively to the letter 'S'. It was just a hunch, an instinct I wasn't sure I wanted to play out. But there it was: 'ES' followed by an Oxford phone number.

I knew it was a long shot – the number must have been over five years old – but it was worth a gamble. I glanced at my watch – it was already nine in the morning and light now flooded the living room. I reached for the phone and dialled the number. It rang for ages. I was just about to give up when a woman answered: older, foreign. In a curt voice she told me that Enrico was currently in hospital but was due home later that day.

I gave her my name and number and asked her to tell him I was the widower of Isabella Brambilla. Widower. The word felt like a tragedy that had befallen someone else. The woman's voice tightened at the mention of Isabella's name, but perhaps I was imagining it.

I put down the receiver, wanting now to escape the history of my marriage, the claustrophobic flat, London itself and my growing sense of being watched.

Outside I heard the sudden noise of someone on the landing. I froze, ready for the pounding on my front door. I sat there calculating how long it would take for me to grab the astrarium and climb out onto the roof. A second later the steps continued down to the ground floor, followed by the slam of the front door – just my neighbour going to work. After my run-in with Hugh Wollington, I was finally completely convinced of the astrarium's value and authenticity. And there was no doubt that Hugh Wollington had shown an unhealthy interest in it, that he had played an odd game by pretending it was a fake. There was a violence about the man that worried me. Who knew what he might do next? I had to get out of London, I needed to assess my position and work out my next move. But the question was whether I had inadvertently drawn Gareth into this dangerous and possibly fatal web.

The ringing of the phone startled me.

'Hello?'

'Hi, Oliver. Gareth here . . . just checking in like I promised.'

My brother sounded totally exhausted, but I was relieved to hear his voice.

'How are you?' I asked, trying not to sound anxious. 'Have you been home yet?'

'Well, I am now. Did you get back to West Hampstead okay?'

'Kind of. Listen, Gareth, have you noticed anything strange – people following you, weird things like that?' Again, I attempted to sound calm and rational, although I was starting to wonder whether I wasn't just a touch paranoid.

'Just the usual groupies. Why, are you paying someone to spy on me?' he joked.

I didn't laugh. 'Just watch your back, okay?'

'*Jawohl*, Herr Kommandant.'

'And take care of yourself.' He knew I was referring to the drug abuse.

'Didn't I say I would?'

His voice was sullen now, hostile; I had to win his trust back.

'I'm going home later, to see Da. Any messages?'

'Yeah, tell him I'm not dying. Then the old bastard might get off my back.'

There was a click, then the dial tone. Gareth had put the phone down but the genetic thread between us was still there, vibrating like a lightly plucked guitar string.

That morning I left via the lane behind the building and walked to the tube station. I had decided it would be easier to lose a tail by immersing myself in the anonymity of King's Cross station and getting a train to go up north. After mingling in with the commuters, I caught a train to my father's village, the astrarium carefully stowed in my rucksack.

The station was exactly as I'd remembered it – the painted sign hanging over the platform, the wooden tubs of roses at each end. A familiar sight that made me relax instantly. The only new additions were a Cadbury's chocolate vending machine placed discreetly next to the ticket office and a brand-new telephone booth installed next to the toilets. Mr Wilcott, the stationmaster, whom I'd known all my life, stood at one end of the platform, a tall, hunched-over individual with a limp from a wound he'd received in the Second World War – a story he used to regale us schoolboys with. After whistling to signal the train's departure, he limped down the platform towards me.

'Oliver, is that you?'

'The one and same, Mr Wilcott.'

'I'm sorry about your wife, lad. I only met her the once but she were a lovely lass.'

The familiarity of his voice hauled me back into safer times, to the never-changing landscape of my childhood. As I listened to his thick northern accent and the small talk about nothing and everything, I suddenly realised how much I missed the unquestioning acceptance, the anchoring, of village life.

'Did Da tell you?' I asked.

'Oh aye, he were very upset, you know. He'll be glad to see you. With us long?'

'Just the night, I'm afraid.'

'Shame. Your da's been ever so lonely since your mother passed. Stay longer – surely it'll do you good to see a few old faces?'

'I'd like to but I can't afford the time.'

'In that case, I'll see you off tomorrow – the 10.45, is it?'

'Aye.'

I walked down the stairs and onto the street, the rucksack hoisted over my shoulder. I'd planned to walk to my father's house through the village – the same route I'd taken every day to and from school decades before. But now I didn't feel like meeting anyone else; I decided to cut through the small field that led onto the row of terraced houses where my father lived and where I'd lived until leaving for university at eighteen. My mother had died five years before and I realised that the last time I'd visited had been for her funeral. It was still difficult for me not to expect her to be waiting with my father at the door of the small red-brick terrace house.

The meadow was filled with buttercups and daisies whose tiny stems bent with each gust of wind coming off the

Fens. There was the faint smell of cow manure and the tang of wet peat. This had been one of the places where I'd done my dreaming as a child, staring up at the sky and imagining each cloud was a magic carpet on which I could escape – to exotic places, to new faces and landscapes. I stood, breathing in deeply, strongly tempted to lie down in the grass in the hope that time would reel back and I'd stand up as a ten-year-old. Cleanly. Innocently. Instead, I hoisted the astrarium back over my shoulder and kept walking.

My father stood waiting at the door of the small terrace house, his frame, once angular and impressive in its height, buckled with gravity, like an ancient tree. It was a shock seeing him so aged, and instinctively I found myself looking for the small frail figure of my mother.

The house was part of an estate built for miners in the 1920s – a harsh grid of narrow streets and small, terraced, architecturally monotonous red-brick dwellings. The rail-way line ran behind the terrace where my father lived, and alongside it stood a neat patchwork of allotment gardens. The one that belonged to my father was filled with mar-rows, tomatoes, strawberries and the occasional rose bush. This small oblong of territory was his pride and joy. It was where he'd disappear to for hours after church on Sundays. It was also a place that we, his sons, were excluded from. Even now it was impossible to look at the allotment without feel-ing resentful.

The house had two bedrooms upstairs, and downstairs there were a front room with a fireplace and a kitchen at the back. There was an outside toilet at the end of the concrete yard; no bathroom, no place to wash except for the kitchen sink. When I was a child we'd bathed in front of the fire in an old tin bath every Sunday night. Da first, then my mother,

then myself, and finally Gareth. I would watch my father
from the other side of the fireplace, his long skinny back
mottled with the blue-black of coal dust, the mystery of his
cock and balls a swinging shadow as he gingerly folded himself into the short tub. This rebirth of his, this transformation
from black-faced Cyclops with the miner's lamp on his forehead to mere mortal was my first memory. I must have been
about one at the time, and it both fascinated and appalled
me. I too wanted to go down into the earth, but I didn't want
it to poison me.

In the early 1960s, at the end of my first year as a successful consultant, I'd offered to pay for an extension to
house a bathroom. My father had been furious. 'I'll not take
charity from me own son,' he'd told my mother. It had been
a year until he'd agreed to talk to me again. But that was my
father – as proud and truculent as the landscape he'd grown
up in.

'I thought you'd come in one of your fancy cars,' he
barked awkwardly from the door. I noticed he was clutching
a walking stick, his huge bluish knuckles knotted over the
wood. He was also wearing a woman's cardigan, the top pearl
button fastened tight, the pale pink wool stretched over his
vest. I didn't dare ask where it was from.

'I took the train,' I said. 'The car's still garaged – I haven't
had a chance to collect it since I got back.'

My father stared at me, his deep-set eyes searching my
face. His skin was hollowed under the cheekbones, the wrinkles a topography of disappointment and anger. Today,
though, the eyes were kind.

'I've had tea on the table for over an hour,' he said. 'But I
can put the kettle on again.'

'That'll be nice.'

Without shaking hands, we both entered the house.

Later that night, we sat in the tiny front room watching an episode of *The Benny Hill Show* – one of my father's few indulgences – on the small black-and-white television I'd bought my parents five Christmases before, mainly to entertain my then-invalided mother. The silence between us was deafening. I'd often suspected this had been one of the many reasons I'd married Isabella – her voice had always run like a stream over my own impenetrable silences. In four hours my father still hadn't mentioned her death. We'd talked about Gareth's health, the weather, the latest disputes the miners' union was having with management, Harold Wilson, Enoch Powell, the failing train services and the state of my father's meticulously maintained allotment. We circled around the subject of my wife's drowning like crows over a recently ploughed field.

The Benny Hill Show finished with the rotund comedian chasing a buxom pigtailed blonde across the screen and my father, who still believed that using the television wore it out, got up to switch it off. On the way back to his armchair, he opened the sideboard drawer where he'd always kept a tin of sherbet lemons. Pulling it out with a rattle, he offered me one.

'So how's Gareth really?' he said.

'Surviving.'

'Well, that's a comfort. How's that musical group of his?'

'I saw them play. They were good, Da. You wouldn't have recognised him. I asked him to stay with me – he refused, but he promised to ring in every day. I think he'll pull through; it's a stage he's going through.'

There was a silence in which I supposed my father was trying to imagine the scene. Then, abruptly, he said, 'I've never said this, but I appreciate you looking out for him. He were always his mother's son, coming so late in the marriage, like. I know that now. Words don't come easily between us, not like me and you . . .'

I smiled, inwardly saddened that my father's perception of our communication could be so different from my own.

'But he's close to you,' he went on. 'You'll take care of him, you know, when . . .'

'Aye, you'll have no worries there, Da.'

We both sucked noisily on our sherbet lemons. The fire spat a sudden ember.

'In case you're wondering, the cardigan was your mother's,' he said. 'Silly, really, but wearing it comforts me. I suppose it still smells of her.'

'You don't have to explain.'

'But I do.'

He leaned across and poked at the few burning coals in the fireplace, as if he were too embarrassed to look at me.

'What's happened is unnatural, son. Isabella were a young girl, she weren't meant to die like that. Promise me you'll not end up rattling about like your old da, not knowing whether it's Sunday or Thursday. Worse still, not caring. It's no way for a man to live.'

My father sat back in his armchair, as if exhausted by the effort of uttering so many words at once. I was shocked into silence. I couldn't remember him ever speaking so intimately to me and it was hard to equate this new vulnerability to the great mythical cliff of a man I'd worshipped as a child.

'She was very fond of you, you know that, don't you, Da?'

'Aye.' He sighed, a long and hollow sound that seemed to contain all the injustices of the world and, worse, his beaten-down resignation to them. He coughed, as if to change the subject, and sat forward. 'You know, I decided to finish that little project your mother started just before she died. You remember how she'd begun to research her family tree – the Irish side?'

'Oh aye.' Hypnotised by the flickering flames of the fire, my lids felt heavy, my many sleepless nights catching up with me. I wrenched open my eyes with some effort.

Sitting there listening to my father ramble on I suddenly remembered a conversation I'd had with Isabella a few years before, after she'd seen me at work on an oilfield in Italy, in the southern Apennines. Her face alight with passion, she'd called me a diviner, told me I had a gift and that I was wasting it. Her conviction had disturbed me. Was it a reaction to my mother's blind, passive faith that had frustrated me so much as a child, or had I been unconsciously frightened of something else? In any case, Isabella must have seen it as yet another occasion when I'd trivialised her beliefs. Little surprise that she'd chosen to confide in Gareth and not myself. Why had I always avoided the issue of her mysticism – was it because I sensed something about my own inherent abilities?

My father had lapsed into another long silence and I could feel the old sense of suffocation and ennui rising up in me; the same restlessness that had propelled me out of the village as a teenager. I didn't belong then, and I knew I didn't belong now. Secretly thankful that I was leaving in the morning, I wished the old man goodnight.

I was sleeping in the second bedroom, Gareth's room once I'd left home. It seemed to be still waiting for a thirteen-year-old boy, with its ancient *Beano* comics, the dusty model aeroplanes hanging from the lamp, a Boy Scouts' flag pinned over the mantelpiece. Mixed in with these were remnants of adolescence – a poster of the band Queen, on the side table an old copy of *Rolling Stone* magazine with

Marc Bolan glaring out from the cover. Sitting on the desk, still in the rucksack, was the astrarium – my talisman of Egypt.

Pulling back the sheets, I squeezed into the single bed.

21

The next morning I tried to ring my brother at the squat. I woke Dennis who informed me that he'd only seen Gareth for a couple of hours in the past two days. This wasn't comforting.

The train back to London was strangely empty. I'd sat in the second-class carriage near the sliding train doors. I was prepared to leap out at the nearest station, but I found myself nodding off, lulled by the rhythm of the train as it rushed through the luxuriantly green English countryside. I would fall asleep then wake with a jolt when the train pulled into a station. I forced myself to sit upright, back stiff against the seat, determined to stay viligant – only to fall asleep again as the wheels rushed over the rails, creating a sound like the roar of a distant sea.

The third time I woke there was a man sitting opposite. Dressed in tracksuit bottoms and an ill-matched zip-up jacket there was something decidedly odd about him. Tall, in his early forties, he had prematurely silver hair and a strangely expressionless face. He appeared to be staring at the rucksack I held on my lap, the rucksack that contained the astrarium. As I tried to work out how long it would take me to bolt to the exit, his gaze shifted to my face, a blank aggressive stare that did not waver. I was just about to get up when he reached down to the floor and picked up a white stick – the kind that the visually impaired use. Ashamed of my paranoia I turned back to the window and the landscape rushing past, trying to still my pounding heart.

An hour later we drew into King's Cross Station. I was amazed to see that the platform was hung with Union Jacks and signs announcing the Queen's Silver Jubilee. Now I understood why the train had been empty. I'd forgotten that it was the seventh of June. By the time I got back to my flat, London was in full celebration. The road was blocked off and the cul-de-sac itself had been transformed. My neighbours must have organised the street party when I was in Egypt.

In the centre of the street, under a canopy, stood a long table covered with cakes, sandwiches, jellies and other manifestations of English home cooking. Small stalls selling a range of souvenirs flanked the display. There were china mugs printed with pictures of the royal family, teacups and saucers with the Queen's face smiling up from the bottom, Silver Jubilee spoons, butter knives, postage stamps and souvenir programmes.

A reggae band playing Bob Marley's 'No Woman No Cry' stood at one end of the street, while at the other end an amateur string quartet played Elgar. Banners strung overhead proclaimed the twenty-five years of the Queen's reign, and Union Jack flags hung out of various windows, fluttering like garish laundry. Neighbours, friends and families milled excitedly around the tables.

Several food stalls were set up along the kerb, one of them selling West Indian cuisine – fried plantains, curried goat and rice – while another offered Indian curries and samosas. A third stall advertised English pork sausages, pickled eggs and jellied eels. The air was filled with a dissonance of smells – curry, hot chips, incense and the occasional whiff of burning toffee.

Two Rastafarians with waist-length dreadlocks chatted to a middle-aged couple dressed as a cockney pearly king and queen, their button-covered jackets shimmering in the sunshine. There was a buxom brunette dressed as Britannia sitting on a throne, sceptre in hand, as several drunken husbands posed to have their photograph taken with her. One old man had dressed his rather plump white British bulldog in a tailored Union Jack jacket.

Families danced together on the tarmac, waltzing to the violins or bopping to the reggae band. Children darted among the intoxicated adults, chasing each other and screeching with excitement. There was something gloriously pagan and uplifting about the whole event and, for a moment, I allowed myself to forget the ordeals of the past two months. Grabbing a sandwich, I half-danced and half-pushed my way towards my front door, almost unrecognisable under the streamers and balloons adorning it. Just then Raj grabbed my shoulder.

'Oliver, there is a man who is looking for you. He has come twice to the house already. Tell me, my friend, are you in some kind of trouble?'

I spun around, scanning the crowd wildly. There was no sign of Hugh Wollington, but it was hard to see anyone over the dancers' heads.

'Is he here?' I ventured, trying not to panic.

'I cannot see him now, but I think so.' Raj looked up at me, clearly worried. Without bothering to explain, I began to make my way towards a clearing in the crowd and an empty side street beyond, pushing past revellers.

Just then I felt a tug on my jacket. Stanley stared up at me solemnly. Then, putting two fingers into his mouth, he gave an ear-splitting whistle. I tried to break free but the child would not let go. Meanwhile Alfred ran towards us from the other side of the road, followed by a thin older man, Mediterranean in appearance.

Holding my arm firmly, Stanley's eyes narrowed accusingly. 'It's an Italian gentleman. He's looking for yer. Probably 'cause he knows you murdered Issy.' His fist tightened around the sleeve of my jacket.

I crouched down so that I was at eye level with the eight-year-old. 'Stanley, Isabella died in a very sad accident—' I started, but was interrupted by a hand on my shoulder.

'Mr Warnock?'

The stranger stood in front of me, awkwardly holding out his hand for me to shake – to the amazement of the watching twins who were obviously expecting some kind of citizen's arrest. The man's face was heavy in the jowls and his mouth had a sensual fullness. He looked like an ageing voluptuary. I guessed he was in his late fifties, but his skin tone was an unhealthy grey and, on closer inspection, his face was etched with a web of fine lines, as if he'd recently suffered some great tragedy.

'My name is Professor Enrico Silvio,' he said in an Italian accent. 'I was your wife's tutor at Lady Margaret Hall, Oxford.'

I closed the window and the sound of the steel drums and bass guitar outside diminished. Professor Silvio stood scanning the living room as if trying to glean the history of my marriage from the surrounding furniture and photographs. Sensing my gaze, he swung back to me.

'It was kind of you to invite me into your apartment, Mr Warnock. I'm sorry if I startled you.'

'It was I who called you initially,' I replied carefully. I wouldn't make the mistake I'd made with Hugh Wollington twice, but the professor's face was so honest and he seemed so frail that I didn't think it would be dangerous to ask him upstairs for a conversation.

'And here I am.' His broad features gleamed with a resigned amusement.

'Besides, if you were going to rob or attack me you would have done it by now,' I added quickly.

'Attack you? Why should I attack you? Are you a man with many enemies?'

'I seem to have acquired a few lately,' I said wryly. 'Hence trying to escape just now. I'm sorry if I've offended you. I didn't know your intentions. I work in the oil business. Isabella's world is sometimes quite alien to me, alien and bewildering.'

'I can imagine.' Silvio sighed and fragility shone out again through the drained, pale skin. 'I've always wondered what type of man Isabella might have married.' He moved to a side table and picked up a framed photograph of her. 'I thought maybe an artist, or some kind of left-wing revolutionary, but never a businessman. She was looking for a zealot, I was convinced of it.' He put the photograph back on the table.

'It sounds as if you knew her well,' I said.

My statement seemed to agitate him. He began to move around the room restlessly.

'I'm dying, Mr Warnock.' There was a brief pause. Then, as if he were making a confession, he went on. 'One of the benefits of confronting one's mortality is a sudden appreciation of the brevity of life. I have no time left for subtlety or nuance. As a dying man I must speak directly.'

'You and Isabella had an affair?' It was just a speculation, but I was amazed at how angry I felt at the thought.

A twitch ran like quicksilver over one cheek. Silvio paused, remembrance clouding his eyes.

'Yes, we were lovers, but to call it an affair would be to trivialise our relationship.' He dropped his head in his hands, then swept his fingers through his hair: the habitual gesture of a once-handsome man. 'You must understand that I am not proud of how I was at that time of my life. I was ambitious, but I had traded too long on the originality of the thesis that had made me famous. Isabella was remarkably lateral in her thinking, even at that age. Her cultural perspective gave her a unique angle on archaeology. For her it was a living subject; it was in her blood. She came to me with the story of this remarkable device she was going to base her doctorate on. She trusted me, but I betrayed her. Yet you have to believe that I loved her.'

He paused again, as if wanting my permission to continue. I waved my hand – a small conciliatory gesture implying an emotion I didn't feel.

'What do you know about her thesis and the "device" she was researching?'

I simply looked at him, not wanting to commit to anything. But he didn't need any encouragement.

'I told Isabella that her thesis sounded too improbable, and that if she continued with this subject she would risk not being taken seriously. I genuinely wanted to protect her, but I wasn't entirely honest.' He sighed. 'I had come across some evidence of the astrarium myself, many years before. While researching in the Louvre, I discovered a small stone naos – a boxlike shrine – that dated from the late Thirtieth Dynasty and had been found at Hierakonpolis. It was covered in hieroglyphs that no one had yet translated. It appeared to be a prayer to Isis asking for her blessing for a skybox that was to be given to Nectanebo II. It was a skybox that could write your destiny and shift mountains and the naos makes reference to the skybox's prediction of Nectanebo's own death date. We don't know what he did in response – tried to destroy the astrarium? Used the prediction for his own advantage? I believed the device Isabella was researching might have been the skybox referred to.'

Despite myself, I inhaled sharply. Yet more evidence of the astrarium's power. 'Quite possibly,' I replied carefully, trying to hide my feelings. I wanted Silvio to continue talking without revealing too much myself. 'Isabella herself had several pieces of research referring to the astrarium as a skybox – though I don't understand why she maintained it was Ptolemaic when in fact it was far older.'

'She might have told you that, but trust me, Isabella had a strong sense of how old the astrarium might actually be. It was around this time that she started having nightmares.'

I remembered Cecilia's description of Isabella's involvement in some of Giovanni's bizarre experiments. 'You know about the dream?'

'I do, and I can't tell you how much I grew to hate her grandfather, a man I never even met. There is some dark history there.'

I sank into a chair, defeated by the knowledge that, again, Isabella had been unable to confide in me, that others had known so much more.

Professor Silvio sighed. 'I made Isabella my research assistant, and then I seduced her. At first it was a calculated move, but then, to my great horror, I fell in love. I promise you that part of the story was not calculated—'

'You appropriated her work and published it yourself?' I interrupted.

I didn't want to hear about the affair. His confession felt like a transgression into a past that Isabella had kept secret –

a decision I felt I should respect regardless of my own emotions.

But he was not to be swayed. 'I even thought of leaving my wife for her,' he went on.

Resigned to having to listen to Silvio unburdening himself, I helped myself to a whisky. He spoke about an angrier, younger Isabella, an Isabella I had glimpsed on occasion but certainly not known.

'She embodied everything I had once aspired to – she was gifted, disciplined, she didn't care about the professional protocols, the stratagems of academia that had castrated me. Being with her broke all the rules that had crippled me over the years, all of them.'

'You stole her work?' I repeated, wanting him to at least acknowledge his treachery.

'She was a young woman and a foreigner. I didn't think the academy would take her seriously. At least, that was my excuse to myself. I didn't appropriate all of it – just a few bits here and there. She never forgave me.'

'So is that why you're here – for absolution? The confession of a dying man?'

'No. I need to see it with my own eyes, I need to know it exists.'

'See what?' I played dumb but I had no intention of showing him the astrarium.

'Please don't be disingenuous, Mr Warnock.' Silvio smiled indulgently. 'Two days ago I received a phone call from the British Museum. After a somewhat heated exchange I told Mr Wollington that I couldn't help him with his inquiries. A day later I swear I was followed in my car. Wollington has some unsavoury allies. For a few years he worked for Prince Majeed, a rather unpleasant individual with a penchant for torture and an unfortunate fascination with ancient artefacts that have theoretically occult attributes. Let me put it this way: hugely ambitious, Majeed would believe in the power of such a device and he would go to any lengths to obtain it. I suspect you have the astrarium. And, if that is the case, you are indeed correct that you have acquired some dangerous and powerful enemies. Let me help you.'

Still unwilling to give anything away, I couldn't help but ask. 'How?'

'You know the astrarium is missing its other half, the object that will make it spring into life. Perhaps if I show you this I will convince you of my sincerity.'

He reached into his jacket pocket and pulled out an object about four inches in length, packaged in tissue. He unwrapped it to reveal a fork-like object with a finely cast stem of iron-like metal. It reminded me of a tuning fork. It had an animal carved at one end and two long prongs at the other. I took it from him and examined the animal: it was a falcon with a tiny human face – the minute head of a Pharaoh.

'It is the Was. The key,' the professor said, watching my face carefully. 'But the portrait isn't of Nectanebo II, this is Ramses III. One of the many pharaohs associated with the Exodus. And engraved on the device there should be two cartouches: Ramses's, and Nectanebo's cartouche carefully stamped below it.'

I struggled to contain my excitement. All the archaeological pieces were suddenly beginning to fit together to give the astrarium its history. The desire to snatch the key away from the professor was almost overwhelming. Sensing my emotional turmoil, Silvio moved slightly away from me.

'Oliver, it's vital you understand what the key actually means. The falcon at the tip symbolises the Ba of the Pharaoh, his soul-bird. You see, the astrarium wasn't only designed to protect the Pharaoh's living destiny; it would also protect his spirit in the afterworld.'

Would it have protected Isabella's Ba too, I wondered. Then I felt surprise that I'd even considered such a far-fetched notion.

'How did you find it?' I asked the professor.

'I stole it.' The brief tug of connection snapped and I almost dropped the Was.

'You stole it?' I echoed.

'From a colleague – an English archaeologist who taught for a semester at my college. She was someone whom Isabella greatly admired.' Silvio bowed his head as if waiting for me to strike.

'Amelia Lynhurst?'

'It is not something I am proud of.' He sighed, his expression full of shame. But it was impossible to excuse the ambition of his younger self. He would have destroyed Isabella if he'd felt that he had to, and that was unforgivable.

'And how did Amelia come by the key?'

'On a dig some years before. She'd never made the find public.'

'Was the dig at Behbeit el-Hagar?' I asked, remembering the younger Amelia in the group photograph I'd found in Isabella's poetry book. The professor nodded, looking impressed.

'So at last the mosaic is beginning to make sense, Mr Warnock.'

'But why there?'

'Behbeit el-Hagar is the birthplace of Nectanebo II – another piece of the mosaic.'

'Did Isabella know you had the key?'

Silvio looked at me, his face drained of colour. 'It is the most appalling thing I have ever done. It was after she'd left me – I thought I could use it to bribe her to come back, but she had already met you.' He paused. 'It is guilt that brings me here. Without the key, the astrarium is nothing. I should have given it to her.'

He sank into a chair and buried his face in his hands, his scalp glimmering palely through his thinning hair. He looked completely defeated and it was almost hard not to pity him. But even without pity, the fact was that I needed him now. This was a crucial moment in my search and he held the key – quite literally – for me to move forward. I could see no other way to get him to produce the Was. I reached for the rucksack.

'Wonderful! It is so sublime in its design. I can barely bring myself to touch it. Do you understand what this means for the three great religions? This instrument was most likely held by Moses thousands of years ago – a Jewish, Christian and Islamic prophet. It was used in one of the great turning points of biblical history – the parting of the Red Sea. It is a living miracle. I can't actually believe I am seeing with my own eyes.' Professor Silvio's face was flooded with a kind of religious ecstasy I recognised from watching my mother when I'd been a child. It was the blind surrender of the faithful, an illuminous transportation into the spiritual that had always made me uneasy.

'We don't know that for sure.' Despite my own pounding excitement I was determined to stay grounded.

He ran his shaking hands lightly across the top of the mechanism. 'I never thought I would live to see it.' He leaned closer. 'You see these three discs?'

I nodded, anticipation clawing at my throat. The astrarium had begun to disturb me, and now, with the key about to activate the mechanism, its power over me felt even stronger.

The professor's trembling fingers caressed the edges of the cogs. 'These dials served to calculate the orbits of not just the Moon and Sun but also the five planets known in those times – Mars, Mercury, Venus, Jupiter and Saturn. Those calculations were used to decide the most auspicious dates for religious festivals as well as for divining purposes. This is where the astrarium becomes an instrument of war. Quite possibly the astronomical calculations were made by the mythical magus Hermes Trismegistus (thrice great) who, in some accounts, was possibly a great physician and contemporary of Moses if those accounts are to be believed. But what are even more extraordinary are these symbols here. They are the Sumerian-inspired cuneiform characters of the Akkadians, a race that pre-dates the Egyptians but who were famous for their magic and astrology. The Ancient Egyptians called upon their craft also.'

Silvio peered down the shaft that formed the pivot for the cogs. 'And, at last the gateway to power, the keyhole itself.'

The Was slipped effortlessly into the slot. We both stood there for a moment, suspended in awe. I was gripped with both fear and excitement, part of me waiting for the outcome of the cipher to manifest itself – for the astrarium to activate or emit a tone perhaps, the singing that Gareth's translation of the cipher had referred to. But there was no movement and no noise. Then, almost involuntarily, I reached my hand towards the key.

The professor's bony fingers locked around my wrist. 'No! Don't turn it until you have heard what I have to say.'

I stepped back from the table. Night had descended and the music outside was punctuated by the distant explosions of fireworks as the Jubilee celebrations reached their climax. There was a smell of fecundity in the air – the aroma of summer that had always made me so restless as a younger man, the sense that something exciting was happening elsewhere and I was compelled to go out and find it, whatever the risk.

I glanced back at the professor. The shadows under his eyes had deepened and his skin looked even greyer, as if he had aged even more in the last few hours.

'I have stomach cancer,' he said, 'an advanced case. I have about two, three months, they don't know exactly. Funny, the Ancients thought the stomach was the seat of all emotion. Perhaps they were right; perhaps I am dying because I have denied my emotions for so long.'

'The facts, professor,' I said coolly, resisting his obvious plea for compassion. 'Something the geophysicist in me can understand.'

'The facts? You have that wonderfully English capacity to make everything sound so dry.'

Silvio pointed to the three hands, each one longer than the preceding one, that rotated across the three dials, like the hands of a clock. 'These mark three time periods – the Ancient Egyptian equivalent of day, month, year. If my translation is right, the hands are currently set at what I believe to be the date of the Battle of Actium.'

'So the astrarium did belong to Cleopatra?'

'From fragments of magical scrolls and reportage in grimoires that existed in the Mouseion, the great library of Alexandria, we know that the astrarium re-emerged three significant times in antiquity. Its construction in the Twentieth Dynasty when it was built for Ramses III. It was then stolen from Ramses's court by Moses himself, who used it to divide the Red Sea. It then reappears in the Thirtieth Dynasty after the Isis priestess Banafrit found it hidden in an Isis temple in the very desert where Moses and his people dwelled for fourteen years. She brings it back to the Egyptian court for her pharaoh Nectanebo. It then disappears for a few hundred years, although its legend grows and scrolls are written advertising its great powers, until Cleopatra, who is then rumoured to have taken it to sea during the battle of Actium. But look here.' Silvio leaned over the instrument. 'If you turn the key, two smaller hands will appear – one made of gold, the birth-year hand; the other made of black silver, the death-year hand.'

'The death-year hand?' I repeated incredulously.

'If you enter your birth date into the machine, it will cal-culate your death date.'

I took a deep breath. So that was what Isabella had wanted to do: try to change her death date.

'But there is more to this instrument. It can bend time and events to serve your desires – actual and unacknowl-edged – fame, fortune, even self-destruction. That makes it very powerful but also very dangerous. Because, let's be honest, how many of us know what we really want? One could describe it as a Faustian device, bringing a judgement of its own.' Silvio smiled, half fearfully, half reverently.

I couldn't believe that a device that was thousands of years old could have saved my wife's life, never mind alter the outcome of events. Despite my scepticism I was fasci-nated. It had to be a metaphor – an object of wish-fulfilment that thousands had imbued with their belief over centuries, and thus made powerful in its own way.

'I'm not a religious man, Professor Silvio. I believe in the Big Bang, evolution and free markets. This device is an enigma, that's obvious. For a start, parts of it are made of an alloy I've never seen before. Then there're the two magnets at its core – they're unusually powerful. Rotating magnetic fields have interesting properties, but affecting destinies? Come on. Besides, if all you've said about this machine is true, then you'd be the first to turn the key – after all, it'd stop your disease in its tracks.' I challenged him, hoping he would call his own bluff.

The academic smiled sadly. 'Indeed it would, but I am not afraid of dying. I am a devout Catholic: God has chosen this path for me and I must follow it. Besides, I suspect there is a twist in the astrarium's promise, a sting in the scorpion's tail.'

'How do you mean?'

'Why do you think the key was separated from the machine before the battle of Actium? I believe Cleopatra was entirely aware, and perhaps afraid, of the astrarium's magical powers. With one turn of the key, she could have influenced the outcome of the battle to her advantage – but she chose not to. The pivotal question is: why?'

I stared at the astrarium sitting there on the table, the soft lamplight picking out the various hues of the metal. Again, I was struck by the sense that the machine appeared to be observing me as I examined it. As I leaned down for closer scrutiny Professor Silvio pulled the key out of the mechanism. He handed it to me, looking at me sternly.

'The key should never be turned. You understand, Oliver?'

I nodded, still not entirely convinced. But staring at his hagged visage now illuminated by the desk lamp, it suddenly occurred to me that he was acting out of love, love for Isabella. Despite my initial doubts, I found myself trusting him.

'And promise me you will hide it somewhere safe – not here in this apartment.' The professor gripped my hands.

'Do not underestimate Hugh Wollington. He has powerful alliances – he is closely linked to Prince Majeed and the Egyptian authorities – and he is ambitious. Watch yourself, Oliver.'

22

The next morning, I picked up my car from where it was garaged near the flat and drove over to Lambeth. I found myself checking the mirror constantly to see whether I was being followed, wondering if Wollington had traced my vehicle. If he knew that Silvio had come to see me, he might suspect that I now held the key – at the very least he'd know that I had all the information I needed. I tried to convince myself it was a combination of exhaustion and stress, but by the time I reached Waterloo my nerves were shot.

Behind the station was a Turkish bathhouse and gymnasium that I'd frequented since my student days. Situated in a small seventeenth-century building sandwiched between two office blocks, the baths had originally been established to service gentlemen of leisure. I suspected they were now used for more clandestine encounters too, but chose to ignore the undercurrent of homosexual flirtation that occasionally drifted through the clouds of steam.

The gym had the most basic of equipment – two bench presses, free weights and a couple of exercise bicycles. A signed photograph of the English boxer Henry Cooper hung on one wall. There was also a steam room, a dry sauna and a large tiled area with plunge pools. I usually worked out, then spent some time in the steam room before immersing myself in the cold plunge pool. It was a brutal regime but one I had become addicted to – it was one of the few ways I could clear my mind of the obsessive analysis that was an integral part of my personality and my job.

But today I was there with an entirely different motive. I knew I couldn't carry the astrarium around for much longer, especially now that the Was had surfaced. I owned a permanent locker in the baths, virtually impossible to find among the other lockers unless you knew the number. The perfect hiding place. I hurried up the narrow stairs, the astrarium in a small bag tucked under my arm. There were several men in various stages of undress in the locker room. A huge West Indian gentleman, his black skin gleaming with droplets of water, was towelling his great shiny back, the rolls of flesh rippling down to his waist. Two young cab drivers, just off the night shift, were exchanging anecdotes about dodgy customers in thick East End accents, while a sullen-looking adolescent in a pair of grubby Y-fronts sat in the corner reading a martial arts magazine that had Bruce Lee glaring out from the cover. They barely looked at me as I unlocked my battered steel locker.

Just then a young Arab entered; lean and muscular, he scanned the room aggressively as if searching for someone. A shudder of fear ran through me and I ducked immediately behind the open door of my locker, hiding my face. I waited a moment before peering over the top. To my relief, the young Arab, having established his territory, was now sitting on the bench. He began stripping his clothes off. I waited until he'd swaggered off in his bathers before placing the astrarium deep inside my locker.

Throwing several layers of gym clothes on top of it, I fastened the lock, stripped and then headed to the steam room.

I settled myself on a bench and stared at the pinewood panelling, thinking over the past few days. The moisture in the steamy air condensed and ran down my forehead. I let my thoughts free-fall and in the drifting steam a vague recollection took shape. It was about seven months ago, just before we were due to leave for Egypt. Isabella had received a letter earlier that day and I'd found her sitting at her desk staring at the scrawled Arabic. She'd looked tense. Worried that it was bad news, I'd asked if it was from Ashraf, who wrote regularly. Frowning, she told me that it was an invitation to a conference from a society of archaeologists she used to belong to and that it had surprised her – she hadn't been involved with them for years. Trying to lighten the atmosphere, I'd joked, asking if it was some kind of coven. To my surprise, Isabella had lost her temper and left the room. Now I wondered whether it had anything to do with the photograph taken at Behbeit el-Hagar. A couple of months after she'd received the invitation she'd gone to a conference in Luxor. Was that the same conference Hugh Wollington had mentioned? My mind wandered to the Egyptologist and our unfortunate meeting. Was he out there, tracking my movements? Would he be waiting for me when I got home? Uneasiness mingled with fear, dark shadows fluttering though my mind, each more threatening than the other. Suddenly I felt a hand on my shoulder. It was the sullen adolescent, his acne-marked face leaning over me.

'The guv'nor told me to tell you there was a bloke looking for you before, at reception, a nasty piece of work, a foreigner. We didn't let him in, though. You being a regular and all,' he said gravely. 'Guv'nor told me to tell you to watch your back. People die in weird places nowadays.'

As I swung the car into my street, I saw Dennis sitting on the doorstep of my building. He was dressed in an old pinstriped suit beneath which the cuffs of pyjamas were visible. Wondering how he'd got hold of my address, I steeled myself for bad news before pulling up in front of the house.

'Something's happened—' I started, but his grim expression cut me off in mid-sentence. All my anxieties about my brother's self-destructiveness shot through me.

'We've been trying to ring you for ages. We didn't know where to look for you. It's Gareth.'

'Has he overdosed?'

'It was an accident . . .'

'No.' The possibility of his death made me reel. Dennis grabbed me by the arm. 'Oliver, Gareth's still alive. He's in a coma, at the Royal Free. Zoë's with him . . .'

Before he'd even finished his sentence I was back in the car.

My first impulse on seeing Gareth lying there so unnaturally still was to tear the tubes from his body, lift him out of the bed and run with him out of the hospital, to whisk him back to my father's house and tuck him under the hand-stitched quilt. To return him magically to the boy I used to read to; mapping out his future with story books filled with adventure. But I couldn't. Gareth had done this to himself, had pushed the life out of his own body until there was almost nothing left but a papery shell.

As I watched, tremors ran under his eyelids, as if he were scanning the horizon of an interior world inaccessible to anyone else. I pulled my gaze away from the clear plastic tube that ran from his wrist up into a drip, terror of further loss rising up in me like bile.

'I knew he'd done too much, and then he wanted a bath – I should have stopped him.' Zoë rocked herself in a chair beside the bed. She looked at me, her face drawn thin around her eyes. 'We had to break the door down.'

I took Gareth's hand. It was cold. I barely noticed the doctor entering the room. He glanced with disapproval at Zoë's unbrushed hair, miniskirt and fishnet stockings, then turned to me.

'You're the brother?' he asked brusquely.

I nodded.

'He's been in a coma for over five hours, I'm afraid. It's too early to tell what the outcome will be.' He waved the chart in his hand. 'The blood tests indicated high amounts of both amphetamine and cocaine. The combined effect plus the heat of the bath most likely caused the seizure. Frankly it's a miracle he didn't drown.'

On the other side of the bed a heart monitor blipped regularly. The guilt of not forcing Gareth to come and stay with me, of not watching him all the time, washed over me. I knew I wouldn't survive the death of somebody else I loved, not now. I wished then that I believed in God, in any kind of afterlife. Dread threatened to overwhelm me. To combat it, I focused on Gareth's appearance; on how ridiculously young he looked without all the fashionable paraphernalia and eye make-up – like the boy I'd known. Someone, a nurse probably, had combed down his hair into an even parting. Gareth would have hated that.

'Will he live?' I asked. 'Is his brain damaged?'

The doctor hesitated. 'It's too early to say. But I must tell you that his brain was without oxygen for quite a few minutes – we don't know how many – and the longer he remains in a coma the worse the prognosis. We must hope he regains consciousness soon.'

I stood up, towering over him. 'For God's sake – is there nothing you can do?'

The doctor stepped back nervously. 'Mr Warnock, you should prepare yourself for the possibility that Gareth may already be virtually brain-dead. We just don't know yet.'

Incredulous, I looked at my brother's prostrate figure. 'Brain-dead?'

'The next twelve hours are crucial.'

Having escaped the oppressive atmosphere of the ward I stood dazed at the entrance of the hospital, watching the rest of the world bustle along in sickening normalcy. The daughters helping their elderly mothers through the glass doors, the pregnant women clutching overnight bags, the ambulances pulling up at the side entrance. Zoë stood next to me. Sighing, she lit up a cigarette.

'Hampstead Heath is nearby – we could take a walk,' she ventured. 'Doesn't have to be for long, but it might help?'

I nodded blankly.

It was late afternoon by now. Pollen smudged the light as dandelion puffs floated through the air like tiny parachutists intent on flight. We walked from South End Green up towards the Hampstead ponds. Above us, a corridor of chestnut trees waved majestically. The heady scent of lilac conjured memories from my youth: of Gareth as a boy playing cricket on the green, of us fishing illegally in the village pond, of taking him out for his first drink down at the local pub. And I was filled with irrational anger – at my brother for his utter disregard for his own life, for the people who loved him; and at the rest of the world that kept on functioning, seemingly indifferent.

Zoë and I walked in silence; words seemed superfluous. She stopped, her settling foot breaking a twig. There was a fine film of sweat on her upper lip and the sunlight illuminated her skin as if she was lit from within; I imagined all the blood corpuscles, her unmarked youth, racing under its surface in an abundance of hope and health. And, despite my fear and anger, I found that I suddenly wanted her.

As if she knew, she reached up to kiss me. I responded, then, filled with chagrin, broke away from her.

She smiled at my mortification. 'It's okay, you know.'

'No, it's not – you're my brother's girlfriend.'

'We haven't got that kind of relationship. Gareth would understand.'

'I don't.'

We'd reached a clearing, a hidden sunlit circle set away from the path, and I threw myself down on the grass. I couldn't help feeling I had betrayed Isabella by desiring someone else. But then I realised I was angry with her too; angry that she'd withheld so much of herself from me – her past, the real nature of her work. I stared up, Zoë beside me. The tree branches above us formed a swaying tent of dark green and lime, of blue and the burning globe of the sun.

'Want a cigarette?' Zoë asked.

'No, thanks, I've given up.'

'Thought you might have.' She lit up, exhaling against the sky. 'Tell me, what's that bird that follows you around?'

Shocked, I sat up. 'What bird?'

'C'mon, you know what I'm talking about – it's like a small hawk. I saw it that night at the gig, just about here . . .' She waved her hand around my shoulder.

'There is no bird.'

'There is, but if you don't want to admit it, that's fine. Is it something to do with Isabella?'

Amazed, I stared at her. 'There is no bird,' I repeated.

'If that's what you want to believe.' Zoë blew smoke into the silvery air. 'Gareth will live, won't he?'

Her question pulled me sharply back into the moment. 'I don't know.' I closed my eyes again, the sun a dancing red dervish against my eyelids.

'I wish there was a way of turning back time,' Zoë said. 'I used to fantasise about that, you know, when my father died. There's the minute before and the minute after. If only it was possible to undo events – or at least to manipulate the outcome. But we can't. We just stumble on, thinking we're in control, until we're confronted with our own death.'

Her words seemed to drift like the pollen in the air. But as she talked on an idea began to manifest in my mind; crazy, irrational but persistent. What if Enrico Silvio's theory about the astrarium were true? If I turned the key, would I influence my brother's destiny? An absurd thought, but, as hard as the rationalist in me argued, I couldn't repress the idea that at least it would be like rolling the dice.

'What if you could manipulate destiny?' I found myself saying out loud.

Zoë turned. 'What do you mean?'

'What if a person's death date is the result of a combination of circumstances – a belief that you're fated to die on that day, which leads to a subconscious vulnerability as you abandon the precautions you usually take instinctively? And what if there's a way of changing that date?'

'I suppose it might be possible,' she answered cautiously.

The urge to get to the astrarium was overwhelming. I leaped up and reached into my pocket for two five-pound notes.

'Here,' I said, handing them to Zoë, 'this is the cab fare

back to the squat. Get some sleep. I'll go back to Gareth,' I lied.

She stared at me, her green eyes questioning.

By the time I reached the Turkish baths it was almost six o'clock. The locker room was full of day workers finishing their evening workouts – amateur bodybuilders, city businessmen looking for a way to unwind. I went straight to my locker and collected the astrarium, abandoning all vigilance.

I ran up the stairs to my flat without looking right or left, thinking only of Gareth. Once inside, I hurriedly unpacked the astrarium and set it on the kitchen table, the key beside it. I felt as if it was coaxing me, calling me in some insidious way. I took the key between my trembling fingers and studied the mechanism.

In the oilfields I had witnessed the potential of belief; it amazed me how many oilmen were susceptible to superstition. I'd even known geophysicists who performed their own special rituals before the final test to separate the oil from the porous rock cuttings – the test that would decide whether they'd hit black gold or not. Men with IQs of well over 150 would cross themselves, kiss a good-luck charm, rub a lucky talisman, before leaning over the UV box to watch whether the dripping perchloroethylene would change the colour of the sandstone chips from milky white to shimmering blue. The more spectacular the hue, the better the quality of oil detected – many described it as the colour of heaven. Was I succumbing to the same irrationality? Despite my inherent scepticism I could feel my own belief system changing, shifting into the realms of the extraordinary. Was this sheer desperation, the overwhelming drive to help my brother survive? There was no time for analysis; I knew I had to act, not think.

Despite Professor Silvio's tutelage, I barely recognised the hieroglyphs on the astrarium, and the Babylonian numbers were completely incomprehensible. I searched the shelves for a reference book that I'd seen Isabella use in her translation work. It contained a graph correlating the Ancient Egyptian calendar with the Christian calendar, with a projection forward that Isabella had boasted was accurate to the day.

I calculated the day, month and year of Gareth's birth according to the ancient calendar then turned on the lamp and directed its beam onto the astrarium's dials. The tiny etched symbols danced under the bright light. Holding my breath, I turned the outer dial so that the marker was aligned with my brother's zodiac sign: the two twisting fish, Pisces. Then I turned the other dials to the corresponding year, month and day of his birth. To my mortification, I found myself muttering the Lord's Prayer and my hand was trembling as I lifted the Was.

I inserted it into the machine and turned it.

I waited. Nothing had happened. Scepticism swept through me; I teetered between disappointment and vindication as the scientist fought the romantic. I couldn't believe I'd let myself be swayed by the power of a mere legend. Then, just as I was about to give up, a faint ticking sounded somewhere within the ancient jumble of cogs. I stood up and stepped away from the machine, amazed and nervous. It was hard not to feel some reverence for the ancient device. I bent down to listen. It was extraordinary, but as I strained my ears the ticking became stronger and stronger. Images of previous owners flashed into my mind: Moses bent over the small bronze instrument as he stood before a churning sea, Nectanebo II dressed in his ceremonial robes, the Pharaonic headdress tilting forward as he too listened apprehensively for the clicking of the mechanism, Cleopatra, her hair streaming behind her, in the bow of a battleship. Disbelief, panic and awe collided in a medley of emotion. What had I set in motion?

Bronze teeth clicked over one another as the cogs moved. As Professor Silvio had predicted, the death-date pointer slid into view: it was blackened silver and tipped with a miniature sculpture of a doglike creature with a forked tail and long hooked snout, like the elongated nose of an anteater.

The death-date pointer ticked past the tiny dashes that marked the decades and arrived at the year 2042 AD. The astrarium had given its verdict. Gareth would live until the age of ninety-five. I exhaled slowly. I'd actually turned the key, invested belief in this ancient tangle of dials and dates. Isabella's desperation suddenly seemed easier to understand than before. I sat back and waited . . . for what? The telephone to ring? For my brother, resurrected, to walk through the door? But at least I had acted. It was a consoling thought.

On the street below, a group of revellers from the nearby pub strolled past. Their conversation was reassuringly pedestrian: one man complained about his sister-in-law, another boasted about his football team's prowess – normal life, twentieth-century realities. Yet here I was, gambling with arcane sorcery, a desperate man resorting to desperate measures.

A slight whirring sound, almost imperceptible, interrupted my thoughts. I bent my head to listen, then peered inside the astrarium. The two magnets were now spinning, revolving around each other at a speed that amazed me. The heartbeat of the machine appeared to have been activated.

I remembered the spinning stones that Isabella had shown me in the dream. If Professor Silvio was right then she had wanted to set the machine in motion to postpone her own death. It should have been Isabella who turned the key all those weeks ago, and perhaps our own lives would have spun on untouched, seamless, innocent.

'If not Isabella, then Gareth, please,' I prayed. I couldn't remember the last time I'd made such an entreaty. And to whom?

23

It was after hours, but the night nurse had taken pity on me and allowed me into the ward provided I didn't wander into any other area of the hospital. I sat by the bed watching the shadowy angles of Gareth's face under the dim night-light. In his unconsciousness the softness of boyhood eclipsed the sharpness of age. I'd been sitting beside his thin, motionless body for over an hour. The astrarium, packed in its rucksack, was on the floor beside me.

Gareth's breathing reverberated through the room like some distant sea breaking on an invisible shore. My mind wandered back over the past few weeks and fastened on Isabella that last night, her face bent over her research, her expression one of apprehension. Her frantic search for a way to cheat death. I reached down and laid my hand on the rucksack, the shape of the astrarium pressing up between my fingers.

I thought of the promise that I'd made to my father. If Gareth died, I would have failed both my father and my brother, in the same way I'd failed Isabella. Was I inherently incapable of protecting the people I loved? The minutes

ticked by as I sat there, gripped by fear and guilt, with the
device at my feet. Suddenly something made the hair on my
arms prickle. I had the sudden and disturbing sensation that
I was being watched. Glancing up at the frosted-glass window
set in the door of the ward, I saw the blurry shadow of a large
man outside. Terrified, I watched as the bulk moved, then
turned left and right. Leaping up, I bolted across the floor,
then stopped and spun around to kick the bag so that it slid
underneath the bed. When I whipped the door open the corridor was empty. The night nurse, her long thin face pasty in
the subdued light, came out of the back room. 'Are you all
right, Mr Warnock?' Her Scottish voice was reedy, and for a
moment I imagined it was also disingenuous.

'Did you see anyone a moment ago, just there by the
door?'

The night nurse smiled patronisingly. 'Not a soul. That's
the danger of the night shift, Mr Warnock – the imagination
is always a little overactive.' I glanced back down the pea-
green corridor – nothing but a couple of empty trolleys and
an abandoned wheelchair. Perhaps I had been imagining
things – but the figure had seemed too real and my sense of
being observed lingered on. I went back into the ward.

No longer able to bear the sound of Gareth's regular
breathing – a deception when he seemed so far away from
life – I took the backpack, retreated to the waiting room and
sat in the dim light, barely aware of the television flickering
on the opposite wall.

A voice from the TV mentioned Egypt and I looked up.
The country was rarely out of the news these days but I was
glad of the distraction. The programme was a late current
affairs one hosted by the left-wing presenter Robin Day,
a man who always reminded me of the armchair socialists
I'd known as a student, annoying in their middle-class

prophesying. Muted, the debate appeared to be in full flight – with much gesturing. To my amazement I recognized Rachel Stern sitting at the end of the panel. I put the sound up – the four panelists were arguing about the situation in the Middle East; a debate that seemed to pivot around the Yom Kippur War of 1973 and its impact on Egyptian–Israeli relations. I recognized the Egyptian ambassador; the other two panelists appeared to be academics. Then Rachel Stern spoke up: 'The situation has some hope – President Sadat is in dialogue, I believe.' The familiarity of her voice flooded through the waiting room. Fleetingly, I had the impression that my life was folding in on itself, youth and adulthood smashing up against each other as if time had become irrelevant.

Robin Day interjected: 'Sadat is making noises that suggest some appeasement towards America. Do you think there might be a peace agreement with Israel itself?'

'I believe he'll make some very unexpected moves in the next couple of months towards that goal,' Rachel said. She radiated a brittle intelligence. 'You have to remember that Sadat wants to push Egypt into the world marketplace. He wants trade and stability. There have been hunger riots in the past twelve months, and there are internal pressures arising from the shift from Nasser's socialism to Sadat's economic policies – this hasn't been an easy transition. Another element to consider is that President Carter wants to make his mark on the Middle East and Sadat has his ear. Of course, there are potentially disruptive factors in the scenario – Colonel Gaddafi in Libya, who has just ordered all Egyptians working in Libya to leave the country by July the first or face arrest; the President of Iraq, Saddam Hussein; President Assad of Syria; and various wild cards. Prince Majeed, for example, has a huge amount invested in disrupting such an alliance. For years there have been rumours that he would like to destabilise Sadat's Egypt and fulfil his own ambitions of taking Egypt back to a feudal state with himself at the head. He has some rather flimsy claim to the old ruling dynasty.'

'Indeed, and we're lucky enough to have some rare footage of the prince . . .'

The screen cut to shaky black-and-white footage of a group of men in battle fatigues on a barren hillside. At their centre was King Faisal of Saudi Arabia, distinctive in his traditional dress, with a bearded young man by his side – Prince Majeed. Another man, obviously belonging to the prince's camp, stood on one side. Tall and swarthy, he looked familiar, startling me out of my trance. I pulled my chair nearer, trying to make out more features in the grainy footage. Suddenly, in a sickening rush of adrenalin, it came back to me. It was the man I'd seen in the car talking to Omar. His menacing persona radiated out of the screen across time and space, and it was hard not to feel pulled back into the threat of Egypt. I stared at the television, wondering about the connection. Had this man hired Omar to be on the boat that day? How much did Majeed know about Isabella's research and the astrarium? Were they behind Barry's death? I shivered in the darkened waiting room, desperately trying to connect all the disparate pieces of information into something I could understand. One thing was certain: everything led back to me.

A hand was suddenly placed over the camera lens and the screen went black. Robin Day appeared again, but I didn't have a chance to hear his comment on the footage. The night nurse rushed into the room.

'Your brother's regained consciousness, Mr Warnock.'

Gareth was still lying flat in his bed but now his face was turned to one side, staring out through the hospital window to the black sky beyond. I was terrified that he might have woken mentally impaired, his mind broken.

'Gareth? It's Oliver.'

'So I'm back on the planet?'

His voice was little more than a whisper. A great wave of emotion rattled through my body and, losing all inhibition, I finally cried – for Isabella, for Barry, for the lost innocence of my marriage.

Gareth, aghast at seeing me so undone, clutched my hand.

Incredulous at the speed of my brother's recovery, the doctors nonetheless reassured me that Gareth's brain patterns appeared normal. At four-thirty in the morning, in the narrow pea-green hospital corridor that smelled of disinfectant, I slipped coins into a payphone and rang the squat. Zoë answered. I told her the news and left her weeping with relief.

As I put the receiver down I glanced along the passage. There was no one except a hospital cleaner pushing a mop across the tiled floor.

Before I went home, I drove to Primrose Hill and climbed to the top. The sunrise that morning was the most inspiring I'd ever witnessed: a huge crimson sphere ascending over London; the streaking clouds catching coral, blue, mauve. Up there I had a sense of absolute power. I felt as though I could dictate who woke and who slept on in the city. It was intoxicating, as if I lived above and beyond the lives spread out before me. Was this how Nectanebo felt? That he had control over people's lives and deaths – a living god? And what of Moses himself, as he stood before the towering walls of water? Was it possible?

I arrived at the flat exhilarated but exhausted. I collapsed onto the couch. On the table next to me, the answering machine blinked. I pressed the button and Johannes Du Voor's voice boomed into the room, demanding that I meet him at the Ritz at ten – a nasty reminder that I was still on the payroll. I hadn't known the South African was in London, but that was typical of Du Voor – he was always showing up at the most inopportune moments. I checked my watch: I had an hour to get there.

Built in 1910, the Ritz was one of those last bastions of old-fashioned service in London. During my first years in the job, as a working-class northerner, I'd always felt distinctly uncomfortable in the large and luxurious arched reception hall with its huge crystal chandeliers and marble pedestals, as if the hotel staff could sense that I was an impostor. But, after studying my clients, I soon learned to adopt the nuances of class, how to at least feign a relaxed indifference, accepting it as natural to be served and waited upon. The CEO of GeoConsultancy, my employer – Johannes Du Voor – was under the impression that such venues still made me uneasy, which was exactly why he insisted on meeting me at the Ritz every time he visited London. It gave me a psychological edge to maintain his illusion. What he didn't know was that over the years I'd stayed at the hotel for the occasional retreat – with and without Isabella.

Johannes shifted uncomfortably, his vast bulk squeezed into the Louis XVI chair, dwarfing the table with its linen cloth, silver tea set and delicate china. He lifted his cup to his lips, then put it down in disgust.

'Jesus, weak as bloody piss. You'd think that here of all bloody places they'd get the tea right. That's the trouble with the English – arrogant and complacent. You should be care-ful – I sometimes feel the same about your bloody hunches.'

'What does it matter if I get the results?'

A waiter holding a tray of scones had hesitated at the sound of Johannes's booming voice. I beckoned him over.

'Have a scone,' I told my boss. 'You know that eating calms you down.'

'Fuck you, Oliver. If you weren't a recent widower, and the best geophysicist I know, I'd have fired you yesterday. My condolences, by the way.'

Johannes's huge paw of a hand swept several scones off the tray and onto his plate.

'Thank you, and thanks too for the wreath.'

'Proteas. Bloody difficult to find in Egypt. I wept, you know, when I heard about Isabella. She was a great girl, strong, fierce, bloody gorgeous – too good for you.'

I watched him pile a huge spoonful of clotted cream onto the scones, followed by a large blob of strawberry jam. There was a rumour at GeoConsultancy that Johannes had become so fat he no longer fitted into a first-class seat and was now looking to buy a private jet with custom-built furniture.

'Why are we here?' I asked him. 'I thought I'd made it clear I was taking a few weeks off.'

'Does it look like we're working?' A rivulet of jam travelled down his chin. Undeterred, he continued to demolish the scones. 'For example, this last job – I looked at the geology, the maps, the seismic but could see nothing at that depth. And yet you insisted on drilling.'

'You're wrong. There *was* something. The data was clear to me.'

'Maybe to you, but to nobody else. You're becoming a real wildcatter, Oliver, reading signs the rest of us just don't bloody see. Even the Dutch are beginning to think you're a mystic. You've begun to rely too much on your gut and not enough on the science.'

'I disagree.'

I knew I didn't sound convincing. Johannes continued his tirade, oblivious to my self-doubt.

'I'll give you another example – that job in Nigeria you were calculating. You sent through the depth and size of the reservoir before the survey was even completed. Explain that!'

'That was just a mix-up in the post. You received my calculations before you received the survey results. You're just confused.'

'Oliver, you telexed your calculations.'

I fell silent. Johannes was right: I had sent in my approximations of the depth and size of the reservoir before the survey had been completed. It wasn't hubris on my part; it was I who'd got the dates confused.

'Look, I'm not complaining,' he went on. 'How can I? You're the best there is. And right now I'm looking down the barrel of a gun and in need of a few miracles myself . . .' He pressed a hand to his chest.

I'd heard rumours Johannes was ill but this was the first time he'd actually mentioned it.

'Heart?' I guessed.

'The good news is that, despite what the ex-wives say, I do actually have one. The bad news is that it's more than a little tricky. So I need a fuck-up on my watch like I need a hole in my head. Oliver, when you get it wrong I'm the one responsible; and the way you're going, you'll get it spectacularly wrong one day – it's inevitable.'

'Is it?'

I didn't want to explain myself. And, as I reflected on all the explorations I'd initiated, I knew I didn't have the language to describe that moment when speculation transmuted into certainty – a gut sense that began as a small knot in my stomach, then flowed through my fingers and feet as I literally felt the hidden folds and ripples of the earth beneath me.

Johannes peered at me, searching my face. It was as if he was looking for some glimmer of understanding – of illumination, something to hope for. I'd never seen him so vulnerable before – it was unnerving: all his confidence had collapsed into a bewildered perplexity.

'How do you do it, Oliver? C'mon, rattle the bars of this old sceptic's cage. Because I'm staring into the void, my friend, and I need something to believe in. Throw the old sinner a bone.'

It was one of those confronting moments when someone I had held at a distance had stepped across the boundary with a genuine need for help – Johannes wanted me to turn him into a believer. But I couldn't answer him. There simply wasn't enough trust between us; or at least that was what I told myself at the time. The truth was, I didn't want to expose myself to what I thought could be ridicule.

'So you want me to be more orthodox in my methodology?' I asked.

A fleeting expression of crushed expectation ran across Johannes's features before he slipped back into his characteristic aggressiveness.

'Do I?' He buttered another scone. 'I suppose I do, yes. I suppose we're all asking for explanations and the nice neat rational ones are the easiest to sell. And, after all, that's what I am, Oliver, isn't it? A salesman who's running out of time. And now you're taking a bloody month off. But in case you're thinking of doing something stupid, remember I have you under contract for at least another year.'

Bill Anderson's warning came back to me: that Johannes was paranoid that I might break away and start my own company. Wasn't it obvious I just needed some time out? A police car screeched past, heading down Piccadilly – another IRA bomb scare, I couldn't help thinking.

'Oliver?' The South African's nasal tones drew me back to the point.

'Johannes, I'm not going anywhere, I promise.'

'Good, but we need you back in Egypt within two weeks – that's the best I can do. Maybe I should get you a decent shrink who specialises in bereavement – you look like shit. Two weeks. No-show after that and you're fired.'

'I'm coping,' I said. 'Isabella left some loose ends and they're a little preoccupying.' A classic English understatement that hung in the air a bit little longer than I'd anticipated.

'Yeah? Well, I just hope it isn't the kind of loose end that's going to upset the Egyptian government. You know how much time, effort and diplomacy it took to set up that relationship, not to mention the money. Destroy that and I'll happily destroy *you*.'

Shifting uncomfortably, I tried to guess whether Bill Anderson had told Johannes about me smuggling an artefact into Britain. Keeping my expression neutral, I answered as innocently as I could: 'Now, why would I do anything like that?'

I stood and picked up my rucksack. Johannes stayed seated and I didn't bother shaking hands with him.

'Don't worry, I've got the bill,' he said, and reached for another scone.

'Have a good flight home, Johannes.'

As I walked away, I heard him bellowing at the waiter for some decent tea.

24

As I turned along my street a police car and an ambulance came into view. I slowed down, not sure whether I should continue driving. Raj's wife Aisha stood by the gate, talking to a policewoman who was scribbling diligently in a notepad. I could see Raj sitting in the back of the ambulance while an attendant wrapped a bandage around his arm. I pulled over quickly.

Aisha, looking tearful and pale, ran up to me as I got out of my car. 'Oliver, a shocking thing has happened. Thieves and no-gooders have desecrated your property! My Raj, he was a hero!'

'I was not a hero,' Raj yelled from the ambulance. 'I just behaved as a good citizen should. But, Oliver, what they have done! It is terrible!'

'What's happened?'

Before Raj could answer, a detective stepped up behind me. 'Mr Warnock?'

The front door of my apartment was ajar, several books and a camera case jammed between it and the door frame. Even from where I stood I could see the extent of the devastation. I hesitated at the doorway, a sense of violation flooding through me.

'We believe the break-in occurred around ten in the morning, sir. It was a professional job, no fingerprints, and they've taken some care to search the premises in an efficient but ruthless manner.'

The detective, in his late thirties, was coolly professional but I found the conciliatory tone of his voice instantly irritating. We stepped over a smashed photograph – Isabella in her wedding dress stared out of the cracked glass.

'Sorry about that, sir.' He picked up the photo. 'Your wife is recently deceased, isn't she?'

'She drowned in a diving accident, six weeks ago in Egypt.'

'That must be difficult. And now this, and you've only been back in the country . . . what, a few days, sir?'

'About a week.' I could hear myself sounding defensive.

We went through into the lounge. The curtains had been ripped from the windows, several pillows lay disembowelled, and the cover of the couch had been slashed, making the white stuffing protrude obscenely. Books had been tumbled from the shelves, an antique clock – the only thing I'd inherited from my grandfather – lay on its side, the wooden back torn from the casing. The invasion of privacy was nauseating. It felt like a kind of rape.

'We believe there was more than one intruder. It was a very thorough job. Your neighbour . . .' he glanced down at his notebook '. . . Mr Raj Ahuja tried to prevent the second man escaping over the back fence. He was kicked rather violently in the arm for his trouble. According to Mr Ahuja, the thief was brandishing a small handgun with a silencer attached. Mr Ahuja thinks he recognised the gun from a

James Bond film.' He smiled patronisingly. 'Interesting, that – the fact that it had a silencer. It would suggest that the intruders had more than theft on their minds.' He looked right at me. 'The odd thing is, sir, even if they have actually stolen anything, they've left behind a lot of objects of evident value, such as your telescope, sir, over there – interesting thing to own, a telescope – and your gold cufflinks on the dresser, and the television. It looks like they were after something specific. Any idea what that might have been?'

Instinctively, I shifted my shoulder so the bag holding the astrarium slipped further behind my back. I looked the plain-clothes officer squarely in the face.

'None at all. I don't even keep a safety box on the premises.'

'I see. Your neighbour told us you work in the oil business. Could they have been after something of corporate significance, information of some kind?'

'Anything like that – survey reports, maps and so on – are kept at my employer's offices. Like I said, there's nothing here of much value other than sentimental.'

'I know this is a distressing possibility, sir, but is there any reason someone might want to harm you?' the detective asked, lowering his voice as if it were an impolite question.

Who *wasn't* out to harm me seemed like a more accurate query. I fought the impulse to touch the bag slung over my shoulder to reassure myself that the astrarium was safe.

'No reason at all,' I said, keeping my gaze steady and direct.

'Then it's a real mystery,' he said, studying my expression.

'Indeed.'

His gaze travelled back to the photograph. 'An attractive woman, your wife. You must miss her very much.'

The police team left an hour later. I sat on an upturned wooden crate in the centre of the living room and stared at the scratched walls, the ripped posters, the torn curtains and cushions, and tried to imagine the fury of the intruders when they'd realised the astrarium wasn't there; how angry they must have been to destroy wantonly the objects around them and risk being caught. Somehow the violation seemed apt, as if they'd deliberately smashed this section of my life firmly into the past tense.

A knock came at the front door. I kicked aside a torn book and a pillow to open it. The twins looked up at me.

'We've got some information for yer,' Stanley declared in a whisper as Alfred scanned the empty hall behind them, as if looking for spies.

'Private information,' Alfred added, before slipping under my arm and into the flat.

They sat on the edge of the slashed couch, swinging their legs. Alfred, eyes wide, couldn't stop staring at the broken furniture now propped up against the wall. 'Mum said Isabella was taken by angels,' he said gravely.

'Underwater,' his brother added, failing to hide the suspicion in his voice, '"cept they don't 'ave angels underwater.'

'Mermaids, then,' Alfred contributed hopefully.

Stanley snorted. 'Alfred believes everything. I know better.'

'We loved Issy – she was an angel 'erself.'

'Shut up, Alfred.' Stanley swung back to me, shoulders hunched. 'This information, it'll cost yer,' he announced.

'What's the information about?' I asked, wondering why I was taking a couple of eight-year-olds so seriously.

Stanley's eyes grew to the size of saucers and his voice lowered to a croak. 'We saw them, didn't we, Alf?'

'Yeah, but we're not tellin' you till we get our price.' Alfred kicked his feet against the couch, triumphantly assertive.

'What's your price?' I asked.

'We want a piece of her,' Alfred pointed to the cracked wedding photograph, 'so we can remember.'

'Done,' I said. 'Now tell me what you saw.'

'There was two of 'em,' Stanley said. 'Big geezers with big ugly heads. We saw 'em come over the wall and past our bedroom window, isn't that right, Alf?'

'And we saw the getaway car outside,' Alfred elaborated. Then he nudged his brother excitedly.

'And that man who was driving, he was the ugliest of them all.'

'Yeah, he had these funny bits down the side of his head – like caterpillars, they were.'

'Ugly red caterpillars hanging upside down,' Stanley concluded helpfully.

The twins left, Alfred clutching a photograph of Isabella. Alone again, I slid down the wall and sat on the floor. If I really thought about it, it was a miracle that Hugh Wollington and his cohorts hadn't broken into the flat before. Trying to convince myself that I was being paranoid I'd felt nonetheless as if I was being hunted down slowly, systematically, as if my pursurers were always one step ahead of me. What did Wollington want with the astrarium? Fame? To claim he'd discovered the astrarium would give him an international reputation overnight. A feasible motivation, but I was more worried by the connection to Majeed that both Wollington and Silvio had mentioned. Was it possible that he was now linked to the sinister face I'd seen with Omar? I felt as if I was now really descending into paranoia, the sense of being squeezed between two factions all-consuming.

I glanced around. The room was a maelstrom of debris. I couldn't possibly spend the night here. Pulling the rucksack over to me I lifted out the astrarium – at least I'd kept that safe. I left it on the floor while I gathered some clothes to pack into the rucksack underneath it.

As I sorted through the chaos, I heard a small thud. I spun around. A metal cigarette lighter on the floor had fastened itself to the astrarium. I pulled it off, placed it back on the floor some distance from the mechanism, and watched it slide across the carpet to stick to the device's side again. The astrarium had become magnetised.

What could have activated the change? Me turning the key after thousands of years? I tried to apply a scientist's logic to the problem. The curious alloys – was there a way of analysing their components without damaging the device? I turned the question this way and that, racking my brains. The jumble of information seemed to mirror the tumult around me, bewildering, disorientating and overwhelming. I no longer knew what I believed in. Had Gareth's recovery been simple coincidence? Had Isabella died in vain?

Staring at the device I suddenly lost my temper, exhaustion and fear catching up with me. 'Damn you! If you have any kind of power, show me! Do your worst, you bloody heap of ancient tin!'

Trembling with frustration, I set the dials to my own birth date, grasped the key and turned it. Again the magnets began to whirl, the cogs clicking over each individual bronze tooth, crossing the centuries. Part of me was terrified that the death pointer would spring up; another part of me defiantly dared the machine to challenge me.

The death pointer didn't appear.

'Just as I thought – a glorified wind-up toy!'

As if in response, a short burst of clicking sounded from the mechanism. Fighting the impulse to kick it, I began searching for the telephone instead. I finally found it under the couch next to a pile of broken wooden chess pieces. To my surprise it still worked.

'Hello? Yes, I need to reserve a room for tonight.'

It was evening, the sky a soft blue, the heat of the day prickling up from under the tarmac. Rush hour had passed and the roads were quiet, but there were people everywhere, enjoying the summer evening. Fleetingly I thought I saw Hugh Wollington's distinctive figure amongst a group of tourists. My hands tightened on the steering wheel as I swung around and just then the man turned fully towards the car. It wasn't Wollington. Worried, I glanced in the rear-view mirror – there was no one behind me. I accelerated anyway.

As I roared past Green Park, something smashed into the windscreen. I swerved, ran the car up onto the kerb and came to a halt. Shaking, I sat with my hands still on the steering wheel. The window had fragmented, transforming the skyline into a thousand pieces of a jigsaw puzzle. Blood rolled down the glass in lazy drips.

I wrapped my fist in a handkerchief and punched a hole through the shattered glass so I could see through the window. The sound of evening birdsong flooded into the car. Climbing out, I began searching for whatever had hit the windscreen. A few yards down the road I found a sparrowhawk, wings spread, head lolling on a broken neck.

Shocked, I kneeled and looked for the band around its leg. The only way a sparrowhawk could be patrolling the

London skies was if it belonged to some eccentric falconer
practising his craft from the safety of a nearby park. As a
child, I'd sometimes found the corpses of such birds on the
Cumbria Fens. But there was no band. The creature's black
claw lay limp in my hand.

Around me, the sky shifted imperceptibly, like a glass
prism that had just been jolted, and I wondered whether I
wasn't still dreaming.

25

The rooms in good hotels have a soundless vacuum-like quality that I found myself craving now: the sealed-off luxury of an anonymous refuge that brought nothing with it – no past associations, no memories – merely the comfort of being one of many to sleep within its four walls, secure in the promiscuity of transition. It is the womb that men like me seek, the place we know we can safely return to during our travels. I had discovered a small discreet hotel tucked into the back of Mayfair. I'd checked in under a false name, but there seemed to be few guests and most of them were not English.

I walked through the hotel room I'd booked, marking out my territory in short paces – past the Louis XVI desk and chair, the gold and blue silk curtains, the canopied bed – then made my way straight into the bathroom and ran a bath.

The waxy white marble tiles jolted me back to the morgue and Barry Douglas's corpse lying on the slab. The Australian would have loved the irony of my setting the astrarium to my own birth date. I could hear his voice cajoling me into an admission that perhaps, finally, my cynicism and deep-seated belief in scientific rationalism were breaking down. The device hadn't set a death date yet, so I might end up regretting my rash impulse.

'We'll see if the damn thing has any power over my life,' I said out loud, answering Barry's grinning ghost.

After the bath, I called to book a flight back to Egypt. Sitting there in the hermetic silence, it struck me that only hours earlier Gareth had still been in his coma. The morning seemed to have receded as if it had been months ago rather than hours.

Wrapped in a bathrobe, I sat down at the small desk that doubled as a dressing table. The curtains were still open; below, cars wound their way through Mayfair. The night was alive. The thin moon pressed against the black sky as delicately as a porcelain fragment, unchanging, eternal. I gazed out, thinking about Isabella, Gareth, the people I loved in my life, working out a strategy that might allow me to regain control of events.

It wasn't just Gareth's carelessness that terrified me but also his vulnerability. His youth gave him that illusory sense that life stretched out for ever, that one never had to be responsible for one's actions. I knew the illusion well: it was how I'd lived for my first twenty years, fallible in my spontaneity, culpable in my impulses. Gareth had survived, but how would he live now?

And what about Isabella, who had lived so much more intensely than I did, despite all my adventures? Her passion and vivacity had sometimes created a gulf between us. Was it my innate trait of stepping back and observing rather than being fully present in a situation that had enforced this final, fatal separation? I didn't know. Perhaps I'd become caught up in a growing obsession with the astrarium as a way of trying to undo past wrongs; an unconscious bid to win her back. Did I think that by solving the enigma of the astrarium I could put to rest all those unresolved arguments? Put her to rest?

Pulling the curtains closed, I shut out the city and the moon, now janglingly bright.

Hours later I was still awake, lying in the bed and staring up at the ceiling. I checked the bedside clock – it showed six a.m. already. It would be seven a.m. in Egypt, and I knew that Moustafa would have already been at the oilfield site for an hour or so. I decided to distract myself by checking on the progress of the well. I rang him on his field phone. The line was bad but in the background I could hear the distant thudding of the drill. The sound swept me right back and suddenly I found myself missing the reality of the field – the frenetic activity, the pungent smells, the shouts and sounds; the physical world I knew.

'Moustafa, it's Oliver. How's it going?'

'Oliver! Fantastic – you are the man I have been trying to reach for days. Du Voor told me you had gone underground . . .'

'It's complicated. How's the drilling going?'

'Wait, I will find some privacy to talk in.'

The shouts of the roughnecks faded as he walked away from the field. A minute later he was back on the phone. 'Oliver, I have exciting news. We have encountered oil-bearing sandstone, and we haven't even reached the main target. But there's more – there seems to have been substantial subsurface movement since the seismic data, and nothing is matching up. You must come back to the Sinai, Oliver. I think we should run another couple of seismic lines.' His words tumbled over each other in his eagerness.

'Moustafa, slow down – this could be bad news, not good news.'

'I don't think it's bad news. We have at least two hundred feet of net oil pay and I believe this new structure could extend a long way to the east, well into the new block. From the helicopter, it seemed to me—'

'Hang on, land formations don't appear overnight.' I yawned; my jaw ached and there was the throbbing balloon of a headache over one eye.

'Of course, but there was the earthquake a few weeks ago.'

'Around the fourteenth of May?'

'That's right – how do you know about it?'

'Fartime told me about it – it was the same tremor that killed my wife. I just hadn't realised the fault line extended that far. Have the original well and field definitely held?'

'There's no leakage – it appears unaffected. But it's this new reservoir rock that is so promising – a trap has appeared, it's like the substructure itself has altered. Even from the air it looks different – you can see signs of the shear. It must have been a thin fault line that ran down from Alex.'

Moustafa usually erred on the side of caution. I'd never heard him so animated.

'Okay, I'll bring my flight forward,' I said. 'I'll be in Port Said in a couple of days.'

'Thank you, Oliver. You won't regret it, I know it. *Inshallah.*'

As I put the phone down I noticed the outline of the astrarium gleaming in the electric glow of the alarm clock.

My suitcase sat in the corner of the hotel room; it contained a couple of pairs of jeans, a suit and an old denim jacket. I would pick up anything else I needed in Cairo. Fifteen minutes later I had a seat on the evening flight to Egypt.

The running man. But running to what?

Gareth's vocals, dancing above the pounding bass, competed with the droning commentary of a football match playing on the television hanging above the bed. The song finished in a lingering note that swept through the hospital room like light. My brother, looking flushed and comparatively healthy, clicked the tape machine off.

'There was a rep at The Vue gig, he's asked us to come in – Stiff Records, could lead to something, you know.' He collapsed back on his pillows.

'That's great, Gareth. The band deserves a break.'

'I get out of here tomorrow – they're just finishing the last tests on my kidney and liver functions. It's all looking pretty good considering I was dead all of two days ago.'

'Not exactly dead. Comatose.'

'Headbanging in Heaven. And thanks for the upgrade to a private room. I feel like a right toff.'

'It's the least I could do.'

On the television, the stadium broke into a roar as Carlisle United scored. We both swung around to watch. I knew that stadium from my childhood: the wooden railings, the old billboard running along the pitch, the hard men of the north up on their feet roaring.

'Da will be happy,' I murmured.

'Happy? He'll be hanging the bloody flag out.'

There was another beat between us; the quiet, undefined pleasure of being with family. Then Gareth spoke.

'Thanks for not telling him . . .'

With my face still turned to the television, I reached

across and took his hand. We sat there watching the football, our hands clasped.

'I wasn't trying to kill myself.' Gareth pulled his hand away, a man again.

'I know that.'

'It won't happen again, I promise.'

'I know that as well.' I met his gaze. 'But this is a chance to really clean up,' I ventured.

To my dismay he sank back into a sullen defensiveness.

'Fuck it, I made a mistake, that's all. I haven't got a problem. I'm going to be a bloody great success, you'll see.'

'Just promise you won't do anything stupid again.'

He stayed silent.

I stood and picked up my overnight bag, the astrarium packed safely inside.

Gareth looked up. 'Don't be away too long this time, will you?'

'I don't plan to be. And remember, if you phone the office they can get hold of me easily enough.'

I leaned towards him, determined to embrace him however awkward the gesture. As I did, I noticed a sketchbook sitting on the side table, folded open to a pencil sketch of a woman's face. She looked familiar. I lifted it up to examine it: Banafrit. I recognised her from the photographs in Amelia Lynhurst's thesis and, more disturbingly, from the shadow that the astrarium had cast that evening in Egypt. The deep-set eyes, the heavy eyebrows and full mouth were unmistakable.

'Who's this?' I asked.

'I don't know. She was in my head when I came out of the coma. Zoë insisted I draw her. It was as if she'd visited me. A face like that could turn a man to crime.' Gareth looked at the drawing thoughtfully. Then he changed tack so quickly

I barely had time to react, 'I was right about the astrarium, wasn't I, Oliver?'

I shut the door and sat down again.

'Listen, if anyone should turn up asking questions, you know nothing, and you've never worked with Isabella, understand?'

'Are you in trouble?'

'Someone broke into the flat – smashed up the whole place.'

'She found it, didn't she, Oliver?'

I barely nodded.

'Christ, do you know how amazing that is!'

'Please, Gareth, this is serious. There are people out there who want it, dangerous people. I want you to forget we even had this conversation.'

'I've already forgotten – but what are you doing going back to Egypt? Surely it's only going to be more dangerous there?'

'I have business to carry out, and I made a promise to Isabella.'

I began to make my way to the door.

'One last thing,' Gareth said. I swung around.

'Don't do something stupid like getting yourself killed, promise?'

'Promise.'

There was an hour of the British Airways flight left and already the Mediterranean was visible below, the shadow of the plane rippling across the blue waves. I glanced back at my copy of the *New York Times*: news of the German anarchist gang Baader–Meinhoff, and the fallout of the Chilean Junta the year before and the horror of the new regime 'disappearing' thousands of young people seemed to fill the pages in a depressing maelstrom of fatalism.

So many events this year had made me feel as if an era was coming to an end. Perhaps it was just that the naive optimism of my generation was now history, to be replaced by scepticism and a growing awareness of a moral void. People younger than myself – Isabella's peers – were angry and understandably disenchanted. Where did I stand in all this now?

Staring down towards Cairo as we flew across the Nile Delta, I realised that I too had started to change. I didn't like to dwell on the real reasons why I had set the astrarium to my birth date; it wasn't just the Newtonian in me challenging the mechanism, it was also a perverse desire to discover whether Isabella could have possibly saved herself. At least by returning to Egypt there was a chance I might resolve the enigma of the astrarium and put Isabella to rest. I couldn't bear the idea, however superstitious it seemed to a non-believer like myself, that she could be trapped in a kind of purgatory.

I glanced up at the overhead locker. The astrarium was safely stored inside. At the departure gate I'd told the airline that I was carrying geological apparatus. Initially suspicious, they had waved me on when I showed them my first-class ticket. I glanced back down the plane. Three rows in front of me I noticed a tall distinguished-looking man of Arabic appearance staring back at me. As soon as he saw me looking he swung back to face the front. I'd first seen him when we'd taken off from Heathrow. Had I been followed to London and now back to Alexandria? How far did Prince Majeed and possibly Hugh Wollington's tendrils stretch? I stared down the plane, torturing myself with the worst possible scenarios, only to be jolted in my seat by sudden turbulence as the plane began its descent. Without warning, it dropped, then stabilised. Stumbling, the hostess steadied herself against the back of my seat. I glanced out the window – Cairo was below, a mirage of high-rise buildings and sandstone. There wasn't a cloud in the sky.

'Clear-air turbulence?' a passenger near me asked the air hostess. 'I fly myself – but usually Cessnas.'

After checking that the other passengers weren't listening, she leaned towards him. I strained to listen. 'Confidentially, there seems to be some disturbance with the instruments. Something's gone wrong with the autopilot; it began at take-off and hasn't corrected itself. So we're landing the old-fashioned way. But don't worry, the captain is an excellent pilot – ex-air force, the best.'

I glanced at the overhead locker again, imagining that I could hear the magnets spinning. Could the magnetic qualities of the astrarium be affecting the plane's navigational instruments?

The jet wobbled again, the fasten-seatbelt sign flicked on and I leaned towards the window. The three pyramids were visible as we passed over Giza. Standing in silent communion, they were a monumental testimony to humanity's attempt to conquer the finality of death. Ten minutes later, the plane made a smooth final approach and, with the usual shudder, the wheels hit the runway.

26

Once I was out of the arrivals gate, I watched the tall Arab disappear without a backward glance, then headed to the set of lockers that British Airways reserved for their first-class passengers. I'd given a lot of thought to where I could hide the astrarium while I went to the desert. After the raid on my flat, I was no longer sure whether it was safest to carry it on my back and I was worried something might happen to it while it was in the oilfield. The first-class lounge was policed and one of the very few places in Egypt I knew that you couldn't bribe your way into. After making sure the cloakroom was empty, I placed the astrarium in a locker, locked it, and then hid the key between the upper sole of my shoe and the leather beneath – a place where I also concealed my money when travelling in Africa.

The next morning, after an early breakfast, I hired an old Honda and drove to Port Said. Every few miles or so was a sign: *Foreigners must not leave the road*. I crossed a bridge and waved at the guard sitting on an upturned wooden crate, his rifle slung casually across his lap. Because of potential military conflict all bridges were guarded and it was forbidden to photograph them.

It was hard to imagine this land had ever been peaceful. On the opposite border at the western edge of Egypt I knew that gun battles had broken out between Libyan and Egyptian troops, and already land and air clashes had started between the two countries. Sadat was at war again.

Meanwhile, here on the other side of the bridge I began to see debris from the Egyptian–Israeli conflicts: burnt-out gun emplacements; old army tanks, some of them upended; the wreckage of a military helicopter half-buried in the sand, the blue Star of David still visible on its side. The tragic remnants of an age-old hostility lay tossed aside like toys that had once belonged to a giant child. I continued along the desert road, a single dirt track, swerving around potholes and the occasional goat. The car engine rattled like a cheap moped and I prayed that it wouldn't break down, troubled by the possibility of ghosts, imagining the faint shimmer of a soldier smiling shyly by the roadside, hitching a ride back to a world that no longer existed.

I turned the radio on – immediately Elvis's deep voice filled the car: 'In the Ghetto' sounded out, broadcast from an American military base in Iraq. I drove on, the desert sky rolling over me. Lulled by mile after mile of track, I felt my recent experiences in London evaporate into the wavering glasslike horizon that constantly hovered just in front of the car. As I travelled, a dust storm blowing up behind the Honda's tyres, a keener sense of myself – stripped back, liberated from memory – settled into the man in the driver's seat. For all its irritations and eccentricities, I now remembered why I loved this country.

*

The four-seater Cessna swung to the left, its wing tilting up to the sun as it circled back over the area we'd just covered. I watched the horizon go from horizontal to diagonal and a thrilling feeling of omnipotence flooded through me, as it always did when I was surveying. It was the exhilaration of seeing the whole formation of the landscape spread out below – the glorious impression of being above humanity, above millions of years of Earth's history, as if reading the topography of the mountains and river beds enabled me to see that remote past and also the faraway future. I could see how the world had stretched and shrunk, how the oceans had eaten the coast, how the continents themselves had moved, how volcanoes had etched their fury down sweeping slopes. More importantly, I could see where the Earth was hiding her treasures in folds of shale and carbonate reefs.

After my phone call to Moustafa from London, I'd spoken to the Alexandrian Oil Company and then to the Ministry of Oil itself. The adjoining block, where the new pay zone appeared to extend, was earmarked for licensing to friendly foreign oil companies as part of Sadat's new economic policy. But I'd agreed with the ministry that we'd use some of our existing equipment and personnel to take a look at the block – whatever we found could only help their negotiations. I decided not to mention the new development to Johannes quite yet. After all, nothing had been confirmed.

Moustafa and I had met in the tiny Port Said airport where we'd sat in the departure lounge – a glorified alcove furnished with an old vinyl lounge suite and a dusty photograph of Nasser in army uniform that hung over an empty counter upon which sat a fan spinning forlornly. We had analysed the Landsat image of the area that the Alexandrian Oil Company had on record. Taken from the NASA satellite in 1972, it covered most of the area east of the Suez Canal.

The section we were interested in showed little geological potential – it appeared on the images as a light-coloured flat area not much higher than sea level. This meant that the ridge we were now searching for from the plane really was new, possibly related to the earthquake. We didn't have the data yet to understand it; we needed to get down there to explore it.

'There it is!' Moustafa, two surveillance maps open on his lap, pointed out of the window.

I looked down. The jutting derricks of the Abu Rudeis oil-fields looked as if they were made of Meccano, the discoloured sand around each one spread out like an ink stain. But the part of the landscape that Moustafa was indicating was a white scar of a ridge that ran for about twenty kilometres directly below. I tapped the pilot's shoulder. The horizon tipped again as he flew the plane down for a closer look.

'See here.' Moustafa traced the formation on the map for me.

I noticed the map was labelled in Hebrew and, surprised, looked at him questioningly. He grinned.

'Israeli – I got them on the black market, dated 1973. Probably military, but they are the best charts.'

The area with the ridge was marked as flat on the sur-veillance map, as it had been on our own satellite images. There was no sign of any external feature, of the edge of a basin or of buried carbonate platforms, the kind of geological conditions that promised a hidden reservoir of oil or gas. I looked out of the window again. Now that we were lower, the ridge was clearly visible – one side a smooth slope, the other side with an incline of about ten feet, giving a hint of the substructure beneath.

'It looks like God has suddenly stamped his foot and the carpet has a wrinkle,' Moustafa said.

'Nicely put but not exactly scientific.' I frowned at the scenery stretched out below.

Moustafa laughed.

I checked the map again; it was the second time we'd flown over the formation and I knew the reference points were accurate. Here it was on the page, flat as a pancake, but through the window the mound was undeniable.

'Has there been instability here before?' I asked, still puzzled. Moustafa pushed the second map towards me; this time the labelling was in Russian.

'This map dates from the late 1950s but you can see it is just the same as the 1973 map. There is nothing in this valley except goats and rubble. Now it looks as if the pay zone we just encountered in the adjacent oilfield,' his finger ran across the map toward Abu Rudeis, 'might extend all the way to here.' He grasped my wrist in sudden excitement. 'Oliver, if this were so, this could be a huge discovery!'

My own oil sense had been ignited the moment we sighted the ridge – it looked like a textbook illustration of where to drill. And there was something about the slight discolouration in the rocks on the far slope that had made my heart rattle with adrenalin. But I'd hidden my enthusiasm. I trusted Moustafa, but before I'd commit to anything I needed to know exactly what we were dealing with, and who else Moustafa had discussed this with. And, of course, I wanted the data. But most of all, I wanted to walk the ridge.

'Let's go down,' I said.

The plane landed on a flat area of scrub just before the slope rose to the crest of the ridge. The terrain was bleak and barren, with twisted bushes clustered around the occasional boulder. Moustafa and the pilot unloaded the gravity meter – an instrument that measured changes in the gravity field

and would indicate whether there was a change in the structure of the crust, the possibility of source rock and, above it,
reservoir rock. There was also a machine called a sniffer that
detected minute traces of hydrocarbons. If any of these tests
indicated a possible oilfield, then we would turn to seismol-
ogy, using explosives to create shock waves that would
reflect off the substructure and allow us to create two-dimen-
sional, even three-dimensional, images of the oil-bearing
strata beneath.

I walked to the top of the crest and stood there looking
over the terrain. I took a deep breath and inhaled the faint
scent of salt, and something else under it that I was beginning to believe might contain that elusive trace of oil.
Thinking it could be coming off the established oilfields to
the west, I turned in that direction, then realised the wind
was blowing from Upper Egypt, entirely the other direction.
I knelt and picked up a small rock that looked as if it had
broken off a boulder. I sniffed it, then licked it – an old geologist's trick – looking for that elusive faint musky taste that
might indicate it was oil-bearing. It tasted promising.

I peered down the other, sharper side of the slope. An
old Bedouin shepherd sat in the shade of the crest, watching
a bunch of scrawny goats graze on the scattered clumps of
desert grass. I shouted a greeting before going down to join
him.

'*Salaam alaikum*,' I then said respectfully.

'*Alaikum salaam*,' he replied patting the flat boulder where
he was sitting to indicate that I should join him. I bowed in
greeting, then sat beside him. He offered me a piece of
chewing tobacco, which I accepted and then slipped discreetly into my pocket.

'How long have you worked this particular piece of land,
my friend?'

'Many years, many years.' He waved vaguely towards the east. 'But now I am confused. I was here four full moons ago and none of this was here.'

'None of what?'

'This.' He patted the boulder we were sitting on, then pointed to the ridge behind us. 'It has grown in the night like mushrooms.'

'Mushrooms in the desert?'

He laughed, which became a hacking cough that finished with a stream of tobacco-stained spittle that bled into the sand.

'There are many things I cannot explain – stars that are older than light, a woman's change of heart, President Sadat's dreams – yet I believe them because I see them with my own eyes. It may be sorcery but it is there – it is God's will, and so I believe it.' He smiled again, pulled out an evil-eye pendant that hung around his neck and pressed it to his forehead.

A dark lump lying on the ground caught my attention. I picked it up and sniffed it. It smelled pungent and rich; a lump of tarry oil, surface seepage probably brought up by the earthquake and already decaying in the air and sun. A pounding sense of excitement rose up in my throat. Concealing my emotion, I slipped the lump into my pocket.

I stood and tracked a stratum of darker sand that finished at a small crevasse. A dead bush sprouted from it. I kneeled and examined the base of the bush; all around it were bird-claw prints baked into what looked like mud. Birds of prey weren't that unusual in the desert, but mud? It had been years since it had rained in this region.

'Oliver!'

Moustafa's voice startled me; he appeared on the crest,

waving a piece of paper in his hand. 'The geophysics look very good! We're close, I know it!'

As I scrambled up the slope towards him, the Bedouin caught my arm.

'This is God's work. It is not to be ravaged without consequence, consequences that will affect us all. Don't forget that you are a mere man, my friend. Allah is mightier.'

Back at the oilfield, I walked around the drilling rig that I'd helped set up months earlier. It had been moved one kilometre to the south-west and was drilling into the same reservoir we had penetrated with the original well, which now rested at over fifteen thousand barrels per day. Mud and oil roared up through the derrick and it seemed clear that the new well would be as productive as the discovery well.

Nearby, the shale shakers – great sieves – were steaming as the hot underground mud rippled out of the drill pipe like the entrails of some subterranean beast. The shale shakers sifted and shook out the mud from the cuttings, after which it showered down into the mud pits, filling the air with the raw smell of oil and pungent earth. I waved at the mud logger who stood over the pit full of drill cuttings, then I pulled Moustafa away from the roar of the generator.

'This new potential field – it's on land leased by IPEC?'

'Naturally.'

'And you haven't spoken to Johannes about it?'

'I work for you, Oliver, not Du Voor, you know that.'

I nodded, then, appalled by my sudden avarice, looked away to the horizon. A truck drove along it, hauling sections of well casing to be used in completing the current well. The sight reassured me. This was industry, commerce, the great cogs of progress. This was a terrain I knew and trusted.

I turned back to Moustafa. 'Let's run some seismic lines, see what they say before telling anyone. I think that might be wiser.'

'I agree, my friend.'

Moustafa held out his hand, and we shook – a sealed pact.

But as I walked away, Enrico Silvio's warning about the astrarium offering a kind of Faustian contract seemed to echo under the thudding of the oil well. No matter how much I tried to rationalise I couldn't rid myself of the disturbing thought that perhaps the earthquake had in some way been a result of the discovery of the astrarium, the releasing of some kind of inexplicable force that reached across time and space. And I was finding it difficult to ignore the coincidence of Moustafa's call about the discovery coming so soon after I had challenged the astrarium. If Moses really had used it to part the Red Sea, if it was somehow related to the tsunami that destroyed the Ptolemaic island of Antirhodos, off the coast of Alexandria, if the astrarium really had that kind of power – then what were the implications of setting the dial to my own birth date?

27

It was late afternoon by the time the silhouette of the camp appeared on the horizon. Already the temperature had started to drop as the desert cooled. As we drew closer the outline of a police car parked outside my hut came into view.

'Oliver, are you in some kind of trouble?' Moustafa asked.

'Perhaps.'

The driver pulled up and we sat in the jeep for a minute.

'Let me deal with the police,' Moustafa murmured in English. 'You know I have connections.'

I glanced at the driver, then, suddenly afraid, I reached down into my shoe and pulled out the locker key. I slipped it into Moustafa's hand. There was no other choice. I had to trust him.

'Take this, Moustafa. If they arrest me, go to the BA first-class lounge at Cairo. The locker is listed under the company name. There's a rucksack inside.'

He nodded. 'I will. You can rely on me.'

The camp quarters were simple – there was a single wrought-iron bed with a striped lumpy mattress, an electric kettle, a bar fridge, a ceiling fan and an old tea chest that functioned as both storage space and a table. I'd never lived more than a few days in such accommodation, but most of the crew weren't so lucky; some spent weeks stationed out on the site. The hut they'd assigned me still contained the possessions of the previous occupant, an Italian-Catholic well-borer. I hadn't bothered throwing them out. A tattered print of the Virgin Mary ascending to heaven on a cloud hung on the wall over the bed. A bookcase made from a plank balancing on two rusty nails held an eclectic collection of worn paperbacks: *Future Shock*, *Roots*, *Fear of Flying* by Erica Jong, *Love Story* (in Italian), *Watership Down* and, I suddenly noticed to my distress, *My Name is Asher Lev* by Chaim Potok, a Jewish writer. The Egyptian military police wouldn't like that.

As Moustafa and I entered the hut, two officers were ripping out the lining of the tea chest. My meagre items of clothing were strewn on the floor beside them. Another officer – obviously their superior – lounged on the bed, watching them. Seeing me, he got lazily to his feet with as much disrespect as he could muster.

'You Mr Warnock, British citizen, yes?'

I stepped forward, blocking the view of the Potok novel. I was afraid they would assume I was Jewish, possibly even Mossad.

'Is there some problem?' I asked.

'Maybe.' The officer shouted at his men in Arabic, ordering them to turn the mattress over, then swung back to me. 'Maybe you spy?'

The old blue-striped mattress fell to the floor in a cloud of dust, revealing two *Playboy* magazines, dated 1968, lying on the rusting base. The officer held them up accusingly. 'Yours?' he demanded.

'Of course not!' I snapped back in the most authoritative tone I could muster.

The officer burst out laughing, his two comrades joining him. Moustafa and I remained stony-faced. Displeased, the officer cracked his baton against the iron bed frame.

'Is funny, no? Very funny.'

Moustafa joined in the laughter. I followed, my heart pounding as the officer flicked through the magazine pages. He stopped at a centrefold displaying a blonde grinning inanely above a pair of enormous pink-tipped breasts. Wearing a leather cowboy hat, she sat astride a saddle perched on a hay bale. He held the page up. The centrefold smiled out at me, her white teeth mockingly perfect next to the officer's stained and irregular grin.

'She your sister, no?'

The atmosphere thickened as the other men, instantly registering the extent of the insult, turned to me.

'Careful,' Moustafa said quietly in English. I remained silent. To defend myself might infuriate the officer further, yet not defending myself undermined my position. I knew he'd been instructed to arrest me, otherwise he wouldn't be taking such liberties.

'Or maybe you like boys?' he went on. 'I'm sorry for you if you do, my friend.'

This time no one dared laugh. I felt my hands curling into fists, the miner's son readying himself for a brawl. But to resort to violence would be suicidal.

Sensing the danger, Moustafa stepped between us. 'Officer, Mr Warnock is Egypt's friend. He is employed by our government. There has been a mistake.'

'No mistake. He is to be escorted back to Alexandria and interrogated.'

'On what grounds?'

'That is between Mr Warnock and my commanding officer, Colonel Hassan.'

Moustafa broke into a warm smile. 'Colonel Khalid
Hassan? From Mansoura?'

Flustered, the officer glanced from Moustafa to me. 'The
same. Why?' he asked suspiciously.

'Then there is no problem. Khalid Hassan is a good friend
of mine. We were at El-Orwa el-Woska together as children.
He will be very unhappy when he hears you have arrested a
friend of mine.'

'We are not arresting him, we simply want to ask him a
few questions.'

I stood frozen in the middle of the room. I'd never felt so
vulnerable before. The thought of the hidden astrarium was
not the least bit consoling, and, for a minute, I wondered
whether this wouldn't be my last day of freedom. I glanced
over at Moustafa – his expression had turned from relieved
to grim again, reflecting the fear in my own expression.

The officer shoved me towards the tea chest and the scattered clothes around it. 'Collect your things – we go now.'

I looked up at the single barred window; the bluish light of
dawn had just begun to thread its way through the night
sky. I tried to measure the time since they had bundled me
into the jail – at least twelve hours. During the short walk
from the police jeep to the cell, I'd recognised the building
from my previous interrogation: the police headquarters on
Al Fateh Street in Alexandria. Behind its austere façade
was a warren of small rooms that ran around an inner courtyard. The atmosphere was dank: the acrid smell of urine
and carbolic soap, undercut by something else – the smell
of fear.

They'd been questioning me for hours. The fluorescent

light above blazed down; I felt as if it was burning actual
stripes across my brain. If I concentrated, I imagined I
could smell my soft grey matter frying like old bacon. I
was beyond exhaustion and my thoughts reeled like a
drunken boxer. The bruises on my face and back were testimony to the rough handling I'd experienced at the hands
of the officer who had brought me in, but so far the investigating officer had focused only on the circumstances of
Isabella's death, reiterating over and over that the dive had
been illegal and had taken place in a restricted military
zone.

'I told you before,' I said wearily, 'on the day she died – I
had no idea the dive was illegal until we were actually on the
boat. My wife hadn't been entirely clear on the matter.'

'She was lying to you, sir.'

The officer, a disarmingly polite man in his late forties,
kept apologising to me; a ploy I'd fallen for until the questioning stretched into hours and I wasn't allowed to rest or go
to the toilet – deliberate tactics meant to humiliate me and
break me down.

'Okay, perhaps she lied to me – what does it matter? She
drowned before we found anything.'

My head sank to my chest. All I wanted was to sleep; my
eyes felt as if they had sunk into pits and my trouser legs
were streaked with urine. Bizarre snippets of phrases kept
popping into my head, along with lines from old pop songs –
The Beatles' 'She Loves You'; The Monkees' 'I'm A
Believer'. Exhaustion and dehydration were sending me into
a delirium peppered with moments of surprising clarity. Did
they know about the existence of the astrarium? They must
not have dared take me at the airport but had they managed
to get into the first-class lounge? Had anyone else been
detained? Hermes Hemiedes? Moustafa? Maybe even

Francesca Brambilla, although I couldn't imagine the matriarch tolerating such treatment.

'Your wife worked with Faakhir Alsayla, a diver?'

I lifted my head and tried to focus on the officer's gaze. His eyes swam around in circles, a swarm of deceptively compassionate brown irises. If only I could grab one and squeeze, I thought irrationally.

'I don't know that name,' I lied.

'So perhaps you know a Hermes Hemiedes?' he persisted.

When I refused to reply, the interrogator nodded and one of the policemen flanking me hauled me to my feet. I caught sight of a man at the glass window of the door, staring in. His face was eerily familiar and through my fog I tried desperately to remember where I'd seen it before. It came to me in fragments. The current affairs show on television in London. Prince Majeed's henchman. Omar's companion.

Another policeman came in and told the officer that Mosry was waiting outside. The name seemed to sear the air like a hot coal. Wanting to memorise it, I held on to the sound, trying it out. Mosry. The officer nodded and Mosry entered the room. Instantly it was as if the temperature had dropped. There was a kind of acidic smell about the man. He stared at me, his eyes boring into my skull, and yet I couldn't turn away. His lack of emotion was utterly terrifying, and the sense of extreme intelligence emanating from him was almost as frightening. I remembered an encounter with a warlord a few years previously in Angola, a man who recruited and butchered child soldiers. Now, for the second time in my life, I knew I was in the presence of evil. Despite my exhaustion a new fear clawed at my throat. The connection was increasingly clear. Omar–Mosry–Majeed. The astrarium. I couldn't be sure, but I suspected their interest in the device was related to Sadat's attempts to open Egypt up to the West, and possibly to President Carter's attempt to negotiate peace in the region. All I knew was that to let the astrarium fall into their hands would be devastating.

The officer gave the newcomer a nod of nervous deference. I started to wonder whether I was going to survive the interrogation. Pulling up a chair, Mosry sat in the corner of the room, watching intently, a slight smile playing across his lips. It was hard not to start screaming.

The questions began again, with a new aggression. 'Answer me!' the officer barked, then slammed his fists on the desk.

'I have no idea what you're talking about,' I said.

'Perhaps this will help your memory.' He reached into a file and pulled out a black-and-white photograph of Hermes and myself at Isabella's funeral.

'May I telephone the British Embassy?' I asked. 'As a British citizen I have rights . . .'

I'd forgotten how many times I'd made this request; it had become a collection of words I clung to like a raft, a means of keeping my fading sanity afloat. The actual words had stopped making any sense to me; they had become a medley of sounds strung together, at the end of which salvation seemed to beckon.

Ignoring me, the interrogator picked up a stubby pencil and drew on a piece of paper, which he shoved towards me. 'Do you recognise this?' It was a crude rendering of the Ba hieroglyph.

'Of course, from my wife's work. That's Ba, the Ancient Egyptian soul-bird.'

'A primitive symbol from a primitive culture – only the West romanticises such fairy tales. It is also the symbol for an organisation – an organisation that is illegal, Mr Warnock. Do you know this organisation?'

By now the room was beginning to spin. I had no strength to feel anything any more. 'Can I sit down?' I asked.

The officer looked towards Mosry as if waiting for an order. The other man nodded and the officer lunged at me, as if to hit me. At the last minute he punched the air and I fainted.

It was her perfume, a spiralling thread of musk and lemon that took me back to the first time I ever met her. If I opened my eyes, she would vanish; it was a magician's trick, a sunspot, the dancing shadows on a lake. I breathed in deeply, wanting to stay basking in her presence no matter how illusory.

The tickling on my face continued, but I fought to stay asleep. I sensed that if I woke completely, pain would flood through my swollen legs and feet. I'd once read of a bereaved neurophysiologist who developed a hypothesis that the dead continued to exist in the way our memory imprinted our experience of them upon our brains. Not an endless loop of disjointed images but a real and ongoing discourse based on decades of observation, of 'knowing' that person. Was this what I was doing now? I didn't care. I held out my hand, blind fingers touching warm flesh.

'Isabella.'

Not a question, just naming the unnameable. She stood over me, her black eyes shining with that wry expression so achingly familiar, wearing the same clothes she'd worn that last evening before the dive.

'Isabella.'

As if in answer, she reached out and touched the prison wall where graffiti was carved into the plaster in desperate scratches. Her fingers outlined the crude drawing of a fish, then a bull, and finally she pointed to a woman's head crowned with writhing snakes.

'The fish, the bull and the Medusa,' I whispered, the images burning themselves into my memory.

Then, as she kissed me, I sank back into unconsciousness.

I woke with a jolt, my whole body a knot of twisting pain. The gaunt face of the guard came into focus as he rattled the keys above me, indicating that I was free to go.

As I sat up I turned to the cell wall. The graffiti had vanished.

28

Henries, the British consul, dealt with the infuriated prison official with icy politeness, then marched me out of the building. As soon as we were out of earshot, he told me that I was indebted to my assistant Moustafa Saheer who had informed him of my arrest and had arranged for a certain Colonel Hassan to pull some strings on my behalf to organise a release.

'You do seem to be leaving an unpleasant trail of half-truths and accidental deaths, Oliver. God knows, losing one's wife is a ghastly experience, but clearing up after you could become somewhat tiresome. I wouldn't want you to become a DBS.'

'A DBS?'

'A Distressed British Subject – the poor dears can float around for decades. A bit like your unfortunate Australian friend Barry Douglas – another headache, but not mine, thank God. I suppose he was a DAS, a Distressed Australian Subject. What a dreadful thought.'

Henries's car was parked along the street, a short distance from the prison entrance. His driver got out and opened the rear door for him.

'Whatever you're up to, stop it now,' Henries told me forcefully. 'I won't be able to bail you out next time, no matter how many phone calls I have to field from the head of BP, Shell or whoever. Even oilmen like you are expendable when it comes to international affairs. You are on borrowed time, Oliver.' He tapped his watch to emphasise the point.

The limousine drove off. I stood on the street, dazed from dehydration. A man stepped out from the shadow of a shop doorway and took me by the arm. I shook him off, then realised it was Hermes Hemiedes.

'Come, my dear fellow, let me escort you to the safety of your villa,' he said.

I pulled him back into the doorway. 'How did you know about my arrest?'

'It's a small country. I had news of your arrival back in Cairo. Naturally, out of concern for yourself and the astrarium, I have been tracking your progress.'

'Are you crazy? You shouldn't be anywhere near here. They asked about you, they wanted to know if I knew you. What's going on?'

'The authorities have never approved of the kind of Egyptology in which I am involved. You must know by now that they felt the same way about Isabella.'

'Hermes, I was questioned and humiliated for hours!'

A short whistle came from behind me and I swung around. Ibrihim, my housekeeper, was standing on the other side of the street some distance away, nervously watching the armed guards at the sentry box outside the police head-quarters. The company car waited next to him. He shot Hermes a glance of utter disdain, then gestured frantically that I should join him.

I turned back to Hermes. 'It seems that my every move really is watched.'

'Possibly more than you realise. Would you like to come with me?'

'No. Stay away!'

He gripped my arm. 'Don't forget: whenever you need me, I'm here.'

I shook him loose and, without looking back, crossed the road towards Ibrihim and the car.

Back at the villa, Ibrihim pressed the rucksack containing the astrarium into my arms.

'Your friend Mr Saheer delivered it. He told me to tell you that sometimes it is better that the heart does not know what the hands are doing. But please, Mr Warnock, I have a wife, and a son at university. I don't want trouble.'

'I promise, Ibrihim, no trouble.'

He looked at me disbelievingly, then shrugged and disappeared into his room.

I carried the rucksack upstairs into the bedroom, then locked the door and pulled down the blinds. After placing the rucksack on the desk, I waited, my nerves rattling, half-expecting a heavy banging on the front door below. My bruises ached as if my muscles were expecting another beating. I was convinced that the villa would be raided at any moment and this time I was sure they would either charge or 'disappear' me. There was nothing but silence.

I lifted out the astrarium carefully and stared into its mechanism. To my surprise, the two magnets were still whirling furiously, the dials turning to activate an avalanche of fate that I had unwittingly begun.

So many people wanted this mysterious instrument, believing it could influence lives, events, even history. An extraordinary but, as much as I'd have liked to deny it, an exhilarating thought. The very ownership of the device made me feel empowered.

I looked around the room, assessing my options. The instrument had to be hidden, but where? After the attempted break-in here and the ransacking of my flat in London, the villa itself felt unsafe as a hiding place. Besides, there were too many people, staff and the like, walking through daily. It had to be concealed somewhere unexpected, too unusual for a seasoned thief to consider. I went to the balcony, pulled aside the blind and stared down into the garden. On Ibrihim's side of the house there was a makeshift yard where Tinnin the Alsatian was kept. Muslims regarded dogs as unclean, but recent events had forced Ibrihim to tolerate Tinnin's presence because he was a good guard dog. There was a kennel there, large enough for something to be buried at the back of it.

Later, after shouting a quick goodbye to Ibrihim as I left, I took a walk along the Corniche. Battling the gusts of wind coming off the Mediterranean, I crossed the road and sat on the sea wall. The scent of roasting chestnuts floated from a brazier nearby, reminding me incongruously of Oxford Street at Christmas. Courting couples, some in traditional dress, others in Western clothes, strolled past, the wind making sails of their garments. The women were beautiful, vivacious, luxuriant in their flesh; the men thin-faced and earnest. Their intimacy suddenly made the absence of Isabella painfully apparent. I was reminded of a walk I'd taken with her only months before. I looked out over the sea. To the right was the islet upon which had once stood that great wonder of the ancient world – the Pharos. Isabella had taken me there, describing the lighthouse in detail, as if she had lived through that era herself. The lighthouse had been built during Ptolemaic times to protect the increasing number of trading ships from being wrecked in the harbour. Isabella told me that the Pharos would have appeared to defy gravity in its soaring height and, for the religious pilgrims of the era, the tower must have been a spiritually transcendent vision with its flaming beacon burning day and night. As she stared out at the site that day, I remembered being struck by how convincing her description sounded.

In the Café Athenios the old men had begun to congregate for the evening, chatting over hookah pipes, small cups of thick black coffee and baklava. I sat at a table outside and ordered a coffee. I needed to put my scattered thoughts into some kind of order.

The police had mentioned that the Ba hieroglyph was the symbol of an illegal organisation. The fact that Isabella and Hugh Wollington both had a Ba tattoo suggested there was a stronger connection between them than I'd first suspected. Were the people in that photograph from Behbeit el-Hagar involved? Perhaps Enrico Silvio was a part of it too. But what kind of organisation was it?

The printed image on the front of the menu caught my eye. The drawing of a woman with snakes for hair somehow resonated. Then I remembered the head of Medusa that Isabella had pointed to in my dream. There had been a fish and a bull scratched onto the cell wall too. Where would one find those three images together? I forced my thoughts back to the illegal organisation. Would Hermes—

'Mr Warnock?'

Startled, I looked up. Aadeel, Francesca's housekeeper, stood at my table, looking flustered.

'I went to the villa in Roushdy – your housekeeper told

me you would probably be here.' He looked at the cut above my eyebrow and lowered his voice. 'You have been questioned again?'

I nodded. 'It was unpleasant but it could have been far worse. I suspect I got preferential treatment as a European.' Aadeel glanced nervously behind him, and I had the sense that he was worried about being seen with me. He indicated that we needed to get going.

'Please, we need to move. I fear the grief is destroying Madame Brambilla. She is losing her mind. Please, you must come now.'

Francesca was sitting in the drawing room, the French doors thrown open to the garden. Despite the warmth of the afternoon she was wearing a blanket around her shoulders. Terrified by my appearance, she clutched at my arm.

'So you have finally come to take my house?'

I sat down on the sofa beside her chair. Her grand authority had been replaced by a childlike bewilderment. It was devastating to witness. 'I'm not going to take anything or send you anywhere, Francesca. You're safe here.' Trying to reassure her, I stroked her hand.

'It was my fault, Oliver, I killed her. It was that woman. I knew Giovanni was a fool to trust her. Do you hear that, Giovanni?' she cried, addressing the empty space in front of her. 'Do you hear?'

She appeared to be slipping in and out of a mild dementia.

'Which woman?' I asked gently.

'The English woman, the one who helped Isabella go to Oxford. She was always scheming.'

'Amelia Lynhurst?'

'Giovanni chose her to be his high priestess . . . they had so much power together, then she wasted it, all of it . . .' Francesca began rocking herself in the chair. 'The body always lets us down so what does it matter? The poor child was already dead.'

I assumed she was talking about Isabella's missing organs. I leaned forward, trying to hold her gaze and pin her to some semblance of lucidity.

'Francesca, who took Isabella's body to the mortuary?'

'The men who work for our church, that was what I arranged. I didn't want the autopsy but the police insisted.'

'And how long did the priests have her?'

Again Francesca appeared to lapse into dementia. 'A Brambilla has never been cremated. We are always buried, like the great kings of Egypt. We are immortalised by our ancestry.' She grasped my hand. 'Isabella was born on a very auspicious day. She was destined for greatness. She was chosen, you know. My husband had her astrological chart calculated; he believed in such matters.'

Reaching into my jacket pocket, I pulled out the photograph of the group that had been shot at the Behbeit el-Hagar dig. 'Do you recognise any of the others in this photo?' I asked.

Francesca pointed to Hugh Wollington. 'This man, he visited here a few times as a student. I didn't like him, but he worshipped Giovanni. A good wife never asks her husband certain questions. Marriage is a mutually agreed conspiracy. Sometimes it is a travesty,' she finished bitterly. 'Come, it is time you met my husband.'

She reached for her cane, then hobbled towards an archway. I followed, a little apprehensively. Where was she going to take me? We arrived at a small door covered by a curtain. She pulled the curtain across, then lifted a key hanging off a chain around her neck and inserted it into the lock. I pushed the heavy door open for her.

'This was Giovanni's study. Only a privileged few were allowed to enter. Nothing has been altered since his death.'

The large room was filled with antique furniture. A Napoleon campaign desk sat at one end, in front of a bay window. On top of it was an oval portrait of a middle-aged man in his fifties wearing the uniform of the Italian Fascist Party, a falcon perched on his outstretched arm. Next to it was a photograph of the same man with a young King Farouk, looking remarkably slim and handsome; the two were shaking hands. A stuffed falcon peered down from a ceiling corner, its glass eyes glinting. A scaled-down model of what appeared to be the family cotton factory, made from balsa wood and matchsticks, stood under a dusty bell jar on a stand to the right of the desk. At the opposite end of the room was a small camp bed made up with sheets and a blanket, set discreetly behind a sofa. It was a poignant sight.

Catching my gaze, Francesca remarked defensively, 'I sleep with the ghosts of my family. They make me safe. But I wanted to show you these . . .'

She led me to a wall covered in framed pictures and pointed to a row of group shots, all men. The photographs were dated in neat inked script from 1910 through to 1954. I noticed that the war years, 1939 to 1945, were missing. All appeared to be taken at the same spot, on the shore of Lake Mariout, an area where many wealthy Alexandrians used to hunt duck and other waterfowl. In one of the latter photographs, dated 1954, a small girl stood proudly beside a middle-aged man who was sporting a moustache and was dressed in a hunting jacket and hat. He had a falcon on his outstretched arm and the child's concentration on the bird transported the viewer straight into the moment: I could almost hear the cries of the disturbed herons as they flapped out of the rushes, the rustling wind in the swaying palms. I recognised Isabella in the child immediately.

'There she is,' Francesca said, 'five years old and already hunting with her father and grandfather. That is Paolo, my son, with the falcon. The other men had hunting dogs, but Paolo had birds of prey. Our family have always kept falcons – since the sixteenth century in Abruzzo. My granddaughter loved that bird.'

She pointed to the stuffed bird hanging from the ceiling. 'That is it there; that ridiculous creature lived longer than my son. That is life: full of banal surprises. After his death, Isabella would take the falcon out herself. "Nonna," she used to say, "why don't I have wings?" She should never have left Egypt; she should never have studied abroad. She would be alive now.'

'How do you mean, Francesca?'

'*Basta*! It is all meaningless now. The line is finished.' Angrily, she hit the leg of an armchair with her cane.

I walked over to a low bookcase and kneeled to look at the titles: *Ancient Astrology*, *The Ancient Art of Mummification*, *The Egyptian Book of the Dead: Spells and Incantations*, *Nectanebo II – Magician or Politician?*, *Moses – the Magus*, *The Writings of Hermes Trismegistus as interpreted by Toz Graecus*.

The old woman shuffled up behind me. 'Giovanni's tomes – they travelled everywhere with him. At first I humoured him. I even joined in with his little re-enactments, but then it got serious . . .' She faltered, as if she had revealed too much. Re-enactments? Could this have been the performances that Cecilia had spoken about? The officer's words about the 'sect' came to mind.

'Serious how?' I asked the question casually, to preserve Francesca's fragile connection to reality.

Her face closed over. 'You can't stop the men,' she said bitterly.

I pulled out a book entitled *Popular Stories of Ancient Egypt* by Gaston Maspero – a name I knew from Isabella's book-shelves. The book fell open at a page relating the dream of Nectanebo, the one that Amelia Lynhurst had described in her thesis. A pressed flower slipped onto the floor. Despite its desiccated state, an exquisite scent flooded the room. I picked up the flower – it was a dried blue lotus, the colour of the petals still faintly visible. I knew it was a sacred flower and was regularly depicted on the walls of the temples and in scenes with members of the Egyptian court poised ele-gantly over the blossom. Isabella had told me it was an hallucinogen.

'Was Giovanni researching Nectanebo II?' I asked.

'The Pharaoh was his obsession. Giovanni was fascinated by the notion of racial purity and Nectanebo II was the last truly Egyptian ruler. Those that followed, my husband described as colonial impostors – the Persians, then the Arabs, then the Turks, French and English. Ironically the next Egyptian ruler was Nasser, but that didn't stop Giovanni's fascination with the pharaoh.'

'There's no such thing as racial purity,' I said, slightly absent-mindedly. I was still looking at the flower, my mind scrambling to try and make the right connections.

'The 1930s were a different time – people looked for cer-tainty then, it made them feel secure. You must understand that we were all desperate, especially here in Egypt. We Italians wanted to belong. Giovanni knew there was change coming; he wanted to secure his family's future, to ensure we would not lose everything.' My ears perked up at the omi-nous note of her last words.

'Just how did he think he was going to achieve that?'

Francesca's head snapped up and she finally looked me in the eye, as if suddenly realising that she had already given away too much. 'Enough! I have told you too much already; I will not betray my husband!'

'I'm not asking you to betray your husband, just to save your granddaughter.' My tone matched hers as we glowered at each other.

'It is too late for that, Oliver. We have lost her, don't you understand? We have both lost her.'

'But is she at peace, Francesca?'

'At peace? Don't be an idiot. Look around you – I am surrounded by the dead, all screaming for retribution. When I die it will be the same.'

I slipped the book back onto the shelf. 'I need to know the name of the priest who handled Isabella's funeral,' I ventured, more carefully now, unsure whether I'd lost her trust altogether.

To my relief Francesca answered my question. 'Father Carlotto, at St Catherine's. The parish has served the family for years.'

Her hand was a collision of delicate bones resting on my arm as I escorted her back to the study door. Once we were in the corridor, she locked the door and turned to me.

'You cannot visit him tonight; tonight your duty is to me. You must accompany me to the opera house. The Bolshoi Ballet is visiting and they are putting on a production of Stravinsky's *Orpheus*.'

Disturbed by her sudden fey tone of voice I thought she might have slipped back into the memory of some past event, but just then Aadeel appeared in the shadows. 'Madame Brambilla would be most indebted if you could accompany her,' he said. 'Truly, it is the event of the year –

everyone who matters in Alexandria will be there. And Madame must attend for the sake of the family's reputation.'

I fingered the cut on my forehead thoughtfully. There were advantages to being seen so publicly – it would be a defiant gesture to my pursuers and might force them out into the open. It occurred to me, somewhat disturbingly, that in this attempt to transform myself from the pursued to the pursuer, I was resorting to using myself as bait. A dangerous ploy but one that just might work.

29

The Sayed Darwish Theatre, known as the Mohammed Ali in its colonial heyday, was a small but ostentatious neoclassical building adorned with great sweeps of gold paint and peeling plaster. From the mid-nineteenth century until 1952, the European diaspora had kept it vibrant with visiting orchestras, ballets and singers. It had been one of the cultural centres of old Alexandria. But since the revolution, the venue had lost much of its original audience and had become a cultural anachronism in the newly affluent Arab-dominated society.

The orchestra struck up and I glanced down the row in which Francesca and I were sitting: it was an eclectic congregation – various European dignitaries, several Egyptian officials and a smattering of tourists. In the row in front of us sat Henries and his wife. Sensing my gaze, the consul turned and tried unsuccessfully to hide his displeasure at my presence.

I felt awkward squeezed into the tuxedo, starched shirt and cummerbund that Francesca had insisted I wear; all had once belonged to Giovanni Brambilla. The shirt prickled the back of my neck, the satin necktie knotted expertly by Aadeel pressed tight against my Adam's apple. And it was hard not to be uncomfortably conscious of the cuts and bruises that still marked my face, drawing stares from members of the audience. I felt very conspicuous, but I guess that's what I'd intended.

On stage, Orpheus, clad in a painted body stocking, sat before Hades and Persephone, the King and Queen of the Underworld, and plucked at a golden lyre. His solo of pirouettes and leaps – a desperate plea to allow him to lead his wife Eurydice out of Hades – was starkly emotional, full of grief and longing, and especially poignant for me.

A rustling to my left distracted me – Amelia Lynhurst, making a late entrance, whispered apologies as she pushed past those already seated to the empty space in my row. Thinking about my pursuers, I was more inclined to fear Mosry and, perhaps, Wollington, but Amelia Lynhurst was a wild card. And maybe her claiming the seat close to me was a sign that she was a force to be reckoned with. I had never trusted her after Isabella's doubts, which were then confirmed by Hermes's comments that she had 'dangerous aspirations' and possibly believed herself to be a reincarnation of Isis. There was the story of the key to the astrarium, too – how Amelia had found it and Enrico Silvio had stolen it from her. And Francesca obviously didn't trust Amelia either – her disdainful words 'scheming woman' still rang in my head. I noticed the matriarch tensing up as she watched the approaching Egyptologist – a flitter of fear crossing her face before she turned rigidly back to the stage. Nevertheless, I knew I had to confront Amelia. During our conversation at Isabella's funeral she had made it clear that she believed I had the astrarium; more importantly, she'd seemed to know a lot more about it than I did, even after my conversations with Hermes, Wollington and Silvio. Her opinion could be an equally significant piece in the puzzle, something that might bring me further towards a solution for the astrarium. But I needed to gain information from her without giving too much away, the mistake I had made with Hugh Wollington.

A musical crescendo interrupted my musings. Eurydice, clad in a diaphanous veil and echoing Orpheus's dance steps with heartbreaking grace, followed her husband to the entrance of the cave that led out of the Underworld and into the living world beyond. Orpheus's frantic yearning to turn and see his wife was evident in the half-spins he made, almost turning but not quite, the choreography teasing out the suspense, the terrible knowledge that if the poet did surrender to temptation he would condemn his wife to a second death and lose her all over again.

My whole body knotted in empathy, his longing mirroring my own desire to have Isabella alive again. And then, with a teasingly slow spin, Orpheus turned, arms outstretched, to embrace his wife as she stood on tiptoe, arched like a willow tree, at the portal between death and a second life – and so he lost her.

Embarrassing to admit, but I actually cried out loud when Eurydice collapsed lifeless again under the gaze of her husband. Mortified by my outburst, I watched on in silence while Orpheus, destroyed by his own desire, traced out his distress in a series of agonised leaps.

There was a reception being held in the foyer. I looked across the sea of people. Amelia was at the far side of the hall at the foot of a majestic marble stairway, half concealed by an aspidistra. I made my way past several Russian ballerinas who were mingling now with local dignitaries, past a table covered with brochures advertising package holidays to the Soviet Union. Without preamble I tapped the Egyptologist on her shoulder.

'We should talk.'

I guided Amelia into a small alcove decorated with a marble statue of Mohammed Ali in his customary fez. 'What do you know about the murder of Barry Douglas – or about my own interrogations, for that matter?' I couldn't suppress the aggressive tone in my voice. Looking slightly startled, Amelia glanced around, then leaned towards me.

'I understand that Mr Douglas killed himself. As for your arrest, I did warn you and you failed to take heed,' she answered in a low voice.

'Barry didn't kill himself and you know it. Why should I trust you? Isabella didn't.'

'Isabella was led into the wrong alliances. That was her tragedy, and now it's yours.'

'"Alliances" – like the sect you belong to?' I said sharply.

To my amazement, she laughed. 'Define sect.'

'A group of people who believe blindly in the same philosophy or religion to the exclusion of all others,' I replied without smiling back. 'One might even call them zealots. Dangerous people.'

'The future belongs to the zealot, whether we like it or not. But I don't belong to any "sect", as you put it.'

I changed tack quickly. I needed some answers and, judging by Amelia's knowing expression, I was convinced she was withholding information that was crucial for me to move forward.

'I want to know who killed Barry.'

'If it wasn't suicide, then I imagine it was the same people who were behind your arrests. All are actions that would require considerable influence with the Egyptian authorities. Think about it.'

I grabbed her wrist. 'Did you know they violated Isabella's body?'

Several bystanders turned at my raised voice, and I could see Henries talking furiously to Francesca Brambilla at the foot of the wide marble staircase. Amelia struggled to free her hand from my grasp.

'I can help you, Oliver. You should know that, like Orpheus's, Nectanebo's is a great love story. Just imagine the clandestine nature of their love. Nectanebo had several wives, all of whom must have hated Banafrit. Banafrit was a secret love, a woman who had access to the all-powerful priest clans and who could spy for her lover and report back on any treachery brewing amongst them. She must have been extraordinary, intelligent, powerful and, by all accounts, beautiful. Both Nectanebo and Banafrit risked their reputations and, possibly, their lives by loving each other.'

'No more myths, Amelia. I've read your thesis. What I want to know is why you want it, just like the others?'

'The astrarium chooses its own keeper and it is my duty to protect that person. Like Orpheus, Banafrit was willing to go into the Underworld to save her lover. Just like you might have to, Oliver.'

'I said enough riddles!'

Over Amelia's shoulder I could see Henries making his way across the foyer towards us. I spoke quickly and quietly, my voice beaded with threat. 'Then tell me, why didn't the astrarium prevent Nectanebo's demise?'

'At the beginning of his reign Nectanebo suppressed a possible coup from the Delta. There was growing dissent within Egypt. Powerful priests claimed that Nectanebo had insulted Isis herself and that the only way to appease the goddess's wrath and save Egypt was to build her an extraordinary temple and find a skybox that had been taken from

Egypt hundreds of years before, stolen from Ramses III by the powerful Hebrew magus Moshe ben Amram ha-Levi.'

'I know all this, Amelia. Get to the point.' I said impatiently. I could see Francesca looking my way.

'Isis was renowned for her magical abilities, so when Moses took it, it was seen not only as an insult to Ramses III but to Isis herself. The legend was well known in Banafrit's time.' After glancing around nervously, Amelia continued, 'The skybox already had the reputation of being a great weapon and sacred object and when the priests claimed that Isis wanted it back Banafrit saw a chance to help Nectanebo by reconciling the skybox with the goddess. She found the astrarium and rededicated it to Isis. One powerful sorceress bowing her head to a goddess steeped in magical myths – it must have been an extraordinary ceremony. But there's something else – a story inscribed on a naos that dates from about fifty years after Nectanebo's disappearance.'

'Professor Silvio's naos?'

Amelia stared at me in surprise, then quickly recovered herself. 'How is the professor?'

I wasn't fooled by her casual demeanour.

'Dying.'

Her eyes widened, whether theatrically or in genuine shock I couldn't tell. 'I'm sorry to hear that; he was once an honourable man. The naos that Professor Silvio discovered described the skybox's prophesy of the Pharaoh's death. After Banafrit rededicated it to Isis, it turned on Nectanebo. The astrarium developed a soul.' At least there was one thing that she and Hermes agreed upon.

'I've heard this theory before – it's absurd. Inanimate objects don't have souls, and why would the rededication trigger such an event?' I retorted, determined not to be drawn into the foggy realm of mysticism.

'Isis represents the unconscious will – the hidden desires. The function of the astrarium was to talk directly to the gods, therefore it became the embodiment of their will. So to the Ancient Egyptians it had a soul, whether you believe it or not. But if you want a prosaic practical explanation I can provide one, not that it's going to help your predicament. Let's just say that one day the astrarium was being transported, something struck it and deep within the mechanism a spring was loosened and the second pointer sprang out. An arbitrary accident takes on meaning – the Pharaoh's death is written in the sky! This would be a deeply powerful and political directive and one that enemies of the Pharaoh might want to exploit. And, of course, it brings up the strong possibility that the magical powers of the astrarium are real and that it can actually be set for killing. But then, you have to be a believer – and you are not.' She looked at me thoughtfully. 'I tell you what, Oliver, I'm giving a lecture on this very topic tomorrow morning, at the Archaeological Society, at ten. It might be useful for even a diehard sceptic like yourself to attend.'

'Could the astrarium have been used for Nectanebo's assassination?'

'Now you are beginning to understand.' Amelia saw Henries coming towards us and started to pull away. I held on to her sleeve.

'So I have nothing to fear.' Suspicion gave way to relief and I almost didn't notice that I was speaking more openly than I'd planned to. Amelia pulled herself free.

'As long as the astrarium remains sleeping. I trust you have not activated it?'

Before I had a chance to reply, Henries joined us. Amelia made an excuse and disappeared into the crowd.

30

The auditorium of the Archaeological Society looked as if it had been designed by some Victorian architect for nine-teenth-century London. It was an airless, mock-Gothic hall panelled in dark wood. A couple of ancient ceiling fans, spaced between arched beams, spun lazily above us and the room was lit by a row of low wrought-iron lanterns. There was a stage set up at one end. Dusty old purple curtains hung closed across the front of the stage and I wondered whether it might have been used for amateur theatrics once. Above the curtains hung a painted portrait of the last king of Italy – Vittorio Emmanuele III – along with a dedication in Latin underneath: 'To know is to be forewarned.' I couldn't help reading it as an ominous warning. Ironically, Emmanuele had been exiled to Egypt in 1946 by a liberated Italy, a penance imposed because of his alliance with Mussolini. He died later in Alexandria. It was hard not to feel horribly vulnerable, sitting there on my own in the near-empty auditorium. I reminded myself that I was there to gather information, the need for which outweighed the risk of encountering others. But I still glanced around nervously.

It was almost ten in the morning and so far there was only a small audience – several French and Italian archaeologists whom I recognised vaguely, one Pole from Kom el-Dik, who gave me a friendly wave across the hall, and Hermes, who sat at the back, dressed rather formally in a caftan and cravat. We nodded at each other. He indicated for me to join him in the empty seat next to him. I declined. I wanted to sit at the front near a small door I'd noticed at the side of the stage, calculating that if I needed to bolt suddenly at any time, this would be the safest and nearest exit. There was no sign of Mosry or Omar, nor of Amelia, who I assumed would appear when the curtains were open. Slowly, the auditorium filled up. About half of the ancient seats were now taken.

A young, earnest-looking Arab youth – a local student, I imagined – pulled the blinds shut. The auditorium was immediately suffused with the dim yellow and somehow ancient light shining down weakly from the lanterns.

It had been easier to feel safer when the hall had been flooded with the strong natural morning light, but I now noticed a projector set up at the back of the hall. Trust Amelia to want a theatrical atmosphere, I told myself, irritated by the Egyptologist's tendency to dramatise. Just then the curtains began to open and there was a thin spluttering of applause. I looked up and saw that Amelia herself now stood at the podium, clutching her notes.

With a flourish she placed her papers on the lectern and, after adjusting the pearl necklace that she wore over her tweed suit, she lifted the spectacles that hung on a chain around her neck and began.

'Some of you have heard me speak on the subject many times and it is well-known that my fascination with Banafrit, Isis and Nectanebo has cost me both my academic position and my professional reputation.'

At this Amelia looked up and viewed the audience defiantly, almost as if she was searching for her detractors. There
was a deathly silence into which the young student standing
at the projector coughed nervously. Amelia dropped her gaze
and continued. 'But before I begin, a note on the Ancient
Egyptian deities, so that even the lay person in the audience
will be able to understand their importance and the great
influence they held over their peoples. If you wronged a god
as an individual – either by desecrating property that
belonged to the god, or by sinning – you could be denied
the afterlife. But if you wronged the gods as a people, their
ensuing wrath could lead to the end of your world. In
Ancient Egypt, the image of a massive flood was a popular
apocalyptic theme – appropriated later by the Christians.
First let me introduce Isis . . .'

Behind her the first slide appeared: an image of Isis – a
massive granite statue of the goddess with the crown of
cows' horns and a sun disc on her head, cradling the child
Horus.

'. . . Isis was the queen of the goddesses; she was both
sister and wife to Osiris and mother to Horus, before Seth
murdered Osiris. She is endowed with great magical powers,
which she gained through the sun god revealing his secret
name to her. She is unique in this magical prowess. A force to
be reckoned with, both inspiring and terrifying. She is the
original revengeful goddess.'

The next slide came up. Osiris, holding the flail sceptres
of a pharaoh across his chest.

'This is Osiris, king of the Underworld and once ruler of
Egypt until his brother Seth murdered him. Seen here holding the djed-pillar, a symbol representing the backbone of
Osiris, he is the judge of all dead souls, ready to punish sinners but humane to those who have led good lives. He plays

a vital role in the most important religious ritual of all – the Weighing of the Heart – in the Underworld after death. Next slide please, Abdul . . .'

The next slide came up with a click and clatter. It was of Thoth, Barry's favourite deity. I immediately recognised him from Barry's home-made shrine and the Australian's colourful description. Looking at the ibis-headed god, I felt as though I was greeting an old friend.

'Another god who is important in the Weighing of the Heart: Thoth, the moon-god, who was considered responsible for the gift of writing. Hieroglyphs were a gift reserved only for the elite and priests. The ibis head is symbolic of the moon, the curved beak the crescent moon. He also appears as a baboon-headed god, as baboons were famous for becoming agitated at the end of the night.

'Then, of course, there is Horus—' Here a quick slide of the hawk-headed god appeared. 'Son of Isis and Osiris, he is the personification of pharaoh-hood, the notion of divine kingship. His early life is beset with attacks by Seth who tries unsuccessfully to destroy him, at least unsuccessful so far . . .' Amelia smiled. Behind me was a thin splattering of laughter, and as I swung around to study the audience, I noticed a new figure standing at the back near the projector – a tall, thin, older man, elegant in his profile. There was something unsettling about him, a kind of regal but sinister presence. I craned my neck but in the dim light it was impossible to get a clear look at his face without moving closer. Filled with unease I turned back to the lectern. Now a slide of Seth himself was displayed.

'And, finally, we have the villain himself: Seth, the most complicated and unpredictable of all the gods. Feared by many, worshipped by all who seek power, Seth is the god of Chaos, War, conflict, storms, winds, darkness and evil, he was also the patron of Upper Egypt. Here I have him in his animal form—'

The slide was of a strange mythical creature – not unlike a large dog but with the curved beak of a bird, upright pointy ears and, most disturbing of all, a forked tail. I stared at it. It was like one of those primordial images that lurk in the back of all nightmares of believers and atheists alike. Amelia's dry voice pulled me back into the room.

'He can also be depicted as a black pig or hippo, usually when he is drawn in battle with Horus. He is also sometimes portrayed as a man with bright red hair, as the Ancient Egyptians saw red hair as evil. He is a foe not to be underestimated.'

The image of Hugh Wollington's flaming sideburns flashed through my mind, an irrational association I couldn't shake off even as Amelia continued. I forced myself to concentrate. So far I hadn't heard anything new about the astrarium, but I knew she'd soon turn back to her favourite topic.

'Seth murders Osiris and fights Horus – but finally Horus is declared the winner. Seth, the god of darkness, is forced to retire after being given two Middle Eastern goddesses as wives by Re – the sun-god.' Another slide appeared. 'Re also makes Seth responsible for thunder in the sky. There are some who claim Seth never stopped fighting, merely took his battle into the Underworld. But that is a whole other story. Back to my hypothesis: Isis always held a fascination for people – the queen of the goddesses, she embodied the ultimate in magical power, so it isn't surprising that she drew in her wake a number of cults dedicated solely to her. One of these sprang into existence around a specific object, an astrarium that originated during the realm of Ramses III – the second king of the Twentieth Dynasty. In Judeo-Christian terms, I'm talking about the years 1198 to 1166 BC. The relevance of this is that I believe that Ramses was involved in the exodus of the Canaanites – Moses's exodus – and that Moses became a great magus at Ramses's court under the tutelage of the pharaoh's greatest magicians and astrologers. It was one of them who designed and constructed a skybox dedicated to Isis, a powerful tool to help the pharaoh to ward off the invasion of the "Sea People" and to fight the ongoing plagues that appeared at this time. It is my firm belief that it was this astrarium that Moses stole from the court to ensure the safety of his own people when fleeing the royal army and confronted with the barrier of the Red Sea. He used this sacred object to part the waters.'

Behind me the projector whirled and another slide came up, this time of a dramatic biblical etching of Moses, hands held out at the edge of the Red Sea, the walls of water towering on either side of him.

'Moses must have abandoned the astrarium later in a minor Isis temple in the Sinai desert, driven no doubt by guilt and, possibly, some residue of respect for the goddess Isis, to appease a wronged deity. And there the device stays abandoned for another ten dynasties until the last dynasty – the Thirtieth.

'The astrarium then reappears in the written scrolls during the realm of Nectanebo II.' Amelia scanned the audience for a response. There was none, just the sound of the Polish archaeologist's pen as he scribbled notes and the whirl of a ceiling fan above. She gestured to her assistant and another slide appeared on the back wall. This time of Nectanebo – a statue of the throned king along with his cartouche beneath, instantly recognisable from his sarcophagus in the British museum. I glanced behind me, curious as to Hermes's reaction – he was sitting at the edge of his seat, looking intently up at Amelia. If I hadn't known better, I would have said his stare was malevolent in the extreme. And, for a moment, I found myself wondering again about the shared history of the two Egyptologists.

'Nectanebo II, the last of the Egyptian pharaohs, was desperate to associate his dynasty with the powerful dynasties of the old and great Egypt. The legend of the astrarium was already well established by then, evident in this excerpt that I discovered in the Dream Papyri, a collection of dream scenarios that the Egyptians thought contained predictions of the future. They date from the Twenty-seventh Dynasty—' Here another slide appeared, this one of hieroglyphs written on thin parchment.

'The hieroglyphs describe a great skybox that had caused the destruction of the king's army and facilitated the escape of a large number of slaves. A skybox that could slay kings and move both sea, earth and sky. A skybox that belonged to Isis, goddess of great magic. You have to understand that Nectanebo ruled a country beset with civil unrest and political intrigues, and to keep control he needed to reach back to greater times to subjugate his political opponents and to resurrect the Great Egypt of the past. He was also under constant threat of invasion from the Persians. He needed a weapon of huge magical and spiritual symbolism. Banafrit, both his mistress and the high priestess of Isis, knew of the astrarium and sent her own hunting party out to the Sinai to locate it. We know she must have found it because there is a line of verse describing it on an Isis temple built by Nectanebo in her honour. But the astrarium turned on Nectanebo. It predicted his own death date. Very little is known about this, so most of what I'm about to say is conjecture. The prediction of his death would have weakened Nectanebo, so he would have done everything to conceal the terrible secret. Another interpretation is that his enemies – and by then, his was a country fraught with tension and political unrest – used the prediction for their own agenda, that is if they didn't create it themselves to build his death into a self-fulfilling prophesy. The last interpretation, and maybe the most fanciful of all, is that they used the astrarium's predictive powers to kill the Pharaoh by getting it to set his death date. Having provided her lover with the most powerful instrument of their times to save his life, Banafrit might have had to watch it defeat her beloved Pharaoh. Ancient Egypt was a place where sorcerers and magicians ruled, dominated by fickle and powerful gods and goddesses. Anything is possible, ladies and gentlemen.

'After that, any mention of the skybox or astrarium vanishes along with the mysterious disappearance of Nectanebo II himself. Then the Persians invade, then Alexander himself.

'The next time the astrarium emerges is during the reign of Ptolemy III. A scroll describing the device and its powers was apparently housed in the great library of Alexandria, the Temple of the Muses or Mouseion. The library was destroyed in 30 AD.'

A medieval illustration of the Mouseion appeared, a projection of what it must have looked like, destroyed along with many of the great written works of mankind in a fire.

'The Mouseion had been the greatest library of antiquity – debatably of all time. It was here that Ptolemy III commissioned seventy rabbis to translate into Greek the five books of the Old Testament that made up the Torah, and here that the greatest mathematical, astronomical and medical texts of the epoch were housed. Manuscripts were amassed in a multitude of languages: Aramaic, Hebrew, Nabatean, Arabic, the Indian languages as well as Egyptian,

reflecting the polyglot nature of the ancient city itself. Every
known account of importance was housed here, Ptolemy III
was known to have had a huge interest in the mystical as
well as the religious.'

A ripple ran through the audience, voices whispering in
low undertones. Slowly, I turned, and to my horror saw that
Mosry and Omar had now entered the hall at the back, peering through the dim light towards the front.

I tensed up, ready to bolt for the exit, when suddenly
four police officers entered the hall from the other end and,
walking down, flanked the auditorium, two on either side.
To my surprise I noticed their presence seemed to deter
Mosry and his henchman from further action. They both sat
down in the back row and, arms folded, stared down aggressively at Amelia, who immediately became flustered,
knocking some of her papers off the lectern. As she picked
them up, I noticed that her hands were now trembling. In a
shaky but defiant voice she continued her lecture, as the
policemen slowly wove their way through the room. I sat in
my chair, paralysed with indecision.

'There is no doubt that the Ptolemaic queen Cleopatra
VII would have known of the astrarium's existence through
scrolls housed at the Mouseion, just as she would have
known about its famed military and magical powers.'

Suddenly I felt the touch of a hand on my shoulder.
Startled, I almost jumped out of my seat, but Hermes's low
whisper reassured me.

'Don't panic, Oliver, and don't react. I have to get us out
of here. I'm just waiting for the right moment. When I say,
follow me.' I glanced back. Hermes had slipped in next to
the seat behind me. Behind him, in the back row, Mosry
caught my eye and smiled – a cold, smug confirmation, as if
he knew he'd cornered me at last. Dread filled me and I felt

frozen, pinned to my seat by the sheer terror of his gaze. I looked across at the projector; the mysterious aristocratic figure that had been there earlier had disappeared yet I hadn't seen anyone leave. Back on the stage, Amelia was concluding her lecture.

'I suspect Cleopatra might have attempted to employ it in her last great battle between her lover Mark Anthony and Octavian – the sea battle at Actium. A hypothesis I owe to my esteemed and now deceased colleague Isabella Warnock, née Brambilla.'

Across the auditorium Amelia looked directly at me, her eyes burning into mine.

'The astrarium has dipped in and out of recorded history and there are great periods of time where it appears virtually to have disappeared. I believe these have been times when it fell under the guardianship of a secret sect of Isis worshippers, whose sole task was to ensure that if the device was used it would be for the good of mankind. As to the whereabouts of the astrarium today or the reality of its ability to wreak either chaos or good fortune – who knows? On that note I conclude.'

As Amelia started to collect her notes the curtains suddenly fell shut. Then lights flickered and blacked out, plunging the hall into total, sudden darkness. The room filled with shouting, people getting up and seats banging against wood. I leaped to my feet, then felt Hermes grabbing my arm.

'This way!' he hissed.

He pulled me forward and we stumbled blindly up some stairs that led up onto the stage, then fought our way through the soft veil of the velvet curtains. On the other side I blinked as my eyes readjusted to the light level. Just before me, an oblong of dim light radiated from the stage floor, illuminating Hermes who knelt beside it. It was a stage trapdoor. Amelia was nowhere to be seen.

'In here – quick!' I bolted over and climbed down the short ladder, followed by Hermes who pulled the trapdoor shut behind him. Using a lighter he guided me through a labyrinth of underground passages. They must have once been the narrow stone lanes of ancient Alexandria, a city famously riddled with subterranean passages. Hermes, holding his lighter high above his head, was almost running as he led me through arched stone and brick tunnels, their walls oozing dampness, the air musky, almost sulphuric. I guessed he must have had an intimate knowledge of the bewildering maze, but his surefootedness amazed me nonetheless. I stumbled and landed on one knee, my trousers now wet with the thin stream that ran down the centre of the floor of the tunnel. Hermes helped me to my feet.

'Are you all right?'

'I'll survive – where are we?'

Hermes lifted his lighter, illuminating an ancient ceiling – the remnants of a Roman mosaic that seemed to feature a throned Zeus. 'Just under the football stadium, not far from your villa,' he replied. Behind us the sound of men shouting suddenly echoed down the tunnel. Startled, we both swung around.

'They're only about ten minutes away.' Hermes pulled me forward. 'We must hurry. They will kill you if they catch us.' His pace intensified and, limping now, I struggled to keep up with him, only terror preventing me from collapsing from pain. After what felt like an hour we arrived at an iron ladder.

'Up there – you will know where you are once you are on the street.'

I stared at him. Indebted, I had no choice but to trust him now. 'Thank you.'

'Do you now believe in the importance of the astrarium, Oliver?'

I couldn't bring myself to speak.

'When you're ready you must bring it to me.'

Suddenly there was the sound of a bullet ricocheting off stone. Hermes pushed me towards the ladder.

'Hurry!'

'What about you?'

'I can take care of myself.'

I watched him bolt back into the shadows. Five minutes later I emerged from a manhole opening into blinding midday light and the frenetic streets of the bazaar. Within minutes I lost myself in the crowd.

31

Ibrihim was waiting for me back at the villa. Gravely, he handed me a note from Mr Fartime who had received a distressed call from my father in England and asked that I ring Da as soon as I possibly could. Fartime kindly suggested that I should use the company's phone to make the call. Touched by both his concern and generosity, I borrowed Ibrihim's Vespa and raced through the back streets of Alexandria, determined to shake off any followers. I parked at the back of the offices and used a tradesman's entrance that was partially concealed by a couple of stalls selling antiques.

The office was empty – it was Friday, the Islamic day of rest – and as I fished out my key I was thankful for the privacy.

Sitting at Mr Fartime's desk, I felt a little like a naughty schoolboy who had broken into the headmaster's office but consoled myself with the thought that I was there with his permission. Ten minutes later the operator had got hold of my father.

'Oliver, is that you?' His voice sounded old and frail, but so close I felt as if I could almost smell the faint scent of pipe tobacco coming off his woolly jumper. In my mind I could see his long gnarled fingers curled around the old Bakelite telephone receiver.

'Da, what's happened?' I steeled myself, anxious about Gareth and my father's own health.

'It's Gareth. He didn't want to ring you himself. He seemed to think you had enough on your plate . . .'

'Is he okay?'

'It's not the drugs, if that's what you're worried about . . .' My imagination leaped ahead but my father's voice interrupted my grim thoughts. 'His house was broken into. He couldn't tell the police for obvious reasons' – he coughed delicately – 'but he told me the burglars had been very specific in their ransacking. They sounded like nasty customers – apparently they roughed up his girlfriend when she disturbed them . . .'

Shocked, I leaned against the desk. So Wollington had caught up with me, and worse, I'd inadvertently dragged my family into this mess.

'Da, listen, I have to get off the phone to ring Gareth immediately. But before I go I want you to promise me not to answer the door to any strangers, you understand?'

'I'm not frightened of strangers, lad. I've fought the best of them in my time,' he replied gruffly.

'Da, I know you can look after yourself, but this is different. They could be armed. Please, all I'm asking is for you to lie low for a while.'

'Oliver, are you in some kind of trouble?' For the first time in the conversation my father sounded scared.

'I'll get myself through it. You have to trust me.'

'Always, lad, you know that.'

As I put down the receiver I fought back tears.

The line rang for minutes but it felt like hours. By the

time Gareth answered I'd convinced myself that Wollington or some hired thug had got there before me and Gareth was now lying dead in the house somewhere.

'Gareth, Dad rang me.' I tried to hide the panic in my voice.

'I told him not to.'

'Never mind all that, just give me a description of the men.'

'There were two, at least that's what Zoë thinks she saw, she was knocked out pretty quickly. Oliver, they took my notebook with the diagrams of the astrarium and my solution to the cipher.'

My heart leaped, my worst fears confirmed. Wollington must have known about the existence of the Was, of course he would – he knew Amelia, Hermes and Silvio – and then followed me to Egypt. Angered by the raid, the urge to protect my brother swept through me.

'Is Zoë okay?'

'A slight concussion – actually, she found the whole thing sort of exciting, but that's Zoë for you. Are *you* okay? I'm worried about you. Who are these nutters?'

'Look, the less you know the better. Can you stay at Zoë's for a while? I don't think they'll be back and it'll only be you that they're after, but I'd feel better if you disappeared for a few weeks.'

'I can do that. I knew Isabella was on to something huge – wasn't she, Oliver?'

'Stay safe, Gareth.' As I hung up, a new loneliness rushed through me.

Back at the villa, a progress report on the new oilfield from Moustafa was waiting for me; the gravity data we had been unofficially collecting looked increasingly encouraging. If I

could secure the finances and the licence, I could end up a
very wealthy man. I debated whether Johannes Du Voor
would support the project, then I remembered his warning
about relying too much on intuition and decided to wait
until I had more concrete data before telling him about the
potential find.

I got up and walked out onto the balcony. I could see the
shaggy outline of Tinnin flopped halfway out of his kennel.
The rucksack containing the astrarium was still buried
behind it. As if sensing my gaze, the Alsatian growled in his
sleep.

My mind returned to the lecture and Amelia's clear chron-
icling of the astrarium's trajectory through time. A sudden
longing for Isabella swept over me and a memory of us
standing besides the River Ganges came into my mind. We'd
been watching the local Indians wash and immerse themselves in the holy river when we'd suddenly both noticed a
baby struggling as it was taken by a sudden current, the
mother screaming in frozen horror from the bank. In a
second, Isabella was in the water. Swimming wildly, she
reached the child and dragged it back to the bank while I
found myself watching in amazement. That was Isabella,
fearless, decisive and able to act in the moment. I wondered
what she would do in my place. What would her next steps
be? I was now as entangled in the mystery of the astrarium as
she'd been, whether I wanted to be or not. Had she been
trying to tell me something when she visited me in my
dreams? Amelia's statement about the astrarium's ability to
cause chaos or good fortune haunted me, and I realised how
far my mind's boundaries had been pushed in my desperation to solve the enigma of the device. Where did the
symbols Isabella pointed to in my dream lead me to? The
fish, the bull and the Medusa. A fish, I knew, was a Christian

image. And then I suddenly remembered Francesca telling me the name of the priest at St Catherine's.

I paused with my hand on the cool wall of the cathedral, thinking about the first time I'd been there, with Isabella. We'd visited it only months before and I remembered her face avid with passion as she told me about its namesake, Saint Catherine. Like many academics, Isabella was convinced that Catherine was merely a Christian appropriation of Hypatia of Alexandria, a pagan philosopher crucified for making her intellectual beliefs public and who was an extraordinary mathematician and cosmologist. Standing there on the steps it was as if Isabella walked before me, her black hair swinging as she described all this to me. Then I realised with a jolt that my second visit to the cathedral had been for Isabella's own funeral.

I stepped inside and felt instant relief from the late-afternoon heat. The high vaulted ceiling was a mosaic of coloured light. I walked towards the main altar, my footsteps echoing in the profound silence. A man sweeping the marble floor spoke to me in Italian, offering himself as a guide. When I asked for Father Carlotto, he disappeared through a side door. I took the opportunity to wander around the cathedral, recalling how it had looked during the funeral, how dreamlike the altars had seemed to me with their gilded wood and lurid stained glass.

I stopped before one window that showed the figure of Christ, the crown of thorns cutting into his forehead, his limbs emaciated. He was reaching towards an older man who was offering him a set of keys, and it was this older figure who had caught my attention. I stared at the grey-haired man, his peasant's face infused with benevolence. I knew him from my Catholic childhood – Saint Peter, the gatekeeper. But it

was the bird that hovered over his left shoulder that fascinated me. I knew it immediately – a sparrowhawk. Then I
remembered Zoë asking me about the bird fluttering around
my own left shoulder. Instinctively, my hand went up to
touch the space next to my left ear. Nothing. What was I
expecting, ghosts?

'Our Saviour handing the keys to Saint Peter. Beautiful,
isn't it?'

I swung around and recognised the short tanned man in
his early thirties from Isabella's funeral. If he hadn't been
wearing a cassock I might have mistaken him for an insur-
ance salesman.

'What is the symbolism of the bird?' I asked.

'The sparrowhawk was the emblem of Saint Peter. Of
course, the early Christians borrowed from the culture
around them and so the Copts assimilated some of the
Ancient Egyptian symbols – the sparrowhawk was important
to them as well. You have an interest in such things, Mr
Warnock?'

'You remember me from the funeral . . .'

'With some difficulty. With that beard I almost mistook
you for one of my Coptic brothers.' He shook my hand, his
palm surprisingly cold. 'How can I help you?'

I glanced around carefully to make sure we weren't overheard. The cathedral appeared empty but I wasn't prepared
to take a risk. 'I wanted to ask you about the body of my
wife.'

'*Scusi?*' He looked flustered, as if he thought he might
have misheard.

'Francesca tells me she organised for your staff to collect
the body from the ambulance before it was delivered to the
city mortuary.'

'Francesca?'

'Madame Brambilla, my wife's grandmother. Surely you know her? After all, your church has looked after the family for decades.'

'No, there has been a mistake.'

'Madame Brambilla told me herself.'

Father Carlotto guided me to one of the smaller enclaves, a family shrine. 'Monsieur Warnock, the Brambilla family was excommunicated many years ago,' he murmured discreetly.

'Excommunicated?' I couldn't hide the shock in my voice.

'In 1946. I looked it up in the records when Madame Brambilla begged me to hold your wife's funeral in our cathedral. I had to have a rather difficult conversation with the Bishop, but we concluded that the sins of the father – or, in this case, the grandfather – had nothing to do with the granddaughter. May God rest her soul.'

'But what about Paolo Brambilla? He died in 1956 – wasn't he buried by this church?'

'He is buried, it is true. But not by this church.'

I looked away to disguise my amazement. My gaze fell on a stained-glass depiction of Saint Sebastian stuck with a dozen arrows, his face twisted in a tragic grimace.

'Why were they excommunicated?' I asked.

'That is a private matter between the church and the family.'

I pulled out my wallet. 'But I am part of the family. And you know, on behalf of the family, I was thinking we should make a donation – say, a hundred dollars. I noticed on the way in that you are in the middle of restoring your roof.'

Father Carlotto hesitated, pursing his lips. Finally, with a certain resignation, he threw up his hands. 'Indeed, and such a generous donation would be most welcome. But, Mr Warnock, you cannot bribe me into surrendering the secret records of the church.'

I picked up a prayer book that had been left on a pew and tucked two fifty-dollar bills between the pages. 'Please, Father, for the sake of my wife. I have reason to believe that her spirit is not at peace.'

I pressed the prayer book into his hands. He stared at me as if deciding whether to trust me or not. Finally he took the book.

'Indeed, I am sure she is most certainly not at peace. Her death was a great tragedy, perhaps an unnecessary one. As to the excommunication, apparently the grandfather had some unfortunate associates – eccentric people who indulged in all sorts of strange pagan rituals. Harmless, really, I suppose, just fanatical historians who got carried away. This country has many echoes; they can creep into your head and make the imagination run riot. My predecessor was prepared to ignore them, but some of the congregation got upset. And then, when Nasser came,' he lowered his voice, 'there was a witch-hunt. No one was safe.'

'And my wife's body?'

'I have no idea. We certainly didn't collect the body. I only ever saw the coffin. I can show you the entry in the record book.'

'That won't be necessary. One other thing, Father, the fish is a Christian symbol, isn't it?'

Father Carlotto smiled, relaxing at last. 'The fish represents the disciples of Jesus, some of whom, as you know, were fishermen. It was used as a secret symbol in the first century AD by early Christians who maintained their faith against the hostility of the Roman Empire. The tradition has continued over the centuries – it has never been easy being Christian in this part of the world. Even now, some of the young Copts here in Alexandria have hidden tattoos to indicate their faith. The symbol also appears in murals in the tombs at Kom el-Shugafa, a place that some of my congregation still believe is haunted.'

He hesitated, then, after checking that the church was still empty, went on in a nervous whisper, 'But there is something else you should know . . . your wife came to see me before she died.'

I tensed. 'About what?'

'She came to me and asked to be baptised so that she could make confession. She was terrified. I baptised her there and then with holy water, then took her confession. Mr Warnock, I believe she had found herself involved in things beyond her control. She told me of the existence of an object, the significance of which would shake up the religious and historical worlds. She asked me whether the church would provide sanctuary if necessary. I reassured her that it would, but I'm afraid I was slightly sceptical. She wasn't the first Egyptologist I'd taken confession from who had spoken of such matters. There was another young Egyptologist, about twenty years before, also a woman . . .'

As I listened I suddenly remembered Demetriou al-Masri's story about the other corpse he'd examined who had also been missing her organs. I shivered as a sudden chill passed through the stone walls of the church. Who was she?

'You knew about the existence of the astrarium?' I asked him directly.

Visibly startled, Father Carlotto crossed himself, 'Please, it is dangerous even to speak the name out loud. But yes, I had heard rumour of such an object. There is a monk I know – not Catholic, he is of the Coptic order – who once told me of ancient documents in his care, both from the time of the Pharaohs and also from the time of Napoleon's invasion, that spoke of the existence of such a device. Father

Mina, he is at Deir Al Anba Bishoy at Wadi El-Natrun. I can make a few discreet enquires on your behalf, if you wish – I owe your wife that much. I don't know if you know the story but there is an account by an early bishop, a Saint John, who claimed that Hypatia herself used both an astrolabe and witchcraft to entice the Roman governor of Alexandria back to the pagan ways. Perhaps this was the very same device – who knows?'

'Isabella was convinced that the only thing Hypatia had been guilty of was being more intellectual than her male counterparts,' I retorted.

Father Carlotto smiled. 'She was a strong-willed woman, your wife. Perhaps if I had suggested she left Egypt . . . But she was almost hysterical, she wasn't really making much sense. I'm deeply sorry now that I didn't take her more seriously.'

'When was this?'

'About two weeks before her death.' He stepped closer. 'Come back to me in a few days – I'll see what I can find out for you. But listen, my friend, if you should need sanctuary at any time, we can help you. My Coptic brothers at Wadi El-Natrun will take you in for as long as necessary. They have helped others this way, and, despite your loss of faith, you are still a Catholic, no? And with that beard you would be almost invisible.'

I examined his open face cautiously, wondering how much he actually knew about the circumstances of Isabella's death. All I could see was someone burdened by a confession and worried that he had somehow played a part in a premature death.

He placed a hand on my shoulder. 'Please, sometimes in life one must simply trust. Remember my offer.' And he left, the prayer book clasped in his hands.

*

I stood beside the huge pipe organ that sat beneath a stained-glass window depicting the trials of Saint Cecily. What terror had compelled Isabella to resort to confessing to a priest? I knew she'd occasionally gone to church but I'd never known her to go to confession. What had she been running from?

The sound of a familiar voice murmuring in English broke my reverie. It was coming from a side chapel: a woman's voice asking about candles. I walked towards it, and entered an alcove with a marble relief depicting a martyred female saint against the far wall. Photographs of children and small offerings of flowers had been placed at the saint's feet. There was even a rusting, unopened can of Pepsi. The woman had her back to me, but I still recognised her. She kneeled and placed a small bunch of gardenias with the other offerings.

'Saint Sabine – isn't she the patron saint of children?' I asked.

Startled, Rachel Stern rose to her feet. 'Do I know you?'

I realised I must have looked fairly intimidating, cuts and bruises slowly fading but still a horrible patchwork on my face, my beard long, my hair tousled.

'Rachel, it's Oliver.'

She regained her composure. 'Oliver! I didn't recognise you with all that hair on your face. What a surprise.'

'A pleasant one, I hope. I'm sorry, I've disturbed you in prayer.'

'Shh, don't tell my rabbi. The offerings are for my sister – she's been trying to conceive for years. Apparently if you genuflect enough, the saint will come to the rescue, although I hope it isn't an immaculate conception – there are enough martyrs in the family as it is.'

She hauled her bag over her shoulder and began walking out of the chapel. I followed.

The sun blinded us for a moment as we stepped out of the cathedral. A young boy in rags slipped out from the shadow of a doorway, stretching out the stump he had for an arm. I pressed a few coins into his other hand.

Rachel armed herself with a huge pair of sunglasses, then assessed my crumpled linen jacket and jeans.

'I heard about your friend Barry,' she said, 'I was so shocked. He didn't seem the type to commit suicide.'

'He wasn't.'

A group of boys in uniform leaving the courtyard of the cathedral school ran past us laughing and I found myself relishing not being alone. The same loneliness I'd felt when I'd put the telephone down on my family came rushing back. I needed company. 'Look, would you like to go for a drink?'

'A drink? Last time we spoke I had the strong impression you didn't even like me.'

'I was drunk and belligerent. I apologise.'

Rachel studied me quizzically. 'No, I don't think so. Sorry, Oliver.' She walked away.

I followed her. 'Please, I just need to talk to someone who knows my history, someone I trust . . .'

She stopped. 'Are you in trouble?'

'Please, Rachel, you can't image how alone I've been . . .'

She hesitated, searching my face for something, perhaps a trace of the idealistic student she'd known, and then linked her arm through mine.

32

The Centro Di Portuguese was a relatively new and exclusive bar in Roushdy, the same expensive suburb as the oil company's villa. The club was a converted villa with an open-air bar in the courtyard and a disco upstairs. The entrance was hard to find and there were a couple of bouncers at the door, well-built ex-security types. The clientele was a curious mix with two things in common – wealth and loneliness.

We sat under a canopy of woven rushes, looking out over the courtyard. At another table, a group of Italian naval officers, drunk, were arguing about who was the greatest entertainer: Michael Jackson or Caruso. Nearby, a white Ugandan (rumoured to be an arms dealer) lifted his gaze away from the buxom young blonde he was flirting with and nodded slightly in my direction, the kind of sly acknowledgement one man makes to another when he thinks the other is involved in some clandestine activity, like infidelity. Aware of the possibility of having been followed I kept glancing around the bar nervously, but I was probably safer in there than in a lot of places in Alexandria. The bar was extremely select, and it was impossible to bribe your way in.

Despite her initial reluctance to join me, Rachel was by now on her third whisky. The only effect the alcohol seemed to have upon her was to make her more talkative. I didn't care. Once we'd arrived I'd found myself growing unusually taciturn. I desperately needed to discuss the events of the last few weeks with someone who might help me reach a more objective perspective, yet I was worried she'd be sceptical, or worse, if I confided in her. I'd already wasted half the evening arguing politics, but Rachel had indulged me, as if she sensed my sudden reticence to talk about personal matters. Our intellectual sparring anchored me to the world I'd known before Eygpt, before Isabella's death – it reminded me of a younger, more hopeful self. And as I sat there listening to her, I suddenly remembered a demonstration we'd attended as students some eighteen years earlier over France's involvement with the Algerian war of independence, and how fervent we'd been – utterly convinced of our moral stance, swept up in that youthful bravado that seems enough to last your whole life. The emotion I'd felt that day, watching the young American woman shouting slogans, echoed in me now – I'd loved Rachel for her political commitment and energy. She still had it. Despite her tough veneer, she seemed to have developed an underlying humanitarianism that appealed to me, as well as a new sense of self-parody, a characteristic that hadn't existed in the younger woman. It was as if she'd become sharper with age. Now there was a muscularity to her thinking that meant I felt slightly at war – a sexy wrestling match that promised to end in orgasm, defeat or death.

'So what exactly happened to your marriage?' I asked her.

'Oh, it's complicated. Basically, although Aaron claimed he loved unconventional women, I don't think he really wanted to be married to one. And you?'

'We are . . . *were* gloriously happy.' Not the entire truth but to say Isabella's name alone would have felt like an infidelity, even though I wasn't even planning to seduce Rachel. 'Tell me, why did you leave all those years ago?' I went on.

'Let's face it, Oliver, we were the most mismatched couple in the world. It wouldn't have lasted.'

'Perhaps not, but it hurt like hell at the time.' I grimaced, remembering my first adult heartbreak.

'As it should at twenty-three,' she retorted, smiling. Our gazes caught in sudden wry reminiscence.

The dance hit 'Disco Inferno' blasted out from above. I glanced up: the DJ, a young rake-thin Arab in a floral yellow silk shirt, was gazing wistfully at the deserted dance floor. Incense curled up from a burner on top of the bar and above us the open starry sky seemed to be looking down with faint amusement. Rachel's perfume drifted across the table with the night breeze, and despite everything, my grieving and my exhaustion, my fears suddenly seemed suspended, diminished.

Rachel sighed. 'Innocent times. I think about them nowadays. When I feel drenched in a kind of existential cynicism. It makes me feel so old. And you?'

'Me? I'm barely surviving from hour to hour.'

She looked at me. I knew she thought I meant surviving the loss of Isabella. She finished her drink, then moved closer, sighed. A moment of hesitation, the beat of blind faith one takes before free-falling into intimacy.

'My marriage broke down because we lost a child. A stillbirth. Aaron was able to deal with it better than me. I just buried myself in work. Then one day at breakfast I looked across the table and didn't recognise him any more. So there you have it – the end of the dream.'

I reached across for her hand. 'I'm sorry.'

'But we're both still here.'

I noticed she didn't remove her hand from my grip. I
looked up at her and suddenly the urge to unburden myself,
to talk to someone was overwhelming, a little like I imagined
had been the motive for Isabella's visit to Father Carlotto,
the impetus for a confession to help lighten the load.

'Rachel, if I told you something astonishing, something
barely believable, could you keep an open mind?'

'Hey, if there's one thing I'm proud to still have it's an
open mind . . .'

I took Rachel back to the villa and, while she waited in the
living room, I slipped out to the kennel and collected the
rucksack. Then, with it slung over my shoulder, we made
our way to the Sheraton Hotel where she was staying. I
needed her to see the astrarium while I told her my story.

In the lift going up to her room, I was aware of a growing
tension between us, a creeping eroticism – her scent, the
warmth of her body brushing against my bare arm. I wondered whether my senses were deceiving me, and if getting
involved might be a way of exorcising the loss of Isabella. It
was a disturbing but tantalising idea.

Catching Rachel's gaze, I realised she was feeling the
same sensations. Without thinking I pulled her towards me
into a clash of tongues and lips. With an almost electric
shock, I realised how much my body had missed being
touched over the past weeks. I vanished in her skin, the feel
of it so completely different from my wife's. Rachel's taste
was green, if I could find a colour for such things. Isabella's
had been a deeper hue. We moved slowly and luxuriously,
tentative in our exploration, my hands finding her nipples
hard against my palms. The lift shuddering to a halt interrupted us, making us both break into self-conscious laughter.

We stumbled down the empty corridor, still kissing and struggling with each other's clothes. Once inside her room, the realism of the pasty green walls and vinyl-covered cabinets sobered me up. But Rachel pulled me back into an embrace, then walked over to the bed.

'I drive this,' she said, with a grin. Then she pulled her smock top over her head, revealing her small breasts, her slim hips arching out of the low-slung jeans like some exotic musical instrument. 'I'm so deprived of touch I think I've gone half-mad; I can't even remember the last time someone hugged me. I always seem to be running – hotel lobbies, press rooms, airports. But oh boy, do I want you now.'

I moved towards her, then paused. In that brief moment of hesitation I knew that I was deceiving myself – I wouldn't be able to escape Isabella in this desperate lovemaking. I wasn't looking for a lover but a confidante. Someone who would convince me that I wasn't going mad. Anything else – sexual or emotional – would get complicated. And if I knew one thing it was that Rachel was complicated.

On the bedside table was an old black-and-white passport photo of a much younger Rachel: her face shiny with the blind belief of the idealist, her curly hair tortured into one long side plait. I recognised her expression. I touched the glossy paper; the faint memory of a smile in a London doorway seemed to come off like a smudge on my finger. Next to the photograph were a seashell and a dog tag. I picked up the shell and held it to the light. It was a small nautilus shell, pearly and ribbed, a luminous subterranean cathedral fated to shine for eternity.

From the bed Rachel looked at me, smiling, her hair spread above her head. Like snakes, like the Medusa.

'That seashell is from the beach where I lost my virginity,' she said. 'The photo's from the ID badge I wore on my first

Democrat campaign, and the dog tag belonged to a soldier I interviewed in Vietnam, who was killed the same day. Love, faith and destiny – I carry them everywhere as a reminder of how far I've come and how precarious life is. But I think you know that already, right?'

I stared down at her; she was so beautiful and desirable at that moment. I groaned inwardly, knowing I shouldn't succumb but knowing also that I wouldn't be able to help myself.

In lieu of an answer, I put the seashell into my mouth and placed it on her belly button with my tongue; the salt taste of her skin caught at my groin in a sudden erotic tumescence. I pulled her jeans and pants below her knees and worked my way down. Rachel gasped, her sex now wet against my face. Groaning, she reached for my fly. Then I was hard in her hand, and then in her mouth. Sitting up, she pulled my hands away from her and concentrated on pleasuring me, her eyes closed in sensual relish. It was as if she was determined to take me, not to be taken.

Trying to control the sudden surge of pleasure, I steadied myself with one hand against the headboard. Then, wanting to give to her, I pulled her up. Pushing her jeans right off, I made her stand as I kneeled. 'No,' she moaned and tried to pull me away, but I held her close, the rich musk of her filling me as I sucked and probed and she clawed at my shoulders. Then, finally, we toppled to the floor and she slowly lowered herself onto me, teasing me, both of us teetering on the edge of orgasm. I felt her bite my neck, her tongue in my ear, each breast filling my hands perfectly, each nipple hard against my palms.

It became a primal struggle of limbs as I threw her onto her back and, with her knees up against my chest, took her violently. With a glorious abandonment each of us surrendered to our own pleasure. She came screaming, triggering my own climax, then, to my astonishment, she broke into gales of laughter. Her hysteria was infectious and soon we were both rolling on the carpet. Perhaps we were giddy with the sheer relief of having experienced intimacy, or perhaps we were both secretly terrified – of our history, of the unspoken understanding that under the surface we were both singular creatures.

A framed poster of the Corniche slid off the wall and hit the carpet with a dull thud, missing Rachel's head by inches.

'You see, we're both watched by ghosts,' she declared. Then she got up, wrapped herself in a bathrobe and walked out onto the balcony. After pulling on my underpants I joined her.

The narrow concrete balcony looked out over the Montazah Gardens. The lights of the palace glimmered on the far side of the park and the tops of the tall palms that ran along the avenues swayed darkly, scratching at the night. Beyond were the fairy lights of the yachts moored at the jetty. It was one of those electric nights with a sense of timelessness, a certain agitation carried on the breeze that seduces fools like me into thinking they're immortal. Only this night I didn't feel immortal. I felt fallible and weak, unable to shake off the idea that I had somehow betrayed Isabella. Suddenly I was filled with that emptiness that often follows meaningless sex. But there was something else that disturbed me, something in the air, a creeping, inexplicable dread.

'I haven't had sex for over three years, not since before my divorce.'

Rachel's statement floated out over the ugly iron railings and down into the street below where it was lost in the steam of car noise and the vitriol of two men arguing at the corner.

'That's far too long.' I wrapped myself into the warmed

wings of her bathrobe. A wave of affection, almost familial, swept through me. It was comforting to hold her but I knew at that moment that we weren't going to be lovers, a mutual realisation that hung, unspoken, between us. 'Rachel, I can't be your lover, I just can't. I need you to be my friend. Could you be that for me?'

She nodded against my bare chest, her cheek a burning tattoo. Below, the two men continued to argue: real time, real life. I gestured for her to follow me inside and reached for the rucksack.

We sat on the bed with the astrarium between us, the story, in all its unbelievable components, now a tangible presence. I couldn't bear to look at Rachel, convinced my disclosure had condemned me entirely. Her hand crept along the tousled bedsheets towards my own.

'It's okay, Oliver, I believe you. You're lucky – if you'd told me these things five years ago I would have dismissed you as simply another Westerner seduced by eastern mysticism. But I've seen some weird things myself. When I was in Kampuchea I watched the Khmer Rouge recruiting witch doctors to terrify the peasants – a campaign that worked, by the way. Then a couple of years ago I was cursed by a Papuan Highlander when my photographer stupidly took a photo of his wives. But there's something else that makes me believe in the power of this . . . astrarium or whatever it is. This Mosry character. If anything, he's the one I would take most seriously.'

I nodded – it was impossible to dismiss Mosry's threatening persona even if I'd wanted to. His presence felt ubiquitious and had left me jumping at every moving shadow.

Rachel watched my expression, then put her hand on

mine. 'Prince Abdul Majeed is the one behind this, I'm sure of it.'

I remembered his glowering face from the TV programme that I'd watched in London. The arrogance of the despot.

Rachel continued urgently, as if to impress upon me how great a danger I was in. 'He's religious, fanatical and dangerous, the kind of man who'd believe in the power of something like this. He hates the West with a fervour and would do absolutely anything to destroy Sadat's peace initiatives. There've been attacks on Western interests in the region – a naval base in Turkey, the US embassy in Damascus, others that you don't even hear about. It's unofficial, but those who should know, know. It's Majeed. Recently his pace has picked up. More and more things are happening, seemingly unrelated. Mosry is his muscle. You can bet that if the astrarium is indeed believed to have such phenomenal influence over events, or even if it is viewed simply as a talisman of an older, more powerful Arabic civilisation, then Majeed will want it and he'll get Mosry to kill for it.'

The memory of Mosry staring into the interrogation room at police headquarters shot through me. Then Mosry smiling at me through a dimly lit lecture hall. I shuddered.

'But what do they want to do with it?' I asked.

'I don't know,' replied Rachel. 'Assume control? Total power? Revert the country back to a kind of feudal state with Majeed as ruler? To be honest, Oliver, Majeed is ruthless. You might want to take some safety precautions,' she said grimly, nodding for emphasis. 'Like get yourself some body armour, a gun, maybe even disappear for a while.'

She turned back to the astrarium, which I'd wrapped up again as she'd been talking. 'But this . . . this is totally amazing: history incarnate. To think the Ancient Egyptians were so advanced in astronomy. I would have liked to have met Isabella – she must have been fascinating.' Our gazes met. Rachel smiled, then looked away quickly.

'But what are we going to do about the astrarium?' she asked. To my surprise I found myself warmed by the inclusiveness of the word 'we', but a shiver of fear passed over me nonetheless. Almost everyone who got involved with the astrarium got hurt.

I sighed. 'Isabella mentioned that the astrarium had a destiny, a resting place. But there are a few pieces I still need to connect. For example, I also need to find out where Isabella's missing organs are and what exactly Giovanni and the group of archaeologists were up to. Then there is the mystery of the actual meaning of the cipher. I'm hoping it will lead to where the astrarium truly belongs, whether that's a temple or a tomb or wherever. I owe Isabella that much. How about strategising over breakfast?'

'Sounds like a good plan,' Rachel said. 'I'll take a quick shower and then we can go.' She stretched, then stood. 'See you in ten.' She disappeared into the bathroom.

The early morning sun had begun to filter through the thin curtains. I glanced at the clock radio beside the bed. It showed 6.30 a.m. I got up and walked out onto the balcony. A strange bird call pierced the early-morning chorus. For some reason it reminded me of London and the sparrowhawk crashing into my windscreen when I'd driven away from the flat. The memory brought with it an increased sense of foreboding, a sudden nervousness. Trying to distract myself, I glanced over at the balcony of the apartment next to us. The curtains were open and the room looked vacant. The sound of a van pulling up drew my gaze down to the front driveway of the hotel. The security guard, looking oddly nervous, stepped out of his sentry box and walked to the van's window. I could see money being exchanged, then, to my amazement, the guard walked away from the hotel. The van pulled up at the main entrance and two men in white uniforms jumped out. Something about the urgency of their movements made me squint, trying to see more clearly where they were headed.

As if sensing my gaze, one of them looked up towards the balcony, staring right into my face before I had a chance to duck down. By the time I'd stood up again, they had disappeared. With mounting uneasiness I went back inside. Rachel stood in the centre of the room, towelling her damp, curling hair. I hesitated, then said 'Maybe we should leave now, I don't know—' Suddenly, outside in the corridor, I could hear the sound of running footsteps. I gestured to Rachel to keep quiet, then went to the door and opened it as gently as I could, peering through the crack carefully. At the end of the corridor were the two men I'd seen outside, now with guns in their hands. I shut the door softly, then grabbed Rachel's arm and pulled her up, away from the door.

'Out – now!' I hissed, sweeping up the astrarium with my other hand.

Rachel looked towards the door, grabbed her travel bag, swept the things on top of the nightstand into her pocket and ran after me to the balcony. We climbed over the low wall onto the balcony of the room next door. The glass doors were unlocked and we slipped inside quickly.

Pressed against the dividing wall I could hear the sound of my own pounding heart and feel Rachel trembling beside me as we both held our breath. Through the thin wall we heard pounding on Rachel's door, then the sound of it being kicked in, followed by footsteps running into the room. They were right next to us and I could hear an exclamation, furious and frustrated. Rachel turned to me in bewilderment. We both

looked at the door at the same time. In seconds we reached it.
The corridor was empty. We slipped out swiftly, then bolted
down the hallway. As we turned the corner we collided with
a bellboy carrying a set of towels. He turned and stared at us.

We were already halfway through the empty lobby when
we heard shouting behind us. In amazement, the desk staff
watched us fly past.

'What the hell, Oliver!' Rachel yelled as she ran beside
me.

'Just keep running! They're right behind us!'

We pushed through the main glass doors and bolted into
the grounds and beyond, on to the sleeping streets. We ran
past a row of parked cars, then ducked into a side lane.
Behind us we could hear the sound of running feet.

Desperate, I glanced around. By a market stall a covered
cart stood, the thin horse harnessed to it chewing on a wad of
hay in the gutter. I pulled up the tarpaulin: the cart was half
empty, a layer of dry cement dust covering the bottom.
There was room to hide.

'In here!' I whispered but Rachel shook her head, looking
around wildly. Opposite us, a clothes stall was just opening
up and the old clothes seller was hanging up the long dresses
and caftans with a hook. Rachel pointed towards the stall.

After slipping the stallholder a hefty bribe we were soon
both hidden between rows of hanging clothes. Nearby we
could hear the sound of running and shouting. We both cowered deeper into the dresses, desperately trying to quieten
our panting breath. Minutes later we heard the men entering
the lane.

'You sure it was him?' one asked in a gruff voice. He spoke
in Arabic with a Saudi accent.

'Absolutely. Mosry had a photo,' the other replied.

Rachel's nails dug into my wrist at the mention of the

name. We waited, motionless, not daring to breathe as they approached the clothes seller.

'You seen two Europeans?' one of them asked the seller aggressively. Frozen, I tried to repress the overwhelming desire to run, praying that the old man would prove trustworthy. Next to me, I saw Rachel blanch.

'I have seen nothing. It's been quiet as a grave,' the old man answered calmly.

'Over here!' the other thug shouted. I peered through a gap in the clothes. I could see both of them frantically searching the cart, the tarpaulin thrown back.

'Must have run on,' the heavier one concluded and they moved off. We stayed hidden for another five minutes. I could feel the pounding of Rachel's heart through her fingers, and the smell of our fear cut through the perfumed fabric of the caftans. Tentatively, I looked out – the lane was empty. We emerged from the layers of hung dresses.

'He said the name Mosry, didn't he?' Rachel said in a low voice.

Her terrified whisper was drowned out by a boom, a flash of light and a shudder that seemed to travel in a wave underneath our feet. Thrown to the ground, we lay there as plaster and debris showered around us. I waited for my senses to be sucked back into the present. Lying on the ground next to us, the old clothes seller sat up, his face bleeding, and immediately broke into prayer.

'What the fuck was that?' Rachel sat up. There were a few tiny scratches on her face, but she seemed unharmed. I checked my arms and face, my fingers touching a couple of bleeding scratches where I'd been hit by debris, then stood and helped the old clothes seller to his feet. Over his wailing I could hear the scream of ambulances coming closer. I sat him down on the edge of his cart and then turned towards the hotel, visible at the end of the lane. One side appeared to be completely demolished, the plaster walls falling away in a heap of rubble and mangled iron girders. Patches of sky showed through shattered windows and door frames. Rachel looked at me, speechless.

'I think they killed two birds with one stone,' I said slowly. 'They were after me and the astrarium but failing that they decided to leave a token. I suspect that was one of Mosry's attempts to ruin Sadat's peace initiatives. They were after the journalists, the foreign press – people like you.'

'Oh Jesus, no.' Rachel froze in horror.

From the street behind us the sound of men shouting came closer. We started running again. Half-dressed and covered in plaster dust, we raced through the dawn streets like ghosts. People scattered away from us, horrified. I clutched the astrarium to my chest, counting the years of my life as a way to distract myself from the thudding of my heart and the roar in my ears, damaged temporarily by the blast. I wasn't entirely aware of where I was going, but some instinctive sense of geography must have been activated – the compass of the survivor – and we suddenly found ourselves outside the shop of a barber whom I knew well. Abdul had been cutting my hair ever since Isabella and I had arrived in Alexandria. A friendly man in his mid-sixties, he was a socialist and a poet and we'd spent many hours debating the failures and successes of various regimes and exchanging opinions on poets such as Seferis, Rilke and Lorca. I knew he would help us.

Abdul and his assistant were prostrate on the floor in the middle of morning prayer. Surprised, they peered up at us.

'Mr Warnock! You look terrible!' Abdul stood, dusting his knees.

'We need a room, Abdul. Please!' I shot him a beseeching glance.

Abdul took one look at Rachel's terrified face and quickly ushered us to the back of the store, shouting at his assistant to close the shop. In the distance there was the wail of sirens as ambulances and fire engines converged on the Sheraton.

33

The room above the barber's shop was equipped with a single iron bed, a small camp stove upon which sat a pot of mint tea, and a low wooden chair. There was a shelf holding several books, including a couple of revolutionary texts and a collection of Constantine Cavafy's poems, and various hairdressing supplies were scattered around. There were two small windows; one looking over the street market below, the other opposite it, looking over a panorama of rooftops.

Rachel, now dressed in a plain traditional caftan that Abdul had supplied, collapsed onto the bed. 'Are we absolutely sure those were Mosry's men?'

'I saw the white van drive up,' I said. 'That's probably where the explosives were. They saw me on the balcony and knew where to look for the astrarium, assuming I had it with me. Then they detonated the bomb when they were sure the astrarium wasn't in the hotel.'

'Oliver, it could have been anyone – the Syrians, the Jordanians even the Libyans. No one wants this peace accord except Sadat.'

'Rachel, you heard them mention Mosry's name yourself.'

She nodded. 'Yes, of course they did.' Then a terrible realisation crept into her eyes. 'Francois Paget from *Le Monde*, Eric Tullberg from *Der Spiegel*, George Del Sorro, the *Washington Times* – Christ, they were all there, Oliver.' She looked at me, her face white with shock, bits of plaster still caught in her blonde hair. If I had had any doubts about trusting her with the whole story, they would be dispelled now. She wouldn't betray me. I knew that now with absolute certainty – to the contrary, with her research skills and her knowledge of the political stakes involved she might be able to help me.

I glanced across at my rucksack sitting on the floor. Following my gaze, Rachel said nothing.

'Don't you think it's a little miraculous?' I ventured.

'What, having your hotel room blown up? I'd say it was very bad luck.'

'I mean having survived.'

'Knowing Mosry, next time we won't be so lucky.' She stood up. 'I have to get to a phone to file the story.'

'Shouldn't you see a doctor?'

'It's just a few cuts. All I need is a shower and a strong coffee. I'll sleep later, if I can find a spare hotel room. I suppose I should be thankful that Mosry's after you and not me.' She smiled grimly and turned towards the small bathroom, separated from Adbul's room by a threadbare curtain.

'Listen,' I said hesitantly, 'I need a couple of favours . . .'

'If it involves confronting two large Saudi gentlemen, count me out,' she said wryly as she pulled aside the curtain.

'Can you take a message to my housekeeper and collect some things for me? Then would you be able to visit the priest at St Catherine's and ask him whether you could borrow a Coptic monk's cassock? If you tell him it's for me, he'll understand. Please, Rachel? I'll be indebted to you for life.' I heard the water splashing, then she reappeared, perfunctorily scrubbed clean.

'For life, huh? That's tempting.' Rachel picked a large piece of plaster out of my tangled hair. 'I guess there's a story in it eventually. Is this barber trustworthy?'

'Completely, although we disagree on the merits of Rilke and he's itching to shave off my beard. So you'll do it?'

Rachel nodded. She left minutes later, with a letter for Ibrihim and some money that I'd borrowed from Abdul.

When she had gone I unwrapped the astrarium. Sections of bronze gleamed dully in the candlelight, and it was hard not to be spellbound by the sheer antiquity of the device. I didn't dare touch it now; it felt as if it were a living creature, imbued with all the power of those who had believed in it before – Moses, Banafrit, Cleopatra – and all those who had died for it. A dangerous seduction, I thought to myself. Amazingly, it was intact, the magnets still whirling. I sat there for a moment, hypnotised by the spinning mechanism. The biggest pointer was still firmly pointed to my birth date. Nothing else had happened. Odd, I thought: Gareth's death date had appeared almost immediately. Was it still deciding? Suddenly I thought I saw a light flicker behind me and spun around, half-expecting to see Banafrit's shadow stretched across the wall and ceiling. There was nothing.

The face reflected back in the sliver of mirror propped up against the wall was almost unrecognisable. For once my Celtic heritage had paid off. My beard, thick and black, covered most of my chin, and with the suntan I'd got at Abu Rudeis only my blue eyes gave me away as English. The robe, shirt and black priest's cap that Father Carlotto had given Rachel fitted me perfectly. It was disturbing that I, a fervent atheist, could take on the appearance of a cleric so convincingly. It was, however, the perfect disguise.

'Wow! You look totally legit.' Rachel stared at me, amazed. 'Even I wouldn't have recognised you.'

I reached into the bag packed by Ibrihim, pulled out a pair of sunglasses and put them on. 'And now you wouldn't even suspect I was European.'

Rachel had had to negotiate the police barricades set up around the city centre and the Sheraton, but had managed to slip by with some hefty bribes. When she'd arrived at the villa Ibrihim had been almost hysterical. The night before, while he'd been visiting his mother, the villa had been broken into, my bedroom and study searched, and Tinnin the Alsatian poisoned. Mosry's men were getting closer. I was terrified but furious also. How dared they terrorise Ibrihim and then vandalise the villa again? I found myself determined to protect the astrarium from these assassins.

'What else did Ibrihim say about the break-in?' I asked.

'It was hard to get much out of him – he was very nervous. He did tell me he'd fired the night guard. He was convinced the guy had been paid off.'

'Better that than murdered. Was there much damage?'

'They'd smashed up some of the furniture, your clothes and books were all over the bedroom, and some of the wall panels had been torn off. Ibrihim told me you should stay invisible for at least another week and keep away from anywhere you're known. Promise me you won't take any unnecessary risks?'

'Promise.'

I looked at Rachel. It felt like a lifetime since we'd made love early that morning, but now, despite the regrets, despite the guilt over Isabella, despite the bruises and scratches I'd collected during the morning, the memory of that lovemaking echoed under my skin.

Rachel left shortly after. She'd taken a room at the Cecil Hotel and was hoping to file a story on the bombing before New York woke up. Within a span of a few hours we had become a team and without her I felt a lot lonelier and, frankly, scared. The fate of Sadat's peace initiative was at stake, together with a lot of other things – my life, for one. I felt the responsibility threatening to overwhelm me; the astrarium had claimed enough lives. I couldn't take Rachel where I had to go – I needed to complete the task alone. It was safer that way.

Ibrihim had followed my instructions perfectly: apart from the sunglasses, he'd packed several changes of clothes, a few of Isabella's reference books, a work diary, money, passport and a knife, which I now slipped into my belt. There was also food: the local Domiati cheese and a hunk of bread. Outside I could hear a street cleaner singing as he went about his work. I had to stay in hiding for the time being, until I had a sense of Mosry's next move and I couldn't carry the astrarium with me. I looked around the small room. In the corner stood a male mannequin that looked as if it dated from the 1940s, a dingy black toupee perched on its shiny plaster pate. Halfway down its torso I noticed a hairline join, as if it might unscrew at that point. I would hide the astrarium until I had figured out where the device's final resting place should be.

Wrapped in cloth, the astrarium fitted perfectly into the hollow torso. 'Stay sleeping,' I found myself saying out loud as I carefully twisted the two halves of the mannequin back together.

I stood in front of the window, eating, still dressed in the priest's cassock. Shoppers and workers eager to return to their families were milling in the street below. Just then, a group of older Arabic women, their shopping piled high in baskets carried on their shoulders, passed beneath the barber's shop. Weaving her way between them was a slim European woman with black hair down to her waist. My heart jolted in recognition: Isabella. If not her, then her double. She glanced blindly up at the window and I stepped back out of sight. When I looked again a moment later, I could see her face clearly. I was convinced it was her, and despite my rational mind telling me that it couldn't possibly be every molecule in my body screamed out for confirmation. She turned and began pushing through the crowd, with that distinctive way of walking I knew so well. Without thinking about the consequences, I reached for the priest's cap and ran down the back stairs of the shop.

I pushed through the crowd after her, but each time I got close she darted on ahead, leading me away from the centre of the city and out towards the old Arab district. Occasionally I caught her half-profile, the strong nose and chin discernible in the fading light. The crowds dropped away, the streets became narrower and more ancient: low mud-brick buildings and the labyrinths of street markets replaced high-rises, neon and the occasional petrol pump. She ran ahead, her long hair tumbling around her shoulders. I followed as closely as I could as she slipped from shadow to shadow, always frustratingly just out of reach.

The gates of the catacombs of Kom el-Shugafa – the catacombs that Father Carlotto had mentioned – appeared in front of us. I called out, but the girl stepped through a side door and was gone. Without hesitating I followed.

The air at the bottom of the central shaft that led down to the catacombs was chilly and damp. The limestone walls dripped with moisture and I was thankful for the electric lights strung up in the corners. I glanced back at the spiral steps I'd climbed down into the shaft, bewildered to find myself suddenly underground. It was almost as if I'd fallen under a spell; how on earth had I allowed myself to be lured into this godforsaken place?

I spun around, staring into the shadows, looking for the woman I thought was Isabella. It couldn't be her, I knew that now, but either way it seemed impossible for a human being to have disappeared so quickly. Was she human or some crazy projection of my own mind? Perhaps the guilt of my night with Rachel was combining with my shattered nerves to play tricks on me.

I tried to gather my rationality around me like armour, scouring my mind for facts I knew about the catacombs that would help me navigate them. I knew they dated from the time of the Roman emperors Domitian and Trajan, when Alexandria was already a Roman colony. The dead had been transported to their tombs via this main shaft, which also provided the necessary ventilation for the mourners, who returned on holy days to celebrate their deceased.

Ahead lay a room called the triclinium – a small square hall with stone benches and a stone table permanently in place – built especially for these subterranean picnics when figs, grapes and cheese would be laid out on the cold stone table top while children and family gathered around, drinking wine and exchanging anecdotes about their dead. Better that than the secret shame we'd made death into in the twentieth century, I couldn't help observing.

My movements were hindered by the long skirt of my cassock, so I stepped out of it and stored it in an alcove; I'd collect it when I left. Now dressed in just jeans and T-shirt, I continued feeling my way. A noise behind me made me jump and I swung around to confront the woman. Instead, a rat scurried past; now I was thankful for the small hunting knife hidden in my belt.

Where was she? I moved forward, stepping carefully over the broken paving stones at the entrance to the catacombs. The doorway was framed by two pillars, with a bas-relief either side showing the Ptolemaic two-tailed cobra god Agathodaimon, the divine guardian of second-century Alexandria. One tail was coiled around the wand of Hermes, while on his head he wore the shield of Perseus that showed the snake-haired head of Medusa. I examined it – here was my first clue. Isabella's double had led me exactly to where the Isabella of my dream had wanted me to be, but why? Was it a trap?

Repressing my fear, I moved cautiously further into the chamber, my heart pounding, wondering if she was now hiding behind one of the stone funereal statues waiting to jump out, perhaps to attack me?

There were two niches on either side of the tomb's entrance. In the left one stood a statue of a woman, while in the niche opposite was her male counterpart, eerily serene in his stance. It felt ominous to me, this timeless preservation. Neither statue bore any inscription but they seemed to be husband and wife: a marriage immortalised. Over the entrance was a carving of the sun disc of Horus, flanked by the wings of the royal falcon. There was mixed allegory everywhere, a reflection of a culture in flux, a hybrid aristocracy seeking legitimacy from both the Pharaonic past and a Hellenistic present, and looking forward towards the Roman future while terrified of insulting anyone – a culture in fear. It reminded me of all the dictatorships in the region, of Majeed and his puppet kingdom. I lifted my head. Had Mosry followed me? The silence was noisy somehow; a thousand ghostly wings seemed to beat beneath the stillness. Thinking that the girl might be hiding behind one of the reliefs, I stepped into the tomb.

Carved into the wall were two reliefs of Anubis, the jackal-headed god of mummification. In one, the grinning jackal's head sat atop the body of a Roman legionary, his muscular torso clad in a leather kilt, one arm holding up a spear, the other resting on a shield. The realism of the statue seemed more sinister than the stylised Egyptian iconography. It was a poignant illustration of how a dictatorship could assimilate local religious beliefs to reinforce its own power. I could almost hear the soldier-jackal breathing, a low growl that threatened violence.

I shivered; it was as if the dead hovered in the chilly air, waiting for some indication of approval of the splendour of their last place of residence. Suddenly I felt something tickling the top of my ear. Startled, I swung around and found my face covered in the thin mesh of a spider's web, the large arachnid now perched on my cheek, its furry legs itchy against my skin. Quickly I brushed it off, then watched it scuttle away into the shadows. Again, the oppressive stillness of the place enveloped me, along with the growing sensation that I was being watched. But how and by whom? Suppressing my panic I moved forward.

In the centre of the burial chamber was the main sarcophagus. It held the body of a woman and was decorated with carvings of floral garlands and Medusa heads. The bas-relief above it showed the Ancient Egyptian burial rite, the embalmed body lying stiffly on the funerary bed. A priest of Anubis stood over the dead woman, and at her head I recognised Osiris, king of the Underworld, wearing his Atef crown and holding the traditional crook and flail.

I reached out and touched the worn features of one of

the Medusas, undoubtedly carved there to scare off grave robbers. She seemed to embody many of the characteristics of the women I was attracted to: fearlessness, curiosity, a beauty that had been frozen into a fierce intellectualism. But where were the other clues that Isabella had pointed out, the bull and the fish?

I heard scurrying. Catching a breath in my throat, I pressed myself against the wall. Sudden silence. It must have been rats, I tried to convince myself. I peered around the dimly lit chamber: nothing moved. Not even the hanging lights or the shadows of the statues.

To my right was a side sarcophagus with a bas-relief above it that featured Apis the sacred bull, a goddess stretching out her wings to protect him. So there was the second symbol. Now I needed the final clue – the fish, the secret sign of the early Christians.

Just then the sound of murmuring voices came from the stairs leading down into the central shaft. My heart felt as if it were a trapped bird flapping wildly as it thudded against the bars of my ribcage. I stepped back out of the light, my hands touching the concealed knife I had in my pocket. I hid in a niche behind a statue as the footsteps grew louder – it sounded like a group. There was a rhythmical beat to their footfalls, almost a ritualised tempo, and I could smell the strong fragrance of burning incense. They were moving towards the burial chamber, towards me.

I held my breath. The footfalls stopped inches away, followed by the noise of stone scraping against stone. Then came the sound of the group descending as each footfall grew fainter – almost as if they had disappeared somewhere subterranean. I was paralysed, frozen against the damp stone. Pulling together every last ounce of my sanity, I exhaled soundlessly, then, hidden by the statue, peered out.

To my astonishment, I saw a figure carrying a blazing ceremonial torch and dressed in the pleated robe of an Ancient
Egyptian priest – the last of the group. But what was most
startling was the ibis mask that he wore. I knew it represented the god of knowledge, Thoth, its curved beak
symbolic of the moon's crescent.

The figure descended into an opening in the stone floor –
the scraping noise I'd heard was the cover being pushed
aside. Curiosity won over fear, but as I moved to see more
clearly I kicked a small rock. The Thoth figure swung
around at the noise, the bird's head staring blindly towards
me. I fell back into my hiding place and breathed silently,
with all my mind willing Thoth to move on.

34

I waited frozen until my entire body seemed to have cramped up. Only when I was sure that the light from the torches had disappeared from the tunnel entrance and I could no longer hear the diminishing footsteps did I emerge from the niche. Looking around me, expecting someone's hand on my shoulder at any moment, I peered down the narrow stone shaft with steps carved into it – I thought it dated from Roman times or perhaps even earlier. I had to try it. I walked softly down ten steps, my hands tracing the roughly hewn walls scarred with chisel marks. A little further down, carved into the rock above my head, was an inscription. Calling on my schoolboy Latin, I translated it: *To descend into darkness is to know oneself.* I shivered.

There was just enough light filtering in from the electric lamps above for me to see the first of the winding steps going further down. Those who had descended before me must have known exactly where they were going – there were no rails, just the slippery walls, clammy under my palm. I touched my hunting knife for assurance before slowly continuing my descent. Despite the cold air, I felt sweat on my forehead. I had never felt more vulnerable, not when diving, not when potholing. The whole tunnel felt as if it were alive, as if its very walls had absorbed centuries of violence, mute witnesses to unmentionable horrors.

About halfway down the light faded away completely and I was plunged into total darkness. It was an unsettling experience; I could see nothing at all, only smell the damp stone and feel it under my groping hands. I paused, fighting off the inevitable claustrophia I felt in such confined locations, then I moved forward tentatively, feeling out every step, expecting to hear the sound of footsteps behind me every second. My breathing sounded unnaturally loud and I forced myself to exhale quietly, the effort making me feel suffocated and panicked. After a couple of minutes I lost all notion of what was external and what was internal. It seemed to me that this profound darkness had become an extension of my body, even my psychology, as if I'd crossed the threshold from physical to metaphysical.

My foot hit the level floor and the thud of the impact seemed to echo like an explosion. I stopped and waited with bated breath. Along the walls I could feel where the limestone fell away to rectangular hollows. My fingers fastened around a long hard object – a stick of some sort, I thought. With a shock, I realised I was holding a bone. I now knew what the hollows were: loculi – horizontal burial shafts, each containing a skeleton. Horrified, I pulled my hands away and relied solely on my feet to guide me.

A breeze coming from deeper inside the catacombs brushed my face. I blinked, my eyes adjusting as they scanned the darkness for light. Nothing, just a seamless, bottomless void that seemed to swallow me whole. Following the direction of the faint wind, I felt my way around a corner. Figures suddenly became visible at the end of a long

passage, moving around each other in slow, ritualised movements, as if choreographed. It was like watching some slow
underwater dance, terrifying and morbid. I felt my breath
rasp in my throat and, in that second, the suffocating claustrophobia was almost unbearable.

Sliding along the wall, I moved closer until I was about fifteen feet away. I realised the figures were inside a chamber;
a blazing torch was set up in each corner. There were five of
them, all dressed like Pharaonic gods. A huge set of scales
stood to the left of the chamber, its ebony and gold arms
stretching a good ten feet from side to side. Gold chains
held the plates of the scales; one tray was empty, while the
other held a single white feather. The pivotal pole was
topped with a carving of the goddess of truth, Maat, recognisable by the ostrich feather she wore on her head.

In that moment I understood what was going on. It was
the Weighing of the Heart, the same ritual Isabella had
dreamed about over and over, the ritual that Amelia had
mentioned in her lecture. It was unmistakable. The scale.
The raised stone platform. Now I knew why I had been led
here by Isabella's double or maybe her shadow. I was transfixed; it was as if I'd been transported into Isabella's
nightmare, into her very psyche.

An African man wearing a jackal mask kneeled by the
scales, his black muscular arms shimmering in the torchlight
as he held a gold platter on which sat a shrivelled piece of
flesh. Anubis. Beyond the scales lay a pool of dark water.
Next to it stood the man in the ibis mask; he held a scroll
and a quill. Thoth would transcribe the good deeds and the
sins of the deceased, whose heart would be weighed against
the weight of a feather. The heart! Horrified, I looked again
at the shrivelled object on the gold platter, the dark desiccated flesh visible in the flickering light. Was it a human

heart? Isabella's? I felt my blood roar in my ears and momentarily I thought I might fall. Could it be possible? If so, what
was the role of the young girl who had led me here to witness this bizarre re-enactment?

Next to Thoth, in the place where the deceased would
usually stand waiting to be judged before the throne of
Osiris, were four Canopic jars carved with the heads of the
sons of Horus. I felt myself gag slightly, noiselessly. I knew
Canopic jars were used to contain the mummified organs of
the dead. Did these jars contain Isabella's organs? Their
bright colours and the hieroglyphs painted vertically on each
one looked completely authentic. The whole theatrical display seemed meticulous in its historical accuracy; garish, yet
sombre with a rigid authority that had kept such a civilisation – with its chaotic underworld – so powerful for
centuries. The purpose and effort behind such a fanatically
correct presentation was terrifying. And judging by the par-
ticipants' concentration they appeared to be convinced by
the power of their own symbolism. They weren't just re-
enacting the weighing-of-the-heart ceremony – they were
living it.

Osiris's throne was a gilded chair on a podium, its base
carved with serpents and jackals. Behind it stood two figures
in profile, Isis and her sister Nephthys, as if they expected
the king of the Underworld to manifest any minute. Isis
wore an elaborate costume that covered her arms and hands,
its long skirt reaching to the ground. Her golden breastplate
was moulded in the shape of a woman's breasts and her face
was a painted mask framed by a long black wig. In contrast,
her sister goddess was unmasked and near-naked – it was
almost as if one goddess was meant to represent artifice, the
other nature. Nephthys looked as if she was in her twenties,
and I peered closer, wondering if this was the woman who

had lured me into the catacombs. But her face did not resemble Isabella's in any way.

I crept forward along the clammy wall, careful not to make any noise. I'd come too far to go back but I was under no illusion what my reception would be if I were discovered. And aside from my fear, I was also curious. Another figure with a falcon mask, Horus, started a low chant in a language I didn't recognise. His stance and stature were vaguely familiar to me. Horus's role was to lead the deceased to the ritual, but as yet the deceased appeared to be absent in the tableau. Had he or she not arrived yet? The other worshippers joined in and the hypnotic monotone echoed off the limestone walls, weaving and blending into one single note that bored its way into my head. I tried to remember the exact order of the gods in the murals I had seen depicting the ritual. Osiris sat on his throne to the right, with Isis and her sister behind him. Here he was missing, the throne empty. Horus and Thoth stood next to the scales that weighed the heart. Horus would read out the sins of the deceased while Thoth would write them down. What did the jackal-headed Anubis do? I thought frantically but I couldn't remember exactly. And there was another god missing – a figure that always appeared at the bottom of the murals, a large crocodile-type creature snapping at the heart on the scales. Ammut, that was it – Ammut the devourer of the dead, a fusion of all the creatures that terrorised the Ancient Egyptians in real life. She had the head of a crocodile, the body of a lion and the haunches of a hippopotamus. Ammut's task was to eat the hearts of those found guilty by the gods, thus destroying any hope of an afterlife for them. Would she appear? Although the monster had a peculiarly comical look, it had always disturbed me: there was something primordially terrifying about the sly ferocity of the reptilian jaw, the jagged teeth waiting to tear apart the sinner.

A great rustling burst up around me. My gaze snapped to the stage. The masked figures appeared indifferent to the cacophony, which grew louder and louder until what appeared at first to be a swarm of black cloth rags came streaming from the back of the catacombs. I looked on in horror at the storm of deadly ancient creatures, flapping darkly like emissaries of hell. They swerved at the last minute to avoid the stationary figures on the raised platform and I was buffeted by a huge wind as thousands of tiny beating wings missed me by inches. Bats. They poured past me and continued towards the tunnel's entrance. I pressed myself against the stone to avoid the flying mass of tiny furry bodies, when I suddenly felt an arm wrap around my neck. I stumbled. Someone pinned my hands behind me and a needle jabbed into my shoulder. I fell back, desperately trying to free myself but my captor hauled me into the full light of the torches and pushed me to my knees. The torches began to spit small meteorites of flame and the masked figures on the podium turned slowly in my direction. They seemed to grow in height as they moved.

Horus stepped forward and his falcon's head sprouted feathers, its beady black eyes swivelling towards me. I tried to speak but my tongue felt too swollen to move. Belatedly I realised I'd been drugged, but the knowledge didn't stop the violent rush of fear as the bird-god stepped down from the podium, his huge gnarled claws rattling against the stone floor. This can't be real, this isn't real, I told myself over and over, terror reverberating through me like the echo of a nightmare drum.

Horus stretched out his arms as he reached me, revealing a small tattoo on his forearm – the Ba symbol. Struggling to stay focused, I racked my memory for the image – I'd seen it recently . . . Hugh Wollington. Was it him behind the mask?

There was so little of the human about the figure now kneeling before me. The falcon cocked its head and opened its beak to speak.

'We welcome you, Lord Osiris.'

I blacked out. When I came to I was strapped into Osiris's throne, my legs and torso bound to its sides. Only my arms from the elbow down were free. The god's tall crown was pressed low on my forehead and his crook and flail were tied across my chest. I was wearing a robe of shimmering fabric threaded with gold. All my senses were heightened by whatever they had injected me with; every movement of the creatures before me carried a multitude of after-images – one sweep of an arm was a thousand arms breaking like a wave, one turn of a god's head made many, the appearance of the players was undeniably real: the fusion of fur and flesh, scale and skin, seamless and horrifically organic.

Horus and Anubis advanced, Anubis carrying the gold platter with the heart on it, two valves trailing from the rippled purple flesh. Ears twitching, the canine fur and flesh fusing into the muscular neck of a man, Anubis held up the plate. Isabella's heart, it had to be. Struggling against my bonds, I tried to shout but again I had no voice.

Horus's falcon head began to speak. 'Oh Lord, we are gathered here in the hall of truth and justice to judge the life of Isabella Brambilla, to weigh her heart against that of the feather of truth, the symbol of the goddess Maat who will tolerate neither sin nor lie. If the deceased's heart balances against the feather, she will be granted a place in the Fields of Hetep and Iaru. But if her heart is heavy with the weight of wrongdoing, Ammut will devour it and the deceased's soul will be condemned to an eternity of oblivion. I seek your blessing, Lord Osiris, as embalmer to the gods and kings.'

Isis stepped in front of the throne. I could see now that

the goddess was wearing a painted mask over her features, bejewelled with turquoise eyes and crimson enamel lips that shone fantastically in the flaring torchlight. As she spoke I thought I recognised the voice – Amelia Lynhurst's, perhaps, only deeper now and resonating with authority.

'My Lord, you must bless Anubis if you wish to save the soul of your consort.'

The heavy black wig covered her torso, concealing the figure beneath the breastplate, but there was something genderless about her shape – the shoulders too wide, the waist too thick. I struggled to remember Amelia's figure, whether it had any similarities. Paralysed as I was by the drugs, it took extraordinary concentration to make any coherent sense of the scene and I kept slipping back into hallucination. I tried to speak again, but only managed a groan. Impatient, Isis yanked the flail from where it was tied across my chest and blessed Anubis herself.

Anubis carried the heart over to the scales and ceremoniously placed it onto the tray opposite to that holding the white feather. The scales balanced for an instant, then tipped violently to the side the heart was on.

'This heart is heavy with deceit!' Horus shrieked, his voice like a bird's cry. Thoth, holding his feathered quill high, started writing on his papyrus scroll, while to either side of me Isis and her sister Nephthys began to ululate in that hair-raising manner of Arabic mourners.

A small wave suddenly ran across the surface of the pool behind the scales. I turned at the movement; it resonated in my drug-heavy mind, echoing some frightening image: Ammut, the devourer. In terror, I struggled in my chair as the air grew pungent with a fishy stench. The water rippled again and this time I was convinced I saw the flaring eyes of a crocodile in the torchlight.

There was a splash and the gnarled horny head of a crocodile lifted out of the water, its long yellowed teeth snapping at the heart. A lion's mane hung from its reptilian scales, a travesty of wet and matted fur.

I retched.

A figure stepped from the shadows beyond the flaring torches and walked towards me – normal, human, dressed in a simple cotton dress. This was no double – this had to be Isabella! Fear slammed into the back of my throat, my heart a rattling cannon. I tried to stand, to walk towards her; my arms tore against their bindings and began to bleed.

'Will you save your consort and surrender Nectanebo's skybox?' Isis whispered.

I was jolted out of the artifice, my mind suddenly coming out of its fog. 'What! What's that got to do with all this?'

The words tumbled out of me as I tried to close myself against the image of my wife, iridescent in its paradoxical ordinariness. Now I could see the spreading stain of dark blood across her chest, oozing from the wound where her heart had been removed. Whose terrible imagination had concocted this?

'Give up the astrarium.' Isabella's voice sounded in my head but her lips didn't move. 'If you do not, I will have no afterlife. I will not even live on in your memory. You will be my condemner, my murderer.'

She had articulated my worst fear: that I had failed to save her and that – equally disturbing – I might forget her entirely. But what on Earth did this have to do with the astrarium? Even with the drugs coursing through me, I knew there was no appeal, no loophole, against the weighing of the heart. Hoping the pain would jolt me into even clearer thinking, I pushed my torn skin against my bonds, but still my mind reeled under the effects of the drug.

'Osiris, speak your judgement. The heart is heavy, the deceased is guilty!' Anubis barked.

Ammut's bulky reptilian body slithered out of the water. I could see that the glistening lion's pelt merged at her waist into the shiny black hide of a hippo. The creature shook herself dry like a large dog – somehow the familiarity of the gesture made it even more frightening. The heavy crocodile head swung from side to side as tremors ran down the goddess's torso.

'Save me! Tell them where it is!' Isabella whispered urgently.

This was why people believed in visions, I suddenly understood, as the realism of the hallucination battled with my intellectual speculation that I was caught up in some horrific drug-induced sham.

'No!' I shouted, my anguished cry solid set against the ephemeral nature of the scene before me.

Her crocodile claws scraping against the stone floor, Ammut slithered closer to the heart sitting on the scales.

Isabella clutched at her chest as if in pain. 'Tell them, I beg you!'

'No! None of this is real!' I screamed. I tore at the rope, if I could only get to my knife.

Ammut lunged forward and grabbed the heart between her jaws as if it were a piece of old meat. She turned her head towards Isis, the heart hanging from her mouth, as if waiting for a command.

'Not real, my Lord? What is real? The waking world or the sleeping one? The world beyond the mind or the chaos that lies beneath order?' Isis's words were like icicles. 'You must fulfil your role or your consort will be denied entry to the afterlife.'

The light flickered wildly as a huge shadow fell across

the blazing torches. The goddess, now silent, was staring at the back wall of the cavern. Across the ceiling, extending down to where the black water lapped the bottom of the limestone, stretched a massive silhouette: a dog-like creature with four slender legs, a long tail with a forked tip, a long beaklike snout and two raised blunt-ended ears. The players all fell to their knees, foreheads to the ground. No one was looking at me, and they seemed too terrified to look at the giant shadow.

With a supreme effort I yanked at my bonds again and managed to slip my knife out. After I'd sawed frantically at the rope, it finally gave. I leaped from the chair, jumped over the figures prostrate on the floor, snatched the heart from Ammut's jaws and bolted down the long corridor towards the steps that led back up to the surface. Behind me I heard chaos erupting – shouts and footsteps.

I raced up the stone steps. Knowing that I was running for my life, sheer terror propelled me forward. At the top a hand shot out. I stumbled but a figure carrying a torch broke my fall and pulled me into an alcove. Faakhir.

'This way!' he cried, waving my abandoned cassock.

We ran towards the light of an open door. Outside, a car was waiting. As I fell into the back seat I managed to murmur the name of the barber's shop before dropping into unconsciousness.

35

☥

I woke sweating in the small iron bed. An embroidered blanket had been thrown over me. Shooting pains burst rhythmically over each eye and it was hard to swallow. The naked electric bulb seemed to swing against the smoke-stained ceiling. My mind was numbed into a sensory jumble that made it difficult to make sense of where I was, even who I was. I lay there waiting as my frenetic thoughts slowly collected themselves. I glanced down at my wrists and the red bands burning around them – the marks of restraint. Flashes of the night before began to flicker across my memory: the catacombs, the ceremony, Faakhir helping me to the door of Abdul's shop, telling me not to look for him but that he would be watching me.

I looked over to the back window. Beyond lay the rooftops of Alexandria. The sun was high; it was about midday, I guessed. Beside the small camp stove sat a bowl of fresh fruit and a bottle of water. Abdul had obviously left some supplies. I reached out and my fingers brushed against a small box on the floor next to the low bed. I sat up and grasped it, slipping my hand into the open top. My fingers hit something sticky and organic in texture. I pulled out a purple lump of muscle tissue; the withered dark flesh bulged out between my fingers.

With a smothered shout, I threw the heart back into the box and leaned over the side of the bed, retching. A few minutes later the shivering finally stopped. I sank back heavily and considered the events of the night before. Why the weighing-of-the-heart ceremony? And why had I been designated as Osiris? Who was the woman who had lured me there? Had it really been Hugh Wollington playing Horus or had that been a figment of my imagination, a desperate attempt to link events and make sense of them? But who else would go to the trouble of creating such an elaborate and macabre charade in order to obtain the astrarium? And if it *was* Wollington, how did he know of the connection between the ritual and Isabella's recurring nightmare? Was it a charade, or was it real? It was impossible to ascertain; the angles of the room still tilted, my thinking blurry. The Coptic robe that Father Carlotto had given me lay neatly folded at the bottom of the bed. Faakhir must have collected it from where I'd hidden it in the catacombs. Had they been watching me the whole time? What was Faakhir's role in all this? And where was Mosry?

I heaved myself out of bed and walked over to the mannequin. Taking it apart and feeling inside I reassured myself that the astrarium was safe. Between the explosion at the Sheraton and the horrific scene in the tomb it seemed more crucial than ever not to let it fall into the wrong hands. I glanced back at the box containing the heart. I wasn't even sure that the heart was human. Then I remembered that I knew someone who would be able to tell me.

Demetriou al-Masri peered through his thick half-moon glasses at the heart on the laboratory dish and prodded it.

His office was a windowless annexe off one of the city morgue's main chambers; I suspected that it might once have been a large cupboard. Dressed in my Coptic robe I'd entered the morgue with remarkable ease, and on seeing my disguise Demetriou had immediately pulled me into his tiny cubicle.

We'd both been staring at the heart for at least five minutes and I was beginning to doubt whether I was going to get a conclusive verdict.

Finally al-Masri cleared his throat and sat back. 'It is a human heart, from a smallish body, quite possibly female. I would say around thirty years of age.'

My own heart started rattling the bars of my ribcage. 'My wife's?'

'It might be, it might not. That is not something I can confirm.' He sighed and began packing the heart back into the container in which I had brought it. 'May I ask how you came by the organ?'

'It was delivered to the villa anonymously.'

The coroner studied me for a moment, then handed me the container. 'Run, my friend, run as fast and as hard as you can. I do not want to find myself staring down at your body tomorrow.'

He opened the door and the room was immediately flooded by the greenish fluorescent lights of the morgue beyond. I glanced back at the windowless room. Demetriou al-Masri followed my gaze.

'I had a view once, but they demoted me. Curiosity can be very bad for one's career. You should be careful. These are dangerous times. Even for a cleric,' he added, with an ironic smile.

I went straight to Chatby Cemetery, clutching Isabella's heart. My air of purpose must have been apparent for the crowds parted to make way as I strode along the thronging streets. I was indifferent to my fate, intent on only one thing.

It was extraordinary to watch how people reacted to me. Some moved respectfully out of my path, others brushed past roughly as if being deliberately rude. Reassuringly, all of them appeared to accept me as a cleric.

The cemetery was empty of living humans, apart from a few gardeners patiently clipping the trees that ran in avenues between the graves. I walked through the dappled light, unrecognisable as the man who had walked the same path a couple of weeks before.

Someone had laid fresh flowers – white lilies – across the marble slab of Isabella's grave. The scent reminded me of the flowers she used to bring back from the street markets in London, filling the apartment with their fragrance. Whispering apologies to my dead wife, I dug a small hole in the earth at the foot of the grave and buried her heart. As I stood up I noticed that the small portal, the miniature door for her Ba, was still there on the side of the gravestone.

In the room above Abdul's shop I pulled the astrarium from its hiding place and unpacked it again, my hands trembling. My experience in the catacombs had unnerved me, had shaken up my old belief system until I didn't know what to believe any more. Anything seemed possible. Staring at the small glinting clocklike mechanism, I could now almost conceive how it might have destroyed kings and saved a people, how it could have ruined nations and made a beggar into a Pharaoh. In a moment of obstinate egoism, I had challenged it. I peered closer. There was something different about it. The pointer was still turned to my birth date and . . . No. It was impossible. There it was, startlingly harsh in its undeniable presence: Seth's death head glinting sinisterly in the lamplight. The small silver-black death pointer had finally sprung up, marking the date of my own supposed death. I didn't dare look. Suddenly nauseous, I steadied myself against the table.

How could the pointer have appeared by itself? I had only put in my birth date; I hadn't even touched anything else. Thinking it must be some mechanical fault, I inserted the Was and tried turning the dials again, but the cogs were unyielding. I forced the key to the point where I was afraid it might snap in half. The pointers stayed immobile: fastened on the date of my birth and, now, of my death. A slow dread filled me. I'd survived the blowout at Abu Rudeis, the explosion at the hotel and then the ritual in the catacombs, but I couldn't deny the very real sense that death had begun to shadow me.

I peered at the death pointer and began to draw the outline of the tiny silver figure at its tip – a doglike beast with an elongated face and a forked tail – onto a blotter. I held it up. Shuddering, I recognised the creature, familiar from Amelia's lecture, whose shadow had appeared on the wall of the catacomb just before I'd fled: Seth, the god of war, chaos and destruction. I couldn't stop myself. Frantically, I counted the tiny dashes running between the hieroglyphs of the full moon on the dial. The next full moon was in eight days. Did that mean my death date was just over a week away?

Suddenly, I had a visceral comprehension of Isabella's blind panic those few days before she drowned. Despite myself, despite my inbuilt scepticism, I felt the same desperation sweep through me. It was all just ridiculous superstition, I told myself. The device had originally been constructed as a piece of political propaganda, a way of intimidating and impressing Nectanebo's followers, of confirming his status as a great magus. Amelia Lynhurst had said herself that the Pharaoh's enemies had turned the device against him and used it to orchestrate his death date. It was merely a toy that could be manipulated any way the user chose – just dials and a clockwork mechanism. It had no control over anything. But I couldn't prevent my mind returning to the same question over and over: could it have stopped Isabella dying on the death date predicted for her?

The impulse to smash the device swept through me – anything to end this madness – but I managed to keep my fists clenched at my sides. To destroy the device would mean that I believed it had power over me. I refused to succumb.

'There is no death date,' I told myself aloud. 'No one is going to frighten me into anything.' My voice bounced back off the walls.

Suddenly sounds and images flooded my mind: Isis's voice, Horus's shriek, Ammut's bloodied crocodile mouth tossing the heart from side to side. I found that I remembered the tone of Isis's voice exactly, as if the drug I'd been injected with had heightened my powers of memory. The vocal inflections had seemed similar to Amelia Lynhurst's yet the voice itself had been deeper. I didn't think it was Amelia – but if not her, then who? And why were they so desperate to get the astrarium? Were they connected with Prince Majeed in any way? I doubted it; I couldn't see Mosry taking such a subtle and complex approach to snatching the instrument.

The ritual made me think of the stories I'd heard about Giovanni Brambilla, the performances he'd got Isabella involved in as a child, which in turn led me to that photograph taken at Behbeit el-Hagar. I already suspected that Hugh Wollington had been behind the Horus mask. What about the other people in that photo – Amelia Lynhurst, Hermes? There was only one person who would know.

A black Volga sat outside the iron gates of the Brambillas' villa. A tall man in flared jeans and a shirt several sizes too small leaned against the boxlike Russian car, smoking and staring blatantly at the house. I recognised him from the Sheraton Hotel – one of the men in the white van. Mosry was obviously having the villa watched. Disguised as a Coptic monk, I decided the best plan was to be as audacious as possible. I slipped on my sunglasses and walked casually towards the iron gates.

As I passed him I greeted him in Arabic. 'Lovely weather, my friend.'

Slightly embarrassed, he dropped his cigarette butt in the gutter and replied, 'It is, Father.'

I continued to approach the villa, smiling back at him – he hadn't recognised me at all. I passed through the iron gates and saw Aadeel on his knees, weeding the enclosed garden. 'Aadeel!' I hissed.

He looked up, his expression suspicious when he saw my Coptic outfit.

'It's me – Oliver,' I whispered.

His look softened and he glanced over at the man watching the house. He waited until we were inside before he spoke.

'Allah be praised. We were worried. Where have you been? So much has happened.'

'I'll tell you later. Right now I need to talk to Francesca.'

'She is resting, she hasn't been well . . .'

I pushed past the housekeeper and strode along the hall into the back parlour. The old woman was sitting in a large armchair facing the open French doors, an old photo album resting on her lap. She continued to stare out vacantly, despite my entrance.

'Francesca, last night I was drugged and forced to take part in a re-enactment of an Ancient Egyptian ritual,' I said bluntly, angry at being ignored.

She didn't respond.

'Is that what Isabella had to endure as a child? The kind of mad nationalism Giovanni believed in – voodoo and bad theatrics?'

I felt a hand on my shoulder. Startled, I wheeled around. Aadeel stepped between me and his mistress.

'Mr Oliver, Madame cannot answer you. I was trying to tell you – she has had a stroke, she is paralysed. But my son Ashraf is here in Alexandria, and I believe he may be able to help you.'

Shocked, I glanced back at the old lady who was still staring ahead blankly.

'Oh, Francesca, I'm so sorry.'

The housekeeper lived in an extension built at the back of the villa. It consisted of a bedroom and a kitchen that also doubled as a lounge room. A photograph of Ashraf in his graduation gown hung proudly on the wall, next to a portrait of Nasser. I sat on the edge of a sofa still covered in its plastic wrapping. Outside I could hear Aadeel welcoming his son.

Ashraf entered, dressed in traditional clothes, the bruise on his forehead the result of cumulative hours spent praying in the mosque – the mark of the devout. I wondered briefly what Isabella would make of her old childhood friend's religious fervour. He greeted me with a warm handshake. 'May peace be with you.'

'And with you,' I replied.

He sat opposite, in a kitchen chair. Aadeel's wife, a silent shadow, handed him a mint tea.

'My father tells me that you want to know about Monsieur Brambilla's . . . special activities?' he said warily.

'Let's call it what it was – it was a cult, wasn't it?'

He stared at me. I knew that, despite his close relationship with Isabella, Ashraf had never entirely trusted me.

'Oliver, you know that Giovanni Brambilla was as close to me as my own grandfather,' he said. 'This family is my family. I would never betray them. But I loved Isabella and she loved you, otherwise I would not be sitting here with you.'

I felt a wave of anger. 'You knew about this as children, didn't you? Re-enacting these ancient rituals in some desperate attempt to conjure up the gods? But for what reason? So he could keep hold of his money!'

'Please, Monsieur Oliver, you are shouting.' Aadeel got up and quickly pulled the window shutters closed, then turned to frown at me. 'You understand, we cannot talk about these things openly. My country is full of spies.'

Ashraf put a hand on his father's shoulder. 'I was the son of a servant so there were some . . . privileges that I did not share. In that respect I was lucky. I saw a ritual once – I must have been eleven and Isabella was eight, I think – her mother had left not long before. It was the year Nasser humiliated the Europeans, when we defeated the invading armies of the British, Israelis and French. I remember the fear in this household. Giovanni Brambilla knew that if Nasser nationalised the Suez Canal, he would eventually nationalise everything, including the cotton. Giovanni was terrified he would lose the mill, the house, his millions.'

Decades of resentment spilled out in Ashraf's voice. His

father put a hand on his arm. 'Please, Ashraf, these things are in the past.'

'And the past has marked us,' Ashraf replied in Arabic before turning back to me. 'We were children, but I was streetwise, I'd seen things. Isabella was the innocent one – she had been protected. He would hypnotise us, both of us. It was his party trick. I knew better. I knew his crazy sorcery, the old man's desperate attempt to manipulate events. His friends and associates, the old colonials, had lost their influence and Giovanni's bribes to the new guard, some of them socialist sons of the fellahin, hadn't worked. There was one young officer who'd taken over the management of the Alexandrian Cotton Mill, run by another Italian – a Jew. Giovanni knew it was only a matter of time before this officer destroyed the Brambilla fortune. He hated him, but Giovanni could do nothing but wait. He was terrified. It was in November – just after the British landed in the Sinai.'

'The sixth of November?'

'Exactly. People were frightened, they didn't know which way it was going to turn. The streets were empty – the young Egyptian men had all run to the train stations to volunteer for the fighting; the Europeans had locked themselves up in their villas. Yet Giovanni and his friends drove out to the catacombs.'

'You followed them?'

'Isabella was with them. In my heart she was my sister.'

Ashraf hid his face in his hands, overwhelmed by grief. Aadeel stroked his head and after a few moments Ashraf collected himself and continued.

'I chased the car on my bicycle, driving through the empty streets, keeping my distance but going fast, trying to keep up with Isabella. When I got there, I followed the sound of voices down the passages. The light of the torches flickered on the walls like the fires of hell, the chanting of the voices like that of demons. I have never forgotten it.'

Ashraf ran his hand across his face, his fingers trembling. Aadeel glanced at his wife and indicated that she should leave the room. She walked out, with a swish of her long skirts. Ashraf took another sip of mint tea.

'There they were, eight, nine of them standing on a stage – all the old gods with their primitive animal heads that I'd seen in the books Giovanni had shown me, books he kept in his study. I remembered the name Horus, because I had wanted to be him. Only it was Isabella there, half-naked and carrying a silver dish with some kind of flesh on it. I almost called out to her, but something stopped me. I knew that what was happening was wrong but I was desperately afraid.

'There was a huge set of scales set up on the stage, and Isabella placed whatever was on the dish onto one of the trays. They all stood there watching silently, like statues in their masks. I recognised Giovanni but the others I didn't know – their faces were hidden. And then . . .'

His face went blank as the memory passed through him.

'Then what?' I prompted.

'There was a terrible screaming. Evil came into that place and it had a shape.'

I didn't need to ask Ashraf anything more and I didn't want to. I had seen the same shape myself, both in the catacombs and carved at the end of the death pointer on the astrarium. Suppressing a shiver, I extended my hand to thank him. His own hand still trembled but he grasped mine firmly as if to reassure himself. I stood to leave. Just as I was about to step out the door, Ashraf looked up.

'That young Egyptian officer who was in charge of repossessing the cotton mills – he was killed by the British on the seventh of November, the very next day. Maybe it was because of Giovanni's old sorcery, maybe not. All I know is – they woke evil and tried to channel it. Ask the Sudanese.'

'Sudanese?' I looked at him, confused.

'The Egyptologist who was a friend of Giovanni's – he was always in the house in those days.'

36

Usta, Hermes's young companion, answered my knock. I pushed past him.

The living room was empty, its brightly coloured cushions scattered across the floor and a hookah pipe still smouldering. From somewhere in the apartment came the sound of Hermes yelling for his companion. I followed his voice.

The bedroom was dominated by a large low bed tented with a mosquito net. Through its fine mesh I could see Hermes lying curled up on his side, his yellowed face in profile against the pillow. His back, naked, looked curiously feminine. I ventured into the room, which was filled with the cloying scent of cologne. Edith Piaf's voice soared out of a record player, immediately evoking both Paris and, bizarrely, the smell of rain.

'Who's that?' Hermes asked.

I flicked up the mosquito net. 'Oliver Warnock.'

Startled, he covered himself with a silk dressing gown incongruously patterned with images of Paddington Bear. His hair, streaked with white, hung loose down his back and his skin was shiny with some kind of cream.

'You're ill?' I asked.

'Fatigued, my dear friend, nothing more. I had to attend an all-night vigil for one of my associates and I am getting too old. Be kind enough to avert your gaze,' he added and made to climb out of the bed.

I turned my head dutifully, although I was perplexed by Hermes's coyness.

'After the lecture I went down to the Kom el-Shugafa catacombs, following a lead,' I began, trying to read his expression out of the corner of my eyes. Hermes was convincingly casual.

'A little too contemporary a location for my archaeological tastes.'

Standing now and wrapped in his dressing gown, he slipped his feet into leather slippers. His eyes were streaked with kohl and two patches of rouge had been daubed carelessly onto his withered cheeks. 'Anything after the first century BC is really rather derivative of earlier times.'

'Contemporary or not,' I said, slightly annoyed by his seeming indifference, 'I stumbled upon a re-enactment of the weighing-of-the-heart ceremony, in which I was forced to take part – drugged and humiliated. You weren't there, were you?' I looked him squarely in the eye.

Hermes sighed heavily. 'An interesting proposition.' He looked at me. 'So, in which role were you cast?'

'Osiris.'

'The king of the Underworld, befitting you as a geophysicist, I think. I did warn you that life was about to become eventful. Come.' He led me back into the lounge, where steaming cups of Turkish coffee now waited on a low table. 'They were seeking the astrarium, no? This was a tactic to frighten you, I assume.'

As Hermes stirred his coffee, I found myself staring at his

painted fingernails, wondering why his vocal rhythms were so familiar. Had he taken part in the ritual? Perhaps I was mistaken in thinking that Hugh Wollington had been Horus. Just then the sleeve of Hermes's dressing gown slipped up as he lifted his cup – there was no tattoo. Besides, it didn't make sense to suspect Hermes. I had already entrusted him with the astrarium and, in fact, with my life. But still – he had avoided answering my question directly.

'Give the instrument to me,' he went on. 'You know it is dangerous. It will seduce you, or those seeking it will destroy you.'

'Too late.' I laughed bitterly. 'Not only has it cost me the life of a friend and made me a fugitive, I've started seeing meanings in everything, everywhere, all linked back to that stupid device. It seems to have taken over my life.'

Hermes laughed, a dry cackle that ended with a cough. 'You Westerners think you can control the weather, that time can be measured by mathematical units, that light travels at the same speed everywhere, and that all that you see in these four dimensions is palpable and finite. It has woken you up, this Pharaonic toy. The sooner you admit it, the better, Oliver.'

'I prefer a world based on solid understanding. Blame my training, if you have to.'

'Then go back to England, to grey skies and red brick, to the godless monotony of commercial enterprise, and leave the astrarium to others.' Hermes took a sip of his coffee and winced. 'Usta! The coffee is not strong enough!' he yelled, then turned back to me. 'The astrarium has given you your death date, has it not?'

I stared at him in surprise. Seeing my look, he smiled, waiting. I found myself not wanting to answer him, not only because of my suspicions but also because, somehow, the fewer people I told, the less of a hold I felt the mechanism had over me. Hermes watched my face with interest.

'Oliver, you heard the history of the mechanism – the astrarium is an irresistible weapon for those who wish to control the events around them. It can and has changed the course of history.' He sighed. 'But you have been foolish. In your desire to keep everything logical, you have challenged the mechanism's power.'

'Perhaps,' I replied curtly, still not willing to reveal the extent of my involvement.

'The scientist's Achilles heel: nothing is real until proven. Newtonian empiricism will undo the world. Oliver, the astrarium is real, whether you can prove it or not, and it will pass judgement on you. The Ancient Egyptians believed that certain raw materials contained the essence of a soul – what you might call, in your dry scientific terms, electromagnetic vibrations, force fields. They constructed sacred objects out of these materials and then brought them to life through incantations. How long has the machine given you?'

The matter-of-fact seriousness of Hermes's tone, his absolute belief in the authenticity of the astrarium, was beginning to alarm me. I'd felt the astrarium take over my life but part of me still wanted to believe that all of this was a terrible combination of recent events, grief and too many sleepless nights. I hesitated, then decided it might not harm anything to give Hermes a few more details.

'The second hand has come up – but it means nothing, and if you want to get literal, the dates could be over two thousand years out anyway.' I shrugged, trying to look casual.

'How long?' he persisted.

'Eight days.'

'I can stop it, Oliver.' He looked at me urgently.

'Isabella couldn't stop it.'

'By the time she discovered the mechanism, it was too late. You know that yourself.'

'All I know is that the information I'm being presented with is so bizarre and unfamiliar that I fear I'm losing my mind.' I heard myself sounding strangely formal and realised that my tone masked a growing terror – I was being pursued by two different parties, both willing to go to extraordinary lengths to get the astrarium, but now I also seemed to be the target of the astrarium itself.

'The moment when you, the staunch rationalist, so adamant about the bricks and mortar of the known world, turned the dial to your own birth date, you revealed your hidden doubts,' Hermes said thoughtfully. 'You have tinkered with the magic of others and now the machine is committed to your fate. I can save you. Give it to me.'

His voice had slipped into a hypnotic rhythm: blues, shifting in half-tones, bumping gently against soft violets. The room had warmed up and bands of sunlight now illuminated the low glass coffee table; a large fly buzzed blindly against the window. Leaning back into the cushions, I closed my eyes. The jarring exhaustion of the past few days floated like a luminescent throbbing mass to the top of my skull. How easy it would be: give up the astrarium, fly back to Abu Rudeis to search for an investor with whom to partner on the new oilfield, return to my normal life. The luminescent mass shifted from blinding white to a deep red, then began to bleed: long languid droplets that solidified into the image of Isabella's heart, then into the crimson of Rachel's lips. Sitting upright, I forced my eyelids open.

'Amelia mentioned in her lecture that Nectanebo disappeared mysteriously. What did happen to him at the end of his reign?' I asked.

'So you are finally using your intuition, Oliver.' Hermes gave me a grudgingly respectful nod.

'Am I?'

Hermes smiled indulgently. 'Officially, Nectanebo's rule ended in 343 BC when the Persian general Ochus attacked Pelusium. According to Diodorus, a series of massacres and other atrocities followed and the Pharaoh reluctantly abandoned the granite palace he'd built at Behbeit el-Hagar, his birthplace—'

'So Nectanebo disappeared?'

'Unofficially, he fled, supposedly to southern Egypt and possibly to Ethiopia. Interestingly, his empty tomb was never raided – almost as if it was left pristine while awaiting his return – for all those thousands of years.'

'But how does this relate to the astrarium?'

'As a weapon of prediction it failed him, as it is failing you now, because he wasn't able to control it. Strictly speaking, and that's why it is so dangerous, the astrarium has no true master.'

'But what happened to him? Didn't the astrarium predict his death?'

'This is the great mystery. There is no record of his death, and there are some who claim that he still walks amongst us.'

'*Some say he still lives to this day.*' Hugh Wollington's comment echoed in my memory. It was an absurd hypothesis, but it was odd that both men had voiced it, almost down to the same language.

'You know that's not possible,' I retorted, trying to keep a grip on the conversation. 'The astrarium can't make you immortal.'

'Can't it?' Hermes replied, with a smile. I looked at him, allowing silence to fall, then stood up abruptly, realising that

I was now infinitely more frightened by the potential of the astrarium than I had been before.

'If you are so convinced that the device has no power then there is nothing to worry about, is there?' Hermes concluded almost smugly. 'Give the device to me for safe keeping, or at least let me be your guide. What do you have to lose?'

I hesitated. Should I trust the Egyptologist? I remembered Francesca blaming Amelia, not Hermes, for her husband's belief in the old ways. Was it possible that Hermes had truly cared for Isabella? But then he would have protected her as a child, kept her away from Giovanni's role-playing, as any sane person surely would have. No, I couldn't afford to trust him, not yet.

I walked to the front door. Hung above it was a papyrus scroll with a hieroglyph painted on it. The image showed the four-legged creature I'd seen twice in the last two days. Hermes followed my gaze.

'That is Seth, god of thunder, chaos and revenge – once the ruler of Ancient Egypt, after he murdered his brother Osiris and overthrew his nephew Horus.'

'I know him.'

'Of course you do. The Christians bastardised him into the lesser form of Satan.'

I locked the door of my hideaway above the barber's shop and unpacked the astrarium again. I sat for a moment, staring at it. Was I any closer to fulfilling Isabella's grand plan? She'd told me there was a destination for the astrarium, but where? I ran through Amelia's lecture points again in my mind – built for Ramses III, taken by Moses to part the Red Sea, then abandoned in a temple in the Sinai, driven by guilt or terror of Isis's revenge. Then sought out and found again by

Banafrit, only to be lost again by Cleopatra, who was apparently too terrified to actually use it. Had she known about its ability to reverse fortunes and change destinies not only in a good but also in a bad way, turning on the user and perhaps condemning him to an early death? And how was the god Seth related to the device? Was he just part of the death pointer, or was he connected to the darker uses of the device? The jigsaw puzzle was becoming more complex by the day, but now I felt I had at least nearly all the pieces – it was just a question of fitting them together to make sense. And I knew who Mosry was working for and why they were after the astrarium. I still needed to know more about the strange re-enactment in the catacombs and about Giovanni's movements twenty years ago. But the most important challenge was to find out what Isabella had intended to do with the astrarium – before my own time ran out. I forced myself to peer into the mechanism. My reluctant gaze found the small death pointer – the date was unchanged. The low ticking of the magnets' movement now sounded like an inevitable acceleration towards my own death. A sudden panic gripped me, and I steadied myself against the desk. Stay rational, stay calm, I tried convincing myself.

I reached for the reference book that I'd asked Ibrihim to pack with my clothes and looked up Seth.

Names: Seth, Sutech, Setekh, Seti, Sutekh, Setech . . . god of destruction, thunder, storm, hostility, chaos and evil. Manifestations: sometimes as a crocodile; sometimes as a four-legged beast with a curved beak, two upright ears and a forked tail. Referred to as the lord of the northern sky in the Book of the Dead, Seth was considered responsible for seizing the souls of the unprepared in the underworld. Son of Nut and Geb, or Nut and Ra, brother of Isis, Osiris and

*Nephthys, Seth battled with Horus, his nephew, after he mur-
dered Osiris . . . According to one myth, every month Seth
attacks and consumes the moon, considered the sanctuary of
Ausar and the gathering place of the souls of the recently
dead . . . In the Old Testament, Seth was the third brother of
Cain and Abel; he also appears in the suppressed gospels
recovered in Egypt in 1945 at Nag Hammadi, in which he is
Sethian, the gnostic god who rules over the thirteenth realm of
the cosmos and carries out the will of the stars on mankind,
regardless of how much havoc that might wreak . . .*

Why had Seth's shadow appeared on the wall of the catacombs during the ritual, I wondered. Had it been meant to
frighten me into believing that Isabella's soul had been
taken by the devil? And why had the other players seemed
so genuinely terrified? Was Seth part of their plan?

I couldn't come up with an answer. Instead, my mind
filled with the unsettling sense that the astrarium had begun
to control not just me but also the events around me.

37

Rachel hung the bag of fruit and other food over the hook on the door, then swung around. She looked exhausted; the events of the past two days were taking their toll.

'It's dire out there, Oliver. The bomb attack on the Sheraton has escalated the political tension and the Americans are talking about cancelling President Carter's visit. At least there's now a ceasefire between Libya and Egypt, thanks to the president of Algiers. I tell you, it feels unsafe simply walking the streets as a Westerner, never mind an American. I tried to glean some info from a friend at the Embassy but there's a blanket silence on everything. Something big's afoot. I can feel it.' She sighed heavily. 'I was real worried about you last night. Why didn't you send a message?' she asked, frowning.

I pulled a chair out for her and poured her a cup of the thick black coffee that I had percolating on the camp stove. 'I went to the catacombs at Kom el-Shugafa,' I told her. 'I was enticed there by someone I thought was Isabella. Total madness, not to mention suicidal, I know. But I was captivated, I had to find out.'

'Oh, Oliver . . .'

'It gets worse. I stumbled across some kind of crazy re-enactment, and the lunatics conducting this little performance injected me with drugs.' I pulled my shirt from my shoulder; the puncture mark had bloomed into a small purple bruise. 'It was an Ancient Egyptian funerary rite called the Weighing of the Heart. I couldn't tell you whether they were Egyptologists, a local cult or just some unemployed actors hired for the occasion, but they acted deadly serious and in full costume.' I held back the gruesome detail of the heart itself.

'And you think this is somehow connected with the death of your wife and with the astrarium?' Rachel asked, her fingers touching the bruise lightly.

'They were trying to pressure me into giving them the astrarium. I suspect that they were the same group Isabella's grandfather was involved with – apparently he dragged Isabella into it as well when she was a child.'

Rachel came closer and looked into my pupils. 'I think you're still wasted. I'd have thought strong hallucinogens would be difficult to get here in Egypt – unless you have military connections. The US Defense Department experimented with extreme hallucinogens in Korea – I wrote a piece on it once. Scary stuff.'

'Any long-term effects?'

'Flashbacks, paranoia, delusions.'

'Great – I was having those already.' I attempted a wry grin.

'There's something else you should know.' Rachel sighed tiredly. 'I spent the best part of today interviewing various members of Sadat's family for *Time* magazine.'

'So?'

'Well, just as I was leaving, an aunt of his told me that

another journalist had visited them the day before, asking all kinds of strange questions about Sadat's date of birth – whether the official date was correct, the hour exact to the minute, that kind of thing. At first, she said she thought he might be considering writing a biography, then she became suspicious because, although he spoke English and claimed he was writing for an American magazine, he looked Arabic – like a Saudi, she said.' Rachel nodded meaningfully, in case I didn't understand the implication. 'She gave me his card and wanted to know whether I'd heard of him or the magazine.'

'Had you?'

'No, it doesn't exist. Besides, I know every journalist covering this part of the world – the guy's a fake. What I want to know is why anyone would insist on getting the absolute correct date and time of Sadat's birth? That's kind of weird, right?'

'I can think of one reason.' The image of the moment when I'd set the astrarium to my own birthdate came flooding back as well as Amelia's ringing voice claiming that the astrarium could be used for both good and evil. Rachel, reading my expression, inhaled sharply as she arrived at the same conclusion.

'Surely not . . .'

'Rachel, the astrarium is legendary in its reputation as a powerful weapon of fate. It can also be used as a political symbol or abused—'

'If it's true that Moses used it to part the Red Sea,' she said sceptically.

'It doesn't even matter if it's true or not, as long as people believe it, and Prince Majeed certainly does.'

'They must really believe it is capable of killing.'

'You mean it can actually *kill*? How do you know?'

'I've used it. Only in my case, it apparently passed

judgement on me and my stupid attempt to defy it, and spontaneously gave me my own death date.'

She stared at me. 'Oliver, you're a scientist – you know that isn't possible.'

It was a question rather than a statement. I didn't answer her. The Seth-headed death pointer indicating my demise floated back into my mind. Rachel shook her head, then pulled out a newspaper from her bag.

'There's something else I wanted to show you.' She handed me a copy of the *New York Times*. 'It's a day old. Isn't GeoConsultancy the company you work for?'

I scanned the front page.

'You might want to turn to page five.' She opened the paper for me.

The article was headlined: OIL CHIEF DIES MID-FLIGHT. I read down the page:

> *Last night Johannes Du Voor, sixty, the CEO of GeoConsultancy, the oil industry's largest independent geo-physics consultancy, died of a suspected heart attack during a helicopter flight north of Cape Town. Shares in the company fell overnight due to uncertainty about future ownership and leadership of the company. Du Voor left no heirs . . .*

Shock ripped through me. 'This happened the night of the explosion?' Ordinarily I would have put Johannes's death down to eating habits and stress levels, but something about the coincidences made me uneasy. Rachel looked at me, her gaze firm.

'Pure coincidence, Oliver, nothing else. Okay?'

I sat there, fear mingling with incomprehension. Johannes was such a large personality, it was hard to believe he'd actually died.

I began pulling on my clothes. 'I have to find a phone.'

'You can't go out there!' Rachel grabbed my arm. 'It's not safe!'

I held up my cassock. 'I've been lucky so far.'

'They're going to catch up with you sooner or later. You've got to get out of town.'

Downstairs, the shop suddenly filled with the sound of men shouting. One voice was raised above the others – gruff, deep and aggressive. It was unmistakable.

Rachel looked at me, her eyes wide with terror. I indicated that she should stay quiet and grabbed the bag with the astrarium, quickly and quietly moving over to the window. Rachel was right beside me. Outside stretched a panorama of rooftops and terraces interspersed with squares of colourful laundry.

The voices downstairs grew louder – one man speaking English was audible above the others. With a jolt, I recognised the chiselled enunciation. Hugh Wollington. So he *was* in Egypt. Determined to stifle the fear shooting through me, I yanked the window wide open. Below us I could now hear Abdul arguing back. There was nothing I could do for him except disappear and hope he'd be able to talk his way out of trouble. We climbed out quickly, dropping the blind back as we left. Crouching, we scuttled across the tiled roof of the shop next to us as quietly as we could, then onto the next, never looking behind. I felt the blood roaring in my ears and heard Rachel's laboured breathing behind me. Any moment I expected the hard nozzle of a gun to be pushed against my back. Suddenly I felt a tug on my shirt and wheeled around. Pushing a sweaty hand across her forehead, Rachel pointed to our left. A fire escape was precariously attached to an old brick wall, its steps leading down to the busy market street below. We half-slid, half-fell down them and onto the ground and were instantly engulfed by a wedding procession that had turned along our narrow lane. A deafening cacophony of drumming and horns filled the air, the guests dancing madly around the veiled bride and bridegroom who were being carried above them on golden painted thrones.

I was in jeans and a T-shirt while Rachel wore a caftan, her blonde hair, wild around her head, drawing curious stares from the jostling crowd.

'We have to get out of here!' Quickly, I glanced around to get my bearings. 'This way!' I said, grabbing her arm.

We pushed our way through the crowd to emerge finally at the other end of the lane, our shoulders and heads covered with flower petals and confetti. From there I knew my way to the only place of sanctuary left to me.

Father Carlotto ushered us deep under the cathedral and to a hidden room at the back of the crypt. We could hear the boys' choir practising upstairs, the thin voices floating down in muffled soprano. The room was situated beneath stone arches that were obviously support structures for the building, and I had to bend my head to walk down the three stone steps into the small chamber. It stank of pipe tobacco and candle wax, and the white paint had begun to flake off the stone walls. By the light of the one lamp burning, I could see it contained a plain wooden desk with church records stacked behind it from floor to ceiling.

Father Carlotto switched on another lamp, his soft features transforming into sculptural planes as he leaned over it. 'You are sure you weren't followed?' he asked.

'We lost them back at the barber's shop,' I answered. 'I think I know who they are. I just hope that Abdul, my friend, is able to persuade them that he wasn't hiding anyone.'

The priest held his hand up. 'I have promised you sanctuary; I do not wish to know anything else. Personally, I have always prized survival over martyrdom, but I have no immediate desire to be confronted with the choice.'

I noticed a large old-fashioned Bakelite telephone on the desk and wondered if it worked. Father Carlotto opened a drawer in the desk and, to my surprise, pulled out a bottle of Benedictine and three small glasses.

'A Christmas present from Saint Benedictus,' he joked. Rachel and I smiled weakly. It was hard to stop the rattling panic thudding through my body, even now, standing still. I reached out and took her hand, the heat of her fingers burning into my own. She was still shaking and I found myself regretting having involved her in the first place.

Father Carlotto filled the three glasses. 'For fortitude. I suspect we shall all need it.'

The liquor burned a path from the back of my throat to behind my eyes, reviving me instantly.

'So now, down to business. I know your situation. Without breaking my confessional discretion, I have spoken to Father Mina. He has agreed to talk with you,' he said. 'How long do you want to disappear for?'

I exchanged glances with Rachel. 'I haven't much time – I was thinking a week at the most. That should give me enough time with Father Mina, and to lose Mosry and his cohorts until I've planned my next move.'

The priest immediately held his hand up.

'Please, I do not need to know who is after you. It is enough that you are being pursued. Besides, the church can shelter you for a week – as long as we agree that no questions are asked and no answers given. My Coptic brothers are closely watched; I do not wish to endanger them more than necessary. And if anyone comes asking, Mr Warnock, I do not know you.'

'How can I thank you?'

It seemed remarkable to me that this man I hardly knew would risk his life to help me. At that moment I would have done anything to return the favour.

'I do it for Isabella, for the confession I did not act upon, that is all. Although I pray that one day you may return to your faith.'

I grimaced. 'I'm afraid I will disappoint you, Father.'

He chuckled and poured himself another glass of Benedictine. 'We shall see.'

I glanced at the telephone again. 'One last request – I need to make two phone calls. I can reverse the charges.'

He pushed the telephone towards me. 'Be my guest. I promise this one is not tapped. The operator is one of my congregation.'

While Father Carlotto gave Rachel a tour of the crypt, I called the operator and finally got a connection to New York – to Ruben Katz, the chief financial officer for GeoConsultancy.

'Ruben, it's Oliver. I'm phoning from Egypt. I just heard the news – I'm so sorry.'

I meant it. As much as I'd disliked Johannes Du Voor, he didn't deserve death.

'Yeah, yeah, it's chaos here. Clients are ringing in left, right and centre.' Ruben was a pragmatic individual, completely loyal to Du Voor. 'I'm afraid the news is a lot worse than what's been reported.'

I steeled myself. 'Tell me.'

'I finally accessed some subsidiary accounts that Johannes had been stalling me on for months. Turns out they had huge borrowings – all guaranteed by the parent company and signed by Johannes. The company's in debt to the tune of twenty million, and most of it falls due in the next few months. We're seriously considering filing for bankruptcy – Chapter 11.'

'What about the Abu Rudeis project?'

'You can carry on for now, but don't make any long-term plans. Meanwhile, I suggest you start to think about your own future. But hey, you're the best in the business, so I wouldn't worry too much.'

'What about the clients, the company's goodwill?'

'The clients care about the people in the field, Oliver. You know that. You want to go independent, you just holler. There are plenty of people here looking for a raft to jump on. Meanwhile, I have to figure out what I'm gonna tell the shareholders tomorrow morning. I tell you this much, it ain't gonna be easy. I'm so sorry, Oliver. I should have seen this coming – Johannes had been acting pretty weird the last couple of months. Some of his recent business decisions have been . . . well, plainly . . . suicidal.' I could hear another phone ringing in the background. 'I have to go,' he said. '*Wall Street Journal* has just rung in . . .' The line clicked off. I was stunned. I had imagined that Johannes's increasing paranoia had been due to his lifestyle, his deteriorating health; I'd had no idea about the debt, the business difficulties. Quickly I dialled Moustafa's sat phone out in the oilfield. Just when I was about to give up, he answered.

'Moustafa?'

There was a silence; I suspected he was checking that the office was empty.

'Oliver,' he whispered then, 'are you okay, my friend? Head office said you had gone missing. Mr Fartime is most concerned.'

'Well, I'm alive, which I guess is good. Seems I've got something a lot of people want.'

'Nothing is worth getting killed over, my friend.'

'Do I sound dead to you?'

Moustafa laughed. 'It's good you still have your gallows sense of humour. But I need you here. The findings for the new oilfield look very promising. When can you come out and confirm them?'

'Give me a week or so. But in the meantime, are you able to visit me in a couple of days?'

'Where are you?'

'Let me contact you. I'll find a way of getting a message to you.'

'I will wait with anticipation.'

It was great just to hear his voice; the familiar realities of the oilfield sounding out beneath it. I put the telephone down with great reluctance. As soon as I did, the now-familiar sense of panic swept through me: I was torn between the excitement of a possible new oilfield and the terror of being pursued. Then there was the ticking clock of my death date. I pushed my fears to the back of my mind and tried to concentrate uneasily on the task ahead of me. Had setting my birth date set my fate in motion in more ways than one? The sea tremor as Isabella uncovered the astrarium, extending as an earthquake out to the desert. The shifting substructures. The new oilfield, promising unimagined wealth. On the other side of the scale, my own life now hung in the balance. Johannes's fortune had been tied into mine but he would also have made my life immensely difficult had I decided to go ahead with the new oilfield by myself, which would have confirmed his deep-set paranoia. Had the astrarium somehow fed on my ambitions and caused Johannes's death, sacrificed him to clear the decks for me? Again, it felt as if I was in free fall, another reality imploded.

Father Carlotto came back into the room and interrupted my racing thoughts. Rachel followed him.

'I have spoken with the abbot at Deir Al Anba Bishoy,' he said. 'You can leave with a group of pilgrims heading to Wadi El-Natrun this afternoon. As long as you are willing to play the part of a monk,' he joked.

I thanked him, then turned to Rachel. It was extraordinary how close I now felt towards her, despite the long hiatus in our friendship and the recent slip into sexual intimacy. As I studied her, her dark eyes filled with concern. 'It's only a couple of hours' drive,' I said, more reassuringly than I felt. 'It should be easy enough to get a message to me if you need to – right, Father?'

'Certainly.'

'Stay safe,' she said. 'I have to get back to my hotel, I have a lead on a secret summit – something to do with all these attacks – and I have to track him down.' She caught my expression.' Don't worry, I can look after myself. I'll contact you in a couple of days, okay?'

She gave me a quick hug and, for a moment, the ground beneath me felt solid.

38

The open-top army truck hurtled down the desert road to Wadi El-Natrun. There were ten of us huddled together in the back: a family obviously travelling to the monastery for a christening, the wailing baby held tightly in the crook of his father's arm; five earnest novice monks who looked frighteningly solemn, their beards barely covering their chins; and myself. We shared the space with one terrified goat and four trussed chickens, including a cockerel that, with every pothole in the road, emitted a loud shriek. It was an exhausting four-hour drive from Alexandria, with only a tarpaulin sheltering us from the afternoon sun and no stops, not even for water.

I'd spoken to no one, in case my accent and my blue eyes betrayed me. As I was older, the novices treated me with respect and mistook my silence for religious reverie. I held the astrarium in a hessian bag between my feet and stared out at the passing landscape, analysing over and over the sequence of bizarre events that had happened since my return to Alexandria. Mosry's face at Amelia's lecture, Hugh Wollington and his link to both Mosry and Prince Majeed, his voice in the barber's shop, the mysterious new oilfield, the earthquake, Johannes's death, even the image of the glassy waters of the Red Sea rising up, all converged and jiggled around in my mind, a collage of images and facts strung together in an increasingly complex narrative. What was real and what was not? I hoped that Father Mina would be able to provide more information. Father Carlotto had been vague so as not to betray Isabella's confidence but I knew he must have grasped the bigger picture and I could only hope Father Mina had a new piece in the puzzle. Either way, a week in the monastery would buy me enough time to work out my next move in solving and, with luck, stopping the astrarium inching towards my supposed death date. Finally, the swaying of the truck sent me to sleep until a few hours later. The sensation of it pulling up woke me with a jolt.

The monastery of Saint Bishoy loomed out of the night sky – its towers with their distinctive domed roofs, the four-way crosses on top, the high walls and the single tower originally built to warn of attacks from the nearby Berbers. Birds circled the tower, attracted by the insects that danced in the beams of light illuminating the keep; they looked as if they were in the grip of some invisible force.

The truck pulled up beside the gate set into the north-facing wall. A couple of monks pushed open the gate from inside and we climbed down wearily. An older man dressed in slightly more ornate robes came out after the first two monks and approached me, his hand outstretched. His wide full face broadened into a smile. The abbot. 'Welcome. Please, come with me.'

He took me to a monk's cell with curved sandstone walls, a narrow high window, a mattress rolled out on the ground, a prayer rug and a kerosene lamp on the floor at the head of

the mattress. A washing stand with a jug of water stood in
the corner with a small cupboard beneath it. Incongruously,
there was a large tin ashtray beside the lamp – a concession
to guests, I imagined. On the opposite wall was an alcove
that held a large wooden crucifix, its tortured Christ's carved
eyes turned upwards.

The abbot lit the kerosene lamp; it ignited in a small
white glow, throwing out long shadows against the domed
ceiling.

'Morning prayers are at four-thirty, breakfast is at seven in
the refectory. It is humble fare – bread, olives, cheese, fruit.
You will join us then,' he stated, before placing the lamp
beside the mattress.

'Thank you. I'm anxious to talk to Father Mina – is he
around?' The abbot smiled enigmatically, wary of my intentions.

'You will find him at breakfast in the morning.' Relief
swept through me – Father Carlotto had obviously been a
good emissary.

'And if I need to get a message to anyone?' I asked,
remembering Moustafa.

'We have messengers coming and going all the time. The
Bedouin will also carry letters for us.'

'I have to contact someone at Abu Rudeis, in the Sinai.'

'I believe there may be a caravan passing through tomorrow. In the meantime, may I suggest you get some sleep
and gather your strength, both spiritually and physically.
Father Carlotto told me you would be with us for a week, is
that correct?'

'Perhaps even less if I can work out a way of making
myself invisible,' I joked.

'A week it is, then,' the abbot replied. 'Any longer could
be difficult for us. These are tense times, Monsieur

Warnock; even out here in the desert we feel the ripples of President Sadat's ambition. May God protect him.'

After the abbot left, I wrote a letter to Moustafa asking him to visit me at the monastery as soon as possible. Then, carefully, I unpacked the astrarium. The faint click of its cogs' bronze teeth sounded out: the mechanism was still working, the death-date pointer as fixed as sunrise. Theoretically, once this night had passed, I had six days left to live.

I felt a surge of fury. Frustrated, I smashed my fist into the hard mattress, hitting it over and over again. The tin ashtray beside the lamp rattled against the floor, then slid across the cement and attached itself firmly to the side of the astrarium. I stopped, both fascinated and horrified. I pulled a safety pin out of my cassock and placed it nearby. It too glided to the astrarium and stuck. Then I held my hand over it and felt a tug on the old iron ring Isabella had given me, as if invisible fingers were reaching up and pulling at it. I jerked my hand back sharply, finding it hard not to imbue the astrarium with a malevolent personality. Don't be irrational, I told myself, this is simply the magnetic force of the mechanism strengthening.

I packed the astrarium away carefully and placed it on the floor of the alcove. Then, without bothering to undress, I lay down on the hard mattress and stared at the domed roof.

I debated the scientific options of measuring the change in the device's magnetic qualities. I mulled over the concept in my mind, forming a mental diagram of all the elements of the mechanism I'd seen so far. I couldn't make sense of it. My mind turned to the abbot's last remark, and I wondered how Rachel was faring with the lead on the secret summit that she'd talked about. Another peace initiative? This ancient community I now found myself amongst had been part of the historical conflicts and intrigues that stretched back centuries. Peace seemed almost a foreign concept here. I was bone-achingly tired but wide awake at the same time. I tossed and turned until eventually I fell into an uneasy sleep.

The next morning I woke and realised that I'd missed breakfast. After rinsing my face in the washbowl, I hid the astrarium in the cupboard beneath the stand. It felt safe here in the monastery, confined and contained, and I felt my uneasiness from last night fade a little. Then I made my way quickly through the cool arched corridors and out into the blinding white light of the courtyard. The Church of Saint Bishoy stood directly in front of me: an impressive series of sand-coloured domes, with a high arched entrance flanked to the right by four smaller arches, each with a stained-glass window from ground to roof. I walked around the church to the main courtyard area on its other side, passing the remains of a mill, a dovecote and a well. Opposite the church was the garden: rows of pomegranate bushes, some olive trees, and various vegetables. Several young monks were busy hoeing and planting. I asked one of them where I could get some breakfast and he plucked a pomegranate and threw it to me, grinning. Then, in a heavy rural accent, he suggested that I might try the refectory as sometimes they fed the very old monks later.

In the refectory I sat down at a low long table bathed in light filtering in through a skylight set in the top of the cupola. A young peasant woman with a wide, curiously blank face placed a bowl of rice in front of me. Across the table, an ancient monk sat eating very slowly from his bowl; he paused, holding his heavy pewter spoon in mid-air, and stared hard at me. I tried smiling, wondering whether this was Father Mina. He guffawed – a sound somewhere between indignation and a cough – then continued his painfully slow meal. I spooned the rice into my mouth. Unexpectedly, it was salty and I spat the spoonful out. The monk burst into laughter. I turned to the peasant woman and asked her in Arabic for some honey, but she ignored me, carrying on with her task of stacking plates.

The monk pushed his bowl away with a clatter and nodded towards the woman. 'She has no ears – deaf!' His wrinkled hands flapped at the side of his head. 'You are the Englishman?' he went on in heavily accented English.

'That's right.'

He sat back and examined my face intently, his raisin-black eyes buried in crevices of wrinkles and creases, empty of emotion. Suddenly he reached across the table and ran his hand over my cheeks and beard. I froze, astounded.

'It is okay, you are good man.'

'I am?'

'You are.' He spoke with such absolute conviction that, to my surprise, I found myself filled with irrational gratitude. 'My name is Father Mina,' he went on. 'And yours, I believe, is Oliver Warnock. Father Carlotto told me you have been looking for me. Come, I am librarian, chief librarian, of our library. It is one of the most famous in our order. Many treasures. You need to see it. Or perhaps I'm wrong – perhaps you are here to take a vow of silence?' He grinned, and I realised he was joking.

'No, no vow of silence and, in any case, I would still be able to read,' I replied, smiling.

'Indeed, to read is to fly over the walls. But perhaps you are here to hide?'

I chose not to reply, and, in response, the monk patted my hand.

'You keep your secrets and I keep my books. Come, my friend.'

We walked across the courtyard. Father Mina was tiny – I doubted whether he was more than five feet tall – and so rotund that it was a miracle he could walk at all. He stopped by the large circular well outside the Church of Saint Bishoy.

'Here Berbers washed their swords after killing the forty-nine martyrs. They threw martyrs in the well, then locked them up in Saint Marcarius Monastery. This is why it is called Well of the Martyrs.'

I stared down into the well. It looked deep, the water just a silver glint at the bottom.

'Always we get fresh water here, always. This is Christ's miracle. But now to library, it is very special.' Father Mina tugged at my arm.

'I have a letter that has to get to the Sinai by tomorrow,' I told him. 'The abbot said there may be a caravan of Bedouin passing through.'

Father Mina nodded, then gave a quick, sharp whistle. Immediately, a skinny fellah boy of about ten appeared from the shadows and ran towards us in a flash of thin legs and grinning white teeth.

'Give me letter, please?' Father Mina commanded. I handed him the letter to Moustafa. He squinted at the address short-sightedly, then passed it on to the boy, barking an order in Arabic. The youth disappeared. The priest read my incredulous expression.

'Do not worry. It will be with the Bedouin by nightfall and in Sinai by tomorrow's sunset. But now to more important matters.'

'The astrarium?' I blurted out.

'Patience, my friend. First let me show you the library.'

The library was situated at the far south-east corner of the compound, next to an ancient mill where the monks had once ground their own flour. It was a narrow room running along the monastery's outer defensive wall, which had been built in the ninth century and stood over ten metres high and two wide. The library was lit from above through openings at the centre of each cupola and was lined with ornate reading stands and floor-to-ceiling eighteenth-century glass cabinets filled with manuscripts.

Father Mina walked me around proudly, describing the historical and religious significance of the texts kept in the cabinets. It was hard to concentrate – I was anxious to see his research, but I sensed that the monk was testing me somehow, perhaps gauging the depth of my sincerity as he lectured me on the importance of the tomes. Finally, we arrived at a small oak chest tucked away in a corner. With a dramatic flourish, the priest pulled out a small key from a pocket in his cassock and opened the chest. He lifted out a hand-bound leather notebook and laid it out on a table. Its stained and yellowed pages were filled with elaborate erratic handwriting that travelled across the page as if being chased – all of it in archaic French.

'This is one of library's great treasures,' the old man said. 'A notebook of Sonnini de Manoncour, the French naturalist and explorer who was part of Napoleon's expedition in 1799.'

My heart began to race. Sonnini de Manoncour – I recognised the name. Instantly I was transported back to Goa, to the passion in Isabella's face as she told me about the letter from Manoncour that Ahmos Khafre had shown her. I'd seen a copy of it myself in the British Museum and the ornate script I'd seen in Wollington's office matched the hand that had inscribed the pages of this notebook. I felt myself starting to smile. Was it possible that the answer to the astrarium's final journey had been waiting here for me all along? Perhaps even a way to both stop the predictive abilities of the device and erase my death date? Mina handed me the notebook, but my hands were trembling too much to hold the pages still. Frowning in disapproval, he gently took it back from me.

Mina's wrinkled fingertip ran down the page. 'You see here there are notes and little drawings. They are of a naos that he found.'

He pointed to a column of tiny ink sketches, each showing a side of a naos inscribed in a language I didn't recognise, something much later than hieroglyphs.

'The naos tell of an occasion when Queen Cleopatra received a present of a star teller, what you called an astrarium.' Father Mina searched my face for a reaction. I nodded, urging him to continue.

'Exactly,' I said.

'This astrarium is wedding gift for Cleopatra's marriage to younger brother Ptolemy XIII from eunuch priest Pothinus. The naos tells us the history of the skybox.' I nodded again to show that I was familiar with these facts. The monk turned a page carefully. 'Sonnini de Manoncour wrote of this machine in letter to Napoleon, telling him that the skybox could give death as well as future, something a great conqueror would naturally be interested in. We had letter here too, but it was stolen by visitor to our monastery in 1943.'

'Ahmos Khafre,' I breathed.

The monk glanced at me sharply, his black eyes surprised, then suspicious. 'You know Khafre?'

'My wife was an archaeologist. She spoke of him.' I kept my voice low and reassuring. Again, I had the suffocating sensation that the astrarium might be controlling my life, connecting the dots itself, pushing me along a trajectory I couldn't see. Had it somehow lured me here?

The old monk pulled me towards him, his breath pungent against my cheek. 'The letter to Napoleon was written but never delivered. Sonnini de Manoncour stayed here in 1778 – we have records of visit. They speak of a great excitement, a great discovery he was about to make. A hundred and sixty-five years later, 1943, just before the end of the war, when all was chaos, Ahmos Khafre came here to research Sonnini's visit. But after he had some strange visitors he became very frightened. He stole the letter and ran. Maybe you know why?' Father Mina looked into my eyes, his gaze direct and unblinking.

I shook my head, suddenly wondering if this was some kind of set-up: a trap to make me reveal the whereabouts of the astrarium.

'I found the notebook after he was gone, hidden in almanac of botanical plants. I spend five years translating this notebook after Khafre left,' Father Mina went on, turning the pages carefully. 'I was sure it contain reason for Khafre's betrayal. We were good friends, so for me a double betrayal. This naos Sonnini write about, it must be linked to letter to Napoleon. But this is most interesting of all . . .' He pointed to a sentence on the last page of the notebook. 'This word here means "poisoned chalice". Pothinus, the eunuch priest who gave the astrarium to Queen Cleopatra, also attempted to have Cleopatra assassinated and to take over the throne himself, with twelve-year-old Ptolemy XIII – Cleopatra's brother – as puppet prince. The astrarium is both a giver of fortune and a taker of lives. A poisoned chalice,' he concluded dramatically, as if pleased with his own performance. I glanced back at the letter: my own death date seemed to dance between the hieroglyphs, taunting me.

'Does it tell us anywhere about how to destroy the astrarium or even where it's true resting place may be?'

The monk looked up at me, both startled and curious. 'Nothing, my friend. Just that the skybox is a sacred object and belongs to the gods – Isis, to be exact. But do not be frightened, this is legend. Myth. I, for one, do not believe in the power of such objects.' He placed a gentle hand on my shoulder. I tried to find the gesture reassuring.

'I cannot believe that the prophet Moses used it to part the Red Sea. The prophet did not need magic. He had God on his side,' Mina said simply, then smiled beatifically.

I retired early that evening, after watching the sun descend behind the ancient keep – debating whether I, like hundreds of monks who must have wondered before me, shouldn't be standing guard at the top, scanning the desert for attackers.

The air was cooling now, and a dry desert breeze brought noises from the nearby village: sounds of children playing, a sudden car horn, a distant radio. Yet here, within the walls of the oblong enclosure, it felt as if time itself was suspended, hovering above a far grimmer contemporary world.

Back in my cell, I left the astrarium packed and hidden. If the dials were still moving inevitably towards my death it could wait until tomorrow. I rolled out my mattress and collapsed onto it, to sleep without dreaming.

39

I spent the next two days arduously trying to read Father Mina's translation of Sonnini's notebook. I was looking for anything, even the smallest clue, that might provide further insight into the astrarium. The work helped distract me from a mounting sense of panic as each day moved me closer to my predicted death. I decided that if I couldn't find anything about how to stop the astrarium I would have no choice. I would have to go back to Alexandria and confront Hermes and Amelia, maybe even Hugh Wollington himself. It was not an attractive proposition.

There was little new information in the notebooks, apart from Sonnini guessing at the mechanics of the device, but there was one footnote that caught my attention. 'Ame' and 'Ombre' – the French words for Soul and Shadow – were written together beside the five elements that Ancient Egyptians believed made up a human soul. Sonnini had drawn a box – a little like a prison – around the two French words: as if they were trapped together, soul and shadow flapping wildly around in a cage. It looked like a whimsical doodle and it was bizarre to imagine the French naturalist bent over the page, quill in hand, drawing as he half-thought, half-imagined. But the small scribble disturbed me; the drawing of the box had an inked spiky malice that was haunting. Other than that, Father Mina hadn't really opened up any new avenues.

My train of thought was suddenly interrupted by a shy young priest, who informed me that my guest Moustafa Saheer had arrived at the monastery.

I went to meet Moustafa at the gates and together we hauled the magnetometer I'd asked him to bring with him into my cell.

Once in the privacy of the tiny chamber Moustafa wiped his sweating brow with the hem of his jellaba, then grinned broadly. 'I knew you were a crazy Englishman but I didn't think you were this crazy. You make a very convincing Copt. I would never have recognised you.'

'And you make a very convincing fellah.'

I had only ever seen Moustafa in Western clothes or overalls. Despite his ethnicity, the Cambridge graduate looked amusingly uncomfortable in his jellaba.

'At least this is my traditional dress, whereas you . . .' He faltered. 'My God, the excuses I've had to make to the company. They think you have gone a little crazy with grief. Lucky your reputation is so sterling.'

'Just don't ask me any questions,' I warned. 'I only need the magnetometer for a day. You can take it back with you tomorrow. Are you sure you weren't followed?'

'Followed? Don't be ridiculous – who is going to follow a man trekking across the desert to get to his aunt's funeral? Besides, I am unimportant in the big scheme of things. I like to keep it this way; unlike you, my friend, who must always be in the eye of the storm. But I have already promised – no questions. I had to see you anyway – I have wonderful news.' He closed the cell door; now only the faint sunlight filtering in through the narrow window lit the room. 'The geophysics have come in.'

'And?'

'They confirm the structure is huge – at least a billion barrels, almost all in the adjoining block.'

My breath caught in my throat and I looked at Moustafa wordlessly. All I could think about was the astrarium. It was as if it was playing a bad joke on me – showing me where to find great treasure yet leaving me, theoretically, with only days to live. Good fortune and death. Or maybe it was directing me somewhere by driving me back to the oilfield. If I simply allowed myself to follow the astrarium, would it lead me to the answers? A vague idea began to form at the back of my mind.

Moustafa, misinterpreting my muted reaction, put his hand on my shoulder. 'My brother, I understand your ambivalence. The news about GeoConsultancy's bankruptcy was in the financial papers this morning. But we are blessed – good fortune has smiled upon us twice.'

I glanced sharply at him. Was it possible he knew something about the astrarium? 'What do you mean?' I failed to keep the paranoia out of my voice.

Hurt, Moustafa stepped back. 'Oliver, please, I am your partner, am I not?'

I put my hand out to reassure him. 'I'm sorry. Lately I've been finding it hard to trust anyone. Tell me about the field. I am excited, really.'

'Firstly, I have spoken to friends at the ministry. The government will lease the block to us for a reasonable percentage, and we can use whatever company we choose, so long as we can post a bond. Secondly, I have found an

investor – a private individual who doesn't want to be
involved directly but will put up all the finance required for
the project.'

'All of it?' I was shocked; it was virtually unheard of for
one individual to fund an exploration. There simply weren't
that many people around with that kind of money. 'Even
without GeoConsultancy's infrastructure behind us?'

'He knows of your reputation, Oliver, and thinks very
highly of you.'

'How does he know of me? Who is he? Is he already in
oil?'

'No, he's a private businessman, an Egyptian, but he's
lived most of his life abroad. Apparently this man, Mr
Imenand, has immense wealth. He is well known in certain
business circles within the Arab world. But – he wants sixty
per cent of the licence.'

I walked to the window. The church bells had begun to
peal and I could see the monks crossing the courtyard with
calm, measured paces, intent yet tranquil. In here, we were
engaged in a whole other realm. What kind of man would
contribute millions of dollars to the initial exploration, all
his own money? It was unheard of: the only explanation I
could think of was that he must completely believe in my
reputation as the Diviner.

I swung back to Moustafa. 'I'm suspicious of people when
I don't understand their motives.'

He laughed. 'Mr Imenand is an eccentric individual who
wants to see this country developed. But he is also a shrewd
businessman. I suspect he will be trying you out for future
ventures. He is enigmatic but of excellent repute. We are
fortunate that he wants to back us. Trust me, this is an amazing deal.'

He unrolled several survey maps and laid them flat on

the mattress. 'We executed the tests you wanted along the points you'd marked. Your intuition was right, except for one thing . . .'

'Which was?'

'You can see the large structure we had already identified here, but we also found anomalies at these two points, which suggests—'

'A further reservoir below,' I finished for him.

'Exactly. Again, my friend, you have shown yourself to have the Midas touch.'

I scanned the new maps: two cross-sections drawn up from the seismic data, and a Landsat image. The change in geology was obvious; the anticline that indicated oil and gas trapped between rock strata was clearly visible. It was extraordinary that the potential oilfield hadn't been discovered until now. But what was even more extraordinary was that there were two reservoirs. It was a risk, but intuitively something was telling me to take it. I was almost convinced now that there was a connection between the oilfield and the astrarium. Perhaps something further would be revealed about the device if I took it to the oilfield? Perhaps it would even stop working? I made up my mind. 'I want to meet the man before I agree to trust him,' I told Moustafa.

'I can arrange a meeting in Alexandria – just give me a few days.'

'It will have to be in the next three days, at a safe house, and I'll have to travel there in disguise.'

Moustafa's dark face was alight with excitement. 'We'll keep the people down to the bare minimum – Mr Waalif from the Egyptian Government Oil Agency, ourselves, and Mr Imenand. Waalif is discretion itself, and we need the EGOA involved – after all, we will be leasing their land.'

'Agreed. But don't say anything to Waalif about where I

am. Keep it vague, and choose a safe house for the meeting at the last possible minute.'

'I understand.' He clearly didn't, but he probably didn't want to either.

'In the meantime, I want you to find out discreetly which rigs are available and look for some decent tool pushers. If we move with Imenand, I want everything in place to begin the exploration immediately. I'll leave the hiring of the roughnecks up to you.'

'No problem.'

'Excellent. Tomorrow we'll drive to the site.'

'Tomorrow?'

'Moustafa, I'm running out of time,' I finished grimly.

I showed Moustafa to the guest quarters of the monastery, made sure he knew where to go for the evening meal, and informed the abbot that I would be leaving with my visitor the next morning. By the time I returned to my cell it was nightfall and I was grateful for the respite that the small, silent room provided. I closed my door, unpacked the astrarium and lifted it out onto the floor.

It seemed to squat there malevolently, staring up at me. Again, I had the impulse to destroy it, to kick it to hell. But how would that help? For all I knew, my death date would continue to exist even after the destruction of the mechanism.

I switched on the magnetometer, curious about the strength of the astrarium's magnetic field, then hesitated with my hand on the lever. The scientist in me desperately wanted an empirical explanation: perhaps the device worked at a quantum level to achieve non-local effects? At the same time, the possibility of proving that the device had extraordinary physical properties disturbed me, especially as I still had no idea of the precise materials used in its construction. And even if I proved that the machine affected its environment, how would that help me to stop it?

I pointed the magnetometer at the astrarium. The detector bleeped wildly and the needle swung off the dial. I'd never seen such a strong reading. Whatever the alloys in the mechanism, I was certain they were unlike anything I'd seen before. Moreover, the magnetic field seemed to have gained hugely in strength since London, even since I came here. What could have affected it? Was it something in the surrounding stone? Whatever the reason, the machine was increasing in power – it seemed more alive than ever before. It wasn't a consoling observation.

I unwrapped the Was, the metal cool against my sweating palm. I hesitated, then made my decision. I would try again. I inserted the key into the mechanism and pushed on the dials, trying to change the dates. The pointer wouldn't shift, and I knew that if I pushed any harder the key would snap. I gave up, irrational fear pounding in my gut. The pointer indicated that I now had just over three days to live. I sat down, fighting an almost suffocating sense of panic. I had run out of options. What I wanted now, more than anything, was simply to be rid of the thing, to return to the remnants of my old life.

A tentative knock came at the door. I ignored it. A young monk shouted outside: 'Mr Warnock, you have another visitor. A woman. We cannot let her into the sleeping quarters – you must come out to see her.'

Rachel sat on the edge of the Well of the Martyrs, wearing a simple white dress. She looked like a young girl despite her air of apprehension. I led her into a smaller enclosed courtyard, secretly surprised at how elated I was to see her.

'Mr Warnock, we cannot allow women to stay within the compound,' called the monk who had told me that Rachel was here.

Rachel squeezed my hand. 'It's okay, I have accommodation at the village.'

'Half an hour of privacy is all I ask,' I called back, and the cleric withdrew.

'Ibrihim found me at the Cecil Hotel,' Rachel said, handing me a letter. 'He has some bad news. There are still men looking for you. Your villa was broken into again, despite the extra security. They even dug up the garden.'

I scanned the letter quickly, trying to find something reassuring. 'He didn't think they were Egyptians,' I noted, without looking up. 'Thugs, he calls them, professional soldiers.' Now I lifted my head to look at her. Her expression confirmed my worst fears. I returned to the letter. 'Also, Hermes Hemiedes's assistant came looking for me – Hermes has been arrested and he wants me to try to influence his release. Apparently, Hermes has dual citizenship and he wants me to go to the British consul on his behalf.'

'From what you've told me about Hermes, it sounds as if he's playing on your fears, manipulating you,' Rachel interjected.

'But why would he bother? He's the one in prison, not me.'

'Maybe he's still trying to get the astrarium.'

I stared up at the moon. The crater-marked crescent was now rising over the wall.

'Rachel, my death date's unchanged. I have three days to go from dawn tomorrow, and the terrifying thing is that I've begun to believe it.'

'Oliver! You have to cling to what's rational, the actual facts . . .'

'The actual facts? The fact is that this . . . thing has hijacked my life.'

'You're not going to die. At least, not in three days.'

I heard her, but I wasn't convinced. Suddenly, I thought of the oilfield again. I felt as if the astrarium was leading me there, but maybe there was more to it than that. It had been born into the present with the same earthquake that shifted the sands in the desert. Maybe, like closing the last link of a chain and joining the beginning and the end, I was meant to bring it to Abu Rudeis, bury it back into the depth of time where it came from? The thought of burying it beneath the sands was suddenly logical, attractive even. How would it feel simply to leave the astrarium behind?

'Listen, I came here for another reason. My source came good – I'm en route to the secret summit I told you about.' Rachel's voice seemed to hang on the still air. 'It's a major break. The scoop of the century – I have to go.'

'What is it?'

Rachel looked around at the courtyard, lowering her voice. 'I've been asked to witness a secret meeting between Sadat and Begin, to record it for posterity.' She swung around. 'It'll take place in Port Tawfiq in a couple of days. I thought I would visit you halfway there. There's a rumour that Sadat will visit the Knesset in person if the initial meeting goes well.' Her excitement was apparent even in her whisper.

'Peace, Oliver. Peace. Maybe Egypt is finally on its way.'

Again, I had the sensation that surrounding events were beginning to line up and converge into a single point. Majeed's frantic efforts to get the astrarium and his increasingly violent focus on Egypt's weak spots began to make even more sense. A strong Egypt would stand in the way of his ascent to power. Sadat's visit to the Israeli parliament, an unprecedented historical event, would be devastating to him.

'Are you serious – Sadat in the Knesset? Do you realise how revolutionary that would be? Neither Syria nor Saudi Arabia would tolerate such a visit.'

'I'm telling you, it's going to happen and I'm going to be there. Fifteen years I've waited for an opportunity like this. Fifteen years, Oliver.'

'You've worked hard for it. You deserve it.'

'I do, don't I?' Rachel grinned, her face alive with an emotional intensity that was unfamiliar and yet not strange. I couldn't help smiling back. Rachel's enthusiasm and courage was infectious and I was glad to have her by my side. Selfishly, I realised I needed her companionship as well as her expertise if I was going to carry through my plan. 'How are you getting to Port Tawfiq? Tomorrow I have to go back to Abu Rudeis with Moustafa to check out a prospective new field. That's only a drive from the Port,' I said. 'We could give you a lift.'

'Will it be safe?'

'Moustafa's an expert on back roads and military road-blocks. By the time we hit the camp itself it'll be night and no one's expecting me.'

'I'm in.'

I pulled her into a brotherly hug and suddenly the task didn't seem so daunting. From somewhere in the shadows came a polite cough, and the fellah boy who had taken my letter to Moustafa appeared. We broke apart, smiling.

'We leave early, around five,' I told her.

'I'll be here.'

I watched Rachel and the boy walk away towards the village that lay beyond the monastery's walls.

40

To our left stretched the Mediterranean in a flat, pale blue monotone – infinity, a place I'd now have liked to escape to. To the right yawned the desert – the coastal track we were driving along was the dividing line. Between the dirt road and the beach were several villas – beach retreats for the wealthy. White sand and scrubland ran right to the edge of the sea – the lip of the ancient world, its desolate beauty captivating.

Moustafa swerved the company jeep around the potholes and rubble. I bounced in the seat next to him, in my Coptic-monk guise and sunglasses, while Rachel sat in the back with the surveying equipment. We made a bizarre group but I wasn't willing to take any chances of being recognised. Moustafa had been diplomatic enough not to ask any direct questions but I could see that the stress had begun to affect him. We'd taken the back roads via Ismailia, then across the Suez Canal and down towards Port Tawfiq, but with the heightened military tension, Moustafa was still worried about encountering army roadblocks. And there were rumours of clashes with Israeli troops on the border, sightings of both

Libyan and Sudanese troops on the other frontiers. Nevertheless, I was convinced that we were going to be fine. So far we'd seen only a few farmers, a couple of tankers and a tourist bus.

The astrarium was in my rucksack, hidden underneath the back seat. There were now fewer than three days to go until my death date and I was acutely aware that the visit to the oilfield was a gamble – if it didn't reveal more information about the astrarium I'd wasted a precious day.

A roadblock loomed up as the road curved around a sand dune. A soldier ran out onto the dirt track and flagged us down. As we drew nearer an army tank became visible, partially concealed behind a clump of palms.

'What now, my friend?' Moustafa asked me grimly as he pulled up beside the trees.

'You are driving me to visit a Coptic family with a dying son,' I said. 'Rachel's a missionary from America working with the church. Understand, Rachel?'

She nodded nervously and I turned back to Moustafa. 'Think you can handle this?' I noticed that his hands, still around the steering wheel, were clenched.

'This is the last time, understand, Oliver?' He sounded unhappy. 'I am getting tired of playing this game. I have asked no questions so far, but there is a limit even to my patience.'

The soldier was now almost at the window. I touched Moustafa's hand reassuringly. 'Thanks, friend.'

After a tense glance at me, Moustafa got out of the jeep and started smiling and talking to the soldier, his arm on his shoulder – a strategy to guide him away from the vehicle and hopefully avoid a search. From the severe expression on the young soldier's face it didn't look as if he was buying Moustafa's story. To my dismay, he called over two other soldiers who were lounging against the tank watching. They put out their cigarettes and sauntered towards us.

One of them, an officer, circled the jeep slowly, staring in at Rachel and me through the windows. We both kept looking straight ahead.

He stopped outside my door and my heart jumped into my throat. I tried to look as relaxed as possible. Abruptly, he pulled open my door. 'You, out!' he demanded in Arabic – to my relief, for it meant he thought I was local.

'What monastery?' he demanded.

'Deir Al Anba Bishoy,' I answered, praying he wouldn't notice my English accent.

He stepped closer, peering into my face. I noticed the glint of a fine gold chain at the neck of his open shirt. A cross?

'I work with Father Mina, in the library,' I elaborated, hoping that my hunch was correct.

The officer smiled slightly, then leaned forward so the others couldn't hear him. 'Father Mina baptised me.' He swung around, bristling with machismo once again, and shouted, 'Let them go!'

The two other soldiers and Moustafa looked surprised. 'But, sir . . .' the younger soldier began.

'I tell you, they're nobodies! Let the jeep through!' A fourth soldier came out from behind the tank, but before they had time to argue amongst themselves Moustafa and I had climbed back into the jeep and accelerated away. None of us spoke for several miles. I heard Rachel exhale slowly.

When the tank was well out of sight, Moustafa stopped and turned to me, his face serious. 'Oliver, this has to stop! I am sorry that you are in trouble, but if you are serious about this new oil prospect I have to have your assurance that we will be okay. You understand?'

'A few days more, I promise you, Moustafa, then all will be normal.'

'Normal? What is normal? We were almost arrested back there, or worse!' He hit the gas and we carried on along the desert track, picking up speed quickly.

'The guy let us go! Moustafa, calm down, you're driving like a crazy man. You'll get us all killed!' I tried to steady the steering wheel.

Moustafa slowed down, then looked at me. I'd never seen him so grim. 'You don't understand. That fourth man, he wasn't a soldier.'

'But he was wearing a uniform.'

'That's just it – his uniform wasn't right. I know the soldiers around here, Oliver, I even served myself. That fourth guy, the young one, I swear he wasn't working for the government.'

'Who, then?'

'Secret police, government, maybe even higher up. Whoever it is, I don't like them.'

'Is that it?' Rachel asked, leaning out of the jeep window.

The mound loomed up to the left of the track. The area had already been fenced off, and the shothole scars where Moustafa's seismic crew had inserted explosives to get the required seismic measurements were visible.

'If you could read the land, you would hear it sing!' Moustafa yelled as he revved the jeep's engine over the rocky ground. 'Tell her, Oliver! Tell her how we are driving over a miracle. How this land will make us both very rich!'

He pulled up beside a boulder and I jumped out. Rachel followed while Moustafa started unpacking the surveying equipment. Opening the back door, I pulled out a shovel and pick. I turned to Rachel. To my surprise she looked uncomfortable.

'What?' I asked, swatting the flies away from my face. 'You don't approve?'

'I just think perhaps natural resources should stay that way,' she said. 'In nature, untouched.'

'Rachel, it won't just be Moustafa and me or our investors who'll make a profit from this. Money will go to the government and in turn to the people. There will be employment for the locals.'

She looked around. 'The locals are Bedouin – shepherds and traders.' She asked, a trace of irony in her voice, 'Do you think they'll be interested in working on an oilfield?'

Ignoring her, I hauled the rucksack from under the back seat and, with the pick and shovel under one arm, strode off towards the far end of the ridge.

'Where are you going?' she asked.

'I don't have time for ambivalence, Rachel!'

Rachel struggled up the mound behind me, while Moustafa, politely ignoring our argument, set up the surveying equipment. His industrious figure disappeared behind me as I clambered over the crest of the ridge.

Rachel, running, caught up with me. 'Don't do something rash just because you're frightened, Oliver! Shouldn't you find out more before trying to destroy it?'

'I can't take that gamble, Rachel – it could kill me!"

In the distance I could see the same Bedouin shepherd I'd met before. I recognised his headscarf with its distinctive pattern. He sat watching his scraggly herd of goats picking their way around a few clumps of long grass. I waved, but this time he didn't wave back.

I put down the rucksack on a small flat area behind a boulder and slammed the pick into the stony ground.

'What are you doing?' she asked.

'Digging.'

'Why?'

I pulled the astrarium out of the rucksack.

'Oliver, you can't bury that – it's a priceless antiquity.'

'So let someone else find it in a hundred years and have it screw up *their* life!'

Fuming, Rachel marched off back to the jeep. I glared down at the rocky earth, furious with her obstinacy, furious with myself, furious with the stony ground. A tiny scorpion stared back at me. Poised with its stinger erect, it was David waiting to take on Goliath. I didn't have the heart to kill it. A second later it scuttled sideways under a rock. I drove the pick into the ground, the reverberation running up my arm.

An hour later I packed the last of the sand back over the astrarium, now buried at least two metres below the surface. An enormous sense of relief washed over me, of freedom, self-determination. Feeling more optimistic than I had in weeks, I joined Moustafa to help him with the surveying. Rachel took photographs of the landscape. The sun – a great red orb like a huge omnipresent eye – hung on the horizon.

'And?' I ventured.

'It's timeless, isn't it? Elemental,' she said finally, avoiding our previous debate.

'The desert isn't timeless. The changes are more subtle but they're there.'

'But without any evidence of human activity you can almost see history reaching back. You could almost believe time wasn't linear.'

'Maybe it isn't,' I replied, momentarily believing it.

'Oliver, do you really think that by burying the astrarium you can destroy its influence?'

'I have a hunch that it might have been responsible for the oilfield coming to light – the skybox that moves Earth, sea and sky. It's a desperate long shot, but I thought that maybe here in the desert is where it actually belongs and maybe if it's at rest its hold over me will cease. But I don't know any more. I've lost my logic. Let's hope it works, otherwise you will be writing my obituary.'

A breeze blew across the plain, foreshadowing the night.

'We should get back before it is dark!' Moustafa yelled from beside the jeep where he'd begun repacking the equipment. Dusting the desert from my hands, I ran over to help him.

It was already night by the time the guards pulled open the large wire gates and we drove into the Abu Rudeis camp. Out at sea, flares from the offshore rigs formed yellow smudges shooting up from a glittering black mirror. Already I felt better, more in control on my own known terrain. I parked the jeep outside my hut and jumped down from the driver's seat, the familiarity of the camp enveloping me. Disco music blared out from a radio in a nearby hut and the air was filled with the distinctive smell of burning fuel and the fecund odours drifting off the top of the mud-logging bins – the signature scents of the oilfield. Rachel grimaced as she breathed it all in. I laughed, watching her.

'It's rough, but you're probably used to that. The other drawback is that you'll be sharing a hut with me.'

Behind us, Moustafa guffawed.

'How many more days did the astrarium give you?' Rachel asked.

'Two, after dawn tomorrow. But it's over, remember? The astrarium is dead and buried.' I smiled, but a hint of concern laced my voice.

Rachel was lying on the bed and I was on the small couch pushed against the wall.

'I once fell in love with a man who got killed by a land-mine three days later.'

'Rachel, you're not making me feel any better.'

I opened a beer and tossed the bottle cap onto the floor, together with the bottle opener, then watched in amazement as they slid across the room and stuck firmly against the side of the chair in the corner. In the same instant the electricity went out, plunging us into darkness, and the door flew inwards, revealing the scrubland outside, beyond a horizon broken only by the flares of the offshore rigs. Rachel screamed. I jumped off the bed and ran for the doorway, thinking we might be experiencing another earthquake. Dressed in knickers and T-shirt, Rachel cowered.

'What was that?'

'Another earth tremor, I think. A shift in tectonic plates . . . Christ, I'm not sure.'

A metal ashtray began to slide across the floor, first slowly, then accelerating as it neared the chair.

'What do you mean, you don't know? You're a geophysicist! You're meant to know!' Rachel pulled the bedspread over herself, terrified.

I found a torch, switched it on and left it balanced on the side table, then tried to shut the door. It wouldn't move.

'It's become jammed somehow.'

'Just shut it!'

But the metal doorknob seemed governed by an invisible force: as I tried to push the door closed, it seemed to push against me.

Staring into the gloom of the room I noticed that the beam of the torch had lit up something in the chair, something that hadn't been there before. For a minute, the shadow behind looked like the outline of a woman –

Banafrit. The skin on my scalp prickled in sudden fear and I jumped. Gathering my courage, I peered closer.

To my amazement, it was my dusty rucksack. I picked it up, brushing off red sand. It was heavy and from inside I could hear the soft whirling sound of the magnets spinning.

Slowly, I lifted out the astrarium, gleaming dully in the darkness, and placed it on the table. The metal objects in the room moved with it.

'What's that doing here?' Rachel said, horror in her eyes. 'Didn't you bury it?'

'I did, I swear.' I stared at the artefact, my mind scrambling to understand.

'What's happening!' Rachel almost screamed the question.

The long shadows of the moving metal objects swung like ghosts across the walls. It was terrifying and disorientating.

'It has some physical properties I don't understand – magnetism is just one of them. It seems to be growing stronger.' I tried to sound rational to calm Rachel, and myself.

'But how did it get here into the hut?'

'I have no idea.'

I sat down heavily, not taking my gaze off the mechanism, thinking over the details of the afternoon. The hole I'd dug was deep. No one had witnessed the burial, at least as far as I could remember. Moustafa had been on the other side of the ridge the whole time. Was it possible that the Bedouin shepherd had seen me bury the astrarium and had then dug it up and brought it back here to the camp? But why would he have done that?

Desperate to find some concrete explanation, I didn't dare examine the terrifying thought that the device might actually have moved itself.

'Okay, so now I'm a complete believer.'

Rachel's voice broke into my thoughts. I looked across and saw real terror in her eyes. Leaving the astrarium on the table, I tried to think of something to say that might be reassuring. Something pinned to a reality that could defuse my fear.

There was nothing.

The door slammed shut again and the torchlight flickered. Then it died, the battery dead. Rachel whimpered. I felt along the edge of the bedside table for the drawer, found a box of matches and a candle that I knew were inside, and lit the candle.

'Isabella knew when she was going to die,' I told Rachel. 'That was the real reason she was so desperate to find the astrarium, so that she could change the date of her death. Call it a self-fulfilling prophecy, but she drowned on the exact date predicted by Ahmos Khafre, a date she might have been able to change if she'd found the astrarium in time. Maybe I could have saved her, but I just didn't know how.'

I was unable to meet Rachel's gaze. A large moth threw itself against the window with a dull thud. We both jumped, then laughed nervously.

41

I lay there staring up at the ceiling. Rachel was curled up asleep on the bed, snoring slightly. I envied the ease with which she'd fallen asleep. I guess it was from sheer exhaustion. My own mind was racing – working out my next step, now that the astrarium had found its way back to me. Obviously I couldn't destroy it and yet I had a moral responsibility not to allow it to fall into the hands of my enemies. Again, I found myself craving Isabella's wisdom and guidance. Restless, I got up.

The cry of a bird broke into my thoughts. It sounded again: *ke-ke-ke-ke* . . . The plaintive cry of a sparrowhawk. Careful not to wake Rachel, I slipped on my jeans and stepped out into the night.

A cloud of insects and moths swarmed around the lanterns. Over to the east, the pale glow of dawn had begun to creep over the horizon. The sparrowhawk cried again, somewhere high above me. I scanned the sky but saw nothing. I sat down on the wooden step of the hut and watched stars so bright that they made me imagine a brilliant cosmos hanging behind a curtain of night.

'Isabella . . .' My voice sounded naked and pathetically human. How does one talk to a ghost? I cleared my throat. 'Show me how to stop the mechanism, to save myself . . .' The utterance felt uncomfortably close to a prayer.

It was then that I became aware of the sensation of being watched – that distinctive prickling at the back of the scalp. Careful not to make any sharp movements, I looked over at the pool of light thrown by the nearest lantern. Just beyond its edge, two yellow eyes stared back. I froze. It had to be a jackal, or a hyena. It was hard to see the animal's body. We stared at each other for only seconds but fear stretched time.

The beast jolted into movement, its haunches lowering in a blur as if readying itself to spring at me. Terrified, I scraped up a handful of stones and threw them. The creature spun and leaped back into the receding night – a swirl of tawny fur and slender legs – and I saw the tip of its forked tail sweep across the sand.

The next morning, Rachel departed reluctantly.

'I don't like to leave you with this,' she gestured helplessly at the astrarium, 'but I have to go.' Moustafa had organised a lift for her with an engineer going to Port Tawfiq where she was going to join President Sadat's anonymous motorcade for its secret mission. She embraced me briefly and I resisted the urge to hold on to her, to beg her to stay and help me. Here, and in this moment, she seemed like my last hope, my one link to safety. Watching her climb into the car and leave, I fought a sense of abandonment.

Later I drove back to the site where I'd buried the astrarium. It was mid-morning by the time I reached the dune and the sun was radiating waves of heat that pushed against my eyes and dried my throat and nostrils. As I began to climb the ridge, I tried to distract myself from the fear of finding something extraordinary by visualising the sedimentary structure I was walking on, the consoling thought of all that black gold beneath my feet. It didn't work and by the time I could see the gaping hole where I'd buried the rucksack my whole body thudded in time with my heart.

Rubble lay strewn around the hole, as if whoever or what-ever had dug up the astrarium had done so in a frenetic manner. I kneeled down. Bird prints ran in a hectic pattern around the edges of the vacant grave, the unmistakable claw marks of the sparrowhawk. I looked up at the sky. It was a void of blue.

When I got back to camp the hut was empty, and accord-ing to the astrarium I had only two days to live.

Later that day, with me disguised once more as a Coptic monk, Moustafa and I left for the safe house he'd organised in Alexandria. I knew I was driving straight into the face of danger and the very real possibility that Mosry would be waiting for me. But with the political situation reaching a climax and potentially only twenty-four hours to go until my death, I needed to force some kind of confrontation – and that wasn't going to happen with me hiding out in the desert.

The drive took twelve hours and we arrived not long before dawn. Our meeting with Mr Imenand was scheduled for that morning. Judging by the crowing roosters and bray-ing donkeys I could hear as we approached the safe house, I suspected it was situated near or above a livestock market.

It was a neoclassical apartment that had seen grander days. Decorated in a glitzy mock Louis XVI style, it looked like the kind of place a government official would procure for his downtown mistress. Moustafa assured me that we had the apartment for the whole day, after which he'd drive

me back to Wadi El-Natrun. I hadn't told him I might not
need the ride back.

At nine a.m. four of us gathered around the long glass-
topped dining table below a large black-and-silver glass
chandelier. Mr Waalif, the official representing the Egyptian
Government Oil Agency, sat opposite Moustafa and myself,
staring at the spreadsheets and surveillance maps that
Moustafa had supplied. A cadaverous man in his late fifties,
whose flat features were covered in an inordinate number of
large sunspots, Waalif had mentioned nothing about the
clandestine nature of the meeting, but that didn't really surprise me. Waalif was famous for two things – discretion and
his own clandestine deals. His approval was essential if we
were to get the licensing agreement.

Sitting at the other end of the table was Mr Eminites, Mr
Imenand's representative, a short Jordanian dressed in a pale
blue jellaba with an expensive tie and shirt underneath. He
wore large black-framed glasses wrapped around his wide
face. Initially he'd seemed friendly, but had frosted up when
I demanded an explanation why Mr Imenand wasn't there
himself. My insistence had shocked my polite companions,
but after Moustafa had murmured something into Mr
Eminites's ear the representative had assured me that Mr
Imenand would be at the meeting but in his own time, and
that we should begin without him. None of which I had
found reassuring.

Waalif cleared his throat. 'So, Mr Warnock, I understand
that you and Moustafa Saheer, in partnership with Mr
Imenand, wish to lease the land for an initial exploration
period of three years, followed by a production period of
twenty-five years at our standard terms. That will mean an
annual land fee as set out in schedule four, production
bonuses as set out in schedule five, a government royalty as

set out in schedule six, and a share of production as set out in schedule seven. I gather the initial work programme is already agreed.'

Mr Eminites glanced at the draft contract in front of him. I found his expression impossible to interpret and without the presence of our enigmatic benefactor it all felt very risky.

'We obviously can't predict the eventual production,' I said. 'But we are confident that the reservoir is there and that we can get the best from it.'

'And who will be the other oil company partnering us?' Waalif went on.

Moustafa and I exchanged glances. Mr Eminites adjusted his tie knot before speaking in polite but heavily accented English.

'There will be no other partners. This is one of the conditions of Mr Imenand's commitment, which, as you can see, is considerable. He also insists that the exploration programme should begin within the month.'

'That quickly?' I interjected, wondering silently if I would myself live long enough to see the work begin.

'Mr Imenand is not a young man and he is keen to see the fruits of his investment.'

'This is unusual,' Waalif said. 'But the Egyptian government is respectful of Mr Imenand's eminence and the significant capital he is offering this project, and we trust our friend Mr Warnock. So we are happy to proceed on this basis.'

Waalif, a pedantic negotiator famous for exhausting his colleagues with endless minutiae, was smiling; his usual arrogance seemed to have been replaced by what I could only describe as reverence. I sat back, trying to conceal my astonishment. Who exactly was this Mr Imenand? The only information I'd gleaned from Moustafa was that he had extensive investments right across the Mediterranean, from Spain to Turkey, as well as in North Africa, and that he'd had been based in Greece for most of his working life. His holdings were complete and, more interestingly, he had no heirs. It wasn't much to go on, but without the backing of GeoConsultancy I knew it would be hard to raise the funds by ourselves for even the most basic exploration, and never on the terms that he was offering. I had no choice but to trust him.

Suddenly I was aware of a change of atmosphere in the room. Mr Eminites had risen to his feet, bowing his head reverently. The others followed suit. I swung around. Behind me, silhouetted in the doorway, was a thin figure.

'Oliver Warnock. It is a delight to meet such a legendary individual in person.'

Imenand's voice was resonant; the bass notes seemed to reverberate right down into my feet. He stepped out of the sunlight and I could see him properly. Lean and around five feet eight inches tall, he was dark-skinned, almost Libyan in appearance, with a finely honed face that had high cheekbones and a long curved nose. His age was hard to guess: I estimated he was somewhere between fifty and seventy – his skin had the well-preserved sheen of wealth. His posture was upright and regal, and he exuded a charisma that I had witnessed only once before – on the one occasion I had met Prince Faisal. He was immaculately dressed in what looked like a Savile Row black suit, with a lavishly patterned cravat and matching handkerchief. The cravat was held in place by a gold tiepin modelled in the shape of an ostrich feather; it was an eccentric detail that suggested a man capable of unconventional behaviour.

Mr Eminites pulled out a chair for the new arrival. 'Mr Warnock, it is my honour to introduce you to Mr Imenand,' he said.

The entrepreneur held out his hand and I shook it. To my astonishment, although the skin on his hand appeared youthful, it felt like that of a far older man.

'Nice to put a face to the enigma, Mr Imenand,' I said.

'And for me to meet the Diviner. Your reputation precedes you – I have been following your career for a while now. You have a very successful exploration record, one of the most impressive on the globe.'

'You exaggerate,' I replied modestly. To my surprise, Imenand seemed to take offence.

'I never exaggerate. Perhaps you are unaware of the full extent of your powers. At your age that is not merely fool-hardy, it is also culpable.'

'I am a scientist, Mr Imenand, no more, no less. I am thorough in my research.'

'We shall see. But I must extend my condolences for the loss of your wife. She was a great archaeologist.'

'You knew of her too?' I felt uncomfortable. I knew so little about this man and yet his familiarity seemed to create an odd intimacy between us.

'I have read several of her papers. I am a collector of antiquities and, one could say, a little of an archaeologist myself – amateur, of course.' He laughed, and the others followed him politely. 'But now, to business. You are satisfied with the terms of the contract?'

Cornered, I became flustered. 'Yes, they are fine.'

'Do not be deceived, Mr Warnock – or may I call you Oliver?'

I nodded.

'Oliver, I shall be taking a strong personal interest in the exploration. I have decided to make you my hobby.'

Again he laughed, and again, like a chorus, the others joined in. I didn't; something in me wanted to resist the allure of that charisma spreading like perfume throughout the room.

'So we have a deal?' I said bluntly, refusing to play along. Immediately the laughter was cut short.

Moustafa glanced at me, his expression pensive as if I had overstepped the mark. Mr Eminites coughed, while Waalif adjusted his wide silk tie. The tension built until finally Mr Imenand broke into a smile, to the others' visible relief.

'We have a deal, and now I have a plane to catch. But we will be seeing a lot of each other in the future, Oliver – that much is certain.'

We shook hands again.

Mr Eminites gathered up our presentation material and placed it in his briefcase. As he moved to open the door, I noticed that he manoeuvred himself so his back was never presented to his employer. Mr Imenand paused in the doorway, and to my astonishment, he winked at me before walking out the door.

42

While Moustafa was out buying supplies for the long drive back to the monastery, I unwrapped the astrarium. Nothing had changed: the mechanism was still whirring away and the tiny pointer with the head of Seth was now only one degree away from my death date.

Carefully, I wrapped the device up again. The meeting with Mr Imenand had disturbed me. Was he just interested in the exploration or did he have other intentions? I needed to get out of Alexandria as soon as possible – but there was one encounter I had to have before leaving.

I waited until Moustafa returned. After asking him to guard the bag containing the astrarium, I stepped once more onto the streets disguised as a Coptic priest.

The prison guard slipped the fifty Egyptian pounds into the back pocket of his uniform and beckoned me into a narrow corridor reeking of urine and disinfectant.

'Mr Hermes, he special friend, maybe?'

Ignoring the guard's grin, I followed him, fighting disorientation and fear as I recognised the peeling plaster and old metal doors from my own interrogation only a week before. We walked past cell after cell – some of them empty and unlit; some with men curled in the corners, abandoned knots of despairing humanity. Some called out for help; others chanted in prayer, rocking themselves backwards and forwards.

At the end of the corridor was a slightly larger cell with a wooden bench and a latrine bucket in the corner. Hermes Hemiedes lay on the bench, wrapped in a grey blanket that he had pulled all the way over his face, almost as if in shame. His old man's legs – pale, with twisting veins encircling the thin ankles – stuck out from underneath, the feet, gnarled with bunions, thrust into a pair of battered oversized sandals.

'Thirty minutes,' the prison guard informed me, unlocking the barred door with a large iron key. 'Normally fifteen, but for you,' he tapped the money in his back pocket, 'thirty.'

He left, locking me in behind him.

'Oliver?' Hermes threw the blanket off his head and sat up. I was relieved to notice that his face didn't appear to be bruised. 'Thank God you've come. I cannot stay here – I will not come out alive!'

'Hermes, please, let's not panic. Tell me first, what have they charged you with?'

'I have been charged with conspiracy to undermine the state. It is a trumped-up lie. And they have attacked me.'

'The prison guards?'

'Don't be ridiculous – the prisoners! They ambushed me in the yard and . . . humiliated me.'

'Really? You look unmarked.'

'You don't understand. For an individual such as myself, with differences . . .'

'Your sexual orientation?'

'My sexual orientation?' He laughed bitterly. 'If only it were that simple.'

Noticing my expression, Hermes slowly lifted his stained prison shirt to reveal pendulous shrivelled breasts – female breasts.

'You're a hermaphrodite?' I struggled to keep the astonishment out of my voice.

Suddenly all the oddities I'd noticed about the Egyptologist made sense: the hairlessness of his skin, the narrow shoulders, the wide hips, the curiously wavering tone of his voice, which now reminded me of the alto voice of an older woman. He covered himself up. 'In this life I have chosen to live as a man.'

'I don't understand . . .'

'I was born over seventy years ago in a small village in the Sudan. We did not have the technology or the medical staff to correct such "abnormality". My parents were horrified. They gave me to the darwish, who brought me up as his apprentice.' He looked at me carefully. 'You might know him – Ahmos Khafre? He's the mystic I sent Isabella to visit in Goa all those years ago.'

I stared at Hermes, a sense of vertigo hitting me as I wondered exactly how much of both Isabella's life and my own had been manipulated from a distance, as though we were marionette puppets jerking at the end of strings. As if he'd heard my thoughts, Hermes said softly, 'So you see, the circle is even tighter than you might have imagined, Oliver.'

'How did you survive?' I asked instead.

'I started to research the history of people like me, whom the Ancient Egyptians had once considered sacred. The perfect blend of the masculine and feminine, we were often chosen to be the high priests. I participate in the most sacred ceremonies.'

Hermes's eyes shone madly and as he spoke his voice seemed to be getting higher, as if he was finally relaxing into his natural ambiguity. My memory jolted me straight back to the catacombs, to the painted features of the goddess Isis shimmering unnaturally, the voice behind the wooden mask. I leaned against the wall, sickened by the realisation. I'd been on the wrong trail the whole time – it had not been Amelia Lynhurst leading the worshippers. I looked at him, but before I could say anything he reached out and grabbed my wrist. 'Oliver, we need each other. No one else can save you. No one else knows how to stop the astrarium.'

'What do you want with it, Hermes? It's not to save me, I know that much . . .'

Hermes smiled cynically and for the second time since meeting him I saw a maniacal side behind those guarded eyes.

'Immortality, Oliver, what anyone would want.'

Horrified, I pushed his hand off. 'You lied to me! You took her heart, you violated her!'

I banged against the bars to get the attention of the guard.

'Wait, I'll tell you everything!' Hermes shouted, pulling me back.

I stopped rattling the bars. Hermes settled himself on the bench and patted the space next to him. I ignored him, preferring to stand.

'Giovanni Brambilla ran a small salon that attracted individuals who were interested in mysticism and the occult. I'm talking over forty years ago, in 1936, when the world we knew was beginning to fragment. None of us wanted to lose power. We were a disparate group – academics, businessmen, archaeologists – but we all had a passion for Egyptology. And those were desperate times in a desperate city.'

So the police had been correct, I thought to myself – a

secret sect of sorts under Giovanni's tutelage. No wonder they'd been suspicious of Isabella.

'At first the re-enactments were innocent, naive attempts to experience some kind of authenticity. But as the years passed I wanted to go further. I was convinced that if the rituals were carried out correctly, we could do something more powerful. It could be real.' He paused, then whispered: 'Sorcery. One day, unknown to the others, I replaced the sheep's heart we'd been using in the weighing-of-the-heart ritual with a human heart.'

'Whose heart?' I asked incredulously, but I thought I already knew the answer. Ashraf had heard screaming.

'A criminal's – I stole it from the mortuary.' He looked at me coolly.

'You're lying again! You had a man murdered, didn't you? Ah, and that young Egyptologist who was missing her organs, like Isabella,' I said, suddenly remembering Demetriou's description.

'They were noble sacrifices! What is important is how that little detail changed everything. That night we conjured Seth, his very being. It was phenomenal – suddenly, we had the power of gods.' Hermes sounded hysterical now, his voice tinged with mania. I took a step back, pressing against the bars.

'That's not possible.'

'Isn't it? Oliver, you've seen it for yourself.'

I shivered, remembering the long shadow falling across the walls of the catacombs. Hermes watched my face with a kind of objective curiosity; a whole other personality seemed to be materialising under his veneer of obsequiousness.

'After that, dissent broke out in the group,' he went on. 'But this was not the debate of a bunch of academic archaeologists. This argument had much broader implications.'

'Giovanni wanted to use the rituals to destroy his political enemies?'

Hermes nodded. 'For a while it worked. I couldn't tell you whether it was the power of all those people believing together or whether it was real sorcery. Then Amelia broke the circle and ruined it all. She took some of the others with her, to pursue their own interests.'

'And Isabella?'

'She did whatever her grandfather wanted, anything. It had been Giovanni who first came across the astrarium in his research; research that he had been foolish enough to share with Amelia Lynhurst.'

'And the excavation at Behbeit el-Hagar?'

'Giovanni organised it. We were all convinced we would find the astrarium there. Giovanni had ideas about using it politically then, as a way of defending the old Egypt and, to protect his assets, warding off the inevitable takeover by Nasser. I thought he was crazy at the time. Now I know otherwise. We found nothing. Instead, Amelia found the Was and fled with it, betraying us. Giovanni persuaded Isabella to dedicate her studies to the mechanism. When she sought out Ahmos Khafre on my advice, he unwittingly pushed her further by giving her her death date. Her urgency fuelled her research and she came so close.'

'What about Isabella's death date?' I asked through gritted teeth.

'Ahmos Khafre was the greatest astrologer the world has ever known. The death date was real.'

'She was just a child, Hermes.' I felt myself getting furious at the callousness of his attitude, at the culpability of involving children, at Isabella's stolen childhood.

'Childhood is such a modern concept.'

At that, I couldn't contain myself any longer. I lifted my

fist; only Hermes's terrified expression and my need to know more stopped me from striking the blow. Relieved, he wiped his sweaty face with a filthy sleeve.

'I was deceived by Mosry. He infiltrated our group and I assumed that he and I wanted the same thing. It was I who arranged for his man to be on that boat when Isabella drowned. I didn't know he was working for Prince Majeed until he murdered your Australian friend – an interrogation gone wrong.'

'I could kill you now,' I said thickly.

'I am ready to die anyway.'

Hermes bared his scrawny neck, as if waiting for me to strangle him. I kept my arms stiffly by my sides. He pulled his collar back up.

'The astrarium has a reputation amongst the military elite, both in Saudi Arabia and Egypt. They believe in its powers. After all, it is known that Alexander of Macedonia wanted it, and Napoleon sent troops to look for it. If Prince Majeed gets hold of the device it will be bedlam for this region – tribal anarchy. He will use it to help create the kind of political chaos he thrives on. Then he swoops in to take over. My needs are far simpler. All I wanted was immortality.' He smiled cynically. 'No use to me now. They will kill me in here. Unless you could be persuaded to part with the astrarium?' He smiled at me hopefully, but I ignored him.

'What about Hugh Wollington? Why does he want the astrarium?'

Hermes's face turned ashen; I'd never seen him look more frightened.

'How do you know about Hugh Wollington?' he asked.

'He was the voice of Horus, wasn't he?' I couldn't hold back – I grabbed a handful of his filthy caftan and shook him, hard. 'He was behind all this from the beginning!'

'He is the high priest. He rules us all.' Petrified, Hermes could barely speak.

'Nonsense. He's just a man like the rest of us. Just give me the facts!' I towered over Hermes, who suddenly looked even more pathetic, almost whimpering with fear.

'If he gets hold of the astrarium he will release Seth, the god of confusion,' Hermes whispered. 'Then may the gods help us all.'

There was a pause and despite myself I felt a frisson of terror.

I turned to call for the guard again. Hermes clutched at my arm.

'Please, you have to understand. You were lured to the ritual deliberately to play Osiris. You are of the Underworld, Oliver, whether you like it or not. You are the deliverer. You must be allowed to complete your task.'

'The deliverer – what are you talking about?'

'At Behbeit el-Hagar we discovered a prophecy written by Banafrit which said that if the astrarium was ever lost the only person able to fulfil the true destiny of the skybox and restore it to the mummy of Nectanebo would be a priest of the Underworld, a follower of Osiris, someone who brought forth the subterranean treasures of the Earth. It was no accident that Isabella chose to marry you,' Hermes concluded, almost with relish, looking at me sideways.

I had to restrain myself from lashing out at Hermes. How dare he suggest that Isabella had married me because she'd been instructed to! Yet, despite my fury, I couldn't contain the tsunami of doubt now roaring up inside me, undermining all I'd ever believed in. Had the astrarium passed judgement on my life?

'You wanted me to take responsibility for the astrarium because of some archaic prophecy?' I said, incredulous.

'You have no choice. But we can't do anything about it if I'm not there. You need me, Oliver. And I need you. Please, please help me.' He reached out. 'I tried to get you to surrender the astrarium in the ritual. If I had succeeded, the power to control it would have transferred to me.'

'You mean that I alone can control it?'

'Until you put your birthdate in it – then you surrendered your destiny to its judgement.'

I felt the blood roaring in my ears and saw a kaleidoscope of images, each one more terrible than the last, dance in front of my eyes – Isabella's heart floating in the water, her lifeless eyes beseeching me, a small pointed hand ticking away inevitably, condemning me to die in two days; the long shadow dancing across the catacombs, coming for me. I knew I should stay, should strike some kind of Faustian bargain with Hermes, but at that moment I suddenly found myself unable to speak. Gulping frantically, I tried to block a rising tide of panic. I pushed Hermes away. I just needed to escape.

I shouted for the guard, my voice hoarse. My calls ignited a chorus of wailing from the other prisoners until the whole corridor was transformed into a cacophony of misery. When finally I stumbled out into the courtyard, Hermes's entreaties still rang in my ears.

43

The iron gates of the prison shut behind me with a clang. I walked towards the main street, calmer now but still reeling from the scenarios swirling around my brain. It was just before noon and the pavements were thronged with people: women on the way back from the market, men sauntering to the midday meal, schoolgirls linked arm in arm. Isabella had loved me, I told myself. But the prism of our marriage was now collapsing into a complexity of shards that I didn't understand. Had my profession been the single factor in her decision to marry me? Had it held some kind of mythical symbolism for her? Everything I had known to be solid, to be real, was evaporating around me. Isabella had been my anchor, the continuity that had given my life foundation for the last five years. To imagine that our shared years of intimacy – of lovemaking, of believing in the life we had, that she loved me for who I was and not what I did – were nothing but mere simulacra was devastating.

And if my marriage hadn't been real, what else was false in my life? I'd assumed myself in control of where I worked and for whom, but now I had to ask just how many of those decisions had been made of my free will? Had I been unwittingly following a path dictated by an unseen master? The idea that parts of my life might have been preordained was suffocating. It was an affront to all my personal philosophies: my atheism, my belief in free will, the notion that a person had control over their destiny. And then there was Hermes's tale of sorcery and sacrifice. In my mind, I heard the quiet ticking of my life ebbing away.

Foreboding travelled over me in waves. I was painfully aware of time passing. Light seemed to bounce off everything – car mirrors, glass shopfronts, even the metal stirrups of the horses. I needed to get back to the monastery. But then what?

Behind me there was the roar of a car engine. I turned; a black Mercedes was trailing me. I could see Mosry at the wheel, Omar beside him and, disturbingly, Hugh Wollington in the back seat. Looking around me wild-eyed, I darted into a side street. The car followed, swerving onto the pavement towards me. People scattered, women screamed, fruit spilled over the street as the car headed straight for me – I closed my eyes, almost glad that it would all be over now, but just before the vehicle hit me a hand yanked me into a doorway, inches clear of the front bumper.

Faakhir.

'Down here!' he said as he bundled me into a side alley and then into a darkened entrance of what appeared to be a halal butcher's shop.

'I suppose you imagined I was the Antichrist incarnate.' Amelia Lynhurst stood at her desk, a vast Victorian construction covered with maps and papers. An elegant cabinet stood against one wall, covered in framed photographs. Several showed a younger Amelia in uniform; one was of her sitting atop a tank, flanked by a couple of grinning British soldiers. *Sinai, 1944* was scrawled across the bottom.

'A sort of a demon goddess in tweed?' She smiled, beginning to stride around the room.

It was a rectangular chamber hidden behind the back of the small halal butcher's shop – the door to the chamber had been concealed by cured goat and sheep carcasses hanging from hooks, and I'd been amazed at how spacious was the room that existed behind the heavy steel door.

The walls were lined from ceiling to floor with shelves crammed with papers and books. One whole wall was dedicated to Jung: I spied *Man and His Symbols, The Archetypes and the Collective Unconscious, Psychology and Alchemy, The Structure and Dynamics of the Psyche* amongst others. Another shelf contained books on physics, including several on the latest developments in quantum physics.

'Just tell me again why I should trust you,' I responded warily.

'Because she allowed you to keep the astrarium,' Faakhir said. He sat down and pulled a cigarette out of his pocket. 'She could have told me to keep it.'

'And how do you fit into all of this?' I asked him, my mind a blur, trying desperately to connect the dots.

Amelia put her hand on the young man's shoulder. 'I had to make sure there was someone close to Isabella who could protect her.'

'But you failed.' I couldn't keep the fury out of my voice.

'This was my tragedy as well as yours.' Faakhir's face was grave with emotion.

'Just tell me who you are!' My patience had finally snapped. I slammed my fist on the desk but Faakhir didn't even flinch. It was obvious that his previous naivety had been a façade.

I was horribly aware of the clock hanging over Amelia's desk, the fine black second hand ticking by, notch by notch. I'd had enough of enigmas, of people who weren't what they seemed.

Faakhir exhaled slowly. 'Let's just say I was trained by the Israeli navy.'

'Mossad?' I persisted.

He chose not to answer.

'None of us predicted the earthquake,' Amelia said. 'We all thought that Isabella would reach the astrarium in time to influence her death date. Faakhir and I had made plans for every eventuality we could anticipate.'

'How do I fit into those plans? Why did I inherit the astrarium?'

'You are the Diviner, you embody Osiris. It must be you who reunites the astrarium with Nectanebo's mummy. This is the only way we can avoid Maat – political and emotional chaos – and the era of Seth.'

She pointed at a black-and-white television in the corner. The sound was turned down but I recognised the footage: Sadat meeting with Assad – the president's last stop before his secret meeting with Begin, the meeting that Rachel would be attending.

'Is that what the era of Seth is – a failed peace initiative?' I asked incredulously.

'Don't play the idiot, it doesn't suit you,' Amelia snapped. 'Your fear keeps you holding on to the small known world you're more comfortable with. Prince Majeed will use the astrarium not only to destroy Sadat but to create a devastating war in the region that will destabilise all neighbouring countries. It will be a version of hell, believe me—'

Faakhir interrupted her. 'Enough, Amelia, we're running

out of time. Mosry is bound to track us down soon. Do you have the Was, Oliver – the key to the mechanism?'

'Thanks to Amelia's old friend Professor Silvio, I do – but then, you stole it in the first place, didn't you, Amelia?'

'I had to put it out of reach of the others. I was frightened they would abuse the power of the mechanism – turns out I was right.' Amelia stopped suddenly, reading the ill-concealed anxiety in my face. 'So you have used the machine. That was very foolish, Oliver. Very bloody arrogant.'

I collapsed into a chair, shattered by the barrage of recent events. 'The sin of hubris,' I volunteered.

'It usually is with scientists. So when is your death date?'

'Can you help me?' I asked. 'I know you were part of the original sect.'

'I left after the first manifestation of Seth. I wish Isabella had, too. From that moment, her whole career was directed by Giovanni – in some ways, even after his death. Then she fell under the influence of Hermes Hemiedes.'

'And he sent her to Goa.'

'When I got that teaching position at Oxford, and once I felt I'd gained her trust, I explained some of the terrible things that her grandfather had done, the events he had manipulated. She wouldn't believe me, couldn't believe me. Then, when you both returned to Egypt this last time, Hermes heard that Isabella was close to finding the instrument. He persuaded her to attend a few of the rituals and, naively, she agreed.'

'I had no idea. If only she'd told me.'

'Would you have believed her?'

I didn't need to answer.

Amelia's expression was one of sympathy. 'I'm afraid, Oliver, that you have a part to play, no matter how reluctant you are. As I tried to tell you at the opera, this is a great love story. You see, when Banafrit, chief consort and sister of Nectanebo, realised the assassination plot, I think she might have died trying to save her lover. Who knows if she succeeded in saving him or not? You can imagine the scene: Banafrit, party to the Machiavellian politics of the priest clan, desperate to reach Nectanebo to warn him. It couldn't have been easy. There were many who plotted against the pharaoh, some in his own family, and the future of a whole nation rested on Banafrit reaching him in time. What I know for certain is that the assassination attempt was organised by a religious cult that worshipped the god Seth; a cult that Hugh Wollington wishes to recreate. Their manifestation of the god is one that thrives on chaos; the personification of amoral evil, the fascistic shadow self.'

'Wait – the manifestation I saw in the catacombs – how was that staged?'

'What makes you think it was staged?'

I didn't answer. The idea that the manifestation might have been real was profoundly disturbing.

'Hermes and his friends' games, a dangerous charade that led to a summoning of arcane evil. Hermes still has some influence and he has gathered a small group of dedicated followers, much like Giovanni did.' An image of the young woman, Isabella's likeness, flashed into my head. Hermes must have picked her for the similarities, knowing that I would follow her.

'You have to remember that when a group of followers come together,' Amelia continued, 'their desire and their will unite. That in itself is a hugely powerful force, an energy that many charismatic political leaders have exploited. Think of Hitler, Stalin, Mao – individuals capable of galvanising hundreds of thousands of people at a time. Jung also believed in the idea of mass hypnosis, an alchemy of faith.

There, Oliver, I have given you a psychological explanation that you may feel more comfortable adopting.'

'I'm due to die in . . .' I glanced at the clock hanging on the wall '. . . sixteen and a half hours. It's hard to find anything comforting at the moment.'

I laughed cynically but the others stayed grimly silent.

'What about Hugh Wollington?' I asked. 'Who's he working for? Was he involved in the ritual that was designed to terrify me?'

'He was. Hermes was playing a dangerous double game. He is terrified of Wollington but he needed him as Horus. I suspect he would have tried to beat him to the astrarium to take it for himself. It wouldn't have worked, poor man. Wollington is too powerful. He struck a deal, I'm sure of it. I imagine he is to get the astrarium after Majeed has abused its power. And, let's face it, if Majeed gets his hands on the astrarium, the consequences will be just as devastating as the era of Seth: a whole country sinking into chaos, darkness, abject poverty, all under a dictatorship – even Seth couldn't do much better. Wollington wants to be the rewriter of biblical history. He is hugely ambitious academically. He also want immortality – just a different sort of immortality to that sought by Hermes or Majeed.'

There was a knock on the door, which startled us all. After a nod from Amelia, Faakhir went to answer it. We could hear him conversing in Arabic. A moment later he came back.

'Hermes Hemiedes has committed suicide. He hanged himself in his cell.'

I buried my face in my hands. 'Jesus Christ.'

Amelia put her hand on my arm, her cool touch reassuring.

'Oliver, concentrate. We have to move fast.'

44

I sent Faakhir to the apartment with a letter for Moustafa, giving him our pre-agreed code word. What seemed like minutes later he returned with the astrarium. Amelia lifted it from its wrapping and I witnessed the same reverence in her face that I'd seen in Hermes's when he first saw the device: an expression of religious rapture. But in seconds she switched back from worshipper to scientist. Using what looked like a dentist's stylus, she pushed at the base from one end. To my amazement, it shifted and slid outwards. She carefully removed it and picked up a magnifying glass to peer at its surface.

'As I thought.'

Amelia offered the magnifying glass to me. A set of hiero-glyphs and a line drawing were clearly visible on the tiny panel: I recognised the symbols for Osiris, the sun god Ra, and Thoth, but that was all.

'This is an Amduat,' she explained, 'a map of the afterlife to help the deceased become an Akh Aper, a prepared spirit. It describes how the spirit must travel to the mansion of Osiris – an early prototype of Hades – and to the Field of

Hetep in a twelve-hour journey that mirrors the journey of Ra, or the sun, in the hours between dusk and dawn. The map shows us how the spirit of the deceased must travel from east to west along a blue waterway across the inner sky. Then back again, from west to east, on a black land-path across the outer sky. Finally the spirit becomes a star in the sky next to the god Thoth. However, I suspect this particular map is more than allegorical; it is a deliberate smokescreen. I have seen this ruse once before on the back of a hand mirror found in the tomb of Nectanebo's uncle.'

Amelia reached over and pulled a cigarette lighter from Faakhir's shirt pocket. Flicking it open, she ran the flame over the metal surface. Shocked, I grabbed her wrist.

'I hope you know what you're doing . . .'

Smiling, she shook my hand off. 'My dear man, of course I don't! It's always ten per cent fact and ninety per cent guesswork. But the flame can't hurt it.'

As the surface of the metal blackened, the lines of another map appeared. I heard Amelia's sharp intake of breath. The distinctive shape of the Nile, like the delicate branches of a wayward tree, was instantly recognisable. At the bottom, Aswan, with the ancient city of Memphis near the top; and the cities of Luxor and Thebes in between, small pale dots on the tiny illustration. A route was etched into the metal, from Alexandria along the coastline to Marsa Matruh, then swinging inland to the south-west near the Libyan border.

Amelia nodded several times. I could see her eyes misting over slightly. 'So, he really was killed,' she murmured. 'This is the true map – added later, I suspect, after Nectanebo's murder – a cartogram describing the route the Pharaoh's mummy was taken along before being placed in a secret tomb. The assassins would never have left him unburied without some ceremony – the danger of angering the gods was too great. Oliver, we have finally solved the mystery of Nectanebo's disappearance.'

'And how will following this map help me?'

'Your role is to return the astrarium to its rightful owner, to place it into the arms of Nectanebo's mummy. The astrarium's soul will unite with that of Nectanebo and the device will cease to function, maybe even to exist. It's not only the one hope for keeping Egypt safe – therein also lies your own redemption, Oliver.'

I peered down at the small soot-laden map – it looked terrifyingly tenuous to me, the silvery etchings of a smoky dream. I still found it difficult to believe completely in the powers of the astrarium, but I had fallen under the spell of the death pointer and its quiet insistent ticks. And, as I noted bitterly, my supposed disbelief hadn't prevented me from becoming embroiled in the events surrounding it. My own ambivalence aside, it was clear that Amelia believed in what the astrarium might achieve in the wrong hands and I had nothing to lose by trusting her. It was a calculated gamble: go with her plan, which might switch off the mechanism, or not. According to the astrarium I had only hours to live.

'Following this map,' Amelia continued, 'Nectanebo's mummy lies somewhere in the oasis of Siwah near the Libyan border. The inscribed instructions aren't only to show the route that the Pharaoh's mummified corpse travelled; they are also our guide through the twelve stages of the journey to the Afterworld.'

I raised my eyebrows and glanced at Faakhir. Reading my expression, he stubbed out his cigarette and said, 'My friend, Egypt is riddled with mysteries. Here the divide between the inanimate and the animate is not the same as in the West. Our land has its own spirits. This is not a new story.'

'If I agree to go, will you be coming with me?' I asked.

Faakhir looked at Amelia, who spoke for him.

'Faakhir has been called away to another mission, equally important. *I* will be your guide and protector.'

Faakhir put his hand on my arm to reassure me. 'She knows the area better than anyone, and she is more of a soldier than I am, believe it or not.'

I must have looked apprehensive but Amelia ignored me. Carefully, she slid the base of the mechanism back into position.

'It's important that you understand the symbolism of the journey before we leave,' she told me.

'Isn't it the soul of the deceased overcoming moral trials and tribulations as he attempts to pass into the Afterworld? A little like a day of reckoning?'

'In the first hour, Ra, the sun god, enters Akhet, the eastern horizon, a place that lies between day and night. The spirit of the deceased accompanies him. In the second and third hours, Ra and the spirit travel through the Waters of Osiris, a realm also known as Wernes. Hours four and five are passed in the world of the desert, Sokar. In the fifth hour, the spirit finds the tomb of Osiris, recognisable by the pyramid mound built over it, a hidden lake of fire beneath the interior enclosure.'

'And will we really be travelling through a desert?'

'Both physically and psychologically. The New Testament also contains a version of this—'

'The temptation of Christ?'

'For an atheist you certainly know your Bible.'

'I blame my mother. What happens next?'

'The sixth hour of the journey is the most crucial. This is when the Ba of the sun god has to unite with his body. If this does not happen, the sun will not rise the next day and such an event symbolises the end of the world. On a smaller scale, the spirit accompanying the god will not pass into the after-life. There is no worse destiny, according to the Ancient Egyptians. The unification of Ba and form traditionally happens within a celestial circle made by the mehen serpent – the snake biting its own tail – which is a symbol of infinity in many cultures. Hour seven leads us into an even more difficult transition. The nemesis of Ra and of renewal – the huge serpent god Apophis – will be waiting to attack and destroy Ra and his spirit companion. Isis is called upon to protect and defend both Ra and the deceased. You will be most vulnerable in this hour. But there is no one who knows Isis's spells from the *Book of the Dead* as well as I do – except Hermes Hemiedes, which now, of course, is irrelevant.'

'And how does this metaphysical journey conclude?'

'At the eighth hour, the tomb gates open to allow the spirit to depart from Sokar. The ninth hour is spent returning back over the waters. Hour ten sees the regeneration of the spirit through immersion in the waters.'

'How dangerous is this going to be?'

Amelia and Faakhir glanced at each other. Amelia answered.

'It's your last hope. Mosry is out there and Hugh Wollington as well – both of them want this more than anything. I suspect that Hugh will have worked out where we're going, although they may not know we've teamed up yet. But I will endeavour to protect you to the best of my abilities.'

'And if I stay in Alexandria?'

'Mosry will kill you,' Faakhir answered bluntly.

I turned to Amelia. She shrugged, then began packing away the astrarium.

'According to the map, by the eleventh hour you will be on an island in Lake Arachie and the god's eyes – and those

of the accompanying spirit – are fully restored. In the twelfth
and final hour, Ra enters the eastern horizon as the dawning
of a new day, while the deceased's soul ascends to become a
star in the sky.'

'Meaning that I emerge having reunited the astrarium
with Nectanebo and my death date has slipped somewhere
to the distant future?' I said. 'I wasn't planning on becoming
a star in the sky.'

'If the gods will it, Oliver,' Amelia said seriously. 'I am of
the view that there are many life paths, all running in parallel. Free will lies in the choices we make, which paths we
step onto at any given moment – but those life paths are
already written. Isabella knew there was a chance she would
die that day in the water. She also knew that you would
inherit her task. The question is: do you have the strength of
character to complete it?'

Again, I found myself thinking about my marriage. The
idea that Isabella had married me because of some prophecy
had been haunting me. Had she really been that obsessed?

I looked at the astrarium, an ancient mesh of cogs and
divination, and remembered how frustrated I'd been with
Isabella's focus on finding it; how absent she had been when
she'd been working, as if incapable of registering anything
outside that circle of intent. I'd begun to view that absence
as a rival. Perhaps my instinct had been right.

And what about my father and Gareth – would I ever see
them again? I glanced at the clock. I'd already been here for
an hour – one precious hour of the few I supposedly had left.

'What have I got to lose if I don't go?' I asked.

'Only your life, if you believe the prediction – or if you
believe in Mosry!'

Faakhir indicated the television. It now showed Sadat's
convoy crossing the Syrian border before it wound its way

across the desert; the same convoy that Rachel was in. 'There's something else you should know,' Faakhir went on. 'We believe that Mosry has details of the secret meeting between Sadat and Begin, right down to the hour. Prince Majeed wants the astrarium now, Oliver. He wants to destroy any possibility of an accord.'

Amelia put her hand over mine. 'We leave in an hour.'

45

♀

The sheikh wore a traditional Berber striped jellaba and sat cross-legged on the rug on the floor of the mud-brick house. He looked about seventy, and had a large scar that ran in a zigzag across one cheek and over his nose. He paused mid-sentence to stare at me dismissively, then swung back to Amelia – with whom he'd been in deep conversation since we'd arrived in the ancient city of Siwah. Although most of their exchange was incomprehensible to me – they were speaking in a dialect I couldn't follow – occasionally I recognised the word 'sister', which made me curious about the nature of their relationship.

I took a sip of the black tea I'd been offered, heavily flavoured with rose syrup, and waited for Amelia to tell me what was going on. Eventually she turned to me.

'Sheikh Suleiman is an old friend and a Berber. This community dates back to 10,000 BC. They, and a few Bedouin traders, are the only people who really live in Siwah.'

The sheikh said something and they both laughed.

'He tells me to warn you about walking amongst the date pickers,' she said.

I was perplexed and it must have shown.

'There is an ancient law here that the date pickers, who are male, must remain virgins until they are forty years old. He thinks your blue eyes might turn their heads.'

Slightly insulted, I glanced at the sheikh who smiled back sardonically.

'Shouldn't we be on our way by now?' I asked Amelia, conscious of the astrarium lying heavily in my rucksack and the insidious hum of a large electric clock that sat, rather incongruously, next to an ornate hookah. I was running out of time. I felt my throat close up every time I looked at the two moving hands inching by.

Amelia put her hand on my knee. 'Patience. The sheikh has a gift we should take with us.'

The sheikh nodded, then stood and left the room.

'Why does he keep addressing you as sister?' I couldn't help asking.

'Because I *am* his sister.' Amelia went over to a low chest that stood in an alcove. 'This once belonged to my husband.'

She opened the chest and took out a photo to show me. Standing in front of a pool surrounded by palms was a young woman in army camouflage and beside her a young Berber holding a rifle. They were smiling at the camera and his arm was wrapped around her waist, but there was tension in their faces, as if this moment was a forced respite.

'The man I loved is buried here,' she went on. 'He was a local sheikh. This was taken in 1943 – we'd been married for two weeks, fighting Rommel for ten. The German troops were notorious in Siwah for desecrating this pool, Cleopatra's bath, by bathing naked in it. The people claimed this contributed to their defeat.'

Amelia touched the photograph, almost a caress. 'He was the love of my life.'

I now realised why, when we'd walked through the streets of the ancient white-clay town with its huts made of palm fronds and its braying donkeys, many of the older tribesmen had greeted Amelia as if she were an honorary male. It was the legacy of her military service in the region during the Second World War.

'He was killed only days after this was taken,' she said, replacing the photograph in the chest.

'I'm sorry.'

'Love while you can. Nothing is certain in life, only this – that nothing is certain in life. Old Arabic proverb.'

The sheikh returned, carrying a couple of objects wrapped in muslin. He sat on the rug and unwrapped them to reveal two handguns, which he pushed towards Amelia. She picked one up. I went for the other, but she stopped me.

'You can't be armed.'

'But it could get dangerous, right?' I insisted, my hand still on the gun.

'For goodness' sake, stop looking so worried. I'm a crack shot.'

Amelia handed the second gun back to the sheikh before tucking the other into her belt.

The sheikh chuckled and put his hand on my shoulder. 'Believe me, my friend, she is.' They were the first English words he'd uttered since we'd arrived.

We stood at the base of the bleached ruins of the Temple of the Oracle, staring out over the valley of thick green date palms swaying like seaweed below us. Despite my anxiety, it was hard not to find the place beautiful. Siwah or Sekht-am, an oasis of mainly date palms and olives, looked as if it had remained unchanged since biblical times. I shivered and looked around, hoping that no one had followed us.

Now dressed in khaki trousers, shirt and a headscarf, Amelia brushed away the flies and gestured towards the waters of Birket Siwah. 'Behold – the oasis as seen by the gods . . .'

The terrain had been spectacular as we'd flown west from Alexandria. The small plane, flying low, had turned inland, heading south-west across the Qattara Depression, then over the sudden emerald of the Qara Oasis before flying on to Siwah. Now the huge salt-water lake, Birket Siwah, shimmered in the sunlight, overshadowed only by the mountains that loomed up like breasts beyond which stretched the dramatic landscape of the Western Desert – the Great Sand Sea, a swathe of white cut only by zigzagging trails, or Masrabs, as they were known.

'This is where our journey begins,' Amelia said and gestured to the temple. Its plain exterior wall loomed above us, an occasional square window breaking the fortress-like façade. 'In Alexander's time, the oracle of Siwah was one of the six most famous oracles of the ancient world. This was the first place Alexander came after landing on Egyptian soil, to gain the blessing of the oracle both as Ammon's son and the son of Nectanebo II – in other words, the son of God. It was a popular motif amongst ambitious men at that time. This temple is the first clue. According to the astrarium's map, it's where the Pharaoh's journey into the Afterworld began.'

She pulled a sheet of paper from her shoulder bag and rolled it flat on a piece of fallen masonry. I recognised the map from the astrarium.

'Here is the ancient town of Aghurmi, and there's Lake Zeitan – a little differently shaped in antiquity. Here, on the opposite side, are the various mountains – Gebel al-Dakrur, Gebel al-Mawta and the twin mountains of Gebel Hamra and Gebel Baydai. But the one that concerns us is this one . . .' Amelia pointed at the hieroglyph of Anubis, the jackal god and protector of the desert necropolis. 'Gebel al-Mawta, the mountain of the dead. But first we need to get to the temple of Amun-Re, built by Nectanebo II himself. Unfortunately there's only one wall left standing, after some Ottoman general blew it up in 1896 to use the stone to build himself a mansion. But the hieroglyphs we need still exist. Is the astrarium secure?'

I nodded, indicating the rucksack strapped tightly over my shoulders. The growing knot of anxiety in my gut had doubled with dusk approaching. Strangely, another emotion had set in – resignation, and reassurance from the fact that I finally had a plan. It might not work, but a plan nevertheless.

'You mustn't let anyone or anything take this from you, Oliver, do you understand? No matter what you see, or what you think you see.'

I scanned the plateau of waving date palms, then looked further, to the edge of the dunes. The only other individuals I could see were a few Berber boys collecting dates. Beyond, on the great sea of sand itself, a black serpent of Bedouins wound its way towards the medieval city of Shali. If Mosry or Hugh Wollington had followed us, they were well hidden.

Amelia checked her watch, then, with her hand shading her eyes, gazed at the sun, a crimson disc starting to dip towards the tops of the palms. 'We have twenty minutes before the journey begins. We should get started.'

I gazed at the horizon. Was this to be my last night alive? The dunes were beginning to cast long rounded shadows that seemed to become more sinister with the fading light. Suddenly a strange haunting birdcry sounded out above us, echoing in the valley below. I peered up at the violet darkening sky. I could see nothing. Yet I had the uneasy and now familiar sensation that we were being watched; not just by unseen enemies, but by the mountains themselves.

I followed Amelia up the mound of earth and rubble towards the base of the temple. Surprisingly small, the building stood high on a hill, obviously positioned to impress an audience standing below and looking up at the priests conducting their ceremonies at the entrance – a smoke-and-mirror show designed to inspire and intimidate. I tried to rationalise to myself that what I was about to experience wasn't dissimiliar – phantoms plucked from my subconscious. They can't hurt you, I told myself, but a childhood memory of being terrified by the images of hell in my schoolbook Bible floated into my mind. I looked at Amelia's broad back ahead of me, her grey hair reassuringly real and maternal. She would be my anchor.

She paused to catch her breath. 'You know, most worshippers never actually entered the temple. Can you imagine what it must have been like for visiting military leaders seeking religious legitimacy? Climbing up here alone, dusty, exhausted, sweating into ceremonial armour, already humbled by the climb, to confront a half-demented seer whose blessing could either make or break your strategies? I came up here myself with my husband in April 1943 to pray to the gods for a victory.' She smiled ironically. 'I suppose it worked, but my prayers had a price.'

The temple's classical portico, flanked by columns, had been eroded by wind and sand; only a few alcoves remained, which must once have held icons or statues. Inside, it was a series of small rooms, no doubt designed to maximise an air of mystery through the use of light and shadow. It reminded me of a De Chirico painting, and I half-expected Isabella or some Grecian goddess to step into the dreamlike interior.

Amelia crouched in the doorway and pulled a flask from her backpack, followed by a small brown envelope. She unscrewed the top of the flask and filled the cup with what looked like wine, then opened the envelope and crumbled a bluish powder into the cup.

'This is for you: the ceremonial cup that will give you the sight of the gods.' She held it out to me. 'You lucky man.'

I eyed the concoction warily, hesitant after my recent experience in the catacombs.

'Oliver, take it. You've got no choice – you must open yourself to other ways of seeing.'

'I have no intention of making myself that vulnerable again. What if we're attacked?'

'I'll protect you.'

I eyed her. Even armed and with her military training, it was hard to imagine her fighting off seasoned killers.

'Oliver, I have the element of surprise on my side, and besides, I know the terrain a lot better than Mosry or Wollington do.'

I shook my head. 'I was lucky to survive the last time. It's too dangerous.'

'Listen, do you think Faakhir and all the others who wish to protect Sadat would have left us to do this alone if they didn't think I was capable of protecting you? You have to see what the priests saw, you have to recognise the symbols when they appear. Please . . . it's too late to stop trusting me now.'

Amelia thrust the cup under my nose; the rich, pungent smell of red wine and a finer perfume, like that of a flower, drifted up.

'This is wine mixed with a bouquet garni of mandrake and blue lotus – you've probably seen them painted in reliefs in the tombs. The Egyptian priests would drink the concoction to attain a state of heightened spirituality. You need to drink it too.'

'I've told you: no.'

Suddenly enraged, Amelia rose to her feet. 'Okay then, I'll leave and you can work out what you want to do next! You can risk your life on the gamble that all this is some elaborate charade put on solely for your entertainment. Or you can decide actually to commit fully to something for a change!'

She glared at me and turned away. I glanced up at the sun; my heart was really pounding now. I had to drink the potion, I knew. My fear pushed me kicking and screaming to do something, anything. Amelia was walking away with a determined stride.

'Wait!' I yelled out, stumbling across the sand.

She still had the cup in her hand. She held it out and I drank the bitter contents.

46

As Amelia and I sat there, our backs resting against the stone that was warm from the day's sun, I found my mind clearing. My memory erased itself into a white blankness. It was as if I had been pushed into the present tense in a way that was infinitely more vivid than I'd ever experienced before. The grain of the stone magnified, the pale mauve of the sky intensified, and the heroics of a large ant carrying a grain of sand across the rock wall by my knee became absolutely fascinating – an allegory for my own struggles.

Something moved at the perimeter of my vision. I lifted my head. Through the stone-framed opening I could see the silhouette of a large ram standing proudly on a boulder just beyond the temple. The sunlight painted his fleece gold and the noble length of his curling horns and his beard marked him as the patriarch of his herd.

'Amun-Re the divine is here,' Amelia whispered.

'Can you see the animal? Is it real?'

'What is real, Oliver?' She smiled. The animal stepped closer. Now I could see the vertical slant of its pupils, the green-golden irises. It stared directly at us, then cocked its

head in the direction of the desert and took a step backwards.

'You must follow.'

The tone of Amelia's voice gave me no choice. The
animal turned and began to leap nimbly over the ruins
towards the remnants of the Temple of Amun-Re. I followed, abandoning any attempt to make a rational analysis of
my actions.

As we climbed, I began to see the temple better: a pile of
toppled columns with one standing wall, one side patched
up with modern bricks. The ram stopped beneath a mural of
hieroglyphs clearly visible on the inside section. Amelia
scrambled to join me about a yard away from the ram. I stood
transfixed by the animal's stare: it was of a piercing intelligence, neither malevolent nor benign.

'What do we do now?' I found myself whispering as if in
church.

'Kneel,' Amelia said, and dropped to the ground.

Rather self-consciously I joined her. The ram disappeared
around the wall and down the hill as silently as it had
appeared.

Amelia pointed to the characters carved into the reddish
sandstone. 'The top row indicates the higher deities.'

I could see the line of gods. In the middle, flanked by the
other deities in profile, stood a figure with both hands outstretched, his headdress adorned with the horns of the ram.

'The central figure is that of Amun-Re himself,' Amelia
explained, 'with Isis on one side, Nephthys on the other,
and on either side of them Horus and Osiris. But concentrate
on the figure of Amun-Re – he is the key.'

The sun's rays formed a perfect half-circle above the top
of the wall, directly above the figure of the god. The light
grew brighter and brighter until the figure was surrounded

by a magenta halo. It seemed to become three-dimensional, suspended in the air before me, and I was filled with an intense sense of well-being and invincibility.

Then a shadow crossed the crescent of the sun. It was a bird, a falcon. It landed on the wall, arched its neck and let out one piercing cry.

'We are entering the second hour.' Amelia's voice had taken on an echoing, reverberating quality. 'Horus is upon us. He will lead you into the Waters of Osiris.'

This time I didn't doubt her.

She grabbed my arm and together we clambered down the rocky slope on the other side of the temple, following the falcon as it plunged into the tops of the palm trees that bordered a lake. We reached the thicket of palms and stumbled through the undergrowth, over dead palm fronds and desiccated dates. Finally, the skyline cleared again as we reached the edge of the salt-encrusted lake. The falcon, swooping like a black arrow, was once more overhead, guiding us. My boots squelched in the marshy ground and were soon covered with the snakeweed and algae that floated in the shallow waters.

A crash sounded behind us and I swung around. 'Is someone following us?' I whispered to Amelia.

We stood still and watched. At a far distance, set against the dusk sky, two torch beams swung across the foreshore, their passage broken by the lattice of palm trunks and low bushes. To me it seemed that the beams of light were being reflected back by the glinting eyes of hundreds of animals crouching in the undergrowth. I began to sweat with terror, as the low murmuring of male voices was carried towards us on the breeze. I was certain that I recognised Wollington's voice and I couldn't shake the thought that he was following close behind.

'Let's go, as quickly and silently as you can,' Amelia commanded in a low voice, gripping my arm again and hurrying me towards a vessel moored to a log. It was a traditional felucca, made of reeds and with a primitive sail hanging limp from a single mast and an oil lantern on a pole at its other end. With a flurry, the falcon landed on the side of the boat, its head cocked, waiting.

Night was falling quickly, as it does in the desert. Only the distant glow of the medieval town of Shali – a scattered shower of pinpricks glowing from those buildings still occupied – lit the horizon. I clambered into the boat after Amelia. She cast off the rope, trying to be quiet, but my clumsy movements sounded impossibly loud in the night air. I looked around, trying to pierce the darkness. I couldn't see anyone but that didn't mean they weren't there. I touched the straps across my shoulders that held the astrarium securely on my back, aware that my senses had become distorted. My imagination elaborated shade and shadow into fantastical creatures; my heightened sense of hearing made it impossible to discern what was close by and what was distant. Above us, the moon, a three-quarter, crater-pocked orb, was now visible. It was as if it was beckoning me – a thousand white arms bending and glowing.

Amelia followed my gaze. 'The Ancient Egyptians believed that the moon was the midpoint for ascending souls,' she murmured.

What had I got myself into? I settled lower into the boat, horribly aware that we were clearly visible from the foreshore.

Amelia pushed the boat off, the falcon took wing, and we floated away from the shore and out onto the shimmering water. Apprehensively, I glanced at Amelia. Her figure seemed to have grown in height and authority and I could see a radiance dancing about her features. She hoisted the sail and announced, 'We are now entering the Waters of Osiris.'

The limp sail swelled and filled like the white wing of an ibis. With a creak, the boat gathered speed, insects trailing behind it as the prow cut a ripple into the huge white spectre of the moon that undulated across the water's surface.

I looked into the moonlit lake. The sound of water lapping against the sides of the boat grew louder until it built into the crashing sound of huge waves against rocks. Despite the noise, I couldn't see anything except gentle ripples on the lake's surface. Fear began to churn my guts again. Irrationally, I kept expecting a tidal wave to appear on the horizon, a massive wall of water. My perception of the boundaries of matter had begun to blur, as if the very laws of physics had altered and the molecular structure of all that I knew had been transformed. I huddled even lower in the boat and forced myself to match sound with vision; gradually the roar of the crashing waves subsided. You can control this, I told myself, you can control the demons. I reminded myself that I was doing this for Isabella and for the Egypt we both loved. I would finish her journey, even if it killed me. The reality of that thought shot through my mind and dissolved into the core of my being.

Then, just as I was congratulating myself at having regained control of my senses, a pale flash of bluish-white broke the surface of the water and then submerged again. I heard the distinctive thud of something bumping against the wooden hull of the felucca. As I forced myself to look over the edge, a body floated into view: white legs, the split peach of a naked vulva at their apex, small breasts barely breaking the surface, long hair streaming over the face. I recognised her immediately – Isabella. The current dragged the hair away from her face and her eyes opened and stared at me.

I shouted her name and leaped to my feet, determined this time to rescue her, to put right the tragedy of her death. This time our lives would play out in the way they had been meant to – our long future together, children, old age. This time she would not have to die. The boat rocked dangerously as I reached out towards those white drifting legs.

'Isabella, here!' I shouted.

Amelia wrestled me back down. 'Shhh. She isn't real! Oliver!'

I fought her, weeping openly now, wanting to pull my wife's body to mine, wanting to stop her growing cold. I leaned back over the side; she was still there, white skin flashing like the underbelly of a dead fish. Her lips opened and she mouthed, 'Help me.'

I struggled to suppress every instinct that told me to dive in. I shut my eyes. When I opened them again, Isabella's white thighs were caught in a spiral of churning water, the ripple of a crocodile's tail cutting the surface in a ridge of jagged scales.

'This isn't happening, this isn't real,' I gasped, panic choking my words. Sweat beaded my forehead and for a moment I thought I might faint. But I held onto my mantra as the wind pushed the felucca across the water to the distant shore.

We were now almost at the centre of the huge pale reflection of the moon. To me, it seemed as though the planet had reached its loudest vibration, buzzing like a thousand cicadas. If anyone was following us they couldn't miss us here. It was then that I noticed a mist rising off the water at the middle of the glinting mirage. It began to twist like a miniature tornado, gathering shape above the lake as if the moon's reflection itself was gaining form. The wind blew us straight into the thickening fog and suddenly there was the beating of a million wings all around me, fluttering insects that smashed blindly against my face, in my hair, up my nostrils, suffocating me. They were moths, large white creatures that twisted and swirled into a single massive cloud. The very air seemed to be raining a soft smothering powder as my hands bashed frantically against the velvety bodies, trying to make space in the cloud to breathe. I felt my lungs squeezing against my ribcage, and then Amelia's arms were around my own, pinning them to my sides.

'Surrender,' she said, and the shape of the word descended on me like the moth powder coating my tongue, the inside of my nostrils, my burning eyelids.

We sat there in the strangest of embraces, Amelia behind me, her legs wrapped around my hips, her arms holding my arms, the astrarium between us, while the felucca moved through the frenetic mass of dazed insects flying in chaotic circles as if they themselves were bewildered by their own predicament.

As I made out the shape of the approaching shore, the wings of the insects surrounding us transformed into a harder, brilliant cascade of hues that glittered in the lantern light. I focused my gaze on the creatures hovering just before my nose, their heavy bodies clumsily defying gravity like bumblebees, their translucent wings a whirl of air, and, with a shock, I recognised them – scarab beetles, the sacred manifestation of Ra, signifying rebirth.

The cloud thinned into a column that spiralled and curved in a path to the shoreline. The boat followed and soon its wooden bottom was scraping along the shallow bank of salt crystal.

Before us lay a lunarscape of sand dunes with the distant

outline of a mountain squatting on the horizon like a giant in repose. Time stretched like taut wire in the darkness until Amelia's voice cut the silence like a bell.

'We are now entering the sandy world of Sokar.'

I couldn't believe that time had passed so quickly – the distortion of the drugs, I guessed. Just then the sound of an approaching speedboat echoed across the water

'Quick!' Amelia said. Grabbing my arm, she helped me out of the boat.

My feet hit a beach made uneven by the drying rock salt and tangled vegetation. The only illumination came from the moonlight and the glistening wings of the scarab beetles as they flew in a zigzagging black-purple snake into the hushed, expectant desert.

Amelia pulled me down behind the cover of some bushes and we watched the dark outline of the approaching boat as it cut across the lake. As we crouched there it was as if the sound of that boat's engine was my own fear curdling at the base of my spine, threatening to burst at any minute into sheer blank terror.

The boat drew up to the bank and I could just make out the faces of the two men sitting by the motor. One looked Arabic, the other European. Were they Wollington and Mosry? I couldn't quite make out their features.

'Wait here!' Amelia whispered.

Keeping low, still holding the lantern, she ran from bush to bush towards the boat. The sound of a twig breaking made one of the men look over. My stomach tightened in fear. Amelia cupped her hands to her mouth and made the call of a marsh bird – a perfect imitation. I could see the guerrilla fighter emerging from the role of the middle-aged woman that she'd played and I realised the years of experience she'd had fighting in this terrain. The man dropped his gaze and got out of the boat to pull it up onto the crusty salt bank.

I could make out Amelia across the way; she was holding a lighter to the wick of the lantern. In a second it was alight. Silently and accurately, she hurled it into the speedboat. It smashed against the wood and the spilled oil burst into flames, which spread quickly across the hull. In that flash of light, I recognised Hugh Wollington.

Shouting, both men leaped into the lake. Amelia bolted back to me. The boat's diesel tank exploded and shattered wood rained down around us.

'Run!' she ordered.

47

We sprinted up the beach and into a thicket of thorny shrubs that tore at our skin, Amelia propelling me forward while bullets flew over our heads. It felt like several minutes of battling the dense foliage before a path opened before us. Amelia pointed upwards: etched against the night sky was the column of glistening scarabs. Following them, we climbed higher and higher, pressing our bodies against the rocks to remain out of sight until finally we reached a moon-drenched plateau surrounded by majestic boulders that looked like chess pieces abandoned by a reckless colossus. Above us, the scarab beetles hovered for a moment, then disappeared into the night sky.

In the centre of this clearing stood a huge antelope, its twisting horns piercing the low moon. A falcon perched on its back.

'Seth in his antelope form and Horus,' Amelia whispered reverently.

Her voice seemed distorted and when I turned towards her she was unrecognisable. She had grown to over six feet in height, her skin had turned to copper, and her grey hair was now thick, black and reached down beyond her shoulders. She wore a headdress of cow horns between which hung a golden disc. I stumbled back, terrified. She had become the goddess Isis. A moment later she switched back to the form I was familiar with, then she was the goddess again. In my hallucinatory state I saw her flickering between the two. She caught my arm just before I fell, dizzy and disorientated.

'Oliver, stay with me. Stay in the moment.'

We heard our pursuers crashing through the shrubs behind us. Bending its head, the antelope pawed the ground, then turned and cantered up the mountain slope in front of us. The falcon flew ahead.

'Come on!' Amelia was instantly after the antelope, clambering up the rocky incline.

I climbed blindly after her, hauling myself higher and higher, tearing the palms of my hands on the jagged stone. Each new plateau accelerated the sense of infinity stretching above and behind me – the huge open cosmos – and I crouched closer and closer to the ground as I climbed, terrified of falling into that void.

As I pulled myself up onto yet another ledge, my foot slipped, dislodging an avalanche of sand. I froze in terror, both hands desperately gripping the rock above me, hanging in mid-air.

'Haul yourself up – you have to!' Amelia's face came over the ledge, one arm extended.

Exhaustion made me panic. I tried to hoist myself up but couldn't. Hanging there, suspended in the void, I made the mistake of looking over my shoulder. Far below, at the foot of the mountain, the moonlight reflected off the tiled roofs and mud-brick walls of Shali Ghali and I realised we'd climbed far higher than I had imagined. The rush of vertigo almost made me let go. I shut my eyes and prayed, still frozen in the same precarious position.

'There is no reversal of fortune. You have to get yourself up here!' Amelia insisted.

With a supreme effort, I pushed down on my right foot and hauled myself up, scrambling and clawing to pull all my body onto the ledge. I lay there panting in the darkness, my heart banging wildly against my chest. I could just make out openings cut into the mountain – burial tunnels. We were climbing Gebel al-Mawta – the Mountain of the Dead – and we were near the top.

In the ensuing silence, punctuated by my short breaths, I could hear the sound of steps, rocks falling. The two men were scrambling up the rock face below us. My limbs felt as if they were moving through treacle, a thousand repetitions of a thousand muscles exploding in effort. My fear had almost transmuted into something else – an ecstasy? Yet part of me was still aware that I was in great danger. I gazed transfixed into the vast cosmos. Could I die now? In some ways it felt as if I had already.

In that second, a bullet whistled past my ear. Amelia pulled me roughly behind a boulder. Lying on her stomach, she returned fire; bullets ricocheted against the flintlike rock, thudding down into the sand. There was a scream as one of the men was hit.

'Move!' Amelia grabbed my arm and pushed me towards one of the burial tunnels before following me inside. I crouched against the stone as two more bullets struck near the entrance.

'Help me!' Amelia called. 'We haven't got long – they'll be here in seconds!'

She indicated a pile of rocks that looked as if they'd been deliberately stacked on a length of wood beneath them.

Together we levered the wood until the rocks fell across the entrance, completely blocking access. Exhausted, I leaned against the cool rock; it smelled faintly of lime. The astrarium was a lead weight across my shoulders.

'How do we get out?' I asked.

'We don't need to.'

'But we'll die in here!'

'Trust me.' Amelia dusted off her hands. 'Come on, we have to keep moving. It's now hour five – the timing is precise.'

She pulled out a small torch and switched it on. The walls and ceiling of the tunnel were covered in brightly coloured murals that, in my drugged state, appeared to be moving. Hieroglyphs and drawings telling of the life of Osiris: here, his marriage to Isis; there, Seth murdering him. On the opposite wall was the story of Isis magically piecing together the fourteen parts of her husband's dismembered body.

Amelia walked in front of me, shining the torch ahead. As I followed her, I could feel the blue lotus pounding through my veins, rippling through my perception. Light glinted off the burnished disc of her headdress and blossoms – poppies, lotuses, lilies – sprang from her feet as she led me deeper into the mountain. Fascinated, I glanced down at my own arms and wondered if I too had metamorphosed. I held my hand up and my fingers danced before me, five, ten, a hundred of them, all moving slowly, as if the air itself had become gelatinous.

We arrived at a thick wooden door carved with a relief of monstrous animals. In front of it sat an old man, his back to us, huddled over.

'The gatekeeper,' Amelia murmured, unable to keep the fascination out of her voice.

The old man turned around. To my horror, it was my

father, naked, his thin, aged body bent, the wrinkled pouch of his sex hanging from his sagging flesh.

Amelia pressed her gun into my hand. 'You must kill him.'

'I can't,' I said, terrified.

'He is not what he appears to be.'

My father whimpered when he saw the gun in my hand. I couldn't drag my stare away from him. Memories ran through me: the first time we flew a kite together on the Fens, my father showing me how to unreel the string and let the kite catch the wind, his pride as I managed to haul it up high into the air; my astonishment and joy at my graduation when I caught sight of my father's figure from the podium after he'd sworn he'd sooner see Carlisle United lose than walk into any university; the last time I'd seen him, only weeks ago, standing at his front door, shrunken and vulnerable, wearing my mother's pink cardigan over his undershirt. I knew that the image before me now was an illusion, but it felt utterly real as I lifted the gun.

The old man cowered, petrified, the whites of his eyes peering out of his dust-covered face. Pleading, he began to claw at my legs, but the sounds that came from his mouth were not human, rather they were the grunts of an animal.

Still I couldn't bring myself to squeeze the trigger.

'Shoot!' Amelia ordered me.

Instead, my arm shaking, I lowered the gun. The creature lunged at me, his hands now reptilian claws, the skin on his wrists darkening and congealing into scales. I smashed the gun against his head, knocking him to the ground, then reeled around, expecting another attack from behind.

Nothing came; just the sound of Amelia chanting what I assumed was a spell from the *Book of the Dead*. The creature's legs began to shrivel and his distorted face flattened into the snout of a hippopotamus as he convulsed and writhed on the ground. Then his jaw stretched wide, cavernous and red, and a sparrowhawk burst out of his mouth and began to fly wildly around my head.

'It's Isabella's Ba,' Amelia whispered. 'You will carry her to the end – you must help her spirit reach the afterlife.'

Awed, I reached out to the bird. The fluttering of its wings formed a thousand after-images that enveloped me in Isabella's scent, in the soft whispering of her voice. Finally it landed on my shoulder.

Amelia took the gun from me and tucked it back into her belt. As she did, we heard an explosion in the distance – the tunnel's entrance being unblocked.

We ran along the narrow passage for what, to my tired limbs, seemed like hours. When I was sure I could go no further, dragging myself along, mustering every last ounce of strength, we emerged into a massive underground limestone cavern deep within the mountain – a vast temple with multi-faceted crystal stalactites glistening like hundreds of diamonds.

'This is where you will meet your Ka, your spiritual twin,' Amelia said.

In the middle of the huge stone floor flickered a large lake of flames that illuminated the ceiling that arched over us like the sweep of a cathedral roof.

'Walk towards the fire,' Amelia told me, and pushed me forward.

Tentatively I moved towards the blazing lake. Curiously, the nearer I got, the less heat I felt on my skin. Encouraged that the flames too were an illusion, I moved quickly closer and stopped about a foot from the edge.

The flames became iridescent and reflective at the same time, winding around themselves to fuse into the smooth surface of a mirror. Reflected in it was an image of myself. I stared at the tousled, bearded man with scratches covering his forehead and cheeks, barely recognising the dirt-stained face, the bewildered blue eyes staring through the red dust. I lifted my hand and he lifted his too. Then, to my amazement, he extended his hand towards me, the flesh becoming real as it reached out of the swirling reflective surface.

I stumbled back and my double stepped out and steadied me. His touch burned, and as his fingers closed around my arm he began to merge into my body. I blacked out.

When I regained consciousness, I seemed to be hovering high above, next to the glistening limestone ceiling. I looked down. Amelia stood below me – an aerial perspective, her figure foreshortened against the stone floor. Shocked, I plummeted downward for a second, then regained my balance. As I did, feathered tips came into my peripheral vision. I had wings. I had transformed into my own Ba. Sensing a presence behind me, I turned my head and saw a sparrowhawk swooping towards me. Isabella.

We flew together, twisting around each other like acrobats, swerving and swooping and narrowly missing the rock walls of the cave. I chased her, revelling in the power of flight, wanting to catch up with her, wanting to feel her spirit engulf me as if we were one being. Memories of our marriage streamed through me: our first night together; her first visit to an oilfield and her amazed expression as she watched me reading the ground; the way we laughed together at an unspoken joke; how we fell asleep in each other's arms. And I knew then that despite all I'd learned since her death, all that Hermes had told me about our marriage being arranged by others, our union had been true, her love for me had been genuine. Isabella might have married me to fulfil the prophecy, but she had loved me above and beyond that – I was certain of it now. All these certainties seemed to tumble with us as we plummeted down to climb again in blind joy. Then, in the grip of my epiphany, I crashed into the cave wall.

I opened my eyes to find myself lying on the sandy ground. The sparrowhawk, perched on my outstretched arm, cocked its head quizzically at me. I tried to sit up. My whole body ached. It felt as if the hallucinogen pumping through my blood was receding.

The sparrowhawk hopped down onto the sand and pushed against my leg with its beak, as if to make me stand. All around me the sand started to undulate.

'Oliver!' Amelia shouted. 'The mehen serpent!'

Two glistening eyes emerged, then a reptilian snout blowing grains of sand. The mottled head of a huge rock python followed, its smooth scaly body now stretched in a huge circle around me. The sparrowhawk dived at the snake with claws outstretched and the snake hissed and lunged back.

I struggled to my feet. The serpent reared up, sand cascading either side of its patterned skin. It stared at me with indifference, as if I were little more than a fly. I held my ground, determined not to show fear. Then, almost as suddenly as it had appeared, the serpent collapsed into dust and I realised that I was standing on a vast mosaic, its design a serpent holding its tail in its mouth.

The last of the blue lotus left my body and I became aware of the cold dampness of the stone tiles, the straps of the rucksack cutting into my shoulders, the sharp throbbing of the scratches on my arms and legs. Uncontrollable shivering gripped my limbs. I looked at Amelia. Her solid figure was also dusty and scratched and very definitely human.

Above us, the sparrowhawk screeched.

There was a whoosh of air as a bullet flew past me, narrowly missing my left shoulder. I ducked, the crack of gunfire horribly real. We bolted to the far side of the cavern as Hugh Wollington, dressed in army fatigues, ran into the huge space, gun raised. Blood stained his left sleeve; Amelia's shot on the hillside had only wounded him slightly.

Amelia had her pistol in her hand and squeezed off two quick shots, forcing Wollington to take cover.

'Over there, Oliver – behind that stalactite lies the entrance to the final chamber of the tomb. The doors will open as you reach them.'

'What about you?'

'This is my fate. Who am I to question it?' she answered, smiling.

Wollington fired again and the bullet caught her in the left shoulder, flinging her body back with the impact. She grunted, but turned back to me.

'Go! Go now!' she told me. 'I'll cover you!'

Blood was seeping through Amelia's jacket. I reached out to help her, but she urged me on. Lying on her side, she kept firing as I darted from one rock to another. As I reached the low archway, barely visible in the shadows, I suddenly felt a searing pain. A bullet had hit me in the foot. Falling to the ground, I cried out in shock and pain.

I rolled over and looked behind me. Wollington was running towards me across the cavern as Amelia worked furiously to snap a new clip of ammunition into her pistol. I watched in horror as he stopped and raised his pistol directly at me, taking careful aim. His stare locked with mine – just a dozen paces and the gun barrel between us.

At the edge of my vision I saw Amelia pull back the slide of her pistol, heard the click of the breech.

A gunshot rang out. My heart jolted. I stared at Wollington, astonished that I was still seeing anything at all, and, as I watched, Amelia's bullet took him squarely in the stomach. Her second hit his temple – spinning him around and dropping him to the floor in a spray of blood.

A scream welled up inside me but I felt and heard it as if I were outside myself. I gasped for breath, hyperventilating with shock, but as Amelia turned towards me, her eyes calm, her hands steady, I felt my own hysteria recede.

I raised my hand and called 'I'm okay,' though I could feel my boot filling with blood.

'Can you move?' she called back.

I levered myself up onto my good foot. Pain shot up my leg. Just then, another shot rang out, the sharp, loud crack of a pistol from the very back of the cavern. Amelia's face, a smile opening across her features, suddenly froze. I expected her to turn and fire back, but instead she pitched backwards, her arms flung wide, her pistol clattering on the stone floor.

In the silence that followed I heard a pair of heavy boots running across the cavern towards me. I was horrified at the loss of Amelia and, for one crucial moment, I dithered. But there was no time to grieve. Dragging myself through the lichen-covered archway as quietly as I could, I prayed that my pursuer wouldn't find the trail of blood I was leaving behind. I looked around for a ready weapon. Reaching for a heavy rock, I lifted it and waited, desperately trying to control my breathing. The footsteps seemed to be coming nearer, but before they reached me a space opened up in the cave wall behind me and I was pulled backwards into it.

48

An old man helped me to my feet and supported me as we made our way to a small rowing boat that appeared to be floating on an underground river. He lowered me into it and I collapsed onto the bottom. Murmuring in a dialect that I didn't understand, he drew a rug over me. As he bent down I noticed that his eyes were white with cataracts.

He cast off and the boat, lit only by a single lantern, began its journey along the dark water, where to I didn't know; the stalactites passing above us were dazzling as the crystals reflected back thousands of shards of light. I felt the blood draining away from my body.

A luminous orange shape pressed against the darker red of my eyelids as external sound and light sucked me back into consciousness. I heard the beat of dripping water, and smelled the acrid odour of manure, damp straw and the distinctive apple-scented tobacco of the hookah. I opened my eyes and realised I was grasping something in my hand. I looked down. I was holding a feather – a sparrowhawk's brown feather.

I was on a low divan that was covered in goatskins. The old man was sitting beside me with a bowl of water on his lap, smiling, his toothless mouth sunk into his wrinkled face. Chanting what sounded like a prayer, he lifted a cup and poured the cold water over my head. Shocked, I spluttered and gasped.

My head ached, but I was aware that, despite a strange feeling of dislocation and a heightened sense of colour, I was now entirely lucid. 'I don't understand you,' I said in Arabic.

'That is because I was using an ancient language,' he replied, also in Arabic. 'Aramaic, the old tongue. Forgive me, the immersion had to be done. It is the tenth hour.'

I sank back against the cushions as he bent down to examine the wound to my foot, now covered with a brown-green poultice of moss. Shocked, I pulled my foot back. The poultice went flying. He scolded me and replaced the moss.

At that moment I remembered the astrarium. My hands flew up to my shoulders; my rucksack was gone. I looked around wildly. Reading my expression, the old man reached for a small woven basket at his feet and pulled out the astrarium, now wrapped in an oiled goatskin.

'Fear not, my friend, the treasure is safe. This is the last hour of your journey and I have restored your health and your sight.' He touched my eyelids in turn, his fingertips pungent with the musk of the poultice. 'I am Yedaniah bar-Ishmael. For centuries members of my family have protected the secret tomb of Nectanebo II, since the time my ancestor was hired as a personal bodyguard by the Pharaoh at Elephantine, long before the living memory of this epoch.'

'You are a Jew?'

'My family chose not to leave with Moshe ben Amram ha-Levi across the divided sea; our hearts were wedded to this land. I was born here and I will die here.' His fingers scraped at the earth floor of the cave, crumbling the soil. 'I am sorry for the death of your companion. The Berbers will collect the shell of her body and they will bury her next to her husband.'

The vision of Amelia's crumpled form swept bleakly through me. Suddenly the death toll, the sacrifice that the astrarium demanded seemed too high. Despair gripped me. Battling rising panic, I tried to calculate how many minutes I had left of my own life – not many.

I looked around. The room appeared to open onto a courtyard, a mat of woven rushes covering the entrance. The bluish dawn light filtered through the gaps between the rushes and I could just make out a couple of goats tethered to a post outside and the outline of a metal water pump.

The cave itself had obviously once been a tomb: murals of the gods hunting and feasting covered the walls. There was a huge stone oven carved into the back of the cave, large enough for a man to crouch in; a blackened copper pot sat atop it. Against the wall was a set of shelves made of wood from a shipping carton – the stickers advertising Siwah Dates were still visible – filled with tinned food, condensed milk and one lonely jar of Nescafé instant coffee. I noticed a radio propped up against a low table that held a backgammon board, the pieces poised mid-game. The prosaic nature of the setting was reassuring and I felt myself becoming calmer.

I looked back at the old man. His skin hung in folds below his chin and his face was a map of moles and uneven pigment. Again, I saw the clouds of cataracts in his eyes. It was impossible to say how old he was – over ninety, I imagined.

'Where am I?' I asked.

'On the island of Arachie, in the cave of Horus. But we must hurry. Ra has almost risen and you must place the skybox into the Pharaoh's arms before then. You know the parable: a king is sacrificed for the greater good of his people, is entombed for a time, then rises again to join his father in the sky. This is the universal story, one that is told again and again.'

He reached up to his neck and, with a jerk, broke the leather thong of the pendant hanging there. He pressed it into my hand. It was a large gold coin embossed with a rearing horse.

'The coin of Nectanebo,' he said. 'This was the first payment made to my ancestor. It will protect you.'

From outside, at some distance, came the sound of running feet. I looked at Yedaniah, wide-eyed with fear.

'They'll kill us,' I said. 'They'll kill us both.'

Yedaniah put his hand on my arm to reassure me. 'Have faith. Come now: it is time you faced your own death.'

I swung my feet around to the dirt floor and he helped me stand. Gingerly, I placed my weight on my injured foot to find that it wasn't hurting nearly as much any more, then slipped the coin into my pocket. Outside, a cockerel crowed, followed by shouting.

'We must hurry,' Yedaniah said. He picked up the astrarium and bowed his head ceremoniously as he placed it into my arms. 'For you and Nectanebo, my king. May the gods bless you both.'

He led me to the oven at the back of the cave, guided me over the cooling coals and pushed against the soot-covered back wall. To my amazement, it opened, revealing a large cavern beyond.

'Quickly.' He bundled me through.

Feeling panicked, I looked around the chamber; there was nothing but the stone walls, a dirt floor and an ancient mural illuminated by two lanterns hanging from the ceiling.

'But where's the coffin?' I asked.

'You were chosen. The gift of Osiris will guide you,' Yedaniah told me, and stepped back into the outer cave. 'May Amun-Re and my God protect you.'

His voice echoed against the walls as he pulled closed the hidden door, leaving me alone in the tomb.

The air was dry and smelled faintly of paraffin. The mural painting showed Seth spearing Osiris; an allegorical declaration of victory by Nectanebo's assassins, I assumed. I put down the astrarium and limped slowly across the dirt floor, my left foot trailing blood. Closing my eyes, I concentrated on the ground beneath my naked feet and, for the first time in my life completely unassisted by science and technology, attempted to read the subterranean geology.

I thought I could hear the distant rattle of gunfire, but I pushed it and my fear to the back of my mind as I concentrated on the earth, sensing its very resonance as it spoke to me. It was as if any distrust of my gift that had impeded me in the past had finally evaporated and I could see the strata in the rock around me as clear as day.

I walked slowly into the centre of the chamber, ignoring the dull throbbing in my left foot. My eyes closed, I pushed my naked right sole back and forth across the dirt. I could feel a ridge in the surface.

I kneeled down and with my fingernails dug wildly at the layers of impacted sand and earth. There was a marked line underneath – it looked like a rectangular corner. I cleared more dirt away and soon I had revealed the full outline: about seven feet by four – the size of a coffin. I brushed away a section in the middle and found a cartouche, one I'd now seen several times: the ostrich feather – Nectanebo II's insignia. But as I kneeled there, my hands flat on the ground,

I sensed nothing; the area felt as dense as the rest of the floor.

I stood up and stepped out of the rectangle, moving several feet to the left, closer to the wall. I felt a tingling under my soles. Here the structure changed radically – I could sense it as clearly as I could see the lights above me. The cartouche was a false lead – a trap to entice tomb raiders to dig in the wrong place.

I kneeled again, running my hands over the floor. Beneath the layers of dried mud and compacted stone dust I could feel a slight bump – the raised indentation of a circle. Scraping with my nails, I unearthed a metal ring and, with all my strength, hauled on it. The wound in my foot screamed in protest, but I ignored it. Time was running out. With a great grinding of stone and metal, a door opened in the floor, revealing a wide, deep grave with a single wooden coffin laid in it.

After jumping in I walked around the simple coffin: its wood was decaying at the corners, the grain eaten by time. The only ornamentation was the painted door for the occupant's Ba to escape. The rest of the coffin was starkly bare, as if Nectanebo's buriers had given him the minimum possible for his journey into the afterlife. I stood over the wooden lid, my legs shaking in nervous anticipation, my body racked with a terrible fear and tremendous excitement. What was I afraid of? Dying? Or seeing the great Nectanebo himself?

I climbed out of the grave and fetched the astrarium. The date of my death was unchanged. The two pointers had almost fused into one, announcing that my final moments were imminent. I had no time to waste – whatever happened to the astrarium, Mosry would probably kill me anyway. My only hope was to complete the task and then hide or try to run.

I stepped back into the grave and used a rock to break the lid of the coffin; the ancient wood splintered, sounding impossibly loud. I paused, listening. Then, reaching into my pocket, I pulled out the feather from Isabella's Ba and placed it into the coffin. If I was to die I could at least try to ensure that she found peace.

Suddenly, shouting came from Yedaniah's cave, then gunfire and the sound of furniture being broken. Frantically, I tore off the rest of the lid. There was a mummy inside, a gold mask over the face. I frowned and looked closer. I recognised the features despite the curl of the royal beard: it was the moulded face of a beautiful woman. I'd seen it on the sphinx that had toppled down onto Isabella, causing her to drown, I'd seen it in the shadow cast by the astrarium. I'd seen it again in Amelia's thesis, and once more in Gareth's drawing: Banafrit, Nectanebo's high priestess and lover. I lifted the mask off and underneath – desiccated, skin blackened like leather but still beautiful – was the face of the woman herself. Now I noticed the outline of breasts under the brownish linen bandages that ran in long lines down the body, a filigree of beaded string stretched over the torso.

Despair washed over me, and I leaned against the side of the grave, staring down at the golden mask I'd left by the side. This was supposed to be Nectanebo's coffin. Had this whole journey been in vain now that I had failed to unite the astrarium with its rightful owner? For a moment, the enormity of my quest overwhelmed me. Then, as I looked more closely at the mask, I noticed a line of hieroglyphs carved into its forehead. I immediately recognised Gareth's cipher. 'When the singing reed is placed in the lion's mouth, the sands will echo.' Now I noticed that the headdress engraved on the mummy's mask looked like a lion's mane. Why was this familiar? I racked my memory desperately, then remembered Gareth telling me that the translation of 'Lion' was also 'Hathor' – the lion-headed revengeful goddess, sister of Isis. What if it was Banafrit not Nectanebo, the feminine not the masculine, who needed to be reunited with her skybox? That still didn't solve the riddle of the singing reed. Outside, the sound of gunfire was very close now. Using every ounce of concentration, I tried to calm my thumping heart. I picked up the astrarium – the key was still inserted into the mechanism, its long thin stem sticking out of the side. Think, think – my mind began putting facts against images against facts . . . Reed. Was. Singing. Quickly I pulled the key out. The key end – the two prongs – was delicate and longer than an ordinary key. It was then that I suddenly remembered my very first impression of the Was: a tuning fork.

The banging from the direction of the secret door to the chamber came closer. I had no time left. I stared at the dial of the astrarium. The black pointer continued ticking towards the moment of my death. I had no choice. I had to take the gamble. I pulled the Was out of the astrarium and tapped it sharply against the stone floor. Immediately, a single note, impossibly pure and clear, rang out from the key. The Singing Reed. I placed the vibrating key between the dried lips of the mummy. The tone intensified: like sunlight, it filled the whole chamber, almost as if the stone itself was vibrating with it.

I lifted the astrarium to place it on Banafrit's torso. Just then the door of the cavern was kicked open. 'Don't move!' a man shouted in heavily accented English.

I froze.

Mosry stood above the grave, his gun pointed directly at me. I looked at the astrarium and the death hand – and it was in that one single moment that I surrendered completely to belief in the device. Waiting for the bullet to pass through my body, I dropped the astrarium onto the mummy. In the same instant, a shot was fired.

I shut my eyes, expecting a searing pain to shoot through me. Nothing happened.

Slowly, I turned to see Mosry sprawled on the chamber floor, blood seeping from a fatal head wound. Behind him in the doorway was Yedaniah, on his hands and knees, cradling an ancient Uzi, blood streaming down his face. The note emanating from the Was suddenly stopped and a terrible silence rushed in to take its place.

Then came a soft but unmissable click from the astrarium. I swung around. As I watched, the small black hand with its Seth figurehead disappeared from view and a strange but liberating mixture of fear, resignation and relief rushed over me. This was the moment. Almost in slow motion, both the astrarium and Banafrit's youthful face began to crumble, until there was nothing left of either but a fine reddish sandlike dust. 'When the singing reed is placed in the lion's mouth the sands will echo.' The prophecy and Isabella's last wish had finally been fulfilled. For one wonderful moment I felt nothing but relief and joy and a wave of post-adrenalin rush. Then I ran back and crouched by Yedaniah's side. Blood was now pooling beneath him.

'Such is God's will.' He groaned in pain. 'You must go. You have succeeded in your task.'

I hesitated, staring back into the cavern, at the plain wooden casket, Mosry's broken body, and the allegory of Seth spearing Osiris.

'Go . . .' Yedaniah fell back as his spirit finally left him.

Outside, the new day was breaking. I collapsed against a rock and stared out over the valley. I would have to go back to take care of the two dead men in the cave behind me and the bodies of Hugh Wollington and Amelia further in but just then, my face flooded with the first rays of the morning sun rising vast and golden over the horizon, I allowed myself to feel a great sense of completion. I had succeeded; I had returned the astrarium to its proper place and fulfilled my promise to Isabella. I had saved myself and I had saved Egypt from certain ruin. Elation quickly mingled with a sense of loss.

A sparrowhawk flew out of the cave behind me. She circled above me, then sailed out over the shimmering lake below, its surface a mass of sparkling diamonds. I watched the bird for as long as I could, until I lost her in the sunlight.

Hours later I sat on the veranda of a café, looking out over the tiny runway at Siwah Oasis. My initial exhilaration had faded and I was exhausted: physically, emotionally, existentially drained. I'd gone back in, retracing my steps, to bury Amelia and Wollington, then Yedaniah and Mosry, and that final physical effort had depleted the last of my energy. Now the real grieving had begun.

Sipping my mint tea, I stared past a plane to the sea of desert that yawned beyond, the horizon with its wavering bands of heat. My odyssey was already beginning to feel like an extended dream, and I wasn't sure what my future held.

Inside the café someone turned up the volume of the television. I thought I heard the word 'Knesset', the Israeli parliament, when shouts of disbelief from my fellow diners made me swing around. The screen was showing live footage of Sadat in the Knesset, one Arab within a mass of Israeli politicians. He glanced almost shyly from under his thick black-rimmed glasses, then began to read a statement in a clear and confident voice.

'In the name of God, Mr Speaker of the Knesset, ladies and gentlemen, allow me first to thank deeply the Speaker of the Knesset for affording me this opportunity to address you . . . I come to you today on solid ground to shape a new life and to establish peace. We all love this land, the land of God, we all, Muslims, Christians and Jews, worship God. I do not blame all those who received my decision when I announced it to the entire world before the Egyptian People's Assembly. I do not blame all those who received my decision with surprise, even with amazement, some gripped even by violent surprise . . .'

So the convoy and Rachel had arrived safely in Jerusalem. The peace initiative would continue, I thought, satisfaction and relief mingling as my fellow diners fell into a stunned silence.

I leaned back in my chair and felt something in my pocket – the gold coin that Yedaniah had given me. I pulled it out and examined the noble profile of Nectanebo II. I tossed the coin into the air, then caught it face up.

Epilogue

21 December 1978

A luminous blue broke into foaming waves as the water rushed under the bow of the speedboat. I watched, hypnotised. It was over a year since I'd left Egypt and even now that time felt as if it had happened to another man – as if my memory and the need to make things logical had started to mythologise those extraordinary events.

In the near distance the outline of Dokos, the Greek island home of Mr Imenand, loomed. Following instructions from his assistant I'd caught a plane to Athens, then a boat out to the home of the entrepreneur. Although he had shaped my life and career over the past twelve months I hadn't seen Mr Imenand since Alexandria and now I wondered why the recluse had suddenly demanded to see me.

A dolphin appeared alongside the boat, its distinctive fin rising and falling in joyful abandon as it raced alongside. The water was a brilliant turquoise – a marine cosmos that seemed to promise both mystery and release.

As the speedboat cut through the Aegean Sea, I couldn't

help remembering that last day I'd spent with Isabella, the day before her death: her face when she emerged from the water wildly excited about discovering the astrarium, her frantic panic the night before, her nightmares.

I hadn't dreamed of her for months. I knew I would always hold her within me but one day I'd woken up and realised, not without sadness, that a sense of her had finally left me; if there was a soul, hers was at rest.

After returning to London I'd moved Gareth out of his squat and into his own flat in London. He was busy recording his first album with Stiff records; more importantly, he appeared to have given up the amphetamines. There was a new intimacy between us, and for the first time since he was a child we both seemed to enjoy each other's company. I even took him up to see my father and treated the old man to a match at Brunton Park – Carlisle United lost but I was busy watching the two of them together. I hadn't seen my father so happy since my mother's death.

I was still regularly in touch with Rachel. She was now back in New York, and her article on Sadat had made the front page of *Time* magazine. We'd spoken a couple of times on the telephone, but the time in Egypt already felt as if it was receding away from us and, like a secret history too extraordinary to share, I could tell that neither of us wanted to talk about it.

Meanwhile, back in Egypt, Moustafa was happily managing the new oilfield full time. And, bearing in mind Bill Anderson's threat of intending to collect on his favour, I'd cut him in on the deal. It was a very small percentage of the profits, in exchange for free disaster-management if we should be unlucky enough to have a blowout, but it was also my way of thanking the Texan. Faakhir had disappeared, but I received the occasional postcard from him from politically interesting places, such as Algiers, Guatemala, Sri Lanka; I never did find out for whom he was actually working. Meanwhile, back in Alexandria Francesca had taken residence in the Casa di Reposa – the retirement home for all the Italian diaspora. The Brambilla villa was now leased, although I had given Aadeel ownership of the flat within the complex; it was the least I could do.

President Sadat and Prime Minister Begin shared the Nobel Prize for peace at the end of that year, and it finally felt as if there might be a whole new climate of optimism.

Life had moved on and I should have been happier.

But my drive to find oil had changed irreversibly. When the second well on the new lease tested at eighteen thousand barrels per day I was pleased, but not excited in the way I once would have been. I'd discovered in myself a need to use my divining ability for more egalitarian purposes. Perhaps Mr Imenand, who had made a commitment to back any ventures my newly formed company might be interested in, had intuited my change of heart. After all, it was he, not I, who had arranged this meeting.

When I was shown into the room where Mr Imenand was waiting for me, it took my eyes a while to adapt to the dimness after the dazzling light outside. I was shocked to realise that despite the size of the space – almost like an art gallery, with its white walls – and the magnificent Persian rug that covered the marble floor, this was a sickroom. The figure propped up against the pillows was bent and old, his face hollowed by illness, dark shadows under his eyes.

'Oliver, welcome.' His voice was impossibly frail.

'Mr Imenand, you are unwell.'

I faltered. Words seemed superfluous for one so obviously close to death. In the silence that followed, Imenand's laboured breathing seemed to grow in volume, scratching at the walls like a caged bird.

'Unwell?' he said drily and laughed. 'I am dying, finally, thank the gods.'

He beckoned me forward. A lamp clicked on, as if my movement had triggered the switch. I could see the room more clearly now. Apart from the bed with its surrounding medical apparatus, I was amazed to see that the only other object was a large stone sculpture of a sphinx. Almost a third presence in the room, it sat against the wall, its face still in shadow.

There was a leather seat at the foot of the bed, angled, I noticed, in a way that meant Mr Imenand did not need to turn any part of his body to see me. A tube ran from under one pyjama sleeve up into a clear glass container hanging off a steel frame. A single pomegranate, half-peeled, sat on a white plate on a side table, the red seeds spilling onto the china.

'I chose you, you know, because you were like me, another Orpheus . . .' he whispered, his voice as pale as parchment.

'Chose me for what?'

'You will be my heir. And my legacy is far greater than just material possessions.'

I looked at him, confused. What was he talking about? I concentrated on the long veined hands lying like old leather gloves against the sheets. They looked abandoned, as if he had already started to vacate his body.

Mr Imenand spoke again, his voice growing in confidence and volume. 'I never thanked you for returning the astrarium.'

Startled, my head snapped up. For a minute I thought I had misheard.

'What are you talking about?' Shock and confusion had made me discourteous. Who was he? And how did he know? I had the disorientating sensation that the strands of my life had pulled together to converge at this one juncture, this moment right now. The old man pulled himself up with great effort.

'Oliver, we have no time for games,' he croaked, his fingers twitching. 'Whether you believe me or not is irrelevant, but I owe you an explanation – the last few pieces of a jigsaw puzzle that stretches far beyond our limited human comprehension. You see, there is another truth hidden behind the astrarium. Please, for now, Oliver, put aside your scepticism. Indulge a dying man.'

Spent, he sank back against the pillows. Anxious that I might hasten his demise by further questioning, I nodded.

'I'm listening.'

Mr Imenand sighed with profound weariness. Then he began his story.

'Nectanebo had many women, many wives, but there was one woman he loved beyond all the others – Banafrit. She was not only his high priestess but also a skilled astronomer and astrologer, who consulted with the greatest engineers of her day, from Greece to Babylon. Over there is a statue made in her honour – a sphinx that has survived to this day. I believe you have seen the companion piece at the bottom of Alexandria's harbour, among the ruins of what was once a magnificent city.'

I swung back to the statue of the sphinx. Now I recognised the patrician arch of the nose, the high cheekbones, the distinctive shape of the face. The mirror image of the stone features of the sphinx that had loomed at me underwater – and that had killed my wife. But the statue before me bore no marks of erosion: it was as if it had been carved yesterday; the features of the face clear and precise. I turned back to the figure in the bed. With a shock, I suddenly realised how the features were repeated in the man before me – his was a masculine, heavier version but the resemblance was unmistakable. A shiver ran through my body. Watching me, Mr Imenand smiled thinly, then with renewed effort continued talking.

'It was so long ago and yet it is still as clear as yesterday. The pharaoh loved his priestess more than his own life, more than his divine right as a god incarnate. But there was mutiny; the priests, the ministers, even some of the army, were secretly aligning themselves with the Persians. And there was a plot, a plot of assassination. Banafrit heard rumour of this and, unknown to Nectanebo, she posed as his double that day, hiding her own features beneath the Pharaoh's golden mask.'

His voice cracked with emotion and he paused before finding the strength to go on.

'Banafrit was killed in the assassination attack, not Nectanebo. That evening, the Pharaoh waited for his lover but instead her servant came to tell him that Banafrit had been poisoned by his enemies and was lying in a coma. Mad with grief, Nectanebo went to his lover and, in the hope of saving her, set the astrarium to her birth date. Isis rules the unconscious and, angry that it had been stolen from her originally, some of her essence passed into the astrarium. The astrarium in turn passed judgement on the Pharaoh, condemning his lover to suffer for eternity and denying him the release of death. And so it was that Banafrit and Nectanebo could never be reunited in the afterlife – until now.' Mr Imenand's breath had become a terrible wheezing sound, as if his very lungs were hollow. But he was determined to finish his tale.

'And so you see, Oliver, you and I have both played Orpheus. I have been doomed for thousands of years to a lingering half-life, a living hell, unable to enter Tuat – heaven – to join my Queen. Until you placed the astrarium into her grave, reuniting her body and soul.'

I stared at him, trying to take in his words. His impending death must have brought with it some kind of semi-lucid senility. Reading my expression, he smiled.

'I said before, Oliver, whether you believe me or not is unimportant. Nevertheless, you have been my saviour; thanks to you, the sorcery was broken. As you see, I am ageing again, rapidly, but I am grateful that I had enough time to find an heir, a talented man who will make his own mark.'

With a supreme effort he reached for my hand – his own hand little more than a bony claw covered with skin. 'Thank you.' His head fell back against the pillow. Then, with his hand still in mine, he spoke again in the faintest of whispers. His tone was one of blessing, even though the language was one I had never heard. Euphoria swept across his face as his eyes focused on a point beyond me – 'Banafrit,' he whispered before exhaling for the last time.

I stepped into the bright hallway, closing the bedroom door quietly behind me.

A servant – a young Greek girl – sat sewing in a cane chair beside an open window. She looked up and smiled. 'You must forgive the old man. He is crazy, completely crazy,' she announced, then bent down to her work again.

The faint jangle of goats' bells floated in from outside, and for a moment I thought I heard the sound of a woman's laughter.

Bibliography

Awad, Mohamed and Hamouda, Sahar (editors), *Voices from Cosmopolitan Alexandria*, The Alexandrian and Mediterranean Research Center, Bibliotheca Alexandrina, 2006.

Callender, Gae, *The Eye of Horus: A History of Ancient Egypt*, Melbourne: Longman Cheshire, 1993.

Davies, Owen, *Grimoires, a History of Magic Books*, Oxford: Oxford University Press, 2009.

Foreman, Laura, *Cleopatra's Palace: In Search of a Legend*, New York: Discovery Books, 1999.

Goddio, Franck and Bernand, André, *Sunken Egypt: Alexandria*, Periplus Publishing, 2004.

Haag, Michael, *Alexandria Illustrated*, American University in Cairo Press, 2004.

La Riche, William, *Alexandria: The Sunken City*, London: Weidenfeld & Nicolson, 1996.

Maspero, Gaston, *The Struggle of Nations: Egypt, Syria and Assyria*, London: Society for Promoting Christian Knowledge, 1896.

Yergin, Daniel, *The Prize: The Epic Quest for Oil, Money, and Power*, New York: Simon & Schuster, 1990.

For further information on the Antikythera Mechanism:
www.nature.com/nature/videoarchive/antikythera

Recommended related fiction:

Durrell, Lawrence, *The Alexandria Quartet*, Penguin, 1991.

Kharrat, Edwar Al, *Girls of Alexandria*, Quartet Books, 1993.

Sattin, Anthony, *The Pharaoh's Shadow*, Indigo, 2001.

Sole, Robert, *The Photographer's Wife*, London: Harvill Press, 1999.

Historical Notes

THE SUEZ CRISIS: On 29 October 1956 Britain, France and Israel began an unsuccessful military attack to secure the Suez Canal after Nasser's decision to nationalise the canal in reaction to a withdrawal of an offer by Britain and the United States to fund the building of the Aswan Dam.

THE EGYPTIAN REVOLUTION: In 1952 there was a military coup d'état that led to the overthrow of King Farouk I and to the establishment of a republic, initially run on loosely socialist principles. Many of the old colonial structures and elite were stripped of their assets and many fled.

THE EUROPEAN DIASPORA IN ALEXANDRIA: There were up to fifty-two nationalities living and working together until Nasser's revolution. The nationalities included Italians, Greeks, Syrians, Jews, Armenians, British, French and Lebanese.

PRESIDENT SADAT'S PEACE INITIATIVES: The Egyptian president Sadat surprised the world and Egypt by visiting the Israeli Parliament – the Knesset – on 20 November 1977 in a gesture of peace and reconciliation after his country had been at war with Israel twice, once in 1967 and once in 1973. A year later both President Anwar El Sadat and Israeli Prime Minister Menachem Begin shared the Nobel Peace Prize; three years later Sadat was assassinated. Both heads of state, witnessed by President Carter, signed the Camp David Accords at the White House on 17 September 1978. The Accords led directly to the 1979 Israel–Egypt Peace Treaty.

NECTANEBO II – ruled Egypt 359/358–342/341 BC: The last independent Egyptian pharaoh, Nectanebo spent much of his reign fighting off Persians, finally fleeing and mysteriously disappearing – probably to perish in Nubia. His tomb always lay empty, a fact that has been the inspiration behind many myths and stories. During that era many Egyptians believed that Nectanebo, who had expanded Egyptian territory into Syria and Cyprus, would return as the great liberator and free them from Persian occupation. As it turned out it was Alexander the Great who liberated the Egyptians from the Persians, leading to the legend that Alexander himself was not the son of Philip of Macedonia but of Nectanebo. Nectanebo himself was known as the Great Magician and was famous for the vast number of temples he had built during his reign in an attempt to rebuild Egyptian self-esteem and resurrect the spiritual and mystical glory of earlier Egyptian dynasties.

ANTIKYTHERA MECHANISM: Discovered off the coast of Rhodes in 1901, the Antikythera Mechanism dates from the first century AD and is the most mechanically sophisticated artefact from classical antiquity ever discovered.

Contained within a boxlike frame it is assumed to have been able to calculate the movement of the sun, moon and the five planets as well as to display the actual orbits of these celestial spheres. It contains at least thirty gear wheels and nothing remotely as sophisticated was made until medieval times. The extent of its functions are still being analysed to this day. As far as I know, no predecessors of the mechanism have yet been discovered.

Reading Group Questions: A Starting Point

After Isabella's death, Oliver discovers a lot about his wife that he hadn't known before. If she had lived, would Isabella have been able to continue to keep these secrets from him?

What do we learn about their relationship in general?

There are many suggestions in the novel that Isabella seems to be haunting Oliver. Is it really her, do you think, and if so, what is she trying to tell him?

Do you think Isabella would have approved of how Oliver uses the astrarium? How would you chart his attitude towards the artefact throughout the narrative? Is there a shift of some kind, and what could be at the root of it?

How do you think Oliver's class and religious background has affected both his agnostic and material attitudes?

Why is Oliver known as the Divider? How does he feel about his own abilities?

How do you see him as a character?

There is a moment in the book when Oliver is seduced by the idea of rekindling his relationship with Rachel. What influences his ultimate decision?

What is the relation between the creation of the astrarium and the different power struggles between the characters?

How does the astrarium influence what lies ahead? Would you say the novel supports the view that you can alter your destiny?

How do you feel about the surprise twist at the very end? A tragic loss or the fitting ending of the ultimate love story?

Acknowledgements

I am indebted to my partner, Jeremy Asher, without whose support and editorial input this book would not have been possible. I'd also like to thank the following individuals for their invaluable contributions. For geological and oil information: Tom O'Connor, Ian Francis, Jonathan Green, Mike Lakin. With regard to Egyptology, archaeology and local culture: Rosalind Park, Gae Callender, Dr Jean Yves Empereur (French Centre for Alexandrian Studies), Dr Mohamed Awad (Alexandria Preservation Trust), Dr Grzegorz Majcherek, Angus Jackson OBE, Heba Tadrios, Farida El Reedy, Victor Politis, Nino Magy, Captain Mohsen El-Gohary, Dr Emad Khalil, Mr Joe 'Giusy' Barda, Mrs Racheline Barda, Dr Ashraf Sabri, David Thomas, Mr M. Rashidy (Cine Egypt), Dr Zahir Hawass (Supreme Council of Antiquities, Egypt), Nina Learner, Rachel Skinner, Paul Schütze. Thanks also go to the Press Office of the Harbour of Alexandria and to the Windsor Palace Hotel and its staff. Finally, thanks to my editors, Linda Funnell, Sarah Golding, Nicola O'Shea, Lydia Papandrea; and to my agents, Rick Raftos, Julian Alexander and Catherine Drayton. Thanks to Nikola Scott and the team at Sphere and Little, Brown UK. And special thanks to Rosalind Park whose insight and feedback got me through the more esoteric aspects of the narrative.

THE HISTORIAN

Elizabeth Kostova

'Kostova captures, beautifully, the turn on a dime
from light to dark' *The Times*

Late one night, exploring her father's library, a young woman
finds an ancient book and a cache of yellowing letters addressed
ominously to 'My dear and unfortunate successor'. Her
discovery plunges her into a world she never dreamed of – a
labyrinth where the secrets of her father's past and her mother's
mysterious fate connect to an evil hidden in the depths of
history.

In those few quiet moments, she unwittingly assumes a quest
she will discover is her birthright – a hunt for the truth about
Vlad the Impaler, the medieval ruler whose barbarous reign
formed the basis of the Dracula myth. Deciphering obscure
signs and hidden texts, reading codes worked into the fabric of
medieval monastic traditions, and evading terrifying
adversaries, one woman comes ever closer to the secret of her
own past and a confrontation with the very definition of evil.

Elizabeth Kostova's debut novel is an adventure of monumental
proportions – a captivating tale that blends fact and fantasy,
history and the present with an assurance that is almost
unbearably suspenseful – and utterly unforgettable.

'A gasp-inducing, breathtakingly dark mystery set in the present
but wrapped around the folklore and history of Dracula . . .
written in an exquisitely delicate and reserved style'
Good Housekeeping

978-0-7515-3728-4

THE SHAKESPEARE SECRET

J.L. Carrell

'An intelligent, thought-provoking, highly readable and
extremely fast-paced whodunit spanning four centuries'
Daily Sport

A modern serial killer – hunting an ancient secret.

A woman is left to die as the rebuilt Globe theatre burns.
Another woman is drowned like Ophelia, skirts swirling in the
water. A professor has his throat slashed open on the steps of
Washington's Capitol building.

A deadly serial killer is on the loose, modelling his murders on
Shakespeare's plays. But why is he killing? And how can
he be stopped?

An action-packed adventure that hurtles from modern-day
London, Boston and Arizona to the dark secrets of
Shakespeare's past, *The Shakespeare Secret* has been acclaimed
as one of the most compulsively readable thrillers of recent
years.

'Plot twists worthy of *The Da Vinci Code* dominate this agile
first novel from Carrell . . . this spirited and action-packed novel
delivers constant excitement' *Publishers Weekly*

978-0-7515-4035-2